Starring in the Movie of My Life

Also by Laurel Osterkamp

Following My Toes

Looking for Ward

Starring in the Movie of My Life

a novel

by

Laurel Osterkamp

PMI Books

Boulder, Colorado

ISBN: 978-1-933826-677

Front cover photo © Robert Remen

Author photo © Richard Fleischman

Published by
PMI Books
an imprint of
Preventive Measures, Inc.
254 Spruce St.
Boulder, CO 80302

Printed in the United States of America

For information regarding special discounts
for bulk purchases, visit our website at:

pmibooks.com 

Starring in the
Movie of
My Life

Part 1

1. Melody

Winter 2006

The girl's restroom is cold, dark and empty. I feel like I'm trespassing. Even the faint scent of cigarette smoke mixed with fruity body spray feels forbidden, and it's how this bathroom always smells. I'm here because I hate to pee in the company of others, and when you're in high school public peeing is an everyday reality. Not tonight. Tonight I refuse to suffer in any way, shape or form. So I told Axel I'd be back shortly, and I snuck up to the English hallway, away from the noise and hustle of the school dance. Here I can pee and primp in peace.

I flush the toilet, straighten my dress, exit the stall, and admire myself in the grimy mirror above the sink. All my effort and suffering has paid off. The hours spent working at Subway to buy this dress, the strategic flirting with the most popular boy in school, the lying to my mom about what I was doing tonight—it's all been worth it. Finally I will no longer just be academically successful. Tonight is the beginning of my social success as well. But even more importantly, if all goes well, I'll have a boyfriend I can count on, and maybe even love.

I take one more appreciative glance at my expensive black strapless gown that, combined with my ultra high heels, makes me look like a slightly shorter Audrey Hepburn. I check that my dark hair is secure in what's supposed to look like a loose upsweep that took no time, and head out to find Axel. I'm startled to discover him standing right outside the bathroom, by the water fountain.

"Hey," I say with a smile. "How did you know I was up here?

Did you follow me?"

"I figured you wanted me to follow you." He steps closer to me, and I can smell the liquor on his breath. When did he have a chance to drink? Was it just now, or had he been drinking before he picked me up? I don't have much time to contemplate because in a moment he is kissing me. Softly at first, but then his tongue is in my mouth, his slobber is on my lips. I turn my head to the side.

"Let's go down to the gym," I manage to squeak out.

He presses into me. "Why? Aren't we having fun right here?"

I play along with a little laugh but gently push him away, creating some space between us. "Well sure, but there's plenty of time for this later. I want to dance." And I want the rest of the school to see me dancing with you, I silently add to myself.

"High school dances are over-rated," he says. "I want to be alone with you."

He grabs me and kisses me again. At first I kiss him back, wondering if this is what passion is supposed to feel like. But his tongue goes so deep down my throat that I begin to gag, and the smell of his breath does not help. I wiggle out of his arms.

"Axel, slow down."

He smiles like he knows some wicked secret. "Don't tell me you're not up for this. You pretend to be all prissy and shit, but I read your notes."

It's true, I did write him sexy notes, ones filled with ideas I got from studying endless copies of *Cosmo*—articles like "How to Drive Him Crazy in Bed," or "His Pleasure Zones (and there are more of them than you think!)." The last note I wrote said, "I need some of your frontal friction to heat up my hot spot." They all said something like that. Anyway, I would slip these notes into his locker during passing time after second hour. Then I would see him fifth hour, where we sit next to each other in History. He would whisper all sorts of things to me, and I would bat my eyes and giggle, although sometimes I couldn't hear or completely get what he was saying. Honestly, I wasn't even always one hundred percent sure of what my notes meant as I was writing them. I am a virgin after all. But I was just playing, flirting really. That's what flirting is.

Then he started asking me out. Other girls would have been thrilled with his requests, but I knew better. When he'd suggest that we meet up after a game, or go for a drive together after school, I would just grin and shake my head, and tell him I was busy. I do have standards, by the way, and my refusal to simply answer a booty-call was finally rewarded when, after several weeks, he asked me to the Valentine's Day dance. Such an invitation proves he not only likes me, but respects me as well. Me, Melody Madsen is going out with Axel Radcliffe, star basketball player and everyone's favorite guy. My stock has gone way up.

Except now things have gotten a little out of control. So I take a deep breath to compose myself, and turn away. I figure if I don't answer but make it clear I'm walking down to the dance, he'll have to follow. Then things will get back on track.

I hear him behind me as he catches up. Suddenly his hand is on my arm and he yanks it, hard, forcing me to turn towards him.

"Ouch! Don't do that!"

His face contorts with aggression and flushes to a deeper shade of red. "Then stop being such a goddamn tease! You know I only asked you here because of those notes."

He captures my body and squashes his mouth into mine; this time he isn't even a little bit gentle. "Come on," he mutters after he comes up for air, "haven't you always wanted to do it here at school? I sure have."

"No," I say.

He doesn't listen. Instead his mouth covers mine again, and his hands cover my breasts. First they are above the fabric of my dress, but soon they are beneath it. Then he pulls my dress completely down, leaving me exposed due to the unfortunate ease of removing a strapless gown.

He stops kissing me and buries his face in my chest. I feel bile rising from my stomach and tears squirting from my eyes. There are two things I pride myself on never doing—crying and puking—and I'm about to do both at once. But then I feel this push from inside me, and I realize it's my own strength.

"I said no!" I yell, and kick him squarely in the balls. He gasps in pain and I begin to run, pulling my dress back up as I go. I don't run towards the dance, to the safety of a crowd. That would be the obvious choice, the smart direction to choose. But instinct or my gut or some unnamed force propels me the opposite way down the hall, and I have only moments to escape.

Because he recovers quickly. "You bitch!" he yells, and runs in my direction. Even in pain he's quite the athlete, and soon he's close enough to tackle me, forcing me to the floor. His hand covers my mouth, but I scream through it anyway, a muffled scream swallowed with fear and nausea. He climbs on top of me, tugging my dress back down, and I think, This is it. This is really going to happen.

Then, like magic, his weight is no longer pressed against me. He's been lifted away, and I open my eyes to see light from a classroom spilling out into the darkened hallway. Mr. Linden's classroom. We are in front of Mr. Linden's classroom, and Mr. Linden has grabbed Axel and shoved him against a wall.

"What the hell are you doing?" he cries, as he shoves Axel again, banging his head and perhaps punching him in the stomach. I can't quite tell. Then he lets go of Axel and comes over to me. Too late I grab my torn dress to cover myself. Mr. Linden looks away but I know what he saw. And I realize I don't care, because in the space of a moment I have discovered what this night is actually about. Tonight is about destiny; it is destiny that drove me towards Mr. Linden's door. I'll be tied to him forever.

"Are you okay?" he asks.

Instantly a fresh batch of tears surface, and they are much more passionate then any I have yet to cry. It's just - I can't remember the last time anyone has cared enough to ask me if I'm okay.

2. Samantha

Early spring, 2006

When I was three years old, a miracle happened. It wasn't quite on the level of seas parting or water turning to wine, but within my own personal context, it was definitely epic. My dad took me to see my first movie, *Cinderella*, and I discovered a more perfect and entertaining version of the world, reflected off that giant silver screen. From that moment on, real life just couldn't compete, and I began to watch whatever my parents would permit me to see.

I'll admit it: occasionally I like to pretend that my life is a movie, and that I'm the star. No problem feels insurmountable if I'm humming a heart-rousing movie soundtrack in my mind. No conversation is too painful or awkward if I can utter a truly quotable line. And no mistake is too asinine if I can imagine an audience's sympathetic laughter at my ineptitude. This used to work for me all the time, but lately, not so much.

You see, there are very few leading ladies over thirty-five. I think it's quite unfair. There's such a double standard in Hollywood when it comes to age and gender. Harrison Ford is almost twenty years older than Julia Ormand in *Sabrina*, and it's a barely mentionable plot point. Yet, in *Prime*, nearly forty-year-old Uma Thurman falls for some guy in his twenties, and that's what the movie is *about*.

Anyway, no, I've haven't been preoccupied with this inequality for my whole life, and I realize there are far more serious concerns to devote my energy to, like curing cancer, ending world hunger, and stopping global warming. However, this particular issue hits close to home since I myself married a man ten years my junior. That sort of thing doesn't happen in movies, and neither does the following:

1. Peoples' eyes immediately darting to my belly whenever I tell them about my sudden wedding. Since my belly is naturally a little bloated, their eyes stay there slightly longer than is comfortable or even decent, in an effort to ascertain whether my belly is in fact, any larger than normal.

2. After deciding that it's impossible to tell whether or not I'm pregnant just by looking at me, they are left with a decision—are they going to be blunt, or indirect? Most people take the latter route, and say things like, "Wow, that's great! You must be so excited to start a family?" But I actually respect directness more, like when my dad said, "Sam. Tell me you married him because you wanted to, and not out of some false nobility that you've never even had."

3. Bad as these questions may be, at the end of the day I'm haunted with another question that nobody has been rude enough to ask—What does he see in you? Even I don't have the answer to that one.

The only person I've shared this with is my best friend, Jane. "You need to trust him, Sam. That's what marriage is about." She says this to me as we're driving home from her nineteen-year-old cousin's baby shower. It's 1:30 p.m. on a cloudy and cold Monday afternoon, and Jane suspects she was only invited to this thing because her aunt thought she'd be working and unable to come. Jane teaches film and television production, full-time, at the local community college. However, Jane has no classes on Mondays. Still, I don't understand why she went, even if she does believe in the value of putting herself in uncomfortable situations to "appease her fears and develop her ability to grow." I volunteered to go with her; nobody should have to grow on their own.

"I do trust him," I say, focusing on what she just said to me. "It's myself that I don't trust."

Jane cocks her head and tightens her mouth into a firm little line. "I can't think why. You're certainly the most honest person I've ever met."

"You are mad, aren't you?"

"Sam, I just think there's a time and a place…"

"I was standing up for you!"

"And I appreciate it. But was it worth it, after the commotion you caused?"

Jane is referring to a comment I made at the shower. You see, her cousin Brittany did not plan this pregnancy. So people were talking about how it must be God's will for her to have gotten pregnant, because God believes that Brittany will be a fantastic mother. After several minutes of this conversation, I couldn't take it anymore, and I broke my silence with, what I still maintain, was a very simple question.

All I said was: "Come on! Do you all *really* believe in this 'God's will' stuff?"

I was faced with a bouquet of blank stares. There was that awkward silent time that went on for a few seconds too long. I kept hoping someone would answer me with laughter in her voice, but it was not to be. So I continued.

"All I mean is, Jane would make a fantastic mother. And God hasn't *willed her* to have a baby. If it is God's fault that Jane hasn't had a baby yet, then I think she has reason to be pissed off."

Jane's aunt answered me. "We can't rationalize God's will. It's not for us to question, but to accept. God works in mysterious ways, and we have to trust him."

All the other women, sans Jane, started nodding their heads in agreement. I know I should have let it go, but the look on Jane's face reminded me of a toddler in the school yard: the littlest one, left out of the bigger kids' games, the one who is trying to be brave but is utterly transparent.

I shook my head. "No. I won't accept that there's some cosmic reason why Jane can't have a baby and Brittany can, not while every year tons of babies are born to unfit mothers who won't love them. The minute I accept that…" My voice trailed off. If I accepted that, then what? I wasn't sure, and being glared at by everyone in the room wasn't making my thinking any clearer. And it also didn't help that I was looking right at Brittany when I said that "unfit mother" thing, because people got really worked up.

Jane and I left the party fairly quickly after that.

Now, I look over at Jane, who is gripping the steering wheel as she speeds down the freeway, weaving in and out of traffic. Jane drives like someone who suffers from ADHD and a bladder problem at the same time. It's her one habit that doesn't fit with the rest of her calm and nurturing personality.

"It wasn't that much of a commotion…" I say.

"We were asked to leave."

"So? You didn't want to go anyway."

She takes a deep breath. I can tell she's trying not to yell, but her words sound like they're being forcefully pushed out of her mouth anyway. "Not the point!"

"I'm sorry! Okay? Really."

She breathes again, and her death grip on the steering wheel loosens just a little. "Sam. It's all right. It's just, are you sure it was me you were sticking up for?"

"Who else would I have been sticking up for, if not you?"

"Yourself."

"Yeah, right."

"No. Really. I was thinking at the time, maybe what they were saying was pushing your buttons."

"Well, it wasn't. That was about you." I brush my hair out of my eyes and turn my face away to look out the side window.

"Okay. Whatever." She speeds up, and honks at the guy to her right as he tries to cut her off. "Where did he learn to drive? Geez." Suddenly, her whole body relaxes. "Oh whatever. You were right. Brittany is going to suck ass as a mother."

We both laugh and the tension in the car evaporates.

"Let me take you out for a late lunch," I say. "There's a Don Pablos over there. On such a gray and icky day we *need* margaritas and greasy Mexican food."

Jane smiles in answer as she exits off the highway.

Later, after two full size margaritas and way too many chips with salsa, I head home. It's 4:00 in the afternoon when I open the door to our apartment, and the first thing I see is Nathan, lying on the couch and reading a book. He's changed out of his formal school clothes into jeans and his college sweatshirt, so he looks like a frat boy.

"You're home early," I say.

Nathan smiles—the type of smile that changes the entire shape of his face—the type of smile I worried I would never elicit from anyone again. He gets up, and crosses the room to kiss me.

"I missed you," he says as he leans down and kisses me. "Besides, I had no meetings, no after school activities, and I'm even up-to-date on my grading. Figured I'd take advantage of my good fortune and rush home to see my wife."

I giggle, as I've done every time he refers to me like that. Wife! Even during our wedding vows the word made me giggle. Good thing the witnesses were people we only met that day at the Wisconsin Dells.

"So what do you want to do? We could go for a bike ride, or a walk, or out to eat for an early supper. You name it—I'm yours for the entire afternoon and evening."

I wrap my arms around him, a gesture made partly to express affection, but mostly to reassure myself that my good fortune is real. He is not just a figment of my imagination.

"I thought you were mine forever," I say.

He hugs me back and kisses the top of my head. "That too," he responds. "That too."

I close my eyes and revel in his warmth. Surely God didn't will Nathan and me to be together. Yet, in his arms, I feel that I've finally discovered what my fate is. It's to love Nathan Linden.

3. Melody

This morning when I get to school I find *whore* written on a piece of paper, taped to my locker. I pretend I don't care while I rip it off the hospital-green metal door. I hear someone laughing behind me, but I refuse to turn around. I won't let them think they're affecting me.

It's been a month and a half since Mr. Linden saved me from Axel and Axel got expelled. But the school hasn't forgiven me for it. The very next weekend we played in our division championship basketball game and lost. Lost—because Axel wasn't there to win the game for us. And whose fault was that? According to popular opinion, it's mine. Mine and Mr. Linden's.

So even though his classroom is way far away from my first hour, I stop in every morning to say hello. Outcasts have to stick together, after all. When I walk into his room I see him sitting at his desk, his blond head leaning over a book, his fingers messing with the collar of his shirt. Mr. L wears a tie to school every day. I'm not sure why because he's always tugging, trying to loosen it. But his ties are his trademark, and I think it's nice he makes an effort. So many people are slobs nowadays, but not Mr. L. Today his tie is dark blue with green polka dots, and it brings out the color of his eyes beautifully.

"Good morning Mr. L."

He looks up, and half a smile teases the corners of his mouth. He can't act too pleased to see me, it wouldn't be professional.

"Miss Madsen, how are you this morning?" Every morning he asks me this, and every morning my answer is a lie.

"I'm great, how are you?"

"I'm fantastic," he beams, "as usual."

This is what we do; it's our code. But I know the truth. He's hurting on the inside from being ostracized just as much as I am.

"I looked for you yesterday after school, but you weren't in your room."

"Yeah, I was actually able to get out of here early for a change. Did you need something?"

My right index finger is twisting itself into the metal wire that loops through my notebook and binds it together. The top part had become unwound from its pages, and now my finger's circulation is cut off. "Well, I was wondering if you could use an aide next trimester."

He frowns and digs his heels into the floor, pushing himself backwards with the wheels of his office chair. His chest raises and lowers with a careful sigh before he answers me.

"Melody, do you really think that's a good idea?"

This is the first time he has ever called me by my first name! Mr. L always, always calls students by our last names. Finally, the moment I have waited for has arrived! Now I know without a doubt that I mean something to him, that I am more than just a student. In my shock and joy I forget to answer his question though, so he continues on.

"I just think we need to be careful. People in this school love to talk, and if I took you on as my aide things could get worse before they get better."

My joy increases—he just referred to us as a "we." *We need to be careful*—it sounds so scandalous! "But I'm fine," I say, wiggling my finger free and holding my notebook tightly to my chest. "And I don't care what people say. Besides, I could do a great job for you." I walk over to his file cabinet and open the top drawer. With a grin I turn to him. "Really Mr. L! This drawer is a mess! I could organize this; I could organize all of these!" I sweep my arm up and down, gesturing toward his cabinets. Then I walk over to his bookshelf. "And these shelves!" I look back over at him, expecting to see him smile, but I'm met with a scowl instead. "I'm sorry," I continue. "I don't mean to insult you. I know you're creative and smart and all, and you don't have time to think about details. That's why you need to let me do it for you."

"Miss Madsen…" he tries to cut me off, but I step in before he can.

"Mr. L, please! Let me do this. Give me the chance to thank you for… you know." I look down, and will my cheeks to flush. I can feel the warmth creeping across my face, and I mentally pat myself on the back for spending hours alone in my room, mastering this skill. After all, older guys like girls who embarrass easily, so that they can feel worldly and experienced.

He hangs his head down momentarily, like he's memorizing the scuffed linoleum floor. "You don't need to thank me any more than you already have. You never needed to thank me. I just did what anyone would do."

"That's where you're wrong," I say. And I mean it. Mr. L doesn't realize how special he is. That's why he needs me. He needs me so much that I'm willing to do anything in order to be in his life. "What you did, it's the nicest, most decent thing anyone has ever done. Please, Mr. L, let me be your aide. I'll work really hard."

His hand creeps up to massage his neck. "I have no doubt you would, but I still think it's a bad idea."

I look down, away, and wipe a phantom tear that, if it were real, would be blocked from his view.

"I see," I say, and start out the door. His voice stops me, just like I knew it would.

"Miss Madsen…" but he doesn't finish. So I take my last, best shot. It's a gamble to play this card so soon, but I'm confident it will work. Besides, it's the truth.

With my back turned, still half way out the door, I say, "It's just, your room is the only place in the whole school where I feel…safe."

He sighs again, this time with resignation. "My prep hour is fifth."

I turn around. "That's perfect! All I have fifth hour is study hall!"

His same half-smile threatens to escape again. "I'll let the office know."

4. Samantha

The phone wakes me up. I pick up on the second ring. "Hello Dad," I say, before he has a chance to greet me.

"How'd you know it was me?"

"I've told you before; you're the only one who calls me this early."

He raises his voice, and I hold the receiver away from my ear. "It's 10:00 a.m.! I've been up for hours!"

"Yeah, but you go to bed at 9:00. I work till midnight."

His voice lowers back to a normal level. "Well, I'm sorry honey. I guess I forget your schedule. You know me. I was raised with the farmer mentality. Early to bed, early to rise, and too much sleep is a sin."

"I think we can agree that sleeping till 10:00 is the least of my sins."

He chuckles like what I just said was a joke, even though we both know it isn't. Then his voice turns serious. "Samantha, it's never too late to change."

I count to three and remind myself how much I love my father. "Did you need something?"

"I just wanted to know if it's okay for me to sell your old bedroom set. I found a second hand store willing to buy it."

"Dad, I've told you twice that I don't care. It's fine if you want to get rid of it."

"I just thought you might want it someday, in case you ever have kids. Now that you and Nathan are together…"

His voice trails off and there's a pause. Sometimes I worry. He's been living alone in Chicago, in the home I grew up in, for most of the last seventeen years. But I left that home more than half my lifetime ago, and he still has trouble accepting that except for visits, I'm not coming back.

"Dad, do what you think is best. If you want the space it's okay to sell it. If Nathan and I decide to have kids there are plenty of cheap bedroom sets around."

"But this is a nice set, been in the family for years. Not like the cheap stuff from that Swedish place you like…"

"Ikea?"

"Yeah. That stuff is made of cardboard. I wouldn't want my grandchild sleeping in a cardboard bed."

"Then maybe you should hold onto my bedroom set. Just in case."

"Fine. I just needed to know, one way or the other. So I won't sell it then."

"Sounds good, Dad."

"Okay, I'll talk to you later."

"Bye."

He hangs up first, then I set down the phone, wondering how many similar conversations we'll have this week. Dad never calls just to chat, there's always a question he needs an answer to. Once he gets the answer it takes him less than thirty seconds to get off the phone, but he'll keep calling back with the same question until he gets the answer he was looking for.

I get out of bed and walk towards the mirror, examining my morning face and hair. Not bad for a thirty-five year old with no makeup or comb. Time has been good to me, better than I deserve. The lines in my face are little ones, around my mouth and eyes, appearing mostly when I'm stressed or tired. My brown hair is still untouched by gray, and it's as thick and shiny as it was in my teens. That's the good news. I look down, away from my reflection, to examine my belly and thighs. Time hasn't been quite as good to me in this area, although still I can't complain. So what if I'm never a size eight again? There are worse things than being a size ten (or a size twelve on my bad days), and at least I have the big boobs to compliment my expanding hips and buttocks.

Truthfully, I've never been more insecure about my appearance than I am now. This is what marrying a man ten years my junior has done. Plus, Nathan isn't just any man; he's one who spends his days with size-two girls who dream up romantic scenarios with him as the hero. Early in our relationship Nathan confessed that quite a few of his students harbor crushes on him, but that's just par for the course, he said. It's what young teachers have to deal with.

I know he'd never take advantage of that; Nathan would sooner die than do something that unethical. But still, most of these girls are closer to his age than he is to mine. That's food for thought, if nothing else.

My reverie is broken by my phone ringing again.

I pick up. "Hi again, Dad."

"It's me, Sam." Through static and background noise, I hear Jane's voice.

"Where are you calling from?"

"I'm in my car. I'm sorry to call so early, it's just sort of an emergency…oh, crap!" A car horn blares. "Watch where you're going, asswipe!" Jane yells. "Sorry, Sam. Are you still there?"

"Still here."

"That jerk just totally cut me off."

I try to make my tone light. "Maybe you shouldn't be driving and talking on your cell phone at the same time?"

But my effort to speak diplomatically is wasted because she snaps at me anyway. "Please don't give me that lecture again, okay? I wouldn't have called if it wasn't an emergency. I… oh crap, hold on a second."

There's hushed swearing while I wait for the return of Jane's phone voice. "Sam?" she says, after a moment.

"Yeah," I say. "Still here."

"Anyway, you'll never believe what happened. This morning this woman from Milwaukee called. She saw our name on one of those adoption lists, and she's having her baby in, like, two weeks. She wants to interview Jake and me, because she's looking for a couple to give her baby to."

"That's great, Jane!"

"Yeah. But she wanted to meet today. No notice—I guess giving up the baby is a split second decision, so I don't know how much she can be trusted. But I'm driving to pick Jake up at work, and we're heading out. Can you cover my class at the college for me?"

"Um, I guess. Am I qualified to do that?"

"You'll be fine. Just show them how to use the video-editing equipment. You could do it in your sleep."

"Okay," I say, with more confidence than I feel.

"The class starts at three. You don't have to work today?"

"Nope," I lie. "It's not a problem. Don't worry about a thing, Jane. I've got everything covered."

"Thanks so much!"

I hear a knock at my door. Since when did I become in such high demand? "Jane, I've got to go. Good luck, and drive carefully!"

She thanks me and hangs up. I go to look through the peephole, and am horrified to see an unbearably familiar face, one that I know better than my own.

Without opening the door, I shout, "Collin, what do you want?"

He yells back, "I just need to check your stove, that's all."

"Why do you need to check my stove? It's fine."

"Sam, I have a key. Either open the door or I'll let myself in."

"Hold on." I run and throw on a pair of jeans and sweatshirt over my nightshirt, not taking the time to put a bra on as well. I cross my arms over my chest and hope nothing is too noticeable. I open the door and there he is, looking how he always looks, sort of like an older, bigger-nosed version of Orlando Bloom, but not like the strong, sexy guy in *Pirates of the Caribbean*. No, he's rather like the defeated yet unfortunately cute loser of *Elizabethtown*. Collin is the manager of our apartment building, and he's also the reason why I wound up in Shannon, Wisconsin, a small city perched on Lake Michigan, a few hours away from my hometown of Chicago.

"Why do you need to check my oven? It's fine."

"Because 2G had a leak. If she hadn't noticed it in time, the whole building could have blown up."

"So just because her oven was leaking gas you think all of them are?"

"They're all old ovens, Sam. I don't think it's a good idea to take chances." He grins. "Don't worry. I'm not making up excuses to see you. Believe me, I've moved on."

"So have I," I remind him.

"Thank God for small miracles" he says, as he moves past me into the kitchen. I follow him, and watch as he pulls out the stove, then bends down to examine the pipes behind it. Without turning to look at me he asks, "How's married life?"

"Great" I say. "Sorry you weren't invited to the wedding. It was really small and quick."

"Hopefully you can't say the same about your husband." He laughs at his own joke, while he raises himself up and pushes the oven back against the wall. Then he starts to fiddle with the stove dials. "Anyway, don't sweat it. I'm the last person you should have invited to your wedding. Although… it would have been nice if you told me yourself, rather than just adding his name to your lease."

I shift uncomfortably. "Sorry," I say. "I guess I thought, after everything that's happened between us, you wouldn't care."

He turns back around and his gray eyes squarely meet mine. "It's because of everything that's happened between us that I will always care."

I look down, switch my weight and hug my arms closer to my chest. "Is the stove okay?"

"Perfect," he says. Then without another word, he strides out of my apartment, so quickly it makes me wonder if his entire visit was a figment of my imagination, sort of like the questions you're left with at the end of that terrible Tom Cruise movie. What was it? Oh yeah—*Vanilla Sky*. I hate it when movies leave you wondering like that. If the entire story was supposed to be an invention of the main character's thoughts or dreams, fine. But at least be clear about it so the audience won't feel like they just wasted $10 and two hours of their life.

Uhgg. I've been awake for less than twenty minutes and already I'm having a bad day, and seeing Nathan is the only thing I can think of that will make me feel better. I look at the clock. It's at least 6 hours until he gets home, and I have to find someone to cover for the first part of my shift (Yeah, I lied to Jane about not having to work. Why complicate things with the truth?).

I stroll into the bathroom and turn the shower faucet on. The water coming out is hot and steams up the tiny space. I stand in front of the mirror, watching as my reflection slowly disappears.

5. Melody

I'm sitting in my fifth hour psychology class, daydreaming about reorganizing Mr. Linden's entire classroom. Second trimester is almost over, and at this time next week I will be putting his life in order. Finally I will be doing something useful with my time at school. I mean really—so many of the classes here are just plain stupid. Like this one. I took psychology because I thought it would help me figure out what other people were thinking, but all I've learned so far is about the id, ego, and superego. Who cares? Give me something practical I can use, not some dumb theory hardly anyone is aware of and even fewer people care about.

At about 2:00 my cell phone vibrates in my pocket. Crap. Almost an entire day had gone by without hearing from her. I know I will pay later if I ignore the call, so I fish my phone out of pocket and flip it open. Normally I'd be discreet about answering, but Mrs. Regis is oblivious, and I sit in the back anyway.

"What?" I say into my phone.

"I need you to stop by the store for me and pick up some things."

"What?"

"Cigarettes, soup, Mountain Dew, and English muffins."

"What kind of soup?"

"Doesn't matter, as long as it has beef, and it's the chunky kind. After that they all taste the same."

"Okay. But I won't be home until late. I have newspaper layout tonight."

"Melody, they don't really need you for that."

"Yes they do Mom, and Ms. Corey will kill me if I'm not there."

"I want you home by five."

I start to protest, because layout won't even begin until at least six o'clock, after all the last minute changes to the stories have been made. But I'm unable to because my phone is snatched from my hand. Mrs. Regis is standing above me. I hadn't even noticed her coming. She snaps my phone shut and drops it in the pocket of her organic cotton dress that's baggy enough to be worn by a pregnant lady. "I'll see you after class," she says.

How could a day that had been going so well suddenly turn so bad?

Mrs. Regis me kept after class for fifteen minutes, lecturing about how I'm not living up to my potential, and is there anything going on in my life that she should know about? Like I would talk to her! She thinks just because she teaches psychology that she's some sort of therapist, and it took all my self-control not to tell her what I really think about her, her class, and her taste in clothing (everyday she wears big dresses with even bigger jewelry.) But I sucked it up, smiled, and told her how sorry I was and I will try to do better.

Then I had to go tell Ms. Corey that I wouldn't be there for newspaper layout. As expected, she freaked. Don't I understand the concept of a deadline, don't I get that there are people relying on me? I'm part of a team, she yelled, and I need to take that seriously. So I buckled. I told her I'd be there at 5:30. That would be enough time to stop at the store and get my mom her food and cigarettes. Once she has them, she'll be happy, and I can tell her I'm going into my room to do homework, then jump out my second story window (I've figured out how to relax into my fall so that it barely hurts) and walk the two mile trek back to school to do layout.

But I'm so crabby from this afternoon's events that I need to do something to cheer myself up. Even though I don't have time, I swing by Mr. Linden's room. When I get there he's not alone; some woman is sitting on his desk, looking down at him in his chair, and laughing.

And he's laughing too. I clear my throat to get his attention, and they both look in my direction.

"Hello Miss Madsen," he says, shifting into his teacher mode. "How can I help you?"

"Um… I just wanted to make sure the office okayed me being your aide?"

"I actually haven't had a chance to notify them, but it won't be a problem."

Then the woman pipes up. "You're going to have an aide? That's great. Maybe she'll help you organize all your stuff."

Mr. Linden laughs again. "Well, hopefully. Sam, this is Melody Madsen. Miss Madsen, this is Sam, my wife."

My stomach dives like it had been shoved off a skyscraper. Wife? "I didn't even know you were married," I say to him.

"It only happened a month ago," he responds.

"We're newlyweds," she giggles, and I look at her again, really taking in her appearance. I'm not impressed with what I see. First of all, she's *old*. Really, she has to be at least thirty. And she's kind of fat too. Okay, her hair is sort of pretty; I'll give her that. But Mr. Linden could do a lot better.

I flash an insincere grin in her direction. "Congratulations," I say. "Mr. Linden is a great teacher and a great guy; you're a lucky woman."

"Oh, believe me, I'm aware. And you're going to be his aide? What's your name again?"

Mr. Linden answers before I can. "Babe, this is Melody. You know. I've mentioned her."

A look passes between them and understanding blossoms on her face. "Oh sure," she says. Then there's a pause, like she's trying to decide whether she's going to make any sort of reference to Mr. L's and my connection. But she simply concludes with, "Well that's great. Hopefully you can help him become more efficient. God knows he could benefit from some help in that department."

I'm tempted to stammer and look away. But I don't. Holding my ground, I look at her squarely and respond. "By the time I'm through, you won't even recognize him."

6. Samantha

I check my cell phone again. It's on ring, not vibrate, so it's not like I'd miss it if it rang. But I called Jane an hour ago to let her know how class went, and to find out about her meeting with the pregnant lady. Then I called her again, about 45 minutes later, because waiting for people to call me back is about as annoying as standing in line at a check-out counter behind that one lady who insists on making small talk with the clerk, asking a million questions and using expired coupons.

I slip my phone into my pocket and let out a long, vocal sigh, which I know is melodramatic, but feels good nonetheless. Work is slow this evening. When I got in, I chose *Some Kind of Wonderful* to play on the store's constantly running televisions. I know Hal, my boss, would prefer me to broadcast new releases, but I'm in a definite John Hughes sort of mood.

Back when *Some Kind of Wonderful* came out, the movie made perfect sense to me. Eric Stoltz blows his college fund to buy diamond earrings for the supposed love of his life, Lea Thompson. In the end he winds up giving the earrings to girl-next-door Mary Stuart Masterson, and he says to her, "My future looks good on you."

I was fifteen or sixteen when the film came out, I can't quite remember. But I do remember believing in its romance, thinking Eric Stoltz was right to follow his heart and not care about his future plans so much, and that his Dad was being a stick in the mud for trying to get him to commit to a college. Stupid old man. So maybe it is the slow evening, or maybe it's the movie, or maybe visiting Nathan at school has put me in this mood. But I'm standing behind the counter at Bravo Video indulging in some introspection. How did I end up here?

I suppose the easiest route is to blame it all on Collin. Since I saw him today for the first time in months that is what I am tempted to do. I have known Collin for seventeen years, but it feels like longer. In fact, it's hard to remember what life felt like before I met him, which was when I was a freshman in college and he was a sophomore. We met here in Shannon, at the branch of the University of Wisconsin campus that we attended. I chose to go to school here because I was convinced that life in a small town would be more profound than living in a big city, and I would still be a fairly short drive away from Chicago and my dad. I pictured myself living simply, like the people do in that movie *Roxanne* (the Steve Martin *Cyrano* take-off) and I'd go to Friday night fish fries and greet old people by name on the street. I should have done more research. Shannon's population is actually well over 100,000, but what did I know? I grew up in the third largest city in the U.S. and just about anywhere else was going to seem tiny in comparison.

Once at school I realized I was just as anonymous there as I had been during my countless commutes on the EL, but in addition, I was homesick and sad. Being at school wasn't the only cause, there was another contributing factor. Right after I graduated from high school my mom moved to Mexico, and has been largely unavailable ever since. Leaving my dad and living away from home shortly thereafter created a loneliness bubble inside of me, and it was rapidly expanding with emptiness. Then I met Collin at a campus showing of *When Harry Met Sally.*

I had come alone, because I needed somewhere to go so my roommate, who I hadn't clicked with, wouldn't think I was the pathetic girl with no friends or plans on a Friday night. I took an aisle seat in the back. Shortly after the lights went down, he walked in, stumbled over my feet, and whispered, "Can I still sit here?" I nodded my head yes. And even though the next seat and the one after that and the one after that we're all empty, he sat right next to me.

Then he acted like we were on a date. Sort of.

I mean, he didn't hold my hand or extend his arm over my shoulders, but his knee rested against mine. And he kept whispering things to me throughout the film.

"I've never understood why people think Carrie Fischer is attractive," he said, keeping his eyes on the screen all the while.

"I thought all straight guys your age are required to be in love with Princess Leah," I whispered back.

He shrugged his shoulders and shook his head.

Later, his eyes still gazing forward, he said, "What's with the Harry Connick Jr. music? Using the original artists would have been so much better."

"Nah," I replied. "Harry Connick Jr. is dreamy. He can sing for me anytime." At that, Collin shifted his eyes from the screen, and stared at me. "Didn't your mother ever tell you it's impolite to stare?" I said, with my eyes focused ahead of me and not on him. "Watch the movie."

When it was over and the lights came up, I got a good look at him and realized he was even cuter than I had suspected while glancing at him in the dark. Olive complexion, hint of beard growth, gray eyes, dark hair. You know the type. But when he looked at me he laughed.

"Oh my God," he said, shaking his head. "You're not Gwen. I only figured it out a few minutes ago."

"Sorry to disappoint you." I replied.

His tan skin grew flushed. "No, I'm sorry. You must think I'm the biggest freak, sitting next to you and talking to you like I know you."

I shrugged my shoulders. "I don't have a problem with it." I said. "But I can't speak for Gwen."

He smiled, and I swooned a little, not in a noticeable way. Then, suddenly, I felt the years fast-forward. We were one of the old couples in *When Harry Met Sally*, giving our testimonial about how we fell in love at first sight.

Me: "I went to see a movie by myself. You were on a date."

Him: "That's right—I was meeting… what was her name?"

Me: "Gwen."

Him: "That's right. Gwen. She looked a lot like you. Of course—not as pretty."

Me: "It was dark in the theater, and you were confused when you sat next to me."

Him: "That's right."

Me: "But by the end of the night we had fallen in love."

"Collin!"

My reverie was broken by the screeching of someone who could only be Gwen (and who I had to admit, did look remarkably like me).

"That's real class," she said. "Not only do you stand me up, but you take another girl to the movie. Thanks a hell of a lot."

Collin stammered. "Gwen, I can explain.'

"Don't bother." She stormed out. Collin remained sitting next to me.

"Oops," he said. "Guess I blew that one."

I laughed. "Let me buy you a cup of coffee. It will make you feel better."

"That's okay," he said, and I wanted to die at the rejection. Then he continued. "I'll pay. I don't want you telling our grandchildren that you paid on our first date."

With those words, sunshine began to radiate from the inside out of me. *Here's what I've been waiting for,* I thought. "I'm Sam, by the way."

"I'm Collin."

"I know." He cocked his head in confusion. "Gwen just called you by name." I said.

"Right," he said with another smile. Then he stood, took my hand, and pulled me gently out of my chair. "Shall we?" he asked. So I followed him out of the theater, and into years and years of heartache and confusion.

Because the next day I moved in with him. He's the reason why I never left Shannon.

At eighteen my entire short life had been spent looking for something to believe in, or be passionate about, or somewhere to feel at home. Collin offered me all that in an incredibly attractive package, and I was convinced he was all I needed. Of course, over the years Collin has done whatever he could to perpetuate that belief, and in the end we resembled a codependency case study. But if it wasn't for him I never would have met Nathan. And I wouldn't be here now.

I switch gears and begin to sort through DVDs, trying to look busy, because I hear Hal emerge from the back office. He walks up to the front counter.

"Samantha, we need to talk."

Hal is younger than me, skinny, with a face that was once tormented by bad acne. Although pock-marked, his skin is usually relatively clear, but right now he has a huge, festering zit on the left side of his nose. I wish I could relieve it of its misery and pop it. I try not to stare and force my eyes to meet his own.

"Sorry Hal," I say. "What new release do you want me to put on?"

"What? Oh. No, that's not what I was going to say. I've been promoted. I'm moving up to corporate headquarters."

"Oh! Congratulations." His zit is taunting me, begging me to pop it. I can even see a hint of white peaking its head out from the top. It would be so easy.

Blah, blah, blah. Hal's voice drones on, something about increased responsibility. I find it hard to listen to him on my good days. I don't even try to hear what he's saying now. I just nod my head, and he finishes with, "So what do you think?"

"I think that sounds great," I say. And I mean it. Hal does work hard; he deserves to be rewarded for it.

He smiles. "Wonderful. Then I'll tell corporate to set up an interview. I think this would be a perfect step for you, Samantha. You've got a lot to offer Bravo Video, and with my recommendation, they just might realize that. I'm going to call them right now." He pats me on the shoulder and walks away. I stand there in a stupor, wondering what I've just committed myself to.

It's close to one o'clock when I get home. My shift actually goes till midnight, but then I need to count out the cash register and close down the store. When I walk into our apartment I immediately drop my bag on the floor and make a beeline to the fridge. I open the door and fish out the peanut butter. Nate thinks I'm insane, but I like my peanut butter cold. He says, "You can't spread it if you keep it cold, it rips up the bread!" I began to worry about his frustration with me over this matter, and spent a whole night several months ago obsessing about it. The next morning I called Jane.

"What should I do?" I demanded. "I've eaten peanut butter this way my entire life. I can't change. I don't want to change. Do you think that means I'm too stubborn to be in a healthy relationship? Am I too weird to keep any normal person around? Should I just call it a day with him before I get really hurt?"

Jane said, "Why don't you just buy him his own jar?

I did just that. "See," I later said to him. "You can have your jar in the pantry, and I'll keep mine in the fridge. Everybody's happy. This can work, Nate. I really think it can work."

"Will you marry me?" he responded.

I smile at the memory as I stand in my kitchen, in the exact spot where Nate and I had agreed to spend eternity with one another. Then I thrust a spoonful of the cold, sweet peanut butter into my mouth, and enjoy eating it as my dad and I have done, for years. After a couple more forbidden spoonfuls I put the peanut butter away, throw the spoon in the sink, brush my teeth, and climb into bed. Nate is sound asleep, and his body heat and steady breathing soothes me more than any memory could. I wrap my arms around him and whisper into his back, "Guess what, I might get a promotion, if I want it. I don't know. Other than you, I don't know what I want."

7. Melody

I walk into the apartment my mom and I share, carrying a plastic grocery bag containing two cans of Campbell's Chunky soup (one each of Meatballs and Rigatoni, and Steak and Potatoes) two packs of Marlboro Lights and two 20 ounce Mountain Dews. Mom is on the couch watching television—one of those shows like *Judge Judy*, but it isn't actually *Judge Judy*. I drop the bag onto the empty couch cushion next to her, and I can smell the stench of alcohol escaping from her pores.

"Thanks Baby," she slurs. She reaches into her bag and pulls out a pack of cigarettes. She unwraps it, fishes out a cigarette, and sticks it in her mouth. Then she starts looking for her lighter, lifting up and looking underneath magazines and old pieces of mail that are sitting on the coffee table in front of her. I walk into the kitchen and grab a book of matches then come back out and hand it to her.

She smiles and lights her cigarette. "Nobody takes care of me the way you do," she says. "How was school?"

"Fine," I answer. "I do need to go back for layout though."

"Why can't they do it without you?" She exhales a puff of smoke.

"I'm part of a team, Mom. They rely on me."

"You need to learn how to say no, Sweetie. You let people take advantage of you too much. You're too nice."

She leans back onto her pillow and refocuses her attention on the television. I go into my room and shut the door. In several hours she'll be passed out on the couch. I know her routine. Once or twice a month she calls in sick to work- mental health days she calls them—and she spends the day drinking, smoking and watching television. Other days she's not so bad, but Mom believes in taking time "for herself." I still don't understand why she thinks that I'm somehow flawed because I work too hard and don't pamper myself the way she does. Because every time I do claim some alone time, she sabotages it. There are days at a time, weeks even, when I've convinced myself that I'd be better off without her. If I lived on my own I wouldn't need to sneak around just to get my work done, and I wouldn't have to put up with her weird habits and needy behavior. Next year when I go away to college all my problems will be solved—but why am I waiting that long to take off? The answer is simple: I don't want to hurt her feelings. When Mom is hurt, she's like a wounded animal, she'll bite and lash out and hurt her aggressor, inflicting far more pain than was inflicted on her. Besides, she needs me.

I sit on my bed and my eyes travel the length of my room. It's not decorated. There are no posters and no snapshots of me acting crazy with my "friends." It looks more like a hotel room than anything—generic décor and everything in its place. I'm not a fan of clutter.

"Melody!" I hear my mom cry my name from the other room.

"What?" I yell back through the closed door.

"Come out here!"

I dig my nails into my fist. What now?

I walk back out to the living room and find her in the exact same spot and exact same position as she was before, only now her face is contorted into a look of frustration as she points the remote towards the television and presses its buttons. Her efforts have no effect, so she shakes the remote, hits the remote, swears under her breath, and tries pressing the buttons again. She notices me and says, "The stupid remote is broken."

"I think it just needs new batteries," I say. "Its power has been weak for a while."

"Do we have any batteries?" she asks.

I walk over to the couch and extend my hand. She gives me the remote, and I walk into the kitchen and open our battery drawer, where I find two double-As. I replace the old batteries with the new ones, and walk back out to the living room, where I hand the remote back to my mother. She points it towards the television and magically, the channel changes.

"You're awesome!" she coos. "I love you so much, honey."

"Do you need anything else, Mom?"

"Not right now, sweetie." She gives me a smile. "But you're not going out again tonight, are you honey? You'll be around in case I need you, right?"

"Mom…"

She sits up and looks only at me. "I'm sorry, Mel. Really, I am. I promise this will be the last time I ask you to skip a school thing for me. But I need you more than they do, and anyway, you need to learn how to say no to those people. Next year you'll be on your own, and how will you get by unless you thicken up that skin of yours? Huh? Think about that."

I've heard this argument before, dozens of times. How could I not think about it? I know I need to toughen up, but blowing off school isn't going to get me where I need to be. Lying, on the other hand, might just work wonders.

I smile back at my mother. "Don't worry," I say. "I'll be around all night, just in case."

It's after 9:00 when we finish the layout for the paper. Once a month this happens—I have to stay late to finish up because the same lame people on the staff of *Shannon High West Tribune* didn't get their stuff in on time and I'm the one to pay for it. It's always the same crew who puts in time right before deadline: me, Ms. Corey, and the other senior staff members, Elle, Trudi, and Meg. And the same thing happens each month after we're done. Ms. Corey takes Elle, Trudi and Meg to Baker's Square, buys them pie and coffee, and they sit around and gossip. I went once, the first time, at the end of September. It was stupid. Elle thinks she's so special just because she was made editor. It's all I can do not to tell her. Last spring Ms. Corey pulled me aside and told me that I was the better writer. "Melody," she said. "I don't think I've ever had a student with more writing ability than you. But you just don't have the leadership skills. That's why I'm making Elle editor next year. I sure hope you stay on though."

I smiled and said of course. And when I'm there, nobody could ever guess how much I resent all of them. I would have made an awesome editor. It's not my fault that Ms. Corey happens to like Elle better. And, it's not fair that Elle gets to put "editor of the high school newspaper" on her college applications. She doesn't need a scholarship the way I'm going to. But I'm not going to ruin whatever chance I may have left of getting a good letter of recommendation from Ms. Corey, so I smile and play along. I draw the line however, at eating pie. It's too much like that stupid idiom—I'd order French Silk, but we all know I'd be eating *humble pie*, and every bite would taste like a mixture of chalk and acid.

So instead I walk out of the school building and pull out my cell phone, dialing the only pre-programmed number I have, other than home. Kelsey answers on the first ring.

"Hey girlfriend," she drawls out her words like she's southern, even though she's lived in Wisconsin her whole life. "How's it hanging?"

"I'm going to stop by, okay?"

"Okay. See you in a few."

I left my apartment this evening by climbing out my second story bedroom window. I've developed a strategy of dropping my feet to a window ledge, then jumping the rest of the way into a relatively soft patch of ground. It's not ideal, but so far the worst I've had to endure is a twisted ankle and a bruised wrist. Anyway, as long as my mom believes I'm in my room she's fine, and she'll pass out on the couch, no problem. But sometimes she wakes up when I come back in, and then I need to make up something about taking out the garbage, and there are only so many times she'll buy such a story. So on nights like this I hang at Kelsey's until I'm sure it's late enough that she's out for the count.

I drop my phone into my backpack and begin the short walk to Kelsey's. She's a really convenient friend. She lives super close to school, so any time I'm there late I can just walk over to her place. She also has a car, and her parents are never home. Back when I used to care about being popular I tried to keep my friendship with Kelsey a secret. You see, she thinks she's really cool, and she acts like everybody likes her. But nobody does. They all make fun of her behind her back. In a way, she's the most embarrassing kind of friend to have. It's better to be tight with someone who knows they're a loser; at least there's some dignity in recognizing how badly you suck.

However, after the whole Axel incident I decided I no longer cared who liked me, because I knew that nobody except Kelsey did anyway. I would continue to be nice to people, but I wasn't going to bend over backwards for anyone. So I started eating lunch with Kelsey, and I let her take me to a movie a couple of months ago. We ran into Elle, Trudi, and Meg at the theater, and I barely was even bothered by it.

I get to Kelsey's door and knock on it. She answers immediately, no surprise. She's probably been hovering in the entryway since I called.

"Come on in! I was just making some popcorn. It's low fat." I enter and follow her into the kitchen. From behind I get an awesome view of Kelsey's huge derrière. She's wearing low-rise jeans that are at least a size too small, so there's a layer or two of her fat that's hanging out. This is emphasized by her short, clinging top. Kelsey always dresses like this; she's like Brittany Spears, who hasn't changed her wardrobe since going from a size two to size twelve. Kelsey takes the popcorn from the microwave and rips it open. The steam that pours out doesn't delay her from reaching in and grabbing a huge handful to shove in her mouth. She offers me the bag and I shake my head. I hoist myself onto a barstool at the snack bar in her elaborate kitchen.

"Are your parents home?"

"Nah. They're at some dinner." Kelsey's parents are high-powered lawyers, and they're always dining with important clients.

"How about something to drink?' I suggest.

"I have been craving a pina-colada all day!" Kelsey squeals.

"Awesome." I say.

Kelsey busies herself with the preparation, pulling out bottles of juice, ice, and rum. She expertly pours the ingredients into the blender and in no time she's handing me a highly-intoxicating frothy drink, complete with one of those little umbrellas and a pineapple wedge. That's one thing I like about Kelsey; she pays attention to detail.

"I am so mad at Bobby," she tells me. "Today in English he was totally flirting with me. Then as soon as the bell rings he takes off to find Abby. When is going to leave her already?"

Kelsey is convinced that Bobby Olson is into her, because sophomore year he took a dare and kissed her at a party. Ever since Kelsey has been following him around like a cat in heat, and Bobby encourages it so he can laugh about it with his friends later.

She continues on. "I just don't get what he sees in her. I'm obviously so much better for him than she is. I'm the one who knows him. And I bet you she doesn't even like him half as much as I do. God! I just wish I could get her out of the way, you know? We only have a few more weeks of school left. If it's ever going to happen with Bobby and me, it's got to happen soon."

"Yeah," I respond, my voice level.

"I mean, I really think he likes me a lot, but he's scared of his feelings. I heard about this; it happens to a lot of guys. They fall in love with someone who, for whatever reason, they think they shouldn't be with. So they channel their feelings into a relationship with someone who's less risky. That way they don't feel so vulnerable. Bobby thinks that just because he weighs less than I do that we can't be together. Even though he likes me more, he's chosen to be with Abby because that's the …

I cut her off. "Where did you hear about this theory, Kelsey?"

"On the Maury show. These guys are all hurting themselves and the women in their lives, and I think Bobby…

"What else?"

"Huh?"

"Was there a psychiatrist on or something? What else did he say?"

Kelsey's face goes blank for a moment. "I don't know. He mostly just told the guys to have some balls and to be with the women they love."

Kelsey takes a long sip of her drink and I stare into mine, swirling the cold, white mixture with my umbrella.

"What you need is a plan," I say.

"Huh?"

"Bobby isn't going to leave Abby just like that. You need a plan. Something not too obvious, but that will make Abby look really bad. Then Bobby will want to dump her, and he'll run straight into your arms."

My words make Kelsey light up. Enthusiasm bubbles out of her like lava. "Okay. What do I do?"

This time it's me who takes a long sip of her drink. I swallow and wipe my mouth with a napkin from the basket nearby. After a significant pause I respond.

"It's nothing that will happen right away. You have to be delicate, so neither of them is even aware of what's happening until after it's over. You'll have to plan each step carefully. You'll have to strategize."

Kelsey gives me a blank look. "But I don't know how to do that."

I smile with confidence. "Don't worry. I do."

8. Samantha

When I wake up it's nearly 11:00 a.m. Nathan crept out of bed this morning as usual at 5:30. I remember waking for a moment when he planted a goodbye kiss on my forehead, but then I fell right back into a deep and dreamless sleep. Now my mouth is dry but my skin is damp—typical symptoms of oversleeping. Oh well. I make a beeline for the bathroom to take a shower. I plan to wash away last night's anxiety along with this morning's general ickiness in one full swoop.

Once out of the shower I take the time to blow-dry my hair, apply makeup, and dress in my favorite pants and the new J-Crew blouse that I got off the sale rack just last week. I'm meeting Jane for lunch. We meet every Wednesday at noon, and I like to look nice because she's the sort of friend who will tell you if she likes what you're wearing or will compliment you on a new haircut. She's good that way.

I'm only ten minutes late when I arrive at the diner near campus, which is our standard meeting place. Ten minutes isn't bad for me, and Jane expects me to be late anyway. Still, I'm getting ready to utter my obligatory apology when I look up and am stopped in my tracks. Jane's face has this radiant look that, as her best friend, I've only seen on her once or twice before. I sit down, cock my head, and squint my eyes at her, which is our code for "what's up?"

"I can barely believe it…" she says.

"The pregnant lady decided to give you her baby?"

Jane squeals in response, nodding her head yes, and sort of jumping up and down while remaining seated. "We're meeting with her and a lawyer tomorrow afternoon!" she exclaims. "Can you believe it? We have so much to do to get ready! It's all happening so fast! In a couple of weeks Jake and I are going to be parents!"

I smile and say, "That's fantastic, Jane! I'm thrilled for you!" But I'm not able to surrender myself to her happiness one hundred percent. Jane's been down this adoption road before, about a year ago, and the mother backed out after giving birth. Well, not right after—Jane and Jake took the baby (a little girl they named Robin) home for two days, but the birth mother had a week to take her back. On the third day, she did. Jane and Jake's hearts were broken, and Robin's name was changed to Celine.

"What are you doing today?" Jane asks. "We need to go shopping. It's a boy; the birth mother, Carrie, found out at the ultra-sound. Of course the room is all ready; I never took Robin's stuff out of the nursery even though Jake kept saying we ought to. So the crib is there, and the rocking chair, and the dresser is already stuffed with onesies and swaddling blankets. But so much of it is pink. I need to get some butch baby stuff. And Jake and I need to figure out a name! What do you think of Robert? Is it too much like Robin? I don't want to be creepy about it…"

"Jane!" I cut her off with more severity than I intended, but if her heart breaks again, so will mine. "Has Jake said anything to you about not getting too excited?"

Her face falls. "Of course. But what fun is that?"

"I just don't want to see you get hurt. Maybe you should wait a little before you, you know…"

"Get too attached?"

"Yeah."

She tilts her head and wrinkles her brow, like she's actually considering the idea. But I know better. "You know," she says, "I read that in colonial days, parents would wait until their children were two or three years old before they started loving them, because infant mortality rates were so high." She leans into the table and her intensity becomes a physical presence that I'm sure I could touch, if I decided to reach out my hand far enough. "Two or three years, Sam. That's so much time lost! First smiles, first steps, first words—they're all priceless moments that can't be replaced." Her voice catches, but she swallows back the tears. "I just can't imagine how they did that. I doubt that if I lived back then that I would have been able to keep myself from loving my baby, no matter how high the risk."

"Well sure, but that's different."

"It's not!" Jane squints her eyes at me. "I loved Robin more in those two days than I've ever loved anyone, and I still love her. I'll always love her, I'll always think of her. And now I love this baby. I can't help it. There's a little boy waiting to be born, and he's meant for me. Not getting excited isn't going to keep my heart from breaking if it somehow doesn't work out. So I may as well go shopping and have some fun, and as my best friend, I expect, no I *require* that you indulge me in this." Now she is crying, and I grab my napkin and hand it over to her. She wipes her face.

My need to make her smile bulldozes over my desire to protect her. "You're right," I say. "We need to celebrate. I say we start by skipping lunch and moving straight to ice cream." I gesture towards the window, which offers a view of Cold Stone Creamery, situated directly across the street. "Let's get huge, disgusting sundaes, then work them off by scouring every baby store in town for the cutest, butchest onesies ever made."

She smiles and I take her hand. We're off.

A few hours later she drives away to get Jake, and to meet with their lawyer and the biological mother. I head to work, where I fritter away the hours stocking the shelves while watching *Thelma and Louise*. The movie choice, in retrospect, was a poor one. I started to get down on myself when I realized that as much as I love Jane, I wouldn't drive off a cliff with her—I don't think I'd drive off a cliff with anyone. Maybe if I was a mother I'd feel differently. I hear most mothers would gladly lay down their lives for the welfare of their children, and without a doubt Jane will belong to *that* mother club.

But not me—I'm too selfish to pay the dues.

Later, when I get home, Nate is still awake, grading papers. He looks up from his work.

"Hey," he says. "Pretty shirt you have on. The color matches your eyes. Is it new?"

I smile, nod my head, and sit myself down on his lap. He wraps his arms around my stomach. "Nate, would you drive off a cliff with me?"

"Right now?" He whispers into my neck. "I'm sorta busy. How about this weekend? We could make a day of it."

"That's okay," I reply. "You don't need to say yes. It's better if you don't."

"But I would, if it would make you happy."

"How would I be happy? I'd be dead. We both would be."

"Oh. So you're talking a really big cliff? I was thinking a small one. Because you didn't specify…"

I cut him off with a firm kiss on the mouth. He returns the affection, and we spend several minutes necking and groping, behaving the way his students most likely do. He pulls away first.

"Sam, I should get back…"

"I know, I know," I say, jokingly waving my finger at him. "Not on a school night!" I get up and walk away, but a smile is still playing on my lips. Someday I'll be worth driving over a cliff for. Maybe someday I'll even be willing to drive off that cliff myself.

9. Melody

The clock reads 12:35 and my plate is full of soggy fried rice and limp vegetables. The problem with third lunch is we're often served leftovers. I try to stay out of the lunchroom as much as possible, but today is an exception. Today is day one of Operation Kelsey and Bobby. Kelsey is sitting across from me, shoveling in a slice of Domino's pizza. It smells good, and for a moment I'm jealous. But one perk of being poor is I can't afford to eat the sort of food that will make me fat. I look at Kelsey's plump, overly made-up face, and feel grateful. Then I look up and see Bobby strolling over to the milk bin by himself.

"Kells! Red alert! Now's your moment!"

She coughs down her last bite of pizza. "Huh? Where?"

"Over by the milk bin. Quick, before he's gone! Wipe your mouth and remember what I told you."

She grabs a napkin and wipes her mouth. Then she strolls over to execute step one of five. Actually, I have serious doubts as to whether or not she can succeed with this plan. It's not like it's foolproof, and besides, nobody says Kelsey isn't a fool. But at the very least I'll be able to iron out the kinks in the system by testing it on her first. I watch as she approaches Bobby. She makes eye contact, then physical contact by placing a hand on his arm as she reaches in for a carton of chocolate milk. As she comes up she sees that Bobby has taken a swig of his own milk and is left with a milk mustache. Then—oh my God—she wipes his mouth with her hand. Is that too much? I can't read his face too easily from here, and amidst all the bustle of the lunchroom I honestly can't tell.

Then out of the corner of my eye I see Mr. L talking to a lunch lady. They're laughing about something. I grab my plate and wander over, pretending not to notice how near he is.

"Excuse me," I say to the lunch lady. "Is it possible to get another egg-roll? They're so good!"

"Sure," she says with a smile, and plops one down on my tray. "But don't tell no one I gave you this. I'm not supposed ta."

"I won't," I say.

"Excuse me, Miss Madsen." I'm so convincing in my act of not noticing him that I am actually startled by his voice and it takes me a moment to compose myself. But only a moment, and by the time I've turned around, I'm perfect.

"Mr. L! How are you today?"

"I'm good. But I'm very jealous."

I smile. He's referring to how I didn't stop by his room like I usually do. So he missed me! Score!

"I was running late. The line at Starbucks was crazy long."

"Okay," he laughs. "I meant about your extra egg-roll. Mary never gives me second-helpings." He shoots the lunch lady (Mary? Do lunch ladies have names?) a mock-evil eye, and she giggles under his gaze. His effect is apparently ageless, because she says, "Here ya go, Mr. L. Now don't ever say I don't do nothing for you."

"Mary, you're a star." He winks at her and accepts the free food, then he and I turn back towards the crowded room. I silently punish myself for my stupid gaffe a moment ago. Of course he doesn't care about me not stopping by this morning. These things take time.

I can't let him think that I'm anything other than super-casual, like the type of girl who never cares too much and always knows the perfect, clever comment to make. But what to say? The only thing I can think of is like, the worst high school pickup line for a student to say to a teacher in the history of the universe: "I didn't know you were a lunch supervisor."

He shrugs his shoulders. "Mr. Rozan is out sick today, so they asked me to fill in."

"Oh?" I phrase my response like a question, widen my eyes, and wait for him to say more.

"So… so I said okay."

"Cool." I keep looking at him. He squirms a little then looks away. I wait a second before I go on. "So why didn't I know you were married?"

He crosses his arms over his chest, a clear sign of self-protection. "I assumed it was common knowledge. You know as well as anyone how word gets around in this school."

I step in closer to him. "Only the bad stuff. But something like this—why wouldn't you want to show off about being a newlywed? You must be so happy! Really, Mr. L., you need to talk about yourself a little more."

He smiles, then answers in his teacher voice. "I prefer to talk about school when I'm at school."

I laugh uproariously, like he's funnier than Jimmy Carey, Will Farrell, and Dave Chappell all rolled into one. "Oh Mr. L, you're so serious. It's a good thing you're handsome, otherwise we'd all think you're a nerd." I brush his hand, which is now resting on the counter, ever so lightly with my left pinky as I say this. It's just enough so he can feel it, but not too much that he couldn't dismiss the physical contact as being accidental. Just then there's wild laughter from the far corner of the room, and a Twinkie is hurled through the air.

"I guess I should be supervising a little more and chatting a little less." He grins at me, then turns his attention across the room, and charges over with a scowl.

I make my way back to our table. Kelsey runs up like she's about to tackle me.

"Did you see? He stayed there and talked to me for like, a long time?"

I give her a genuine smile—I don't need to fake it at all. "Yeah, you were great."

Kelsey looks down at my tray. "Hey, how you'd get an egg-roll?"

"The lunch lady gave it to me. Do you want it?"

"Sure!" Kelsey reaches over, grabs it, and shoves it in her mouth. "So did you see," she continues with a full mouth, "The flirting went well, huh?"

"Yeah, it was fierce."

"How much longer with step one?"

"Be patient, Kells. These things take time."

That afternoon I come home early because for once, I don't have to stay after for the newspaper or work a shift at Subway. Plus, my mom said something about going out tonight. That means I finally, *finally*, have some sweet, precious time when there's nothing I need to do. I figure I'll take a hot bath, cook some ramen noodles, and use the time to work on filling out financial-aid forms. Wherever I end up going to school next year, one thing is ultimately clear; I will be in desperate need of money. I have my books and papers pressed to my chest as I walk in, and the first thing I notice is the sound of Jimmy Buffet playing from my mom's bedroom. That means she is in a good mood—always a bad sign.

"Wasting away again in Margarita-ville" she sings to the music as she sloppily applies thick black eyeliner and alternately puffs on a cigarette. She's wearing one of her favorite outfits: a pink suede camisole top with tight acid washed jeans. I've tried, believe me, to update her wardrobe to the twenty-first century, but the clothes I pick out are never trashy enough for her, so they always end up in my closet. From the mirror she sees me lurking behind her and turns around.

"Hey honey," she croons. "How was school?"

"Fine," I utter, trying not to sound scared. But I know from experience how destructive her happiness can be.

"You're home early," she chirps.

My answer is slow and deliberate. "Yeah, well, I thought it would be nice to have some time to myself."

If she catches my gist she doesn't let on. She smiles, a big toothy grin, which lets me know instantly that she wants something. "Perfect! Cause Kenny's sitter cancelled, and I need you to watch his kids."

Kenny is her on-again/off-again boyfriend who lives in a trailer park with his two-year-old daughter and four-year-old son. He has sole custody because his girlfriend, the kids' mother, had to be institutionalized for schizophrenia. Kenny's desire to date my mother is proof that some of us are doomed to make the same mistake over and over.

"I can't, Mom. I have work to do."

"You just said you have nothing going on."

"No, I said it would be nice to have time to myself…"

"Same thing!"

"It's not!"

She throws her mascara on the floor like a two-year-old having a tantrum. It rolls its way to the corner of the room because the floors are uneven in this crappy little apartment. "How can you be so selfish? Kenny and me just got back together and we need some time alone! What is so important that you'd deprive us of that?"

I look at her, her hair poofed and sprayed, her face painted on, and I hate her. I shouldn't hate my own mother; I realize that. But sometimes, I do.

"Mom, you and Kenny are always getting back together. And I have to work on these forms for next year; I don't have time to watch Penny and Petey!"

"You're just jealous," she says. "You're jealous because I have a life and you don't."

"Yeah Mom, that's it. You're right. I'm sooo jealous!" I laugh, a superior little chuckle. "I wouldn't exchange lives with you if someone paid me."

"At least I have a boyfriend," she taunts. "You've never even dated, have you? Have you even been kissed, Melody?"

My face turns bright red; I know because I can feel the warm blood gathering underneath my cheeks. It may be possible to blush on command, but I still haven't mastered stopping a blush from happening when I don't want it to.

Mom sees me and laughs in response. "Hah. I was right. Don't worry honey, someday you'll find a man. I just wouldn't hold your breath is all." My embarrassment turns to anger. I never told my mother about the incident with Axel. The school tried, but I found ways around it. For a moment I'm tempted to tell her now, but the thought of her sympathy makes my stomach turn. So I snap at her instead.

"You think I couldn't date a guy like Kenny? I just happen to have some taste. Make no mistake; I could date any guy I want!"

Instead of getting angry and taunting me even more, my mom starts to giggle—a light-hearted, schoolgirl sort of giggle that slowly transforms into a belly laugh. "Oh honey," she says between breaths, "don't get so worked up. It's not worth it." She laughs more, and I stand there, speechless. "I mean really, what has winning an argument with me ever gotten you, other than the evil eye from yours truly?"

She turns back to her mirror and starts to apply her lipstick. I stand behind her, unmoved by her buoyancy, and we speak to each other's reflections. "Mom, I really can't baby-sit tonight. I have too much to do."

"Okay," she says with a smile.

"Really?"

"Sure. You have things to do. Kenny and I will take the kids to McDonald's play-land or something. It's no big deal."

"Great." I turn to walk away, and she turns around too.

"What are all those papers?" she asks.

"Homework."

She smiles and squints. She always reminds me of that evil doll, Chucky, when she gives me that look. "I know what homework looks like, sweetie. Those don't look like homework, it's more like official forms or something." She steps in closer and grabs one of the forms—an application for a University of Minnesota scholarship that I picked up in the guidance office this afternoon. After looking it over, she says to me, "Melody, I thought we talked about this already. You can't go to college far away. I'll miss you too much."

"Mom…" The words I've formed over and over in my head, all my reasons for why I have to go away, they all stop dead in their tracks when I see her face.

"You can go to school here in town, sweetie. Then we can still see each other every day."

I want to be rational and tell her this town is suffocating me, that I'm meant for something better, and the idea of getting away from here and her and this stupid version of myself is the only thing that keeps me going. But my words would be wasted, so I resort to anger and meanness.

"You can't stop me!" I yell. "You can't stop me from leaving you if I want to!" I run into my bedroom and slam the door, but it doesn't have a lock, and she follows me right in. She looks down at me, lying on my bed like a frustrated child. This is what she reduces me to, *every single time!*

"You'd be surprised," she says. "I can stop you, and I will. Don't put it past me neither, because once I decide to do something, I'm shameless. We have that in common."

She's right. I've learned how to manipulate from the master, and deep down I know that if she wants to keep me here next year, she'll find a way. Her secret weapon is guilt and my downfall is a conscience. Sure, technically she can't keep me against my will. But if she needs to, she'll resort to some mystery illness or financial ruin or a nervous breakdown or whatever: anything to manipulate me into staying. My problem is I let her ploys work, even though I realize she's roping me into taking care of her yet another time. But I can't help myself. She's the only person in the world who actually sort of loves me. What I need is for her to just let me go with no strings attached, but at this moment, that feels like an impossibility. I'm still her marionette.

So I don't answer. She sits down on my bed and strokes my hair. I'm such a fool that I let her.

"There, there. It's not so bad."

"Yes it is. I want to go to college."

"No. You're not ready. You think you're so smart, and maybe you are. But honey, book-smarts are different from street smarts. There's so much you need to learn about the world before you take off on your own."

I sit up to face her. "Mom, I'm eighteen, and I can take of myself. Believe me."

"How can I, sweetie? You've never even dated. You set out and I know what will happen. The first guy who's nice to you will sucker you in, and take advantage of you. You'll wind up pregnant, heartbroken, and on my doorstep in six months, guaranteed. I love you too much to let that happen."

"You're wrong. I'm a lot smarter than you think."

She sighs, and collapses onto my bed. We're lying side by side, like sisters. She's still stroking my hair. "How do I know that sweetie?"

I sit up. My five-step plan. If anything would impress my mother, that's it. "I'll prove it to you."

"How?"

"I'm going to get my hot young teacher to leave his wife for me."

Mom sits up in interest, smiling. "Yeah, right."

"No really. I can do it."

"What makes you so sure?"

"I have a plan."

She raises her eyebrows. "What sort of a plan?"

We sit on my bed, cross-legged, and I take her through, step by step, the plan I've devised. Mom can't hide her pride at my scheming, and she even offers me some pointers. I take notes.

"Well," she says, after we've discussed it all, "I'll be surprised if it works. But who knows? Maybe you'll actually succeed at something worthwhile and make me proud."

"And if I do," I say, ignoring her jab, "I'll have proved to you that I'm ready to be on my own, and you'll let me go to college."

She shrugs her shoulders and hops off the bed. "Sure. Why the hell not?" She exits my bedroom, and I hear her pick up the phone. After a moment she says, "Hey honey. Good news. Melody said she'd baby-sit."

I lie back down on my bed, kicking all my books and papers onto the floor.

10. Samantha

Saturday mornings are my favorite time of the week. The weekend is stretched out like the promise of a sit-down holiday meal, ready to be hedonistically accompanied by drinks, naps, and sex. Yum! So I lie in bed with Nate, watching cartoons, eating cereal from the box, and gently gnawing on his toes.

"Ouch," he cries when I accidentally bite down a little too hard. "Slow down Captain Crunch! Is it necessary to have my feet for breakfast? Can't you just stick to that sugary non-food you eat?"

"Sorry, Mr. Linden, it just doesn't fulfill me. Not enough protein."

The tinge of annoyance in his voice sounds real. "You know I hate it when you call me Mr. Linden."

I stroke his injured toe. "But it's your name. All your students call you by it."

"Exactly. And you sound just like one of my students, which is a little disturbing when we're in bed."

I give him an overly indignant sigh, meant to be funny. "I guess I should find that encouraging. It's better than the alternative anyway."

He raises an eyebrow at me. "Meaning?"

"Well, I'd be worried if you got off on it, like in that movie with the skinny girl from that show."

"Huh?"

"You know, the one where she's the manipulative student and the teacher doesn't actually come on to her but it turns out he gets aroused by the idea and asks his wife to dress up like a school girl and call him Mr. so and so. And then after the whole thing blows up she leaves him, even though he's innocent."

"Oh, that one!" He smiles and shrugs his shoulders. "Don't think I ever saw it."

"Yeah, you did. I brought it home from Bravo around a month ago."

He speaks to me in his slow, patient voice. "But I didn't watch it. I never watch movies set in high schools. You know that."

I scrunch my face as I begin to remember. "Oh. Right. Maybe I watched that one on my own."

"You must have."

How could I have forgotten? Nate won't watch any movie that has to do with high school. Either they're completely idealistic and thus, unrealistic, or they're so real they're depressing. Either way, Nate says he gets enough of high school at work.

"Sorry, I forgot," I say, and I gently ruffle his hair. He reaches up and pulls on my arm, his cue to spoon. I settle into his embrace, content to play with his fingers rather than eat his toes. He strokes my hair, and the only sound in the room is our breathing and the soundtrack to *A Shark in the Park*, the Saturday morning cartoon playing on TV.

"I still don't understand why a shark is living in the suburbs," he says softly, stroking my arm at the same time. "Wouldn't he happier in the ocean where he belongs?"

"Probably. I think he's doing it for love though, kind of like the ending of *Splash*, only reversed. He wants to be with that girl, but in a platonic way of course."

"Ah, the things we do for love." Nate gives me a final squeeze, then he gets up to go to the bathroom. I lay in bed, half watching *A Shark in the Park*, which, if you have never heard of it, is about a little girl who has a very pleasant shark (who both speaks and sings) as a pet. They have all sorts of adventures together. I'm wondering, is this really the message we ought to be sending to our youth? They're going to grow up believing that even nature's worst predators have a soft side. I know from experience, that just isn't so.

My musings are interrupted several minutes later when Nate emerges from the bathroom, looking guilty.

"We need to call the super," he says.

I spring up at attention. "Why?"

"The toilet. Again."

"Can't you just plunge it?"

"Hon, believe me, I tried. It won't go down."

I laugh despite myself. "My God, Nate. What did you do in there?"

He gives me his mean teacher look, a look that used to shut me up in the past, until I caught on to what he was doing. My chuckling continues, so in defiance he says, "You're the one who insisted on Indian takeout last night."

"Eww! Don't be disgusting."

"I can't help it. Sometimes life is disgusting." He unapologetically moves towards the phone. As he lifts the receiver my panic sets in.

"Wait! Don't call Collin over this. He hates toilet-plunging calls."

Nate's face wrinkles in offense. I tell myself to take his irritation seriously, but he's wearing his Shannon high soccer T-shirt and his dirty-blond hair is sticking out in different directions; he looks like a teenager. "I don't care!" Nate waves and points the receiver at me to emphasize his point. "He's the super, that's his job. Besides, this is the second time in a month that the toilet's backed up. There's something wrong."

"Yeah, your poop is too big!"

Nate tries not to laugh, but his smile breaks out. "You want to plunge the toilet?"

"No."

"Then why can't I call him?"

I have no good answer. Sure, at one point I mentioned to Nate that Collin and I used to be together, a long, long time ago. But I never gave him the whole story; there were too many complicated reasons for why I shouldn't. Now, standing here arguing over a backed-up toilet, I decide that this is not the time to fill him in.

I shrug my shoulders and he starts to dial. I plop back down on the bed, but only for a moment. If Collin is coming I want to be wearing a bra this time. I get up and get dressed, also stopping to comb my hair, and using the kitchen faucet to splash some cold water on my face. After a couple of minutes I hear a knock on the door. When I answer it, of course Collin is on the other side, his longish dark hair tied back and his shirt sleeves rolled up. With his industrial strength plunger grasped in his hand, he's ready for action. If there's emotion behind his steely eyes I can't read it, and when he speaks his voice is annoyingly neutral.

"Hey, Sam. Your husband just called?"

"Yeah, come on in."

Collin enters and Nate emerges from the bedroom, a welcoming smile plastered onto his golden-child face. My stomach is already doing a dance.

"Hey man, sorry to bother you with this. I tried to get it un-plugged, but I guess I need help from the expert."

Collin says nothing, walks past Nate into the bathroom, and he sets to work on the toilet. Nate's eyes meet my own, asking me the silent question, "How friendly should I be?" I shrug my shoulders, because really, I don't know.

Nate shrugs his shoulders too; then he turns toward the bathroom. I take a seat on the living room couch. Our apartment is small enough that I can hear all of what transpires.

Nate speaks. "Sam tells me you hate toilet-plunging calls. I don't blame you. I'm thinking maybe we should call the plumber. It's not the first time we've had trouble with this toilet."

Collin grunts. Nate continues. "I mean, I'm sorry, dude. I'm sure you don't get paid enough for this."

Silence. I'm sending out a psychic message, telling Nate to shut up, but he doesn't hear me, and after an awkward pause, he continues. "So, do you think we should call a plumber?"

Nate waits for Collin to answer, but all I hear is the sound of rubber squishing in water, accompanied by a song about friendship from the television. The shark is singing—"*Oh, how good it is to be, friends with the land and the sea. It doesn't matter if you walk or swim, if your name is Guppy or Jim. We may come to different ends, but you and I will always be friends!"*

I get up to turn off the T.V. just as Collin gives a final grunt and flushes the toilet. "That should do it." Collin says, and he walks right past Nate. I have come back into the living room, and Collin faces me as he reaches the front door. Before I can thank him, Collin says, "I can't believe you married a guy who says 'dude.' What the hell has happened to you?"

My mouth drops open in shock as I am momentarily rendered speechless. Nate, unfortunately, still has his voice. "Hey man, you're out of line."

Collin turns around and finally acknowledges my husband. He squints at Nate. When he speaks it sounds like the effort necessary to form his words isn't worth the trouble. "I've known Sam for half her life. I understand things about her that you will never begin to grasp. And I just plunged your shit down the drain—a job you were too weak to handle. I'm out of line? You don't even know where the line is."

Nate's face turns bright red, and he looks like he's about to lunge towards Collin and rip him a new one. But he doesn't. That's what I love about Nate—he may be young, but he's the most mature guy I know. Nate just says, "Thanks for your help," then he walks out the door—past me, past Collin, to I don't know where.

I'm left facing the man whose history I can't forget.

"Thanks," I say. "You've been a huge help." My sarcasm flows out like sicky-sweet goo. I only wish it was possible to hurl out enough to suffocate him.

But Collin is immune to my methods. He just laughs. "Come on, is that any way to treat the guy who did you a favor? I just spiced things up for you! You need a little drama in your relationships—otherwise, you get bored. You'll see; in a little while, you'll be thanking me for real."

"No, I won't."

His fake happiness hardens into something more sinister. "Come on Sam. You really think you're going to be happy with this guy? You were never meant for settling down. The thrill of the chase has always held way too much allure for you. That's why we were together for so long."

"I've changed. I grew up."

"Nobody changes that much."

I try to remain calm, James Bond-ish, like a calculated assassin. "People can change, Collin. You just don't realize that because you're incapable of changing yourself."

"If that's true, why are you still here talking to me instead of running after him?"

I have no response. For a moment we glare at each other, his eyes issuing a silent challenge that I don't understand and cannot accept. But if our stare-down is a competition I'm definitely the loser, and I grab my keys from the entryway door and push past him. Once out in the hallway I turn around. "You know, I was just about to leave to go find him. I'm not doing this because you suggested it."

Collin laughs. "You're hopeless, Sam."

I head downstairs, through the lobby and outside to look for Nate. It occurs to me that finding him would be a hell of a lot easier if I weren't already so lost myself.

11. Melody

I have no idea who my dad is. When my mom got pregnant with me she was nineteen and sleeping with three different guys interchangeably. Karl was her old boyfriend from high school, she worked with Jesse at Pizza Shack, and Oswald had been her dad's best friend. She tried to convince each one of them that I was his, but none of them bought it. She's still angry about that.

So she decided to have me anyway, even though she knew there was little chance of ever getting any help from anyone. Mom said that all men are jerks anyway and that I should take whatever I can from them, because I won't get much if I just sit around and wait to be rewarded. Mom had a terrible childhood—her father was a big, scary son-of-a-bitch (her words). I guess he drank a lot, and got violent when things didn't go his way, like if somebody forgot to take out the garbage, or made chicken for dinner when he was in the mood for hotdogs, or if the Packers lost. Most of his violence was directed towards my grandmother. But sometimes Mom became the target, which is why she ran away at sixteen. Several years later they died in a car accident; he was drunk behind the wheel. Mom says she was never sad about it, but I trust little that Mom says.

"I learned to take care of myself," she says. "And I became a better person for it. Most people who got hit by their parents end up hitting their own kids," she says. "Not me. I've never hit you, and I never will." So in other words, I'm just really lucky, and Mom's "Mother of the Year" award is simply lost in the mail.

I don't know about that.

But I've never been big into self-pity. It's a waste of time. And let's face it, even on my worst days I have it better than 90 percent of the world's population. I pay attention in Social Studies, and I'm aware of all the suffering that goes on: the hunger, disease, poverty, and oppression. So what if my mom is a head case and I'm not popular at school? I'm the only one who can change my situation, and sure, from the outside, I can see how a plan to steal another woman's husband might seem evil. But I truly believe Mr. Linden will be happier with me, and I can tell just by looking at his loser wife that she'll never rise to the occasion. I mean come on, she's so old, and what has she done with her life? By the time I'm her age I'll have conquered the world. Just watch.

Anyway, it's late Saturday morning and I'm at school, after getting back from a Key Club outing to bag groceries at Piggly Wiggly. (Ick. I'll be so glad once I'm in college and I no longer have to pack junk food for fat women on food stamps in order to pad my resume.) Anyway, Katie, who is also in Key Club, gave me a ride back to school. She offered to drive me home, but I lied and said I needed something from my locker so she wouldn't see the crappy apartment building we live in. Once we were in the school parking lot, I had to go inside to make my lie seem real. Then I decided to just wander the halls. School is sort of peaceful when nobody's here. Plus, and I know this is going to sound weird, it helps me to walk around when I know nothing bad is going to happen. I still haven't completely gotten over that Axel incident, and sometimes I like to be here when nobody else is around. I guess I could call it facing my demons.

And the really funny thing is I was going over my plan in my head as I was strolling past all the lockers and silent classrooms: "Step one: flirt. Be around him a lot, then become unavailable. Always make eye contact. Do nice things for him, then act helpless so he'll do nice things for you. Step two: temptation. Boost his ego. Make yourself…" Then, in the middle of my silent diatribe, I notice it. The light is on in his classroom. And I'm almost as happy to see it now, as I was the other time that his light was there just for me.

I wander in, pretending to be calm, when really my heart is beating at twice its speed and my underarms are all damp. He's standing at the blackboard, his back to me. He is so intent on what he's writing that he is unaware of my approach.

There are two columns. One has quotes—"To thy own self be true," "Goodnight sweet prince," "Get thee to a nunnery," and so on. On the other side is a list of characters: Hamlet, Polonius, Horatio, Gertrude, etc. Mr. L stands back and examines his work as if it holds the answer to one of life's greatest mysteries—like whether or not Carson Daily is gay or how Ashley Simpson became a star. I knock gently on a desk so as not to startle him, but the sound still gives him a start. He turns around abruptly, and for a moment I see a flicker of emotion on his face. Like he's glad to see me. Then he quickly puts on his strict teacher face, which clashes with his messy hair and the shorts and T-shirt he's wearing.

"What are you doing here?" He puts down his stick of chalk.

"I could ask you the same question," I say, making myself comfortable by hopping up and sitting on the top of a desk.

He puts his hands on his waist in a slightly defiant stance. "I just have some work to finish up."

"On a Saturday? Shouldn't you be home with your wife?"

Mr. L blushes—it's so cute! I had no idea it would be so easy, too easy, to embarrass a twenty-five-year-old man. "It's work that needs to get done. If I do it now then I can enjoy the rest of the weekend."

"And your wife doesn't mind?"

"Of course not." Mr. L strolls over to his desk and starts shuffling through papers. He's like the textbook example of a bad liar, the way he's creating a diversion to prevent eye contact.

I hop off the desk and stroll over to stand close to him. "Well, you're newlyweds. Doesn't she want you to spend time with her? If you were my husband, I'd nag you all the time and tell you to stay home and pay attention to me."

Mr. L sits down and takes out a red pen. As he starts paging through the stack of tests he picked up he says, "Sam isn't like that. She's not the nagging type."

I lean my weight in his direction. "Oh, you're lucky then. Whoever I marry is in for it, because I'm going to nag him constantly. Not about stupid stuff, like bills and cleaning. But about spending time with me, I'll nag him all the time about that. It's how I'll show him that I care."

Mr. L looks up for a moment, like he's going to say something then thinks better of it. After a moment he switches courses by saying, "You still haven't told me what you're doing here."

"I was bagging groceries for Key Club, and Katie dropped me off at school because I forgot my trig homework."

His eyes stay on me, but he blinks a couple of times before speaking again. "Shouldn't you go and get it then?"

I feel like a huge whoosh of breath is about to burst out of me. It would feel so good to let that happen, but I push the explosion down with a breezy smile. "There's no rush. Why don't I help you grade those tests? Do you have an extra answer key?"

"Miss Madsen, I really think…"

I cut him off with probably more force than necessary. "Mr. L, it's Saturday, nobody's here, and with everything that's happened, don't you think you can call me Melody?"

He just looks at me. For a long time, as if he's seeing something in me that he hadn't noticed before. I'm tempted to look down or away, but I don't. I maintain the eye-contact as if it was a staring contest, and I'm refusing to blink first. I always win these types of things. So without averting my eyes, I continue. "I promise I won't tell anyone."

Then—miracle of miracles—he smiles. A big, genuine, toothy grin spreads across his adorable face. "Fine," he says. "Melody. I would love for you to help me grade these tests."

12. Samantha

Of course one of the first places I look for Nate is at school. Sometimes I think he loves his job too much. It's like he won't know who he is if he's not a teacher. Or maybe I'm just jealous because I don't have something that I'm really passionate about.

When I enter the building it is quiet and dim. I notice a sign for a swim meet, and I can hear the muffled sound of cheers. The smell of chlorine hangs in the air. Silently, I wander the halls—a prowler on the loose, afraid of being caught. I feel like I have entered a world where I do not belong.

I make my way up to Nate's classroom and see the light from his classroom many feet away. And I hear voices. His voice, and a female voice.

I know this is stupid, but I freeze in my tracks. I tell myself that whatever is going on is completely harmless, yet somehow my feet are stuck to the floor. "It's probably just a student from the swim meet. She wandered up here for some reason then stopped in to say hi. Why are you freaking out like this?" These words run through my mind, and they make sense, yet my body refuses to respond. Finally, after standing there, listening to the laughter coming from Nate's room for what seems like a really long time, I turn around and walk away.

The trek back to my apartment passes in a haze. I barely notice my surroundings as I walk. Instead my mind wanders back to a time nearly a year ago…

That night I had walked into the church basement with a hint of shame. It had been months since I attended a meeting. Collin and I weren't together anymore and I had convinced myself it was no longer necessary to come. Then he started making appearances in my dreams. I hate it when that happens. I guess it's more possible to expel someone from your life than it is from your subconscious.

I went to take a seat, and noticed there was a new face among all the familiar ones. He looked remarkably like Owen Wilson, funny nose and all. Of course, upon further inspection I realized that the pretty boy was too young to be Owen Wilson. "Sure, Sam," my mind raced on. "Otherwise, it could have been him. Owen Wilson attending an Alanon meeting in Shannon, Wisconsin makes *perfect* sense."

I told myself to focus but let's face it; my attention span has never been my most remarkable quality. I kept looking over at him. I wondered if he was going to speak.

He didn't. But towards the end of the meeting, when I stole what must have been my one-hundredth glance at him, I found his eyes staring back at me. Then he broke into a grin—a huge one. It transformed the shape of his cute little face with the endearingly crooked nose and the big blue eyes.

Once the meeting was over he approached me. "Do I know you?" he asked.

"Not yet." I replied. "Do you want to know me?"

His lopsided smile crept from the corners of his mouth. "Sure," he said.

We went out for a drink—hey, it's not like we're the ones with a substance abuse problem. We're allowed a drink if we want one, and perversely, those meetings always leave me craving alcohol. Nate ordered a beer and I ordered a G&T, and we sat across from each other, still grinning.

Of course, it was necessary to get a certain conversation out of the way first.

"Who did you come for?" he asked.

"My ex. It's over now between us, but I guess I still need a little bit of support."

Nate took a swig of his Miller Lite. "Is he a drunk?"

"Sometimes. When it comes to substance abuse he's spanned pretty much the entire spectrum. Although he swears he's not using now. What about you?"

"My Dad's an alcoholic."

"Oh. That's too bad."

Nate smiled at my inane comment. "Yeah. It really is." Then he took another swig of his beer, finishing it.

"Have you heard that alcoholism can run in families?"

Nate shook his head and adopted a false look of concern. "Nope. Never heard that before."

"Really?" I asked, not sure if he was being serious or not. Hadn't everybody heard of that?

Nate put down his empty bottle. "Next you're going to tell me that alcoholism is a disease."

I smiled. "Actually, there is a rumor to that effect."

"Well, I'm not worried." He leaned in and lowered his voice, poised to share a secret. "Want to know why?"

"Why?" I asked.

"Because I'm adopted."

I started to laugh. "Really? You're adopted?"

His endearing face looked momentarily puzzled. "Why would I lie about something like that?"

I instantly stopped laughing, and gave him a serious answer. "I don't know. Perhaps to ease my guilt, so I don't feel like I'm corrupting you? Going for a drink was my idea."

He smiled, and his eyes crinkled in such an charming way, that it was impossible to imagine him ever experiencing or being responsible for a moment's worth of pain. "And it was a good one," he chuckled. "Can I get you another? I'm going for another beer."

I shrugged my shoulders, resigned. "Sure."

He got up, and I watched him at the bar, enjoying the giddiness I felt. The gin was working its magic, but so was his company. We stayed at the bar for some time, sharing stories and laughing about things that shouldn't have been funny. It was getting close to midnight when Nate looked at his watch.

"Wow," he said. "It's getting late."

My oversensitivity immediately jumped into overdrive. Was he already tired of me? "The bars don't close for a couple of hours."

He nodded his head and answered in an overly patient tone. "Yeah, but I have to be at work at six."

My jaw dropped. "Really? My God. What do you do?"

"I teach high school English."

"That's admirable," I said.

He stared into my eyes like he could see something behind them. Then he replied, "It's only admirable if I'm doing it for altruistic purposes. I'm not. I guess I'm just weird, but I love my job."

So! He had passion and purpose. Suddenly I wanted to be as close to him as possible, as if by doing so I could somehow absorb those attributes.

I put my elbows on the table that separated us and leaned into them. "I'd walk you out to your car," I said, "but you'd probably get the wrong idea and think I'm inviting you to kiss me."

He shifted back, away from me. Raising his eyebrows, he responded with, "It wouldn't matter. There's no chance I'm kissing you tonight anyway."

"Why not?"

Half of his mouth arched up in a smile, creating a dimple on the left side of his face. "I don't kiss girls in bar parking lots. It's tacky."

"Oh. Okay. Well, let's go then," I said, valiantly trying not to show my disappointment. "I'll walk you out."

We got to his Jeep and stood there, facing each other. He spoke first. "I'm the one who ought to walk you to your car—make sure you leave safely and all."

"I'll be fine," I said. Then with vixen-like bravado that I don't normally possess, I reached up, wrapped my arms around his neck, and leaned in. He responded by giving me a warm, firm kiss—on the forehead.

"I'll call you," he said with a chuckle. Torn between shame and glee, I pulled away and walked towards my car without saying goodbye. I wasn't mad, but I wanted him to think I was. I figured that way he'd be more likely to call.

I was right.

Once back at our apartment I sit down on our still unmade bed. Slightly over an hour ago we had been lying there, content, with the promise of the weekend and time together looming ahead of us. Now I feel the opposite of the happy lightness that I experienced earlier today. I turn the television on and start flipping through the channels until I find a rerun of Mystic Pizza playing on TNT. Lilly Taylor, Julia Roberts, and Annabeth Gish are all young and beautiful, living in an adorable New England tourist town that they are dying to leave. I saw the movie for the first time when I was a senior in high school and fell in love with the romance of their situation. But what would their characters be like now, if they actually existed and had grown into their thirties? What if their life hadn't stopped once the music swelled and the credits rolled? I wonder if any of their dreams would have come true.

13. Melody

I turn off the television with a snap of the remote. Kelsey leans back in her dad's easy chair and stretches her arms out. "That is the most romantic movie ever!" she says. "I would kill to be Hillary Duff and have Chad Michael Murray in love with me." She sips on her Malibu Coke and sighs.

I try not to let my exasperation show. After all, watching movies on a Saturday night in Kelsey's lavish basement with a huge flat screen TV and free pizza and booze is way better than hanging out at home with mom in our depressing apartment, where all I'd get for dinner is some Ramen and Sunny Delight. But just once, I'd like to pick the movie. If we have to watch a stupid romance, why not something like *Love and Basketball*? I like the end where she challenges him to a game of one-on-one to win his heart. In the movies Kelsey likes, the girls are always clingy losers.

Personally, I'm not a big movie fan anyway. What's the point of wasting your time watching made up stories with people pretending to feel emotion they don't really feel? Then, after you watch it you're supposed to talk about the movie like it's something that actually happened. I just don't get it.

"Kelsey, it's getting late. Maybe we should go over the plan for Monday."

The blissful smile vanishes from Kelsey's face. "Oh yeah, right. I suppose we should."

"What's wrong? Aren't you still into Bobby?"

"Of course I am," says Kelsey. "But come on, let's be realistic. It's never going to work."

"Sure it will. My plan is fool proof. I guarantee it."

"How?" She says. "How can you guarantee it? Have you ever used this plan before?"

"No," I admit. "But…"

She cuts me off. "Will your plan make me five-foot-two, ninety-five pounds, perky, and blond with a cute little nose and pouty lips?"

Every once in a while Kelsey decides to live in reality. It's always very unexpected, and tonight is no exception. I know I need to be careful, because she looks like she'll burst into tears if I say the wrong thing. But it's important that she uses my plan, so I can test it on her and iron out the kinks before I use each step on myself with Mr. L.

"Kelsey, you're being silly. You look great."

She swivels in her chair so that she's facing me. "Uh, reality check. Were you not just watching the movie? I look nothing like Hillary Duff. I'm like one of the overdone stepsisters. And using a quote, plan," Kelsey makes air-quotes with her fingers to compound her sarcasm, "to try and get Bobby—that's totally an ugly stepsister sort of thing to do. And you and I both know that in the end the cute, gushy blond girl always wins the guy. So what's the point of trying?" She collapses her weight into the chair, and pouts.

Good God. Selling her on my plan shouldn't require so much effort and diplomacy. Is this the sort of thing I have to look forward to, once I hit the workforce? I keep my voice even with a smile on my face. "The point is that you and Bobby belong together. You don't have to look like Hillary Duff to have a guy fall in love with you. Besides, we're talking about real life here, *not* the movies. In real life guys sometimes need an extra little push so they can see that it's the unexpected girl who they're actually in love with. And didn't Cinderella use a plan? What was all that stuff about dressing in disguise and going to the ball just to get Prince Charming's attention? If that's not a plan, I don't know what is. If you ask me, the definition of ugly stepsister is 'girl without a plan,' because they're the ones who are going to end up alone."

Kelsey takes a moment to consider my words, then the tension she was wearing evaporates and her body relaxes. "Fine. You've convinced me. Let's go over step two."

"Good girl. Now we're talking." I take out my notebook where I've recorded all the details. "So on Monday, you need to act helpless and put him a situation where he's forced to protect you…"

Kelsey and I choose gym class for her plan of attack. There are two reasons for this. One, it's the perfect environment to promote victim-hood. Two, and more importantly, Kelsey, Bobby, and I all have gym class together, so I can observe her in action and give her feedback afterwards. Of course I don't tell her this, but I also need to watch her so I can serve my own purposes as well.

We're running laps. Kelsey waits until Bobby is very close by, then pretends to be distracted, and runs full-steam into a bleacher. (I specifically told her not to do the twisted ankle thing, it's so tired.) She falls on the floor knee first and yelps in pain. Several kids laugh and call out to her. "Nice going!" one guy shouts.

"Lose a few pounds and you'll be more graceful," I hear Becki Birkland remark.

She doesn't even have to fake the tears. I go over to her, because Bobby has already passed by. "Are you okay?"

Kelsey is smiling and crying at the same time. "Yeah, fine. Just feel really stupid."

"Do you need help getting up?"

"Please."

I pretend to struggle with helping her up, then give up just as Bobby is making his way towards us again.

"Bobby!" I shout. He stops a few feet away from us. "How about a little help here?"

His face looks like murder but he wanders over. Kelsey says, "No really, it's fine. I can get up on my own." She pretends to stand up, then collapses in pain. Mr. Severson, the gym teacher, has now approached the scene. He takes one look at her knee, then turns to

Bobby and slaps him on the back.

"Wilson, I need you to escort this young lady to the nurse. Can you do that for me? Thanks. You're a champ."

Wordlessly Bobby helps Kelsey up, and with her arm around his shoulders, they walk out of the gym towards the nurse's office. On their way past me I hear her say, "Sorry."

His face is bright red, probably because all his buddies are laughing at him, but he replies, "Don't worry about it."

I'm so proud of Kelsey I could spit. I know later on I'll have to reassure her; Kelsey will need to be convinced not to worry about all the mean comments that everyone made. And sure, Bobby heard them and was no doubt embarrassed. But the important thing is he came to her rescue. Any time a guy comes to girl's rescue he feels important, no matter how he feels about the girl. Now all we need to do is capitalize on this, so he associates Kelsey with feeling important. Shouldn't be too tough.

I wipe the smile off my face as I approach Mr. L's room. Today's rehearsal is over; now it's time for tonight's performance.

14. Samantha

I never expected Nate to call me after he refused my advances in the bar parking lot. But he did. The first time he called was to ask me to a movie (*Casablanca*), and the second time was to go snowshoeing (along the shore of Lake Michigan.) The third time was to ask me to attend the annual Shannon Schnee Days Winter Dance Party.

I felt like Marcia Brady, about to have a dreamy date right after my nose got hit by Peter's football. No courtship of mine had ever been more wholesome, awkward, and thrilling all at once. When Nate, wearing jeans and a green crew-neck sweater, picked me up on the night of the dance I was sure I was over-dressed in the black cocktail dress I've owned since 1998. But he smiled in appreciation and said, "You look great!"

Once we got to the dance I was even more convinced that I was out of place. There were a lot of families; parents holding the hands of grade school aged children, or middle-school kids pretending they didn't know their parents, running around in packs. There were a lot of sixtyish-looking participants, enjoying the music of Richie Valens, Buddy Holly, and the Big Bopper. Nate had told me the evening's music was a rendition of their concert tour right before that fateful plane crash.

"Won't that be bad karma, to attend something like that?" I asked.

Nate chuckled. "I don't believe in bad karma."

"I do."

"Does that mean you don't want to go?" he asked.

"No," I replied.

So there we were, semi-slow dancing to La Bamba, and I was trying to ignore the chuckles of people around us. Nate didn't seem bothered by it, but I was sure it was directed towards us. "Are any of your students here tonight?" I asked.

"Nah. They're way too cool to attend something like this."

"But we're not?"

Nate reached down and stroked a lock of my hair. "Sam, are you having a bad time?"

"It's not that. I'm just not sure what we're doing."

"We're dancing," he said.

"Maybe we shouldn't be," I said as I pushed away from him, finding my way through the crowds of young and old, hoping to find some sanity in a quiet hallway. Nate followed me. The air was suddenly much colder, as we were closer to the outside doors and away from the heat of the pack. I shivered.

"What's wrong?" he asked me.

I felt like I was about to push off a very pleasant cliff. But I had to know. "How old are you, Nate?"

"I'm twenty-five."

How could he not be? Standing in front of me, his skin glowing, light bouncing off his hair as if he wore a halo, his looks mirrored his personality. After three dates I couldn't figure out what was wrong with him, except for his refusal to kiss me anywhere other than on the cheek or forehead. "I wish I had a script writer that good for my life," he whispered to me during *Casablanca*. And he bent his head down and sniffed my hair. I looked up and met his eyes in the darkened theater. Then he didn't kiss me. "I love fighting with the snow and cold; maybe I was a Viking in a past life", he said over hot chocolate after our snowshoeing expedition. His fingers traced my own, and I could feel the heat kicking between our hands. "You have an eyelash on your cheek." He leaned forward and brushed it away. Then he didn't kiss me. "Don't you love to see people dancing in large groups? It makes me believe in the human race, to see people made so happy by something so simple," he said, as he pulled me onto the dance floor when we arrived earlier that night. He held my body close and my gaze even closer, as he mouthed the words to *That Will Be the Day That I Die.* Then he didn't kiss me.

"I'm ten years older than you." I said, facing him in that hallway, naked in my black dress.

"Okay."

"And I've made a lot of mistakes in my life," I continued. "I'm not a good person like you are. I'm weak. I make decisions without thinking things through, and I have no direction. All your purpose, your drive, your sense of right and wrong, that's not me. I'm not like you at all."

Nate shrugged his shoulders. "What's your point?"

My heart lurched and pressed against my rib cage. I was convinced this was the easiest way, less painful than prolonging it would be, but saying goodbye now would be like returning a beautiful ball gown because I had nowhere fancy enough to wear it. "I just don't see the point of us spending time together," I said, blinking back tears of frustration.

Nate stepped in, close to me. He put his hand underneath my chin and tilted it up, so our eyes met. "I see a lot of point."

"Why?"

"Because," he said, "You're real, you're honest, and you're beautiful." Then, finally, he kissed me. Wrapped in his arms, I knew with absolute certainty that this kiss far exceeded any kiss between Humphrey Bogart and Ingrid Bergman, or Tom Hanks and Meg Ryan, or even Clark Gable and Vivien Leigh. I had been waiting my whole life for my first Hollywood quality kiss, and now that I had it, no way I was giving up my chance for more.

It's Tuesday morning and I'm stocking the shelves at Bravo Video, as memories of Nate's and my early days dance through my mind. I still haven't heard whether or not I got the promotion, but I thought my interview last week went well. Yet, it's not at the forefront of my concerns, even though it would mean I'd no longer be relegated to menial tasks like the one I'm performing now. Right now, I'm too pissed off with Nate to think about much of anything. Even recalling our best moments together doesn't help me let go of my anger over our fight last night.

And I had thought the evening was going to go so well. He had promised me yesterday morning that he would be home for dinner since it was my night off. We were going to have some time together, and after our strained weekend it felt necessary. So I went grocery shopping and got some fresh catfish, which I was going to marinate and serve with biscuits and steamed veggies. It's one of Nate's favorite meals that I make, and I had thought to pick up Stella Artois (his favorite beer) and key lime pie (his favorite dessert.) We still had the latest episode of *Project Runway* recorded; I envisioned us having a leisurely meal concluded by quality time on the couch and then in bed. But it was not to be.

At 3:30 I got back from a run and found a message on our voice mail. "Hey, it's me," he said. "Something came up and I won't be home until late. I'll explain later. Love you…" click.

I instantly started steaming. I thought about calling him, demanding an explanation, but it felt better to yell at him self-righteously in my head. "You're the one who said we need to communicate better. How are we supposed to do that if you're always putting your job first?" Or, "Yeah, Collin is still in my life, but I think an ex-boyfriend is less threatening to you than your job is to me." Or best yet, "Were you hanging out with Melody? You know, I stood outside your classroom last Saturday, and I could swear it was her laugh that I heard combined with your own. What's going on, Nate?" Nate had told me all about how he had saved her from being raped. But since then he can't seem to get rid of her. And on Saturday, when he got home after hiding in his classroom for several hours, he never mentioned she had been there with him. Then we had a long conversation about how we need to work on our communication. Healthy, huh?

So last night, at 8:30, when he finally came through the door I was so worked up I could barely speak. But I didn't want to bring up the Melody thing, not yet. I knew I would be crossing a line if I did.

I looked at him. His tie was askew, his sleeves rolled up, and he had replaced his contacts with his glasses at some point during the day. And although he wasn't smiling, he looked more relaxed than I had seen him look in a while.

"Where have you been?" I said.

"Didn't you get my message?" he asked, as he strolled over to me on the couch, kissed my cheek, then plopped down beside me.

"I got it, but you didn't say where you were going."

"Oh, right. I had to have dinner with a student."

I gulped back my anger. "Why?" I asked.

"She's having trouble finalizing her college plans. Her mother, who sounds crazy, had decided she didn't want her to go. I needed to go over to the girl's house and eat dinner with them. You know, talk some sense into the mother."

I leaned away from him, creating enough distance to prevent our arms from touching. "Why was it your job to do this?"

He turned his head toward me. "Hon, she was in tears. It's her dream to go to college and make something of herself. She didn't ask me; I just noticed something was wrong and asked her what was up. I sort of had to pry the story out of her. So I offered to go. It was just one of those things."

"What about our plans to eat dinner together?"

He shrugged his shoulders. "I figured it could wait."

"Nate! You promised we'd spend time together tonight! Why is it that I can wait but Melody can't?"

"I never said it was Melody…"

"Well, wasn't it?"

"No," Nate said, a little too loudly. Then his face turned bright red. He looked down at the couch cushion and squinted. I got up.

"So it was some other girl," I said, as I paced into the kitchen to get a glass of water. "You just went to some female student's house to eat dinner and mess with her life. Do you really think that's professional?"

"Wow," he replied, with the warmth of dry ice smoking above his head. "I don't think I want to answer that."

He stood up and walked into the bedroom door, closing it behind him. I followed, finding him lying down on the bed. I sat down on the edge, my back to him. I played with his foot as I spoke.

"Sorry," I said. "I didn't mean to sound like I must have sounded. But I had been looking forward all day to our evening together. I had planned a really special dinner—all your favorites."

He spoke into his pillow. "Why didn't you call and tell me? If I had known I would have come home."

I sighed. I felt betrayed, like how Molly Ringwald was in *Pretty in Pink*. It wasn't enough for Andrew McCarthy to take her to the prom—he had to *want* to take her to the prom. I wanted Nathan to want to come home, whether he felt obligated to or not. Nate took my silence as an answer, and continued on.

"You know Sam, I think part of the problem here is you. You need something other than me to be important to you. Then our evenings together wouldn't be such a big deal. I hate to say it, but sometimes I feel burdened."

I shoved his feet out off my lap and leapt up from the bed. "Well, the last thing I want to be is a burden." The anger that had been brewing inside of me all day was now bubbling over. "And you're right, I need something else. You're so lucky that you have your job, with all those adoring students who you serve so well. You must feel so good about yourself. If only I could aspire to be like you Nate. If only we all could!" Nate's face registered shock, but not much else. I stormed out, much like he had done last Saturday.

I walked through the streets of our neighborhood, his words echoing in my mind. Of course he was right. I don't have his sense of direction. I don't really have a sense of direction at all, a fact which was proved to me as I got lost roaming the streets that I've lived on for years. It was much later once I finally got home, cold and exhausted. Nate was sound asleep. I grabbed a blanket and slept on the couch, then pretended to be asleep several hours later when he got up to go to work.

Now at work myself, I finish putting the DVDs away and wander over to the bulletin board at the store's entrance. I pull down a notice that's been up for over a month and read it, even though I've memorized what it says:

Attention Amateur Film Makers!
The National Institute of Film and Photographic Arts
Is hosting its 3rd annual short-film competition.
First Prize is $25,000 and a year long internship position!

The contest deadline is in two weeks. The internship position is in Chicago. There is no way I could possibly take the position on the off chance that I happened to win. I have no idea for a short film, no equipment, and other than some investments made for me by grandmother before she died, no money.

"Sam, can you come here for a minute?"

I look up to see Hal poking his head out of his office. With utter clarity, I know he's calling me back to tell me whether or not I got the promotion. If I get the job it means more money. But more than that, it means I finally, at thirty-five, have a real job. People might actually respect me. On the surface, it will seem like my life has direction.

I look back down at the flier in my hand. But if I get the job, I won't have time to make this film that I have to make. Before Collin, before Nate, before everything that got in the way, I did want something for myself. And for the longest time, I've thought it was too late. But maybe it's not. Maybe I still have one chance left.

"Sam!" Hal's voice breaks my reverie. "I really need to talk with you. Now please."

I take a final look around the store, ending at Hal's pimply face. Goodbye safety net. "Sorry," I say, as I grab my bag. "I quit." Then I turn around, and while still fiercely clutching the film competition notice in my hand, walk out of Bravo Video for the last time.

15. Melody

I was twelve years old when I learned about the power of words.

I had decided to enter the school spelling bee. While I thought the whole concept of spelling bees was a little silly and over-rated (anyone with half a brain can look up how to spell something) I liked the idea of gaining respect for something so easy. To succeed in a spelling bee all you need is the discipline to memorize, and the ability to think well under pressure. I have both, so of course, I won.

Not that it was effortless. There were many sleepless nights where I sat in bed with a flashlight and a dictionary, reciting back in a whisper the spelling of the most difficult words I could find. And of course I was nervous, standing up in front of the school, spelling words most of the kids had never heard of. By the end of it my left palm was bleeding, because my nervous habit of digging my nails into my own palm. However, the bleeding was pretty mild and if I kept my hand in a fist, which I did, nobody was ever going to notice.

Anyway, my school-wide victory permitted me to move on to the city's competition. For that, I practiced even more, and I went door to door asking people if I could rake their yards or do other odd jobs, so I could raise money to buy something decent to wear for the competition. I was able to come up with $35, enough for a smart light blue blouse off of Macy's sale rack, and a wool pinstriped pencil skirt from Savers, which was too big, but I took it in and it looked fine. On the day of the competition I said a prayer that I wouldn't embarrass myself, and that if I didn't win, that at least I wouldn't be the first one out.

I don't usually pray, but on that morning it seemed necessary, because my naïve twelve-year-old mind actually believed that I could earn respect by standing up there, composed and mature, spelling words like "abstinence," "chutzpah" and "homogeneity". Also, the prize for winning was $500, which would have been lovely to have. I decided I would open a savings account for myself at the bank, so my mother would be unable to touch it, and I'd have an emergency fund for those weeks when she "forgot" to give me lunch money, or insisted I do the grocery shopping without giving me any money to shop with.

I didn't tell my mother about the competition for obvious reasons. On the day it took place I rode the city bus down to the public library, which is where it was being held (in one of the conference rooms). Lots of kids I knew were there, because Carter Wilkin, who took second place in my school's competition, had been permitted to compete as well, and they came to show him their support. You see, my school victory was not without controversy. Carter's last word had been "a cappella." He spelled it correctly, except he didn't include the space between the *a* and the *c*, so he was out and I won with "onomatopoeia." But Carter was really popular, and the whole school thought it was unfair that he lost so they started a petition to that effect. Some kids took their protest a step further by suckering all the sixth graders into standing up at their desks at exactly 10:05 a.m., at which point Rachael Peterson, who is the sort of girl who: (a) never shuts up, (b) believes everyone is interested in what she has to say, and (c) thinks she's always the most important person in the room (because probably nobody has ever told her otherwise), stepped forward and said, "We're not sitting down until Carter is declared the winner."

Nobody would have cared about Carter and the stupid spelling bee, but his parents owned Fantasy Land Skating Rink, and he was always having these awesome (or so I heard) private parties and everyone wanted to be invited to them. So the principal, who took social protest very seriously, called the city competition officials and explained the situation, and they decreed that Carter could compete. And I never let all the uproar bother me, because back then I honestly thought that if I won fair and square, the kids would like and respect me for it.

I was wrong.

The competition started out okay. The bus I had taken ran late, so I was a little rattled walking in, but my mature, classic outfit gave me confidence. I looked way more composed than the other contestants, in their outfits from Gap Kids. When I stood up to spell my first word, "conquer," I spoke with such confidence and clarity - I was sure that conquer was exactly what I was going to do.

But after round three she walked in. I had tried to keep the competition a secret from her; later I found out the contest officials had called that morning when I wasn't there on time. It was before noon when she arrived, but it was clear she had already had a drink or two. I could tell by her smile and the slight stumble to her step. "Excuse me!" she shouted. "My daughter's up there. I need to find a seat!" She stepped over people, loudly muttering her apologies, until she found the one empty seat that was up at the front. Once she finally sat down, she waved to me. "Hey, Melody baby!" Never had I wanted to melt into a puddle more. Not ironically, my next word was "embarrass." "E M B A R R A S S," I said to judges. Then to finish, I focused the last part on my mother, sitting in the front row. "Embarr –ASS!"

After the fourth round there was a break. I hid back stage, but the room was small enough to hear my mother talking to Rachael Peterson's mom. I peaked out from behind the curtain, and saw Rachael standing there too, with a smirk on her face. Rachael had never liked me, because when we were in second grade I started a rumor that she ate her own boogers after she refused to let me borrow her Swan Lake Barbie pencil sharpener. Now was her chance to gain retribution. "Oh, I'm so proud of Melody," my mother yelled. "She looks so damn mature up there. Seriously, just last month she was still wetting her bed. Now look at her!"

I was tempted to make a run for it. And by the way, I had stopped wetting my bed when I was seven. It's not something I'm proud of, because yes, seven is rather old to still have such a problem. However, it's not nearly as bad as being a twelve-year-old bed-wetter. But my mother has a selective memory, especially when she's drunk. Anyway, I was still contemplating walking out of the competition when the signal for the end of intermission was given and the contestants were instructed to walk back out on stage. So with my heart in my throat, I took my seat.

Three more rounds. I was doing fine, despite everything. At the end of the seventh round Carter got out on "poignant," forgetting to put in the *i*. Such a stupid mistake! Suddenly I felt vindicated. Surely everyone would now realize I deserved my spot, that I was in fact the superior speller, and the entire school would cheer and celebrate my victory. At the beginning of the eighth round I stood up for my turn, my head held high, my shoulders back, and my composure intact. The judges asked me to spell "odious." I hesitated for only a moment, but it was long enough. Rachael took my pause as her chance to shout out, "Hey Madsen, why don't you spell out 'bed-wetter'!" Her mother turned to her with a punishing glare, but it didn't matter. My mother, who loves any joke that's at my expense, started to laugh. Later she would explain that she had been laughing with me, not at me. But at that moment, her obnoxious snickering was enough to cause a ripple effect, and soon everyone (or at least it felt like everyone) in the audience had joined in. I stood there, frozen, wanting to be sick but unable to open my mouth. The lights were beating down on me, and the bare stage widened; there were no borders, no offer of support. It was just me. Any help would have to come from within.

It seemed like an eternity, but finally the crowd quieted down. Still, I stood there, silent. Finally one of the judges said, "Miss Madsen, I'm afraid we need your response."

I fought back tears as I answered. "Bed-wetter. B E D dash W E T T E R. Bed-wetter." Then I ran off stage, out of the building, and as far away from my life as I could. Of course, eventually I had to return home to my mother, and two days later to school, where I had a brand new nickname.

So it was then that I realized - on their own, words are nothing.

They are just a group of random letters put together to form sounds that we label as language. People often think that the longer the word, the fancier or more profound or smarter it is. But I learned that day that a word as simple as bed-wetter is in fact far more odious than the word odious itself. Words are nothing without the meanings behind them, and I was done learning about their composition. From now on I would focus on their emotion, their meaning, their power, and put all of it to my own use for my own emotional well-being, my own meanings, my own power.

I also vowed to stop praying. I would look to no one, not even God, to take care of me. I would take care of myself.

Even if it killed me.

It's Friday morning and I'm waiting at Kelsey's locker to hear how step two went. Yesterday I overheard Bobby asking a buddy of his for a ride to school. Abby is on the spring band trip, so his usual mode of transportation is missing. But his friend is grounded from his car, so in Bobby's own words, he was going to be "hoofing it" this morning.

It was the perfect opportunity. Kelsey had already completed step one of my "How To Get a Guy to Leave His Significant Other For You" plan. Step one was multifaceted, including lots of eye-contact, acting helpless and letting him rescue her, then completely ignoring him for a while. Kelsey, on strict orders from me, had been ignoring Bobby for several days, ever since he escorted her to the nurse's office. But this morning she was supposed to drive down Bobby's route to school and offer him a ride. During said ride she needs to have tempted him and imply that she is indeed, available. Of course it makes me nervous that I couldn't supervise her during step two, so I am eagerly awaiting her arrival.

Finally I see her approach, cheeks flushed and smiling.

"Hola, Chica!" she says as she grabs me in a hug. I pull away instantly; we've been friends for months and yet she still doesn't realize how much I hate hugging.

"How did it go?" I ask.

"Oh, it so totally worked," she squeals.

"Describe," I command.

"Okay, so I'm driving down his street, and there he is! So I pull over and I'm like, 'Hey, need a ride?' And at first he's all, 'What are you doing on my street you stalker,' but I laugh and say 'get in' and he does! So we ride to school, and I said that thing you told me to say, about how if he's ever looking for a hook-up with no strings he should call me."

"Did you say …"

"That he would be fulfilling my graduation fantasy by doing me? I totally did! And his face got all red and he sort of laughed, then he said he'd keep it in mind. Then we got to school, and he saw one of his friends and took off. But not before he thanked me for the ride."

My shock and annoyance keeps me from responding right away. Kelsey looks like she was just crowned Queen Princess, that's how pleased she is with herself, and I want to wipe the smug look of triumph off her looming, smug face.

"Kelsey, you cow, I never said to say that! I said to ask him about his fantasies. That was it! You were supposed to ask him about his fantasies, listen to him, smile, and that was it! You came on way too strong. You ruined the whole plan!"

Her face falls. "I'm sorry. But I thought you said…"

'You thought I said! You don't listen, do you? Forget it. I can't help you if you're not going to help yourself."

I storm away before I say anything harsh to her.

Of course, I have been simultaneously executing my plan on Mr. Linden while Kelsey's been fumbling it with Bobby. It was easy to convince him to come for dinner last Monday. All I had to do was bring my financial aid forms with me to work on during his prep, then start silently weeping as I'm filling them out. He asks me what's wrong, I say some story about how they're due but what's the use, my mom doesn't want me to go, my dream is ruined, if only I could get her to see reason, blah, blah, blah. He practically invited himself over.

Dinner went great, too. I cooked up some pork chops, green beans with bacon, and mashed potatoes. He got the chance to see that I'm capable of taking care of a husband by cooking him good meals. I bet his fat wife only feeds him pre-packaged junk food. But the best part was how good he felt about helping me. I got my mom to agree to play along ("You owe me big time," she said) and she let him "convince her" to permit me to go away to college. Then after dinner she left, and Mr. L stayed to help me with the dishes. I said, "Thank you so much. You really are my hero." He blushed and pretended to act all modest, but I could tell it gave his ego a major boost.

Then for the last few days I've made myself as unavailable as possible, telling him they need my help down in the attendance office during our hour together, and being too busy to stop by before or after school. This gives him the chance to miss me. But screw that. Kelsey can't handle executing my plan, but that's not my plan's fault. It's a great plan, and I owe it to both the plan and to myself to see that it's done right.

So fifth hour I head to his room instead of making my way down to see Edith, the secretary in the attendance office, who basically runs the school. She always has extra work that needs to be done, and I like her style of intimidation. It's actually been sort of fun, helping her the last few days, but enough is enough. I have a man to catch.

Mr. L's head snaps up when I walk in, and his hand raises to his head as he absently strokes his hair off his forehead. He's practically primping when he sees me. Should this be so easy?

"Miss Madsen, I thought you were helping Edith this hour."

"I was going to, but the guilt crept up on me, and I told her I had to come back to you."

He smiles and utters a silent chuckle. "Not necessary. I'm sure she's busier than I am. There's no reason to feel guilty."

"But it's the weekend. You don't want to have to take work home."

"True…" he says.

"What would you like me to do?" I'm standing before him, looking good in my blue sweater that brings out the color of my eyes and my tight khakis that I found on sale at Old Navy just last week.

"Um, you could grade these worksheets," and he hands me a pile—they're on types of verbs. I settle into grading and there is silence between us for quite a while. In fact, I wait until I am done with the stack of papers before I say anything else. I get up and walk back over to his desk, placing them on the one clear spot.

"All done," I say. "Is there anything else you'd like me to do?"

"Actually, I can't think of anything. The only other stuff I have to grade is journal assignments, and I can't let you grade those."

"Why not? Too private?"

His mouth curls up in a crooked smile. "No… well, that's partly it. It's just that with any writing assignment, I need to grade it."

"Right. I understand. And I wouldn't want to invade anyone's privacy. I'm sure lots of your students write you all sorts of things that they wouldn't want anyone else to see. There's just something about you that makes people want to open up."

Mr. L shifts in his seat. "I doubt that's true."

"No, it totally is." I pause for several seconds and just gaze down at him as he is sitting in his desk chair. He looks up and our eyes meet.

"Miss Madsen…" he begins, but I cut him off.

"No, just let me say this. I know you're going to tell me that I shouldn't, but after I'm done you can pretend that I never said anything."

He jumps up from his chair and walks around to face me. "I don't know what you're going to say, but don't say it."

"Relax! All I'm going to say is that after everything, well…"

"Melody, please don't…"

"…you're my best friend. And if you ever need anything from me, you've got it." I laugh and punch him in the shoulder. "There. That wasn't so bad, now was it?" I laugh again. "What did you think I was going to say?"

He smiles in relief and shrugs his shoulders. "I have no idea. It's just, well, you know…"

The bell rings, signaling the end of the day and the beginning of the weekend. Voices fill the hall outside, and I remind myself that timing is everything. "Don't worry," I say. "I'd never do that to you."

I smile, punch him on the shoulder again, tell him to have a great weekend, then walk away.

Eat that, Kelsey. This is how it's done.

16. Samantha

I've never been a fan of birthdays, even when I wasn't yet worried about growing older. They have always seemed a little unnecessary, like the warning label on a package of cigarettes. We all know smoking is bad for you, just like we all know that everyone is going to grow older and die; it's inevitable. So what's the point of celebrating the passage of time? I told Nate this theory, and he said I was morose.

"Lighten up," he scolded. "There are good things about growing older, you know. I see plenty of reason to celebrate."

"People also find reasons to smoke. That doesn't mean it's a good idea."

He laughed, and took his hand off the steering wheel and placed it on my knee and gave it a squeeze. "You're silly."

I crossed my arms and pouted. We were driving to his parents' house, west of Shannon, in Plymouth, Wisconsin. "I'm nervous. What if she doesn't like me? What if she's still not over the fact that we got married before you introduced me to her?"

"Then I guess we'll divorce." Nate paused for dramatic effect for about two seconds before he started laughing.

"Ha, ha, ha, Mr. Smarty Pants. I'm serious here. Have you thought about the wisdom of bringing me to meet you mother on her birthday? She's going to be in a bad mood already because she's a year older…"

"My mom loves birthdays…"

"And she's meeting the woman who took her son away from her…"

"…and she loves me."

"If she hates me it could really ruin her day," I finished. "I think you should turn the car around. It's not too late. You'd only be a little late if you take me home and then go back."

He sighs. "Sam, I'd be over an hour late at this point. And anyway, you're being ridiculous. Mom wants me to be happy. She'll see that you're the person who makes me happy, and she'll instantly love you."

I didn't believe him, but I didn't say anything. We drove on in silence. My mind began to wander to other things, and I played with the strap of my new fake Burberry clutch that Jane had brought me back from her trip to New York. Outside it was raining the way it does in February, a light sleety sort of rain that is worse than snow. The windshield wipers were swooshing it all away, but that was not enough to make me feel warm and safe.

I looked over at Nate, and noticed his jaw was clenched. I reached up, and ran my fingers through his hair. "Sorry," I said. "I know this is important to you. I'll be good, I promise."

"Just be yourself, Sam. Anyway, it's not you or Mom that I'm worried about."

"Your dad?" I asked.

He nods. "Let's just hope he doesn't get completely plastered. The last thing I want to subject you to is a sloppy display of how much he loves me, loves my mom, etc. That will occur right before he loses his temper about something stupid. Happens every time."

"Hmm." I said.

"What?" Nate responded.

"I'm just wondering—do you think part of our mutual attraction comes from our dysfunctional families?"

Nate arched his neck at my question, quickly darted his eyes at me, then back to the road. "What are you talking about? You and your dad get along great. And he's one of the sweetest guys I've ever met."

Nate may have been idealizing my relationship with Dad slightly, but I let it go because I wanted to believe he was right. "I'm not talking about my dad. I'm talking about my mom."

"But you don't really have a relationship with your mother."

I pushed my exasperation down, and made an effort to sound

diplomatic. "That's my point. *Not* having a relationship with my mother is pretty dysfunctional."

Nate again momentarily took his eyes off the road to glance over at me. "When was the last time you spoke?"

"I don't know. A year ago, maybe?"

"Wow."

"Yeah, I know."

Nate had heard my mom story already. It was May 1989 and I was eighteen years old, about to graduate from high school. Mom, Dad, and I had been living as a tight trio for my entire life. I thought we were happy. Then one lovely spring evening over dinner (tuna casserole, which to this day I still can't stomach) she announced that her life lacked meaning. She decided she needed to help people in need, so she was leaving for Mexico to be a part of the hunger relief effort. Despite my tears and my dad's pleading, a month later she boarded the plane, promising she would be back when she felt she had made a difference.

Three years later she returned. For six months. Then a friend who she had worked with told her about a relief effort being organized in Guatemala. "I hear they desperately need my help," she said. That time she was gone for nearly five years.

And so the pattern was formed. She's been all over South America, she's learned to speak Spanish fluently, and I can only guess about the lovers and adventures she's had. Every few years she'll come back, and live with my dad just long enough to keep him hopeful and in love with her. Then she'll disappear again, claiming she has an obligation to the world and she's sacrificing her comfort for the greater good.

Every now and then I hear from her, but it's hard to communicate when she has no phone, computer, or reliable post service. She used to call me on my birthday and Christmas, but that stopped once I turned twenty-one. One year she actually came home for Christmas, but by that time Dad and I had formed our own traditions that didn't really include her. We tried, all three of us tried, but it was the sort of trying that feels like being at a party and getting stuck talking to someone that you only sort of know and like for way too long. Meanwhile, my dad and she are still married. Dad believes she'll come back for good some day, though why he would want her to is beyond me.

"Anyway," I said to Nate. "It's a good thing you and I are never going to have kids. With the parents we've had as role models, I'm sure we'd be a disaster."

Before we got married I told Nate that I didn't want children. He said that was okay, as long as he had me, he'd be happy.

But now he responded, "We might not be so bad."

"Yeah, right. Can you imagine me as a mother?" I laughed, but Nate didn't join in.

"Actually, yeah. I could," he said.

I wasn't prepared for a big time fight, but this was a big time issue. "Nate, you said you were fine with not having kids. I really hope you haven't changed your mind about that."

"What if I have?"

"Well, then we have a problem."

"Sam…" his voice trailed off. "You never really told me why. Why don't you want kids?"

I squeezed my eyes shut, hating myself for lying. "There's no specific reason. I just don't."

"You know what I think?" he said. "I think you believe you're somehow unworthy. Like you don't deserve that sort of happiness."

I turned my head away and stared out the passenger window. So many cars on the road on a night like tonight. Where in the world was everyone going?

"Sam?"

I sighed because I had to answer. "It's more complicated than that," I said.

"But I'm partially right, aren't I?"

"Yeah."

"Honey." He pulled the car over to the side of the road, and turned the ignition off. With it went the sound of the radio, the defroster, and the windshield wipers. The car was now filled only with our breathing, and he took off his seat belt and captured me in a hug. "Listen to me," he muttered into my hair, "Nobody deserves happiness more than you. And you would be a fantastic mother."

Tears mixed with gratitude, love, and frustration ran down my face. How is it possible that he understands me so well without really knowing me at all?

That was several months ago, and since then I have acquiesced and told Nate we could have kids. I'm trying to believe him, trying to adopt the right mind set for being a mother. Maybe what I need is to do something truly great first, something where I make a difference in the world. Then I won't feel the need to take off on my family, like my own mother did.

I've just left Bravo for the last time. I'm in my car, driving towards the school, rehearsing in my mind how I'm going to tell Nate about my newest career change, when my cell phone rings. It's Jane.

"Hey," I say. "You'll never guess what just happened. It's going to sound crazy, but I'm really, really happy."

I pause as I make a turn at the light; it's then that I hear the crying on the other end of the line.

"Jane?" No answer. "What's wrong? Can you tell me what's wrong?"

Her voice sounds strangled and unnatural. "It's the baby, Sam. The mom changed her mind."

Instantly I'm crying too. But my tears are silent; I have to be strong for Jane. "I'll be right over," I say. At the next stoplight I make a U-turn, and drive off in a completely different direction.

Twenty minutes later I'm sitting on the couch, holding Jane in my arms as she sobs into my shoulder.

"I just feel so stupid!" she wails. "How could I have been dumb enough to think it would work out this time?"

She cries. I rub her back with the palm of my hand. "You were excited. There's nothing stupid about that."

"No!" she demands. "You were right when you told me not to

get my hopes up. I should have listened to you. Now I have his room all ready, I washed all the baby clothes so they wouldn't irritate his skin, and they're all laid out, ready for him. And I can't return any of it now. Plus I told everyone about him, and now I'm going to have to tell people that it's not going to happen, and I'll have to deal with their sympathy. Oh God!" She lifts her head up and shouts into the ceiling. "How could I have been so completely stupid?"

She cries harder. Of course she'd rather think about non-returnable baby clothes or the social awkwardness of having to tell people. It's easier than thinking about the baby she's not going to be a mother to. But I know the real pain won't set in until she does think about him.

"Jane…" I say, and I stop, unable to complete my thought. Nothing will help, not unless I have a baby to give her.

"He was never mine," she says to the ceiling. "So why do I feel like I lost him?" She shakes her head and wipes away more tears. "No. I have to stop doing this to myself. I can't let myself believe anymore. Why did I believe this time?"

My response is to grab her hand and give it a squeeze. She continues. "I mean, isn't the definition of insanity when you keep committing the same action over and over, while each time expecting a different a result?"

"You weren't wrong to believe, Jane."

"Yes I was." Her voice rises in volume and aggravation. "Obviously I was wrong. Obviously I am always going to be wrong. Maybe my family is right, and God just doesn't want me to have a baby."

"You don't believe that," I say.

She sniffs—a pathetic little whimper of a sniff. "I don't think I know how to believe in anything anymore." She looks at me, and it takes all my strength not to look away. The pain I see swimming in her eyes nearly breaks my heart. "Why do I have to want a baby so badly?" she pleads. "Why can't I just be one of those women who doesn't care?"

Then there is an unspoken question that neither of us dares to utter. Was she referring to me? After an eternal moment, I say the only thing I can think of to say.

"What can I do?"

Her tear-stained face contorts into an unnatural smile. "I don't know. Have a baby for me?" She fakes a laugh.

The floor shifts underneath me as I realize she's half serious.

"I can't do this adoption thing again," she says. "Next time it has to be Jake's and my baby. That's the only way that it can't be taken away from us. But since I can't carry a baby to term, we need somebody else's uterus to do the job for us."

I carefully form my question, and it comes out in a squeak. "So it would be your egg and Jake's sperm, growing inside me?"

She looks up, surprised. "Sam, I'm not actually asking you to do this. If Jake and I decide to go this route, we would hire somebody. There are lots of surrogate mothers out there; we'd just need to find one.'"

"Is that easy to do?"

She shrugs her shoulders "I don't know. It's not like finding a cleaning lady, you know? I mean, I have trouble with the idea of hiring someone to come to into my house when I'm not here, and this is way more personal. What's more intimate than someone else carrying our baby? Jake wanted to do it this way all along, but I've resisted because it just seemed too weird."

Jane takes a sip of her tea, and places her cup down on the table. She wipes the tears off her face with her sleeve, and forces a smile. "But enough, I'm sick of thinking about it. Tell me about the crazy thing that you're so happy about."

In an instant an idea barges into my brain and takes hold so strongly, it's impossible to make it let go. I know I should keep my mouth shut; this sort of decision should not be made impulsively. But what the hell? My mouth opens, and the words fly out.

"Jane, what if I said we could make both our dreams come true at once?"

She squints at me. "What are you talking about?"

More than anything, I want to erase her pain. I know this kind of pain, and it's unfair that somebody as good and deserving as she is should be going through this. But I could change that, with just nine months of sacrifice, I could change her life forever. So I say, "Let me carry your baby." She starts to shake her head no, so I continue, because of course there's something in it for me too. "And let me make a film about the experience! It could be amazing! You'll get the baby you've always wanted, and I'll have the film subject of a lifetime—all tastefully done, of course."

"But… there's no way." Without realizing it, Jane was speaking the truth about the film contest I was dead set on entering less than an hour ago. This film would be impossible to finish in two weeks. But screw the contest. I would make the film anyway, and with any luck, the film would end up making me as well.

I grab her hands and tuck my knees under me. "This is my chance to do something for you, and I'll admit, for me too. This is my chance. Let me carry your baby." Jane laughs, and pushes me away.

"You're insane."

"I'm serious."

"Sam, no, I can't…"

"Why? Is it that I want to make a film of it? Are you worried about your privacy?"

"No! After all the adoption proceedings and fertility treatments I've been through, I don't even know what privacy is anymore."

"Then what? Are you worried that it would be too weird, that I'd become attached to the baby or something?"

She blinks and looks down. "How could you not become attached? When a baby is growing inside you, you're going to feel like it's yours."

I force my emotions down. "I could handle it, though. I know I could."

Jane sighs, and squeezes my hands in her own. "Sam, I love you. And I appreciate your offer more than I can ever express. But you're not thinking this through. And no offense, you do have a tendency to be impulsive."

I smile and shake my head. "You think I'll change my mind halfway through? I won't. I couldn't. Besides, didn't you say you'd do anything for a baby? I can't believe you're not willing to take a chance."

She knits her brow, forming a tense little line right between her eyes. "This is a baby we're talking about, not a lottery ticket. The stakes are high."

I look at her straight on. For reasons that extend beyond my film or any discernable logic, I know I have to do this. Now it's my turn to cry. "Jane, you know I've made more than my share of mistakes. Doing this for you, it would be like correcting a really big one. Let me do this for you. Let me do something truly good, so at the end of everything, I'll know there was at least one positive mark I've left in the world."

I can feel her resolve falter. After a moment she says, "I'd have to talk to Jake."

"Of course," I say.

"And you'll have to talk to Nate."

All of a sudden I remember Nate. My husband Nate. Oh yeah, him.

I smile and squeeze her hands again. And with self assurance borrowed from the air around us I say, "Don't worry. He'll be fine with it."

Part 2

17. Samantha

I was late getting home. It had been a difficult day of serving tables and I was ready to relax with my feet up and a beer in hand. *Thirtysomething* was on that night, and I was hoping to find out whether or not Nancy was going to survive her cancer. I tried to remember if there was still a frozen pizza left in our freezer. There should be, unless Collin had eaten it already.

I walked into our apartment and immediately felt relief. There was no residual cooked pizza smell, as there always was after baking one. My pizza was safe and I now knew my evening would be complete. Yet my euphoria quickly evaporated as I realized he was experiencing a euphoria of a different sort. I saw the mirror in the sink, and I knew. Then I heard voices from the living room, and I was tempted to turn back around and exit the apartment. But where would I go?

"Sam, is that you?"

I shrugged my jacket off in defeat and shuffled into the living room. Collin and some guy in a light blue polo shirt were pouring over their business and marketing textbooks with an intensity that was almost funny. A few months ago Collin and I had rented *Wall Street*, but he fell asleep before the end. He didn't see Charley Sheen getting hauled off to jail, and I was convinced that if he had he wouldn't have switched his major to business with the goal of becoming a millionaire by the time he's thirty. Collin swore the movie has nothing to do with his recent life-style change, but I was skeptical.

"Hey babe, you remember Marty, right?"

Unfortunately, I did. Skinny with overly styled blond hair, he would have been good looking if he hadn't resembled a ferret. "Sure. How are you, Marty?"

"Great. Good to see you, Sam."

I couldn't say the same, so I just kept quiet. I looked over at Collin, and I could tell they had snorted fairly recently. He always had an altered look in his gray eyes when he was high, like the guy I loved had taken a break and someone else had taken residency in his body. It was nothing blatant, I'm not trying to get all *The Exorcist*–like here, but I think when you know someone intimately you can sense any little difference and it thus becomes magnified, even if it's only to you.

"How was your day?" Collin asked me. There was a fake glow underneath his olive skin, and his smile was so wide he ought to have been in a toothpaste commercial.

"Long. I'm tired."

"Then let me take care of you." Collin shoved his books away, jumped up and pulled me over to the couch, forcing me to land in his lap. He planted a big kiss squarely on my mouth, and I pulled away without trying to be subtle. I struggled out of his arms.

"Collin, no."

"What's your problem?"

"I can't even begin to answer that."

Collin laughed as if I was being sarcastic. I couldn't stand to look at his glowing face, so I looked down at his foot, and I noticed a huge hole in his sock. His big toe was sticking out, and there was a hair on it. Up until that point I was sort of unaware of how angry I was, but seeing his big toe with that single, grotesque hair sprouting out of it drove home my frustration at break-neck speed. Suddenly I wanted nothing more than to cause his toe pain. I hated his stupid hairy toe sticking out of that stupid hole in his stupid, stupid dirty sock. So impulsively I bore my weight down, then jumped up and landed directly on his foot, forcing the majority of my weight onto his toe.

His laughter abruptly stopped as his face contorted in pain.

"Son a bitch! What the hell did you do that for?" He pushed me off him and I landed on my behind—a painless fall. "God damn it,

Sam! I think you broke my toe!"

"Huh," I said, dispassionately. "Sorry, I don't know what I was thinking." His toe did look kind of crooked and purple. "You know, I'd take you to the emergency room, but I've heard there's nothing they can do for broken toes. Guess you'll just have to suffer."

Collin looked over to Marty. "Do you have any more?"

"Yeah, sure." Marty got up to retrieve the mirror from the kitchen.

"No. Not while I'm here. You promised me at least that." I yelled this to Collin.

"Well if you hadn't broken my toe..."

"Take an Advil!"

Marty came back into the living room, with the mirror in one hand and his bag of blow in another. He sat down and prepared it just like they do in that Michael J. Fox movie that I thought was so bad. I sat there passively, as if I was watching TV rather than a real life guy doing something I detest. Collin was still writhing in pain.

"Hurry, man."

Marty handed the mirror over to Collin, but I was still sitting on the floor. Unexpectedly my arm had a mind of its own, and I reached up and knocked the mirror out of Marty's hands. It went flying over the couch, landing on the floor, cocaine scattering everywhere, destined to mix with the rest of the dust that covered our apartment.

They both stared at the fallen mirror, stunned. But the moment didn't last, and they directed their attention back to me. I got up, thinking I'd make a run for it. Marty thought otherwise, and he grabbed my arm, stopping me. He twisted it into my back and I yelped in protest.

"Do you have any idea how much that cost? Who gives you the right to do that?" He said this softly into my ear, pulling on my arm even harder as I struggled to get away. I realized I was powerless, and admitted defeat by crying out. "Collin, please. Help."

Collin climbed out of his pain, shock, and anger to see me in trouble. I could see the struggle on his face, but he said, "Marty, let go of her. I'll pay you back for it."

Marty released my arm, and I dissolved into tears. I looked over at Collin, and now his face was unreadable. "Get out," he said.

So I did. And it was over. For eight whole months.

That was fifteen years ago. Now I am sitting at my apartment window, watching as Collin on the ground below plants tulips and daisies in the boxes around our entryway. It's springtime and everything is in bloom.

Sometimes my mind jumps to the potholes in the ever-bumpy road that was my relationship with Collin, just to remind myself of how good I have it with Nate. Our relationship has been a remarkably smooth ride in comparison.

For instance, he was so cool about the whole me-carrying-a-baby-for-Jane thing.

"If it's something you have to do, then it's something you have to do." That's what he said, after I had pleaded my case over dinner at Timber House Steak Lodge. I thought the comfortable environment and family atmosphere would put him right in the mood to hear me out, plus Nate loves a good steak at a reasonable price. So I had arranged all the bullet points in my brain, ready to shoot them out when necessary:

- Yes, I'm getting up there. But women over thirty-five have a better chance of conceiving and carrying a baby to term if they've already had one.
- Jane has always been such a good friend; she's given me so much. What better way is there to pay her back?
- I've been looking for meaning in my life. Now I know how to find it.
- Think of the film I could make!

But it turned out to be unnecessary. Nate hardly seemed concerned at the idea, and said, "It's your body. I'll trust you know what you're doing."

"So you're not worried about us having kids one day?' I asked.

He leaned forward and took my hand. "Sam, there's nothing I want more than to have a baby with you. But I know from experience; trying to keep someone from doing something important is like kicking yourself in the foot." He smiled at me then, his eyes crinkling in that adorable way that first made me fall in love with him. "I have to accept the whole package, don't I? I love that you're kind, and giving, and impulsive. But the flipside to that is putting up with the inconveniences caused by your generosity along the way."

So the next day I called up Jane, and told her we were on. And Nate didn't bat an eye when I told him I quit my job. We agreed it was smart for me not to work for a while. Nate has good health insurance, so we had nothing to worry about in that regard, and Jane and Jake were going to help fund my film by giving me a fraction of the money they would be paying a professional surrogate or by going through with an expensive adoption. The whole thing happened really fast, and was unexpectedly successful. I guess artificial insemination is a big financial risk, but for once luck was on Jane and Jake's side, because I got pregnant on their first very expensive try. I'm now in my sixth week. Sometimes it all seems too good to be true.

Maybe it is. I have done research on surrogate motherhood, mostly for background information for my film, and it seems I'm not the ideal candidate. You're supposed to have kids already; I guess because you're less likely to become attached to the one you're giving away. Also, you're not supposed to rush into anything. There are even lawyers who specialize in forming contracts between surrogates and potential parents, just so everything is laid out and official. But doing things that way just isn't my style, and it would have felt weird anyway. I mean, Jane's my best friend.

But then I get hormonal or nauseous, and I lose perspective. Like today. This morning I got up and felt like I was going to be sick, but I didn't throw up. This happens most mornings, and it's not what I was expecting. In movies pregnant women can be going along perfectly fine, then all of a sudden they run out of the room with their hand over their mouth, and return a couple of seconds later with the sound of the toilet flushing in the background, acting like throwing up is no big deal and barely crimps their style. I *hate* throwing up. I have a hard time permitting my stomach to let go, so even if my guts are pleading with me, I hold on with great tenacity. I wish I could be some other way, but I don't know how. The result? I feel like I'm about to puke all the time, yet I never do. On top of that I feel like I have the worst case of PMS ever, complete with mood swings, tender breasts, and a strong conviction that I am fat. And this is only my sixth week. I read that symptoms aren't even supposed to start until around your seventh or eighth week. Nate suggested perhaps my symptoms are exaggerated since I am so focused and aware of my pregnancy, and I started to cry.

"What are you saying, Nate?" I said. "Are you calling me a hypochondriac? You think I'm making all this up?"

"Sweetie, no. But the only thing you're focused on right now is your pregnancy."

"And my film! I don't just sit around and watch *Dawson's Creek* all day, you know. I'm working on my film!"

"But your film is about pregnancy. That's all I'm saying."

I couldn't defend myself because he was right. Pregnancy is all I think about lately, except for when I'm watching TV. (I actually have been watching an awful lot of *Dawson's Creek*, it's on every morning when I'm usually feeling sick, and it takes my mind off the nausea.) Yet I have been working on my film. I've made a lot of progress, setting up interviews with other surrogates and doctors, and of course, filming weekly testimonials with myself, Jane, and Jake. Nate agreed to do monthly testimonials, which I thought was generous, considering the circumstances.

But my biggest accomplishment so far has been telling my dad. I was going to try to keep it from him, but Nate convinced me to come clean. Last week Dad called me with a question over whether Nate and I were coming to Chicago for Easter. We had already had two conversations about this, and I had told him no, an answer which he found to be unsatisfactory.

"Sam, honey. I just thought you might want to go to Ruth's Kris for brunch. I know how you love it. But you need to let me know so I can make a reservation."

"Dad, don't worry about that. We're not coming. Nate only gets the Friday before off, and besides, I don't feel that well."

There was a pregnant (no pun intended) pause before he replied. "Why, what's wrong with you?"

I laid down on the bed, flat on my back, staring at a watermark on the ceiling, caused years ago by a leaking toilet. I forced myself to focus. "Dad, you need to hear me out. Promise not to interrupt until I'm done, okay?"

"Now you have me worried."

"Dad, promise."

He grunted his reply, and I was hit with a strong pang of guilt for putting him through this.

"Dad, I'm pregnant." I heard him gasp in delight, so I hurried out my next words before he could congratulate me. "But it's not what you think. I'm a surrogate for Jane and Jake. Jane can't carry a baby to term, so they're using my womb to carry an embryo made from her egg and his sperm."

Long pause. I could hear his breathing - proof he was still alive, and hadn't yet collapsed from cardiac arrest. That was something.

"It's only for nine months," I said, after I'd figured out he was refusing to say anything. "Then I can have another one, one for Nate and me."

Another long pause.

"I mean, how often do we get a chance to do something truly wonderful for another person, you know? Jane will be such a good mother. I feel really great about this."

Long, long pause.

"And I'm making a film about the whole experience. It's going to be my seminal work, Dad. If it's good, maybe I can sell it to HBO or the Sundance Channel. It's the sort of thing that will attract tons of publicity."

Excruciating pause.

"Dad, please say something."

He sighed, letting out a breath as if he was letting go of something precious. "Sam, tell me you thought about this for more than a few seconds before you agreed to it."

"What? Of course I did. I wouldn't commit to carrying a child without thinking it through all the way."

"And have you thought about how you'll feel when it's time to give the baby up?"

"Dad, it's not my baby. I won't be giving away my own baby, it's not like that."

"I get how it works, honey. But this baby will be a part of you for nine months. I know you; you're incapable of not falling in love. I just worry that when it's time to hand that baby over, your heart will break."

"Well don't worry. I know what I'm doing Dad. I'm not going to let my heart break."

My dad sighed again. "Oh, Sam. I've just heard you say that one too many times."

18. Melody

I'm sitting in bed doing my homework when I hear my mom come home. I consider turning off the lamp on my bedside stand. If she thinks I'm asleep then it's less likely she'll come into my room and bug me. I've had a difficult day and I'm not in the mood to talk to her. But I hesitate a moment too long before turning off my light, and her footsteps approach.

"I have news!" she announces, standing in my doorway.

"I don't even want to try and guess what it could be," I say. "Just tell me so I can finish my AP Calc and hopefully get to bed before three."

She smiles and enters my room. She's practically skipping as she gets to my bed, sits, and starts bouncing. With her brown hair up in a clippie thing, and tendrils hanging down in curls, she looks almost pretty. "Kenny proposed! His divorce came through, and he's free! He doesn't have to pay for his crazy wife anymore, and we can be together! Isn't that great?"

I keep my head down, buried in my work. "Sure. Congratulations. Just don't expect me to baby-sit Petey and Penny any more than I already do. Can I get back to my homework now?"

She reaches over and slams my book shut.

"Mom!"

She pretends not to notice how annoyed I am. "Come on honey," she says in her best cheerleader voice, "this is the best thing that's ever happened to us. It means we can finally get out of this town. Kenny has a job all lined up in Green Bay, and he wants to move us all out there. Isn't that fantastic?"

I work against my instinct, and decide not to lash out. Instead I keep my voice calm, although I can't help tapping my pencil nervously against my textbook. "To you, Mom. It's the best thing that's ever happened to you. I'm not going to Green Bay."

She just smiles down at me. "Of course you are. Where I go, you go."

In frustration, I throw my pencil over the side of the bed. "I graduate in a few weeks! Then I'm going to college, remember?"

"I remember. And I don't see any evidence that you've hooked up with your teacher. Isn't that our deal?"

"Give me time. I'm working on it." I hold eye contact with her for an extra moment, enough to make anyone but her feel uncomfortable. Then I pointedly open my Calculus book back up, determined to figure out these stupid equations. I wish I still had that pencil. It would look so undignified to try and retrieve it now.

Mom continues. "Are you? Two months ago he came for dinner, but I haven't heard anything about him lately."

My mom doesn't understand taking things slow; she rivals Cookie Monster in her need for immediate gratification. I'm not even going to attempt to explain to her the time commitment that hooking in Mr. L requires. Sure, it's been two months since we became BFFs, but those two months have been time well spent. Every day he relaxes a little more and opens up in new ways while he learns to trust me. If I throw myself at him too soon it will ruin everything.

I keep my head buried in the equations. "It's going to happen, Mom. I just need to go at my own pace."

Mom lies down, spread eagle, across my mattress. Her legs carelessly knock into my work, sending it flying off my bed. "Melody honey, get real. The man is married. I'm not saying that you don't got it going on, but he's a teacher. There's no way."

I look at her face, upside down beneath me. She looks like one of those weird Picasso paintings from this angle. "I'm making real progress, Mom."

She sits up and laughs, then literally pats me on the head. "That's what you think. Have you even kissed him yet?"

I consider lying, but there's no point. Mom is the one person who can read me like a vision test. When it comes to me, she's always been 20/20. "No," I say. "But I can tell he's getting tempted."

She laughs again, harder. "Sweetie, give it up. You're coming to Green Bay with us. This is a good thing. You're meant to be living in a real city. Trust me, you'll love it."

I sigh. "Okay, let's just say for a moment I would consider this. When we would be going?"

"Kenny's job starts in two weeks."

"Are you insane? I can't start at a new school right before I graduate! It will ruin everything. All my hard work…"

"Don't be so dramatic. It's just high school."

"It's my future, Mom. All the advanced courses, everything I've done to try and get into a good college. Enduring all the morons and rumors—Mom, you can't pull me out now."

"Why not? You hate that school. Anyway, colleges don't care about what grades you get during the last part of senior year."

"That's not always true. Besides, I'm late getting my applications in, so they'll look at it all."

Mom purses her lips into a superior looking line. "Well, I guess you should of thought of that sooner." She gets up from my bed with a triumphant little hop. "You have two weeks, hon."

I get up too, and when I reach her I grab her by the shoulders, forcing her to look me in the eye. "Mom, please, don't do this."

She lifts up her right hand and cradles my cheek in it. "I would be a lot more sympathetic if I knew you weren't lying. Admit the real reason why you want to stay."

I can't move my head, so I force my eyes down. "I don't know what you mean."

"This man who saved you, you're in love with him." I try to hide my astonishment; she knows about Mr. Linden saving me. I thought I had been successful at keeping the whole incident under wraps. Is it possible that she knew all along and just didn't care enough to mention it?

If my mother can read my mind, she doesn't let on. "You wanting to stay isn't about proving me wrong, or going to college, or proving to yourself that you're desirable. This is about you needing to be around him."

I break away from her touch. "You underestimate me."

She folds her arms across her chest and shifts her weight to onto one hip. "Really? So I'm the only one here who is stupid enough to fall in love? You're better than that?"

"I know what I'm doing, Mom."

"Maybe. But you don't know why you're doing it."

I shake my head, partly in an effort to shake off these thoughts. She's wrong. I know what I want; I want college, and I want to be with him. But if I admitted to wanting it all, she'd laugh in my face. "You'll see!" I assert. "My plan is going to work and he's going to leave his wife for me."

She walks out of my room, but pauses once more in the doorway. "Only if you can make it happen in two weeks."

The next morning I find Kelsey down in the cafeteria, eating French toast sticks and drinking an icy orange juice cup. "Hey," I say. "I need to ask you a favor."

Kelsey and I haven't been on such great terms since I called her a cow several weeks ago. At first that was fine with me. I didn't see the point in continuing on with the plan after she offered Bobby her no-conditions-required-services. Doesn't she get that *anyone* can get a guy to sleep with you if you do that? My plan is about so much more, and I didn't see wasting it on her. So we were barely talking for a while. Then I started to miss having somewhere to hang out when I wasn't working or at home, so I pretended to be sorry. I'm actually surprised she didn't come to me first, but whatever. Anyway, we're back on track now, but not going at the same speed as before.

I sit down across from her and give her my sweetest smile. "Hey, I need a favor."

"What sort of favor?" she asks. If I didn't know better, I'd say she sounded weary. But it must be my imagination, because Kelsey would do anything for me.

"A sort of big one. My mom wants to get married and move to Green Bay, in like, two weeks. Can I live with you until graduation?"

Kelsey's eyes grow wide and she gently places her orange juice down. "You seriously want to live with me?"

"Only until school is over. I wouldn't be any trouble, I promise. And this way we could really put 'Operation Get Bobby' into full swing. We haven't done much in the last few weeks, and it's time for you to take the next step."

Kelsey's face turns pink. "I thought you said I messed it up. I thought we were through with the plan."

"No, of course not. We just needed to give the plan some room to breathe. But I think you're ready for phase two, which is to discredit the other woman. I worked out all the details last night, and …"

"I'd have to ask my parents!" Kelsey blurts out.

"Huh?"

"About you moving in." She says. "I don't know what they'll say. They can be kind of strict about that sort of thing."

I laugh. "Whatever! They're never home. They wouldn't even notice I'm there."

Kelsey tilts her head and tugs on her blouse. "Come on, Melody."

"Alright, just tell them it's a sleep over that got out of control. Please, I need you to do this for me. And it would be fun, don't you think? Like we're sisters?" I lay on all the charm and I can feel her starting to melt. She even gives me a half smile.

"I'll ask them," she says.

19. Samantha

I don't know what you want me to say."

"I want you to say what's on your mind. Just be honest. That's all." Nate smirks at my response, but I choose to ignore it. I've booked the television studio at the Shannon local access channel. I have a membership, so I can use most of the equipment and studio space for free, in exchange for letting the station air my work to fill time.

Nate is sitting underneath the Fresnel lights, looking about as comfortable as a cat in the bathtub.

"You want me to be honest about what it feels like to have my wife pregnant, but not with our baby? And you plan to air this on the local access channel? Did you take a hallucinatory for breakfast?"

I talk from behind the camera. "Honey, nobody watches local access. It will be fine."

He hunches up his shoulders into two tense little knobs, almost so they're touching his ears. "Remind me again what I'm getting out of this."

I smile and give him my "come hither" look. "What would you like to get out of this?" I say.

He reaches his arms out, a signal for me to come and sit on his lap. We are alone in the studio so I comply. I climb on top of him, and he wraps his arms around me. "It's a good thing you're so cute," he says, "because you're also a real pain in the ass."

"That would make you an ass lover," I joke.

"You're logic doesn't fit. I'm not an ass lover, I'm lover of a pain…"

I cut him off with a kiss. Nothing turns me on more than the way he can examine and dissect the meaning of a sentence. As our mouths meet in a sweet embrace, I feel so warm and cozy that I ought to be sitting by a roaring fire, rather than in a sterile talk show set. But then I a catch a whiff of Nate's after-shave, and my stomach turns. Any sort of strong scent has been offensive to me lately; it's a pregnancy thing. After a moment I have to push him away.

"Sorry," I say as I get up off his lap. "But we only have the studio for an hour, so we should get this done."

Nate sighs but doesn't seem too annoyed. "That's fine. The sooner this is over, the better."

"Great." I adjust the lights one more time, then step behind the larger stationary camera. From behind it I speak to him. "Okay honey, I'm going to turn on the camera, and I want you to just talk about how you feel. Got it?"

"Sure."

"Great. Okay, the camera's on. So go ahead."

Nate adjusts himself and sits up straight. Then he begins to speak. "Well, Sam is in her first trimester, and I guess things are going pretty well. She hasn't had a doctor's appointment yet. She told me that she's not supposed to until, like, her tenth week. So, um… yeah. She's been feeling a little woozy and cranky…"

"Nate!" His head jerks up.

"What?"

"Talk about your feelings. I don't need you to summarize how I've been feeling."

"Sam, I'm a guy. I'm not supposed to talk about my feelings."

"Come on, please."

Nate shifts again in his fake leather armchair. He looks pale and so young under the harsh light. "Fine. I don't know how I feel, okay? My wife is pregnant, and it's something I should be happy about, something we should be sharing, but instead it's something completely different." He suddenly stops talking, and adopts an expression that I see him wear only when he's concentrating really hard, like on a Scrabble game or the *New York Times* crossword.

"Can you tell me more?" I ask.

He continues. "My family thinks I'm crazy for agreeing to this. But I told them—that's Sam. She's the most generous person I've ever met. It's why I love her. And I guess I have to believe that if she'd do something this huge for a friend then, what will she one day do for me? I don't know. But I figure we have our lifetime together to find out."

I start to speak but my throat catches. Nate goes on. "But I might need to find out sooner rather than later."

I manage to get words out. "Nate, my God. You know I'd do anything for you."

He gives me a half smile. "Would you live in poverty?"

"Huh?"

"They're talking layoffs at school. All non-tenured teachers are in danger."

Nate has explained the whole tenure thing to me already. You automatically get it after your third year, if they hire you back. But before that time, you're really easy to fire. "But you're such a good teacher. They wouldn't fire you; jeez—nobody is more dedicated."

"It doesn't matter how dedicated I am, Sam. It's about seniority. And politics."

I step out from behind the camera and walk over to him. "What do you mean, politics?"

Nate sighs. "The administration doesn't like me. I'm too outspoken at meetings and they don't think I'm a 'team player'. They're going to look for any excuse they can find to get rid of me."

"Well, they won't be able to find one. What could they possibly fault you on, Nate?"

Nate looks up at me, a bunny in his cage wanting to be lifted out, held and comforted. Or at least I think that's his expression. Maybe it's something else.

"They can always find something to fault you on if they want to."

I climb back into Nate's lap, not caring about his smell or anything other than how much I love him.

"Well, I certainly can't think of anything."

He kisses me, then pulls away. "Tell me this won't be aired on public access."

I laugh, and all of a sudden the mood is light. We leave the television studio, go eat at Applebees, and pretend like all our problems are surmountable. I almost believe they are.

The next day I am lying on the couch in my pajamas, watching the episode of *Dawson's Creek* where Joey and Pacey finally decide to have sex. I try to remember what it was like to lose my own virginity, but it's not as vivid a memory as it ought to be. I was drunk on prom night (a cliché, I know), and afterwards I felt cheap. The rest I've blocked out.

Why is it that my life is so mundane, and on *Dawson's Creek* everything is so epic? I realize I only have myself to blame, that all my choices have led me back to Shannon, like I'm plane in a holding pattern.

And I'm trying to decide if this thought process is a result of hormones or if it's actually justified, when there's a knock at my door. I open it, and somehow it seems perfectly natural to find Mr. Holding Pattern himself standing there, holding a goldfish bowl in one hand and a box of fish food in another. Other than that he looks the way he always looks: dark longish hair pulled back, two day beard growth, wearing his standard uniform of ancient Levis and a plain white T-shirt.

"Hi, Collin," I say.

"Hey, sorry to bother you, but I'm going out of town for a couple of days so I need you to watch Cheshire."

I haven't said more than a passing hello to Collin since the toilet plunging incident, but ours is one of those relationships where time is irrelevant. Weeks or months can go buy without us talking, yet when we see each other again as if we're resuming a conversation from the day before. I take the fishbowl from him and walk into my apartment, placing it on the coffee table. As Collin has followed me inside, I turn *Dawson's Creek* off.

"I'll look after your fish," I say, "But I'm not guaranteeing that I won't accidentally kill it."

Collin plops down on the couch, making himself comfortable. "It's important that you keep Cheshire alive. I need to prove that I can commit to another living being. If you kill him that will screw everything up."

"So this is a twelve-step thing?" I ask, as I sit down across from him.

"Sort of."

"But if I kill him it isn't your fault…"

"Just keep my fish alive, okay?" Collin's voice has an edge and urgency that he doesn't use everyday. I know that when he uses it, it's my signal to shut up. Yet somehow my inclination is always to do just the opposite.

"Well if this fish is so instrumental to your well-being, why trust him with someone like me?"

He takes a deep sigh. "I told you, I have to go out of town. It's important, and not the sort of trip where you can take a fish."

I let a giggle escape. "Are there trips where you can take a fish?"

"Sam… will you just do it? Please?"

"And I'm the only person you can ask."

"You live in the building. Fish don't travel well—not even down the street."

I could make more of an issue, but what's the point? "Okay. But if you ask me, Cheshire is a stupid name for a fish. It's like you're asking for trouble. You wouldn't name your baby 'Kidnapper' would you? So why name your fish after its number one predator? That makes no sense."

Collin looks at me and shakes his head. "You still don't get me, do you?"

"I get you, Collin. I just wish that I didn't."

He laughs even though I said nothing funny. Then he gets up, places the box of food on the table, and says, "Only feed him once a day. Don't worry about changing his water; I'll be back before it needs to be done again."

"How do you know it's a him?"

Collin ignores my question and strolls out my door. After a moment I rush out into the hallway, stopping him with my voice. "Hey!" I shout, and he turns around. "When exactly will you be back?"

"Saturday."

"And where did you say you were going?"

He smiles. "We both know that I didn't say."

"So…"

Collin waves. "See you Saturday. Have fun with Cheshire."

20. Melody

I'm sitting outside Kelsey's house, waiting. Waiting sucks, especially if you're waiting for someone. I look at my watch again, wondering where in God's good name she could be. I swear, I really have been trying to be more patient with Kelsey, but she makes it so difficult sometimes. I told her 6:00. She's over fifteen minutes late, and that's just flat out rude. Kelsey doesn't know what it's like to have a mother who depends on you. I need to be back soon, before my mom is home from work. Mom works as a receptionist at a furnace cleaning company, usually from 10:00 a.m. to 7:30 p.m., but she calls in sick a lot. Anyway, if I don't have dinner waiting for her, I'll certainly pay for it later, and I can do without guilt trips and not-so-subtle forms of manipulation for the next few days.

I'm contemplating just taking off when Kelsey's metallic green Echo pulls into the driveway. She hops out and walks over to me, with a definite spring to her step. "Hey, have you been waiting long? I am so sorry! I was at the mall and I saw the perfect shoes to go with my new Juicy Couture top, so I went to stand in line, but there was only one person working and there was this foreign couple ahead of me who wanted to return something. So they like, called the manager out. And she's like, 'can I help you?' as she opens up a new register, and I'm like, 'finally!' And then, I'm not kidding, the cash register breaks! So I'm thinking no pair of shoes is worth this, so I left. Sorry I'm so late."

Kelsey walks past me, unconcerned about whether or not I'm

accepting her apology, and unlocks the front door. I follow her in, not saying anything.

"What do you want to drink? I'm in the mood for something simple, like a Citrus Absolute and cranberry Juice? Doesn't that sound good? Spring like, you know? And we can have veggies and dip to go with it. We'll be healthy for a change."

Kelsey makes her way into the kitchen and opens up the refrigerator. I say, "Actually Kelsey, I'm sort of in a hurry, so can we just get down to business?"

"What is this business again? Remind me."

I've told her three times already, so I can't help sounding pissy when I say, "The background check, remember?"

Kelsey reaches into the freezer, fills two glasses with ice, then closes the freezer door. After putting the glasses down on the counter, she retrieves a bottle of Vodka and a bottle of cranberry juice, and starts mixing our drinks. "Um, yeah, about that. I don't know. Is it really necessary to dig stuff up about Abby and spread it around school? Isn't that sort of an evil thing to do?"

Not again. We've already had this conversation twice, but oh well. One more time won't hurt. "You're thinking about it all wrong. This is retribution, Kelsey, for all the times Abby or her friends have been snotty and bitchy by not inviting you to their lame-ass parties, or have looked down at you just because you're not exactly like them."

Kelsey hands me a drink and I take a sip. The cool warmth travels down my throat. Kelsey's reply comes out in a squeak. "Um, Abby has never been all that mean to me..."

"Maybe not to your face, Kelsey. But come on. You know her type. Girls like her say mean things about everyone. You think she doesn't talk about you behind your back?"

Kelsey's face goes blank. "Have you heard her say stuff?"

I walk towards her, and put a consoling hand on her shoulder. "Well, yeah. But you shouldn't worry about it. You shouldn't worry about any of it, that's my whole point."

Pink splotches appear on Kelsey's cheeks. She had been mixing Cool Ranch dressing mix into sour cream, but she despondently drops the spoon. "What did she say?"

"Are you sure you want to know? Can't we just…"

"I want to know!" Kelsey picks her spoon back up and starts mixing the sour cream with fervor. "Tell me what she said."

"Alright. But just remember, you asked me to tell you. So don't shoot the messenger."

"Huh?" Confusion clouds her angry expression momentarily.

I shake my head and exhale. "Never mind. Anyway, we were in the locker room after gym, and you were drying your hair. Abby went over to your locker and started looking through your stuff. She must have checked out what size your pants were, because she goes, 'Oh my God, she is SO not a size eight. I'm surprised she can even squeeze her fat ass into these pants.' And Becki Birkland, who was there too, started laughing. So Abby tried to make her laugh more, saying something like, 'The girl is so delusional. I'd feel sorry for her if she wasn't such a loser!' Then Abby was going to throw your pants into the showers, saying the water would make them stretch out, but I was there and I told them to stop it, and I took your pants back and put them in your locker before you came back. And I would have said something to you before, but I didn't see the point until now."

Okay. So I'm stretching the truth a little. Fact is, it was Becki Birkland who laughed at Kelsey's pants, but she never suggested that we throw them in the showers. Abby giggled a little, but never really said much. And me—well I was more of a passive observer throughout. But whatever, in this situation, the truth is inconsequential. It's not like Abby wasn't involved, so if the facts are altered a little, who's to say that on a different day she might not have been the truly guilty one?

It's so quiet in the kitchen that all I can hear is the hum of the refrigerator. I watch Kelsey, her head down, still twirling her spoon through the sour cream, although without any of her original force. Not looking up, she finally responds, tears in her voice. "I can too wear a size eight. The fashions today are supposed to be tight. And Abby doesn't know anything about me. I'm not a loser."

Kelsey shifts her weight from foot to foot, and I can tell her mind is starting to shift too. Here's my chance for the deal sealer.

I keep my voice soft. "Look, maybe you're right. I'd hate to do something bad to someone who doesn't deserve it. I guess that's why I thought of the background check; we'd only spread truth, not rumors. Then anything we did would be totally justified."

Kelsey twirls her hair, deep in thought. "What if we don't find anything?"

"Then we let it go." I don't feel bad lying to Kelsey. Of course we're not going to find anything about Abby—an eighteen-year-old who has lived in Shannon her whole life. But if Kelsey is gullible enough to buy that, then that's not my problem.

Doing the background check with Kelsey on Abby was originally meant to serve two purposes. One, I could research the type of information I could expect to find when I did one on Mr. Linden's wife. There's all the standard stuff: past addresses, marriages, criminal records, possible aliases, etc. But the site I found goes the extra mile if you're willing to pay the price. They'll give you medical records, a psychological profile, and what they call "a dating and romance report" if you shell out the big bucks. They also require a signature for release, supposedly from the subject of the search. That's a laugh—wanna make a bet on how many forged signatures this place has received? Anyway, my other goal was to copy down the credit card number Kelsey used when doing the background check, so I could go to an internet coffee shop, minutes after leaving Kelsey's house, to do the background check that I'm really interested in. That way, on the off chance Kelsey actually looks at her statement, she'll just think the credit card company charged her twice.

So imagine my surprise when we actually find something on Abby. It turns out she has a DUI.

"So what?" Kelsey says. "Bobby would probably think that's cool. He drinks all the time."

"Let me think about how to spin this," I say. "We can turn this into something good, I'm sure."

"But you said we'd only tell the truth," Kelsey whines.

I squeeze Kelsey's shoulder, then I grab my backpack, preparing to head downstairs and out the door. "Kelsey, you need to learn the difference between lies and spin. The sooner you do, the sooner you'll toughen up and grow a pair."

She gives me another one of her clueless expressions, so I just pat her on the back. "Give me twenty-hours. I'll come up with something good. Bobby will be yours in no time. I gotta go! See you tomorrow."

I race out, stopping only to write down the credit card number before I forget it completely. Learning to memorize numbers took less time than learning to blush on command, but both skills are proving to be useful. I practically sprint to the coffee shop because I don't have much time if I want to get home before Mom does. I enter, the smell of coffee unnecessarily jumping through my nose. I'm already wired. I park myself at the nearest computer, open up my backpack, and retrieve my notebook, where I wrote down the maiden name of Mr. L's wife. It had been easy to find out what it was; I asked Mr. L for it on the pretense of her seeming "sort of familiar."

Soon I have called up the screen, typed in all the needed information, and after forging her on-line signature (what's the point of requiring someone to check a box saying they've signed something?), voila! Samantha Linden's life is displayed before my eyes. And what's there before me is just too good to be true.

21. Samantha

I looked at the clock, then at my suitcase, then back at the clock. 5:47. No taxi. I rubbed my hand over my stomach, hoping that action would calm the sick butterflies of indigestion. No luck.

I ran to the kitchen, and opened up the cabinet underneath the sink to find a paper bag. I needed a small one to breathe into, like how Holly Hunter did in *Broadcast News* when she was freaking out over William Hurt. But there were no small bags, only large ones. I tried to make the large bag fit tightly around my mouth, and I breathed in and out, hoping it would work, but I only felt ridiculous on top of feeling panicked.

Then there was a knock on my door.

I opened it, and of course, there was Collin.

"What do you want?" I asked.

"We need to talk," he said, invading my apartment, practically pushing me aside so as not to be standing out in the hallway.

"There's nothing to talk about. It's over. You need to accept it and move on."

He stood by the window, bathed in light. I had to squint to be able to look at him. So I looked down.

"Sam, don't give up on me. It will be different this time. I promise."

Like I hadn't heard that before? It was 1994, and Collin and I had been broken up for five months after being back together for over two years. For a while everything had been great. He had abandoned his dreams of big business, after a friend of a friend who worked on Wall

Street had a nervous breakdown and needed to be institutionalized. "I'm tired of the whole lifestyle," Collin told me. "I'm tired of it all." By "all" he meant coke, and he was true to his proclamation. When he begged me to take him back, I said I would on the condition that he would give up doing drugs.

"Sam, I figured it out," he had told me. "You're what makes me happy. You're what I need. Give me another chance, and I promise, I'll make *you* happy."

For a while, he really did. We finished college and life was easy. We both were taking time to figure out who we were and what we wanted to become. I worked in a coffee shop and wrote screenplays with the intention of entering them into competitions. Collin managed his uncle's apartment building, so we got free rent. Collin also played guitar for a garage band, which enjoyed a small local success and actually brought in some money. I would go to his gigs, dressed in my baby-doll dresses, flannel shirts and Doc Martens, drink cheap beer and cheer whenever I heard Collin's sweet voice and skilled guitar playing. When he dedicated his songs to me, I felt like the luckiest girl in the world.

Then the realities of being poor and aimless began to sink in. I dealt with it by researching ways to move out of Shannon. Collin dealt with it by spending more time with his band, rehearsing and performing every night in some smoky bar. "There's no way I'm leaving my band now," he would say whenever I'd suggest relocating, "we're on the brink of real success."

We came to an impasse. I wanted to leave; he wanted to stay. Perhaps that played into Collin's decision that it was too hard to enjoy the rock-n-roll lifestyle without partaking in all of its pleasures. "It's just pot," he would tell me. "It's not even addictive."

That may be true, technically. But soon our apartment reeked of that strong, sicky-sweet smell all the time. Collin would wake up in the morning, and light up a joint right away, and he would keep on all day. If his stash ran out, he would re-smoke the reeds. It got so he was always high. When he got busted while trying to buy, I went down to the jail to bail him out. That was when I told him it was over.

"Give me a break," he said. "Kurt Cobain just died."

His face was passive, barely even registering what I had said. I wanted to shake him until he exploded. "What does that have to do with you, or with us? It's not like he was a friend of yours."

"Sam," he said, as if I was very small, slow child, "he was the voice of our generation. And he's dead. It's like our generation has killed itself. Forgive me for wanting to mourn my own death a little."

There was so much I could have said at that moment, so much I wanted to say. All the promises and plans we had made while lying in bed together late at night, holding hands and playing with each other's hair. All the times I had looked into his eyes and believed what he told me, believed that he could fix whatever was wrong with my world, it all seemed void—as if our relationship was a bad check with a stamp over it. "Sorry, insufficient funds."

"Collin, I'm sorry. But I'm still alive, even if you're not."

I went home and packed up my stuff. My boss had an empty room above the coffee shop where she let me stay while I figured things out. I decided it was urgently important for me to leave town for somewhere far, far away, as soon as possible. My solution? I signed up to volunteer as an optometrist's assistant for two months in Ghana. This program was so desperate for volunteers that they accepted me despite my lack of experience or my inability to speak a second language. After my volunteer stint I planned to travel and work odd jobs for as long as possible. It only took me four months to get through the application process, and to procure all the necessary shots, and immunizations, and my passport. Sure, I recognized the similarity between what I was about to do and the path my mother had chosen. But don't we all eventually turn into our parents, whether we plan on it or not?

And as I was waiting for my taxi, it seemed I had one more obstacle to overcome before I could finally leave town.

"Sam, don't give up on me. It will be different this time. I promise." His words echoed in my ears, and I looked back up at him.

"It's too late, Collin. I'm going."

He ran his hands through his hair, yanking on it slightly. Then he rushed over to me, and took both my hands in both of his. I let him lead me to the couch. "Okay," he said. "I get it. But I need to tell you something first."

I sighed. "There's nothing you can possibly say…"

"Sam! Come on. Just give me half a chance here."

"You've had more than that. I think I've given you more than your share of chances."

His face grew all red and pinched. "I just need to tell you one thing!"

I yelled in exasperation. "Well then just freaking say it instead of asking for permission! Just say it for God's sake!"

"Fine!"

Then there was silence, as he collapsed back on the couch, slumped over in defeat. "Well?" I demanded.

He exhaled loudly then sat back up. "Okay, here it is. I didn't get it before, but now I do. I figured it out. I'm an addictive personality. I've admitted it to myself and now to you. And I'll get help. I'll move with you - anywhere you want to go. Just please, Sam. I love you. Don't give up on me now."

The taxi pulled up; it was honking its horn on the street below my window.

"Collin, I'm leaving for Ghana now."

He grabbed my hand again, this time his grip was so strong I couldn't imagine how I'd convince him to let go. "When will you be back?" he pleaded.

"I don't know." I paused. And because I couldn't think of anything better to say, I simply added, "I'm sorry."

I got up from the couch and retrieved my suitcase from the bedroom. I was ordered to pack light, but even still, it was sort of heavy and my shoulder sagged from the weight. Collin was standing in my doorway, blocking my exit. "Sam, please. You're the only one who gets me. You're all I have."

I pushed him away with all my strength. "And you choose now to come to this realization? When I'm about to go?"

"I ran into Kelly at the grocery yesterday. She told me you were leaving. I've been up all night thinking, and now, here I am."

"Well, like I said, you're too late. I'm going."

I tried to get past him, but he grabbed my shoulders, tilted his head down, and trapped me in a kiss. I violently pulled away.

"You think that's going to work? You're not Clark Gable, Collin. You can't convince me to stay by making me swoon."

Me and my suitcase struggled past him, making it down to the curb. Collin followed me, and yelled out as I handed the taxi driver my luggage.

"Sam! Your door isn't locked. You forgot to lock your front door."

"I don't care!" I yelled back. "I have nothing worth keeping here! I'm probably never coming back!"

He didn't respond. I started to get into the taxi, but then I made my fatal mistake. I took one more look at Collin, and I noticed the tears running down his face. In the five years I'd known him, this was the first time I'd ever seen him cry. Suddenly a combined force of emotion, nature, and weakness was pulling me towards him, and I was wrapping my arms around him in a goodbye hug. My senses were overwhelmed with how familiar it was to be in his arms: the feel of his body, the warmth of his skin, the smell of fabric softener combined with his deodorant, the worn texture of his favorite flannel shirt. My mind was hit with the realization that I have been missing him terribly, and the hug quickly turned into a kiss, and then my body remembered how much I missed him. Whether our relationship is in a cold or warm stage, this one thing between us had always been hot, and I couldn't, I wouldn't pull away from him this time. Instead, after a moment, he pulled away instead.

"Can't you just delay your trip for one night? They'll understand. And it will give us a chance to really say goodbye."

My desire to go was dwarfed by my inability to let go of him. "Just one night," I said. "Just one night."

"I guess I don't get it. Why does it have to be you to take care of his fish? Doesn't he have any friends?"

Nate and I are eating dinner, and my mind fast-forwards back to the present, twelve years ahead of where it had been. "I don't know. I mean, sure he has friends but they aren't responsible."

Nate laughs. "If you're the most responsible person he knows, then he's got much bigger problems than his fish's well-being to worry about."

I drop my fork, and it clatters against my plate. "That was a mean thing to say, Nate. I'm responsible."

Nate takes a bite of rice then a drink of water. "Sure you are, honey."

"Okay, don't condescend to me."

"Oh, Sam, lighten up. Your ex-boyfriend stills lives in our building…"

"It's his uncle's building, Nate."

"…and he drops by all the time…"

"To fix our toilet."

"Now he wants you to take care of his fish?"

I raise my voice, permitting all my frustrated tension to escape as I speak. "What's the big deal? It's just a fish. I'm going to sprinkle some food into its bowl once a day for a few days, then give it back once Collin returns. I'm doing a favor for an old friend, and I don't see how that merits your insulting me."

Nate swirls his spinach into long green streams on his plate. We don't talk, so the dinner music that Nate chose fills the room. Bruce Springsteen croons away about cars and redemption, and it does nothing to relieve the tension that has risen between Nate and me. I stare at him, waiting for an apology. He keeps his head down, playing with his food. In this moment I feel more like a mother than a wife, and I'm glaring at my spoiled, petulant son. Never has our age difference been so, well, palpable.

Just when I think there's no way I'm winning this one, and I'm about to give in and break our silence, he looks up and says to me, "Honey, I'm sorry. Of course you're responsible. Don't mind me; I'm just having a bad day."

I exhale "More work stuff?"

"Yeah. Things are tense. One of us English teachers has to go.

We're just waiting. Meanwhile my head is on the chopping block."

"Is there anything I can do?"

"No. Just be understanding when I'm a crab."

I smile in answer, and he smiles back.

We finish eating in silence. However, the tension is gone and now the air between us is peaceful. Lately I have been so tired, I feel like my limbs are made of lukewarm lead. I guess that's normal for women in my stage of pregnancy. Nate is used to my fatigue, and allows for my wilting early in the evening by not demanding much of me.

"Are you done?" He asks.

I nod. Nate clears our plates and does the dishes. I move into the bedroom, collapse onto the bed, and watch television for a couple of hours while Nate grades papers in the living room. Another normal evening in the Linden household.

The next morning I meet Jane at a coffee shop close to campus. We find a table near the widow. She has a double latte and a biscotti. I have decaffeinated tea and a rice crispy treat.

"Are you still feeling nauseous?" Jane asks.

"Yeah," I say. "According to *What to Expect When You're Expecting*, morning sickness peaks at around twelve weeks. So I have another month or so of this, and it will get worse before it gets better."

Jane stretches out her arms, grabs both sides of the table with either hand, and leans forward. "Sam, I'll never be able to thank you enough for this."

"You don't have to," I say. "Seeing you as a mother will make it all worth it. Just think, in a few months, you'll have a baby!"

I take one of her hands and give it a squeeze. She smiles at me. "And you'll have an amazing film to distribute! Have you thought about selling it to HBO? It seems like the sort of thing they'd be into."

I laugh. "Let me actually produce the thing first. Then I'll worry about selling it."

Jane sips her latte and wipes foam from her mouth. "How is the filming going?"

"Okay," I say. "I've been looking for other surrogate mothers to interview, and I also want to interview moms and dads who had their kids through surrogates. I've been doing a lot of research online, but it's slow going. Even if I find these people, how do I convince them to be filmed?"

"Through your charm and wit?" Jane quips.

"Yeah. Whatever. Lately I've been feeling tired and bloated and about as far away from clever and charming as I've ever felt." I sip my tea, contemplate taking a bite of my rice crispy treat, but decide against it. "Oh well. This too shall pass. At least I got a good testimonial from Nate the other day."

"Oh yeah?" Jane leans back and crosses her legs, therapist like. "And how are you and Nate doing?"

"Fine!" I say, with a touch too much volume and enthusiasm. Jane raises her eyebrows. "You know. I'm tired. He's stressed. But he's been great. So supportive and understanding! I couldn't ask for much more."

"And Collin?" Jane asks.

It's a good thing I wasn't drinking my tea right then, or I would have had one of those comedic movie moments where one character says something shocking in the middle of another character's swallow, and she spits out her beverage in surprise. But luckily my teacup is safely on the table, and the only clue to my embarrassment is that my voice rises an octave when I answer her.

"What does Collin have to do with anything?"

Jane tilts her chin down and simultaneously raises her eyebrows at me. "Come on Sam, this is me you're talking to. Does he even know you're pregnant?"

"No."

"Don't you think you ought to tell him?"

I open my mouth to answer, but am saved by the bell. Or, to be more exact, the ringing of my cell phone. I look at my phone to see who is calling, then look back up at Jane.

"Speaking of the devil," I say. "He's calling me. Hold on, he's probably worried about his fish."

I flip open my phone. "Hey, Collin. Cheshire is fine."

His voice sounds far away. "Oh, great. But that's not why I'm calling."

I know his voice well enough to know that something's wrong. "What is it?" I ask.

"It's your dad," he says. "You need to come to Chicago."

22. Melody

Today is one of those rare days when I am sure everything about me is wrong. My hair is flat and I wish I had pulled it back this morning before I left the apartment. Instead it's down, brushing against my shoulders, and every time I feel it I want to yank all of it out. I also hate what I'm wearing. Why did I ever buy Capri pants with no back pockets? So what if they were on sale—no fashion trend of the last five years is more guaranteed to make your butt look big than pocketless Capris. I wouldn't have even worn them, but I had no time to do laundry this weekend and everything else I have is dirty. To top it all off, I have a cold sore on my lower lip. Even though it hurts, I can't stop rubbing it with my tongue over and over and over, like a self-punishing, pain-loving idiot who doesn't know any better.

When I walk into my first hour class, frustration is practically dripping from my skin. The weather is beautiful and spring fever has made everyone, especially the seniors, a little crazy. I'm no exception, but I expect I'll take my misery out on other people rather than internalize it. I'm not trying to justify my actions in advance or anything, I know I'm not always a nice person. But it's better to at least be honest with yourself, isn't it?

Class is due to start in a couple of minutes. I take my seat next to Becki Birkland and her best friend, Lana Gretch. They are perfect in nearly identical T-shirts from J Crew or some other store where I can't afford to shop. They each have their hair up in an effortless ponytail that showcases their beautiful, professionally done highlights.

I hate them both.

"I still can't believe he hasn't gotten busted," says Lana.

"Totally," replies Becki. "He was so drunk on Saturday night when he left Kevin's house. I was sure he'd get pulled over."

I have no idea who they are talking about, but I do know they are referring to Kevin Finkstein's eighteenth birthday party. Anyone who was anyone was there, so it's a safe bet that Abby and Bobby attended.

"Did you hear that Maya tried to stop him? She like stole his keys and everything, saying 'I don't want you to die, Justin!' When he left anyway she started sobbing. Swear to God."

"What a drama queen," said Becki. They both laugh, and I join in, loud enough to make them look at me.

"Sorry," I said. "Couldn't help but overhear. I had to laugh, because it's just all so hypocritical, isn't it?"

"Excuse me?" says Becki.

"Hypocritical," I say. "It means not practicing what you preach."

"We know what it means," says Lana, in a tone that oozes snot, "but just who are you calling a hypocrite?"

"All of you," I say. "Did you even check to see if Abby was sober when she left the party? She's supposed to be a good friend of yours, and you haven't even realized that she's the one with a serious problem."

Becki laughs. "You barely even know Abby. You say hi to her a couple of times in the hallway, and that gives you the right to say stuff about her?"

"I know what I see, I know what I hear, and my mom is an alcoholic, so believe me, I know how to spot it in other people. There have been tons of signs in Abby, and if you two want to ignore them, fine, but if something really tragic happens it will be on your shoulders."

Their futile struggle against asking for more reads clearly across their faces. Lana gives in first. "Okay. What signs?" She asks with a sigh.

"At Key Club she's had alcohol on her breath several times. And just last week I had a bathroom pass in the middle of third hour, and I saw Abby with mascara streaks down her face, and she was chugging from this water bottle that she threw away as she left. So I picked it up and sniffed it and Vodka had obviously been in there…"

Becki interrupts. "Gross! You sniffed her water bottle that had been in the garbage!"

I stare at her with laser hot eyes, long enough to make her squirm. Then I say, "Yeah, I did. The garbage was full of paper towels, nothing gross. And I only did it because I'm worried about her. Even if we're not friends, I've always liked Abby. And after her DUI this fall…"

"How did you hear about that?" Lana asks.

"Brady Williams told me." Brady is the school's notorious bad boy, and I happen to have World History with him and Abby. Through assigned seating they sit next to each other, and I've seen her let him copy her homework.

"Okay, you're lying. There's no way Brady knows about the DUI."

I smirk at her. "Just shows how much you know your friend. They're like, always together in World History. And they come in together all the time when I'm working at Subway. Usually they look like they're about to pounce each other."

Lana and Becki exchange questioning looks, and I continue. "Anyway, I'm pretty sure that he's the reason she's drinking so much."

"No way." says Becki.

"Look, if Brady didn't tell me about Abby's DUI, how else would I know? Besides, what motive do I have for lying? I'm only telling you because I know you're her friend, and maybe you can help her stop this self-destructive behavior. Everybody knows Brady is bad news, and it was around the time they started hanging out together that I noticed these signs in Abby."

Lana shrugs her shoulders and looks at Becki, who is at a loss for words. "Poor Bobby," says Lana. "I wonder if he knows."

Lana and Becki whisper to each other with great urgency. As Mr. Vincent finishes attendance and begins class, I make a mental note to talk to Brady Williams ASAP. I'm sure if I offer to write his final term paper for World History, he'll have no problem backing up my story.

After school on Thursday afternoon I'm hanging out in Mr. L's room, putting up a new bulletin board display of famous quotes by

American authors. He has a whole set of posters with these quotes, each one showcasing the author's face and vital stats about them. I found the posters hidden in the corner of his teacher closet, rolled up and forgotten about. "Why aren't these up?" I asked. "They're so cool!"

"I've been meaning to put them up for a while," Mr. L replied. "I just never seem to get around to it."

So I smiled at him and he shook his head, laughing. He knew without being told that I was going to put them up for him, and there was no point in protesting. After weeks of working together, we don't talk with words as much as with our eyes. It's just one of the reasons why we're perfect together.

That was two days ago. Now I am stapling construction paper letters to the cork wall, letters that I took pains to develop last night after I was done with all of my homework. They spell out: "Made in America! Great Quotes by Great American Authors." On each letter I drew the outline of an old book, as if they have pages. And the letters are in red, white and blue, but I used faded colors in order to give it a more antique-y feel. This is going to make his room look as good as he does.

But Mr. L isn't paying attention to the progress of my display. He's on the phone, leaning back in his chair with his feet on his desk. With one hand he is fiddling with his stapler, his other hand is twirling the phone cord.

"How are you feeling? Are you still nauseous?" He waits for an answer, and says, "Well that's good. Eat some saltines for me." Then his face tightens a little, as does his grip on the phone cord.

"Uh, huh, but what did the doctor say?" Mr. L's face looks concerned, like anyone's would after they are hearing the answer to that particular question. "Do you want me to come out?" I'm guessing he's talking to his wife, and she must be giving him a long answer, because it's after a minute that he says, "Oh. Okay."

He pauses again, this time for not as long. "Hon, don't worry about it. It's not your fault Collin happened to be there. I understand he and your dad are still close. Just worry about taking care of your dad and yourself, and call me if you need me…Yeah. I love you too…

Okay, bye."

He hangs up. For a moment he is silent, lost in thought. Then he remembers that I am in the room and says, "Wow. That board is looking really good."

I blush and look down, pretending to be shy. "Thanks," I say. Then I sort of hesitate, again faking a bashfulness that I do not feel. "Is everything okay at home?"

"Oh, uh, yeah. My father-in-law is having some health problems, so Sam had to leave town rather suddenly."

"And Sam? Is she okay?"

He looks confused for a moment. "What? Oh, yeah, she's fine. It's just a pregnancy thing."

My pulse starts to race. "Your wife is pregnant?"

He removes his feet from the desk. "No! I mean, yeah, she is, but it's not our baby. She's a surrogate for her best friend. It's… it's complicated. So please, don't spread that news around, okay?"

"Sure," I say with a smile.

My pulse and my body have relaxed in relief. As long as he's not having a baby with her, I could care less what his wife is up to. But wow, their relationship seems less and less normal every day.

He resumes his silence and stares off into space. I continue to work on my bulletin board, but my mind is racing. So Collin is there with her, huh? I know all about Collin from the background check, and any idiot can see that his being around really bothers Mr. L. So when do I bring up what I know? I look back over at Mr. L in all his introspection, and decide, what the hell?

"Mr. L?" His head snaps up and towards my direction. "Are you sure that you're okay?"

"Yeah, I'm fine. Just worried, that's all."

"I understand," I say. "But you shouldn't worry—I'm sure you that your wife loves you, not that Collin guy I heard you mention just now."

"What?"

Behind my back I make a fist, digging my nails hard into the palm of my hand. It hurts, but the pain keeps me in control. "I'm sorry, I couldn't help but overhear. And I think it's great that you're so understanding. I don't know if I could trust someone in the same situation."

Mr. L's cheeks turn pink. "I… I think you misunderstand. Collin is just a friend of Sam's. I'm actually glad he's there to give her support."

I put down the poster of Ernest Hemmingway and sit on top of the student desk that is opposite of his own. "Sure, of course you are right to trust your wife. But this is me you're talking to, and I've heard…" I look at his face, and am pleased to see innocence staring back. So he doesn't know. Perhaps I should save this for just a little while longer.

It's too good not to.

"…You know what? Never mind. I'm sure I just heard wrong."

I hop off the desk and start to collect the posters into a pile. "Wow, look at the time. I've got to go. My shift at Subway starts in twenty minutes."

"Melody!"

I turn back around. His feet are off the desk. He is leaning forward. "What did you hear?"

"Nothing, just gossip. And you and I both know how silly listening to gossip can be."

"Tell me anyway."

I tilt my head toward the floor and shuffle my feet. "Okay, without going into detail…" I pause for effect. "I heard that your wife has a past. That's all."

Outside the classroom students are leaving school, slamming their lockers shut for the day, making plans and talking on cell phones. But inside the classroom it's only him and me. And his cheating wife, who is obviously so much on his mind, she may as well be there too. Don't worry, Mr. L. Once you've dumped her for me, you'll be so much happier.

But of course, I save those thoughts for later, and I keep the rest of what I know to myself.

Mr. L is staring past me, and he looks like he's trying really hard to process what I've just said. I gently tap his shoulder. "I have to go.

Can we talk about this more tomorrow?"

He breaks out of his trance, and gives me a forced little smile. "Of course. Thanks for all your help, Miss Madsen."

I smile back. If only he knew how much I love him. If only he realized how much he's going to love me.

23. Samantha

I'm in my old room in my father's house, lying on the bed that he didn't want me to give away. I rub my socked foot along its carved, golden wood frame and glance over at the matching dresser. They are one of a kind, distinctive antiques. Dad was right to hold onto them. Why do I always take so long—too long - to realize the beauty in things?

For the fifteenth time today, tears travel down my face. I sniff and wipe them away.

Turns out there's a problem with my dad's heart. He had been experiencing chest pain, occasional nausea, and shortness of breath. But he was either too scared or too stubborn to take it seriously. He never said anything about it to me, but for some reason he mentioned his symptoms to Collin, during one of their frequent phone conversations. My dad and Collin have become close over the years; it's like a pseudo father/son relationship that didn't end even though the love between Collin and me did.

But no matter. The important thing is that Collin dropped everything, drove to Chicago, and took my dad to the doctor himself. And it's a good thing. The doctor said dad has serious heart disease, with three blocked arteries. At the rate he was going, a fatal heart attack was most likely imminent. Now they are recommending triple coronary artery bypass surgery. It should fix the problem, they say, but I'm worried he might not survive the surgery.

I roll over, sit up, and grab a Kleenex from my nightstand. How is it that Dad thinks to put boxes of Kleenex in rooms that nobody ever uses, but I can't manage to have them around my own apartment? I inspect the box. There's a kitten, surrounded by faded pink flowers. The plastic at the top has a layer of dust. Could it be that this Kleenex box has been on my nightstand since before I moved out, seventeen years ago? Surely I have visited home enough to go through more tissue than one box could hold, but perhaps not. Now I feel even worse.

My cell phone rings. My first instinct is to ignore it, thinking it's Collin calling, wondering why I'm not at the hospital yet this morning. But the caller ID says it's Jane, so I pick up.

"Hi."

"Hi! How are you? How's your dad?" Her voice is full of concern, and her sympathy makes me sort of start to cry again.

"I'm okay. My dad says he's fine, but he isn't." I take a profound sniff and wipe my nose with my sleeve. "His surgery is in two days."

"But that should fix the problem, right?"

"Supposedly. As soon as the doctor took one look at his heart they admitted him to the hospital, amazed he wasn't already dead from cardiac arrest. Now they keep trying to put a positive spin on everything, saying they detected the problem in time, that he's lucky he came in when he did because they can still fix him."

"So? Isn't that all true?"

I suddenly feel very tired, even though I haven't exerted any energy yet today. "Yeah, I suppose." I know how defeatist I sound. "But he has to have major heart surgery and he could die from it, so where's the luck in that?"

"Sam, the doctors have to prepare you for the worst possible outcome. But people usually get through those surgeries just fine. Bill Clinton did."

"Okay." I don't know what else to say, so I leave it at that. The silence between us is comfortable, nurturing me as if she was here, holding my hand.

"Do you want me to drive up and be with you?" Nathan had offered the same thing, but I turned him down. How would it seem, to let my best friend be there for me, but not him? So even though I am tempted to say yes, I respond with, "No. That's okay. I'll be fine."

"Are you sure?"

I sniff once again. "Yeah. I appreciate the offer, but I think it's better not to have a lot of people here. Dad might think we're making a big deal out of it, and get freaked out."

"So Nathan's not coming out either?"

"No, he's really bogged down with work. He offered, but I told him not to."

"And Collin?"

"Collin is already here. You know that."

"Okay. But does Nathan know?"

"Nate knows Collin is here."

Pause. "Sam, does Nathan know that Collin is staying with you, at your dad's house?"

I bite down on the inside of my mouth to suppress my anger. Whether I'm angry at Jane or at myself is immaterial. Her question has brought to surface a situation that is almost more troubling than my father's health.

"Sam?"

I run my hand along the comforter on my bed. It's light pink with an ivy leaf print on top. The fabric is worn and softened with age, and I lie down so I can feel it beneath my cheek—a child caressing her security blanket. "With all the talk about my dad it just didn't come up."

"Sam!"

"What was I supposed to say, Jane? With everything else that's going on, I just couldn't talk about Collin." Her silent disapproval on the other end of the phone causes me to babble. "Look, I never said that he *wasn't* staying at my dad's house. It's not like I'm lying, and it's not like I can ask Collin to go. If it weren't for him, my dad would probably be dead. Besides, my dad wants him here. But if Nathan were to come up, everything would be all tense and awful. And if I tell Nate about Collin, he'll know that's the reason I don't want him to come. So where does that leave things? It's better to just not say anything."

"But he'll find out eventually. It's bound to come up at some point—your dad will mention it, or Collin will, or you'll slip up and say something. He'll find out, and you'll look like you were hiding something; then the situation will be a million times worse because you'll be caught in a lie." I pull my comforter up over my head, and settle into the fetal position. I'm wrapped in a dark, tight cocoon, yet I'm not protected from the truth of Jane's words.

"I can't think about that now."

"Sam, I really think you ought to…"

"Yeah, okay thanks. I have to go." I don't usually hang up on people, but before I know it I have snapped my phone shut. I break free from the covers and sit up. For a moment I stare at my phone, shiny and slick, fitting perfectly in my hand. Nothing should be allowed to look so neat and tidy when my world is a complete mess. Without thinking, I hurl it across the room. It lands against the wall with a thud and a crack. From where I'm sitting it appears that it's broken. I hang my head and start to cry yet again, but in a moment my tears are interrupted by the ringing of my phone. I jump up, hoping it's Jane. It isn't.

"Hey Sweetheart. I'm just calling to see how you are." Nathan's voice is far away.

"Hi. I'm fine. I was just about to go see my dad."

More static. "Hon, I'm having trouble hearing you. I think our connection is bad."

"Sorry. Can you hear me now?"

Nathan starts to answer, but his voice cuts out and my phone goes dead. I guess we'll have to talk later. As I'm standing in the middle of my childhood bedroom, I catch a glance of myself in the large mirror hanging over my dresser. My hair is sticking out in clumps, my face is blotchy and tear-streaked, and my stomach bulges with the extra baby weight I have already accrued. Not a pretty picture. I take a deep breath and square my shoulders. With all the resolve I can manage I head to the shower. I need to pull myself together before I see my dad.

An hour later I walk into my father's hospital room. He is sitting up, watching *The View*, and chewing on a piece of dry toast. "They won't let me eat anything good," he says as soon as he sees me.

"Yeah, well, get used to it. The doctors say you're going to have to drastically change your diet." I give him a hug and sit down next to him on the bed. "What's Barbara Walters talking about this morning?"

"Nuclear proliferation in North Korea."

"Wow. I didn't know they covered such serious topics on *The View*."

My dad reaches for the remote and changes the channel. He keeps flipping through, rejecting everything that comes on, including the morning showing of *Dawson's Creek*. "Why is everything on television such crap?" he says.

"Well, we don't have to watch TV. We could play cards, or go for a walk. Or do you want me to get you something to read?"

"Where's Collin?"

"Huh?"

"I haven't seen him since yesterday," my dad says. "Do you know where he is?"

"No. Sorry."

Dad turns off the TV and pushes away his breakfast tray. "The food here is awful. I think they are trying to starve me."

Dad has been in a terrible mood since he was admitted to the hospital. I guess I'm in no position to pass judgment, but he is making it difficult to help him.

"I know!" I say. "The TV has a DVD player. Do you want me to go rent you a movie or two? I'm sure I could pick out something you'd enjoy."

Dad barks out a laugh. "I would hope so. All those years of college, and your biggest achievement is working at the video store. If you can't pick out a movie for your own father, then you really are a failure."

I get up off the bed. "Thanks Dad. That's sweet of you to say." I wander over to the window and pull open the shades. "It looks like a beautiful day out there. Do you want to get some fresh air?"

"Nah. Maybe later. Where did you say Collin was?"

I look over at my Dad, sitting in his hospital bed, wearing pajamas. He's pale with bags under his eyes. He says he feels fine, but I'm guessing the stress of the situation is taking its toll. How can I be mad when he's never been more vulnerable? I can't ask him why, *why*, he chose to trust Collin and why he now seems to prefer him to me—I can't do it. There will be time for that later, when he's well. Then I'll yell at him good.

"Dad, do you want me to call him? I'm sure he's around."

"Yeah. Give him a call. Tell him to bring me an Egg McMuffin while you're at it."

I reach for my phone, remembering too late that it's broken. "Dad, I'm going to have to use the pay phone. I'll be right back."

I start to leave, but stop in my tracks when Collin enters the room.

"Hey, Phil! How are you this morning?"

"Fine, but the food here is crap! Can you bring me something decent to eat?"

Collin laughs. "You know I can't do that, man. Sorry. But I'll bring you some hard candy. How does that sound?"

Dad grunts and Collin turns to me. "Can I talk to you alone for a second?"

Dad answers Collin before I can. "No, no. No private conversations. It is probably about me, so just say it right now, right here."

"Sorry Phil. This will just take a minute."

Collin grabs me by the arm and leads me out into the hallway. I yank my arm away once we are out of earshot. "What's going on?"

"Look, I know your Dad's heart is weak, and I didn't want send him into a serious state of shock. So I thought I should tell you first."

"Tell me what? What are you talking about?"

Collin opens his mouth to answer, but I hear someone else from behind me first. "Hello, honey. I'm back."

It's been years and years, but her voice is still familiar, like looking at an old photo album. I turn around. Her face is older, but her eyes are unchanged—blue, yielding, and bottomless. "Mom," I say, more of a guttural sound than a word. Suddenly, randomly I remember a college physics lesson, and I realize I'm Newton's first law of motion come to life. Long ago her departure sent me spinning aimlessly, unable to stop; now here she is, my external and unbalanced force standing in front of me, providing a safe harbor as I run into her arms. Finally I can be still.

24. Melody

"Yeah, give me a foot-long meatball sub on white." My kazillionith customer of the night stands before me, ordering a sandwich which, judging by his large belly, he clearly doesn't need. It's ironic that so many customers at Subway are fat, when they advertise the whole Jared-Subway-diet-thing. Then again, maybe Jared is on his way out, because last time I saw him on TV he was looking pretty pudgy himself.

I put on my plastic gloves and cut open a twelve-inch piece of white bread. "What type of cheese do you want?" I ask.

"Uhm… what are the choices?"

"American, provolone, cheddar, or pepper-jack."

"I just want the white kind."

"Except for cheddar, they're all white." Is he retarded? Jesus.

He scratches his *Pump and Munch* T-shirt-clad stomach, and shakes his head. "That's gay. Why are they all white? How are you supposed to tell them apart?"

"Sir, I have no idea what the cheese-makers were thinking, making them all white, but they are and there's nothing we can do about it. Now, what kind of cheese do you want?"

"The regular kind."

"American?"

"No. Whatever you normally put on sandwiches."

"That would be American."

"Fine. But if I don't like it, you're making me another."

I don't reply, but start making his sandwich. I've spooned on the meatballs and asked him what vegetables he wants when he stops me. "Wait a minute. What kind of bread is that? You used the wrong the kind of bread."

"It's white bread. You said white bread."

"No, I said white cheese. I wanted the cheesy bread."

Did he? I stutter in confusion and anger, "I don't think so?"

He leans into the counter. "You don't *think* so? Nobody is paying you to think. You're getting paid to make sandwiches, so if you wouldn't mind making me the sandwich that I actually want, that would be great."

I imagine throwing the white bread, white cheese, and bright red meatballs in his pudgy, pale face, and the satisfaction it would bring nearly causes me to do so.

But I don't. Instead I throw the sandwich in the garbage and take out a piece of baked cheddar bread and begin his sandwich again. He wants all the vegetables except lettuce, and I have to scrape them all off and put on new ones after he insists that I put on too much salt and pepper. Finally, after getting him an extra-large cup for his drink, and a bag of chips, he pays for his meal and goes away.

Why do so many people believe they are superior to you, simply because they are standing on the other side of the counter? My mom has worked in one form of the service profession or another for her entire adult life, and I think it explains a lot about why she is how she is. Years and years of people who aren't as smart as you looking at you like you're furniture, and assuming you're less intelligent than the chair they sit on. No wonder she's mean; she could have been so much more. As I refill the empty green pepper and pickle bins, I promise myself that the same thing won't happen to me.

I head into the back, where my co-worker Kyle is baking more bread.

"Do we really need more bread tonight? We only have an hour before closing."

"You can never be overly prepared, Melody." Kyle says this as he slides the tray of dough into the oven.

"Yeah, but they told us not to waste the bread. If we end up not using that tonight Bonnie will be mad cuz we'll have to throw it away."

"You're hardly one to talk about throwing food away. I saw the last sandwich you made, Melody."

I could make a catty reply, but actually, I don't mind Kyle. At least he thinks for himself. He doesn't automatically buy into everything our manager, Bonnie, tells us, and that's refreshing. However, I wish he wouldn't *always* say my name at the end of every sentence that he speaks to me.

"Whatever. If we end up throwing bread out, it's on you." I look in the refrigerator for more American cheese; Mr. Pump and Munch used up the last slice. Actually, he used the last slice on his first sandwich, the one I had to throw away. I used pepper Jack on his second one. It is white, after all. I'm just praying he hates spicy food.

I hear the "ding" that sounds every time our door opens. "We have a customer, Melody," says Kyle.

"Yeah, I know. I'll get it if you want to start cleaning up back here."

"No problem. Thanks, Melody."

I come out through the double doors. They swing back and forth as I grab another pair of plastic gloves and put them on. I turn around, but I'm putting the American cheese in its spot as I say, "Hi, welcome to Subway. What can I get you?"

"Actually, I was hoping I could buy you a coke or something."

His voice shocks me into looking up, and there he is—beautiful eyes, crooked yet charming nose, tussled blonde hair, and a smile that melts me like butter. I'm not prepared to see him, and I'm instantly aware that he is seeing me in my stupid Subway shirt and visor. Uhg!

"Mr. L! Hi." I stammer. This time my embarrassment isn't faked, and he laughs.

"Hi Melody."

A couple of minutes later I'm sitting in a booth across from him. My visor is off, but I'm conscious of how messy my hair must be, and I'm compulsively running my fingers through it. The fluorescent lights, sterile table tops, and bright yellow décor does nothing to detract from Mr. L's beauty, but I doubt the same is true in my case.

I take a sip of the coke he "bought" me (truth is, I can drink soda here for free), and say, "So, what's up?"

"I have a favor to ask you," he responds.

"Oh?"

"You said something about rumors going around about my wife."

"Yeah."

He swallows, and his face looks like he's about to deliver bad news. "I want you to promise me that you'll never tell me what they are."

I laugh because I'm sure I either heard him wrong, or that he's kidding. But his face doesn't flinch, nor does it turn into a smile. "I don't understand," I say. "Why would you need me to promise you something like that?"

He scratches his head, and his hand travels down to massage his own neck. "Because part of me is desperate to know what others are saying."

"Well, if you're desperate I can tell you."

"But the other part of me, the mature, wiser part, knows that no good can come from it."

I scratch my head in real confusion. "But what if they're spreading lies? Don't you want to know so you can protect her honor?"

He gives me a half-smile. "Melody, this might not make any sense to you, but I'm more worried about protecting my marriage than I am in protecting her honor. If I'm going to find out something bad about my wife, I need to find it out from her."

"Why?"

"It's hard to explain. I just don't want to accuse her of something she didn't do."

"But what if you accuse her of something she did do?"

He looks off into the distance, and his voice grows soft. "That would be almost worse. There's got to be a reason why I don't know about it, right? If that's the case, I need to let her tell me in her own time."

Something inside me snaps. "Okay. I don't get it. How can you be so naïve?" As soon as the words escape I regret them. The look on his face has one clear message—*you're not allowed to talk to me like that*. But he's too nice to actually tell me that, so there is silence for a moment as I decide what to say next. Should I tell him what he wants to hear, or what he needs to hear? "Mr. L, I'm sorry. I didn't mean to overstep by saying that. It's just that the world doesn't work that way. Surely you realize that."

He squints at me, and leans back as far as the booth we're sitting in will allow. "Is that so? Tell me, Miss Madsen. How does the world work?"

I don't miss that he's being condescending; his tone reminds me of how he talks to Alex Cleveland, the student who gives him the most attitude. He's good at putting Alex in his place, but I'd like to think I'm a little tougher. "Well," I reply, "for one thing, people don't get rewarded for being good, or nice, or respectful. They're rewarded for being clever or for staying one step ahead of everyone else. Also, people aren't going to return the favor if you're good to them, or if they do, it will be out of some sense of obligation, not because they want to. If you want love and everything that goes with it you have to prove that you're worthy of love, and you do that by refusing to take any crap. It's the only way. Trust me."

He wrinkles his face and a line appears between his eyes. "Why should I trust you? You've been married before?"

"Obviously not."

"Have you even had a serious boyfriend?"

I could lie; perhaps it would be smart to make him think other men have desired me. But I decide it's more sensible to let him know he'll be my first. Guys like that sort of thing. "No," I say, looking him squarely in the eye. "I'm picky. I'm waiting for the man of my dreams to come along."

He shakes his head. "If you don't mind me saying so, that's not a good idea. How are you going to know who the perfect guy is, if you don't put yourself out there a little, and learn about how relationships work?"

I take a sip of my coke, stalling as I form my answer. "I know plenty about relationships; I've witnessed all of my mom's screw-ups over the years. She goes from guy to guy, and every time it ends up getting ugly. I vowed a long time ago that I would never be like her. I have no interest in going through a lot of losers just to get to Mr. Right. I'd rather skip to the good part."

Mr. L is still leaning back, his head is motionless and his neck is arched. Yet his eyes move all around, resting for a moment on my face. "But how are you going to recognize Mr. Right when he comes along?"

Our eyes lock together, and I decide to accept the challenge of his question. "That's easy," I begin. "He's the sort of guy who will rescue me from danger." Mr. L's eyes flicker when I say that, but he doesn't look away, so I continue. "He's smart, big-hearted, and highly principled. So principled, in fact, that it might be hard for him to recognize that he needs me, because it's easy to see that I'm not as good a person as he is. But sooner or later he'll realize that I'd do anything for him, not because I feel I ought to, but because I want to. Because somehow we're soul-mates, and if I spent the rest of my life making myself worthy of him, well, that would be the most wonderful fate I could imagine." I think I see him wanting to smile, so I smile too. "And I'd certainly never lie to him, or do anything to make him doubt my devotion." I lean towards him as I say this, and the air between us is electric and uncertain. I can't read his expression, but at least it hasn't changed. At least he hasn't moved.

There's still that wrinkle between his eyes, but he's not in his fright or flight position. "But you just said that people don't get loved for being honest and good."

"True."

"So tell me how that works," he whispers.

My heart is beating at twice its normal speed. His hand is resting on the table. Touching him would be scary and superb, like stealing something wonderful even though I have the money to pay for it. My fingers graze the warmth of his knuckles; I've never felt anything better. He clenches his hand into a fist; then he rolls it from underneath my touch, and now his dry palm is covering my own. His hand squeezes my mine before he pulls away.

When I realize I'm biting down hard on my lip I relax my mouth and answer him. "I guess my plan is flawed. Hopefully he'll love me anyway."

Mr. L shifts in his seat, finally, and he looks down, away from me. "Well, love is flawed. That's all the wisdom I can offer you."

I laugh as though what he said was funny, and he laughs too. The tension is broken.

"Well, anyway," I say. "I promise I won't tell you what they're saying about your wife and her ex-husband. You must really be concerned if you came all the way here just to ask me *not* to tell you something."

I punctuate my sentence with a giggle, but this time he doesn't laugh along. "You're mistaken," he says. "My wife was never married before me."

Jackpot! I erase the smile on my face, but my insides are bouncing around in glee. "Oh, right," I stutter. "Well there you go, that just goes to show how off base everybody is!" I get up, and standing over him I squeeze his shoulder. "Well, thanks for the coke, Mr. L. I should get back to work. I'll see you tomorrow?"

He nods and I exit to the back room, but I peek through the door's window, watching him as he sits, unaware of my gaze. He looks like a little boy who has just been scolded for dressing up in his dad's clothing—he's slumped over, his tie is crooked, his sleeves are rolled up too far and his shirt is un-tucked. But most noticeable is his look of defeat where one of victory clearly belongs.

"It's time to clean up. We should get started, Melody."

"Sure thing, Kyle. Why don't you go close up, and I'll get going on the dishes."

Kyle smiles at my suggestion; I never offer to do the dishes. He charges out to the storefront while I saunter over to the sink. As I tackle the task at hand, lyrics from one of my mom's favorite songs come to mind, and I sing about being cruel to be kind, confident that the running water will drown out the sound of my voice.

25. Samantha

September 11th, 2001

My morning started out as usual. I got out of bed, and stretched out a little while watching CNN. Nothing too important was going on, except primary elections. I reminded myself to look for and read the page I had saved from the newspaper—the one that explained all the candidates' positions, before going to the polls later that day.

I changed into sweat pants and a T-shirt, and put on my relatively new running shoes. I had been running every morning since the day after my thirtieth birthday, which had been in June. I never thought I would be thirty and alone, but here I was. The only thing I could think of that could have been worse was to be thirty, alone, and fat. So I ran.

Soon my feet were hitting the pavement, and I silently praised myself for my discipline. Honestly, I was in one of the best places emotionally that I'd ever been. Daily exercise was just the beginning—I was also eating right and getting enough, but not too much, sleep. I had a good job, working for an after-school program at the YWCA. It didn't pay much, but they offered to train me as a lifeguard so I could at least supplement my hours by working in two different programs. And, I'd signed up for a beginning video production class at Shannon Community and Technical College. It met on Wednesday and Friday mornings, and I had free access to cameras and editing equipment.

Life is good, I said to myself, as I ran through the neighborhood lined with tall, leafy trees and bungalow style homes. Of course, there was room for improvement, but who couldn't say that about their life? Things were nice. Sure, they would have been nicer if I'd had a man around. I wasn't ashamed to admit it. But I worked with kids in a predominately female environment, so I didn't meet many eligible guys there. Nor did I meet many guys at school, or if I did, they were ten or more years younger than I was. I didn't see much potential for a relationship when that was the case.

Slap slap slap. My sneakers moved in a steady rhythm, and my heart was beating quickly but steadily. *Oh well, at any rate, having no guy in your life is better than having the wrong guy.* I'd come to this conclusion many times during my morning runs. I always began to rehash the drama of my relationship with Collin while I was running. It was like channel flipping and finding the last fourth of *Gone With the Wind.* You know that Scarlet will plummet down those stairs, and that Rhett won't be able to keep Bonnie from falling off her horse, and that Melanie will still die, and in the end, everyone is alone and nobody gave a damn. Yet there's something fascinating about reliving how it all fell apart.

After I agreed to stay "one more night" with Collin, we of course got back together and I never made it to Ghana. Collin swore off pot, and I was impressed with the strength of his resolve. I moved back in with him, and he continued to manage the building his uncle owns. His band dissolved, which I was silently happy about. It meant less temptation and fewer situations to his test his ability to stay on the wagon. Plus, I had him to myself now.

I believed things were good. Shannon didn't seem as small as it once had. I was working for a temp agency, and I liked changing jobs and meeting new people. On weekends we would take short road trips to tourist towns along the Great Lakes, or to Chicago or Green Bay. A couple of times we even splurged on plane tickets to more exotic locations, like San Francisco or Toronto. Life was easy and breezy, and I believed that if I was happy, Collin had to be too.

Until one Tuesday evening in March. I was standing in the kitchen, heating up nacho flavored frozen rice that came in a bag from the grocery store. The nacho part was in little orange circles, and they were supposed to melt into something that resembled cheese. As soon as they did, I was going to add in leftover chicken and fresh onions and tomatoes, but at the moment I was concentrating on moving the orange circles around the bottom of the pan so they would liquefy more quickly.

Collin walked into the kitchen. "I'm depressed," he announced. "And I need to do something about it soon, or I'm going to go crazy."

I dropped my fork into the rice/cheese combination and looked at him. He looked as familiar as ever in his jeans and flannel shirt, but unfortunately, in the space of less than twenty words he had changed into someone else.

"I thought we were happy," I replied.

"You thought wrong."

I turned off the stove and stepped away from it, towards the sink. "But… what about all the good times we've been having? The other night when we ordered pizza and watched *Futurama*– were you just pretending to have a good time?"

He leaned up against the olive green kitchen wall, holding his arms across his chest. "I wasn't just pretending. But is that as good as it gets? TV and pizza on a Sunday night?"

"What's wrong with TV and pizza on a Sunday night? Lots of people would kill to have that."

Collin tilted his head and looked down at me. "They'd kill to have that? Really?"

"I don't see what good sarcasm is going to do you." I puffed.

He returned to his normal, neutral tone. "I'm not being sarcastic. And I'm not discounting the value of pizza and TV. But there has to be something more."

I needed a moment before responding, so I put my finger under the nozzle of the sink, which had a slow drip. My finger acted as a dam, then water began to seep out anyway and a variety of answers ran through my mind as I debated which one to say. I opened my mouth and what came out was not what I was expecting. "Something more than me, you mean. Something more than you and me."

"Yes."

I burst into tears.

Under normal circumstances Collin would take me into his arms and tell me that everything will be all right. But he kept his distance, and simply said, "This isn't about you, Sam." Then he walked away, shutting himself in the bedroom for the rest of the evening.

Shortly after midnight I brushed my teeth then entered our bedroom, where the lights were out and he was pretending to be asleep. I climbed in next to him, and spoke to his back. "You begged me to drop my plans and come back to you. I did, and now you're saying I'm not enough. How do you think that makes me feel?"

"It's not you," he said. "I just need something more. Something that's mine."

"Like what?"

"A career. Something I can do where I feel like I'm contributing, and not just taking up space on this planet for no reason."

"You contribute everyday. What about the apartment building?"

"Sam, if the most ambitious thing I can accomplish is managing the apartment building my uncle owns, while living off my family's money, then I'm a failure, and no one can disagree."

I wrapped my arms around his back, taking comfort in the warmth of his skin. I pressed my mouth between his shoulder blades. "You'll never be a failure to me."

He turned over and wrapped his arms around me, so there was a mere centimeter or two between us. "And that's huge," he said. "It just isn't enough."

Pushing aside my resentment, I could sort of understand how he felt. Nonetheless, Collin having something of his own meant there would be a part of his life I that couldn't control. I knew from experience how bad things could go when that was the case. Days later I tried to express this to him, and he replied diplomatically. "Okay. But at some point you're going to have to trust me. Otherwise, what future do we have?" I couldn't answer. Sure, he was right, but I felt like I was riding shotgun without a seatbelt or airbag while Collin drove recklessly down a curvy road.

So, speaking of scary driving situations, his solution was to work as one of those guys who rides in ambulances and helps out. He needed to get his EMT training first, so he found a two-week course in Madison and signed up immediately. Once he got back, certificate in hand, he volunteered fifteen hours a week. "I'm fulfilling a childhood fantasy," he said. "I can't tell you what a rush it is. And I'm actually helping people."

I had to admit that this new fascination was much healthier than his previous ones. And he perked up. The light behind his eyes turned back on, and Collin no longer spoke of being depressed.

It didn't even matter to him that he wasn't getting paid. Of course, with his family's fortune in casinos and real estate, money had never been a worry. However, months later when he was offered a full-time paid position, he said we should celebrate. We went out for seafood, and Collin insisted on ordering us the lobster. We also had cocktails (a Cosmo for me and a dry Manhattan for him). It was the first time since we had gotten back together that I had seen him drink, but I didn't say anything because I didn't want to spoil the festive mood.

"To us," he said, holding up his drink.

I lifted mine up too, and our glasses clinked. "To our life together," I added. And he smiled.

What could go wrong?

Then one day Collin rode to the site of a car accident. He was trying to remove a 200-pound unconscious guy from a crashed vehicle when the guy came to, and started writhing in pain. He thrust forward and backwards in Collin's arms, causing Collin to throw his back out. He landed in the hospital for several days, and was prescribed Percodan to help.

At first I was accommodating and doting—rubbing his feet and bringing him scrambled eggs in bed. I bought him all his favorite magazines and ones he didn't like as well. I let him watch sports and Comedy Central 24/7, even though it was May sweeps and all my favorite shows were airing their season finale cliff-hangers. I even went to the liquor store for him when he requested beer.

But the weeks turned into a month and after two months Collin still wasn't better. Then I began to slowly realize; Collin is two people. There's good Collin, the guy I love. He is gentle, giving, and sweet—the sort of guy who would think nothing of climbing a twelve-foot tree to save a kitten in need. But introduce mood-altering substances into the picture, and bad Collin emerges. He's the sort of guy who is lazy, ambivalent, and who refuses, at all costs, to take responsibility for himself.

I know. It doesn't take a genius to have figured that one out, right? Okay, fair enough. But accepting a harsh reality about the most important person in your life is almost as hard as admitting to your own fatal flaws. The truth hurts.

Collin sat on the couch in his sweat pants and grayish white T-shirts, watching bad daytime television, for weeks. "Leave me alone, I'm in pain," he'd say every time I'd try to get him to get up and do something, anything. They wouldn't have him back as an EMT, even after his back was, for the most part, healed. Unfortunately there was permanent damage, and they saw him as too big a liability. "I finally do something useful with my life, and I screw it up." He said this over and over, like a mantra.

It would be easy to blame our ensuing breakup on the Percodan, but I know it's not that simple. Collin got as many refills as the doctor would allow, and after his doctor said no more, he tried without success to find another doctor who would prescribe him some.

"Nobody understands the amount of pain I'm in!" Collin would whine as he went from one doctor's office to another. Then he'd go home and drink beer, feeling sorry for himself. After another couple of weeks of this, I decided enough was enough.

"Collin, you have to get a grip. This is not the end of the world, even if it feels like it is. Don't you think it's time to move on?"

He looked at me with disgust. "For years I've wanted to be a better man than the guy you see sitting before you. I finally figured out how, and it's taken away. Plus, my back hurts. I know you don't believe me, but it does."

"The doctors said you were okay."

"The doctors don't know crap," he grunted.

"Right, so it's the doctor's fault."

Collin threw his empty beer can on the floor, but I could tell he would have preferred to have thrown it at me. "This isn't about fault. I feel bad, okay?"

His wallowing in self-pity made it impossible not to condescend to him, even though I realized it would set him off. "Oh, I see. Guess what? Everyone feels bad from time to time. That's life, and you have to learn to deal with the bad patches. I hate to say it, but worse things have happened to better people."

I was standing in our living room, on top of the brown shag carpet, staring down at Collin, who was sitting on the brown corduroy couch. All of a sudden I could no longer see him, the lines that separated him from the rest of our drab living room had blurred, like I was staring at a muddy impressionist painting. His voice jumped out at me, though. "You think I'm just a drunken, drugged-out loser without any direction, don't you?"

"Yes." By this time, breaking up with Collin had become so old hat that affirming his question was not hard to do.

"Well," he replied. "That's useful information."

Then he grabbed his keys, and walked out. All I could think of was, "Oh God, not again. We didn't just break up *again*." But we had. The signs were all there, and the next day Collin knocked on our door.

"Hey," he said. "I just wanted you to know that I've moved upstairs. Since most of our stuff is yours, I figured it would be easier for me to leave."

"That's very considerate of you," I said.

Then there was a long, icky pause as we both stood there, grasping for words that would express our feelings, but in the end, we let the dead air floating between us do the job. Sometimes silence says it all.

"See you around," he said.

And I saw him a lot.

He'd stop up because he had left something in our apartment that he now needed, or I'd see him in the hallways, changing light bulbs or vacuuming the entryway. Each time I encountered him I felt like our eyes should meet and lock, like Hubbel and Katie's do at the end of *The Way We Were* and then we should have this incredibly simple conversation about mundane things that was loaded with double meanings and hidden emotions. But no, our conversations were really just about the weather or getting his name off the phone bill or whether or not I had found his favorite green sweatshirt while I was cleaning. Nothing behind them, they were the very definition of boring.

One time, I was walking in right as Collin was leaving with this young, skinny blonde who looked sort of like Hillary Duff—all apple pie cheeks and girl-next-door-ness. He casually threw his arm around her, and he must have said something funny, because she blushed and laughed simultaneously.

Then Collin looked up and saw me. "Oh. Hey, Sam. How are you?"

"Fine." I said. Then I raced into my apartment without returning the question. I sat down on my ugly brown couch and willed myself to cry. But try as I might, no tears would come.

"You're over him," I said to myself. "Move on."

Slap Slap Slap. My feet slowed down until they were silently hitting the pavement, and my heart and breathing returned to their usual steady pace. It was a beautiful morning, the bright sun was promising the optimism of a warm day. So I shouldn't find it necessary to rehash the negative Collin stuff. If I was truly over him, why did I still think about him?

I reached my building, walked inside, and mounted the stairs up to my apartment. Once there I headed directly to the shower, where I washed while singing that Neil Diamond song about heart lights. It had been in my mind for the last two days, after hearing it on the oldie's station. You know you're getting up there when songs you enjoyed as a sixth grader are being played as oldies.

I got out of the shower and got dressed. It was Tuesday. Excellent. On Tuesdays I got to spend time using the editing equipment down at SCTC, working on my projects for class. In addition, I'd probably run into Jane, my favorite instructor. She was my age, and

I could tell we had a lot in common. Maybe we could go for lunch or something, since I didn't have to be at the Y until 2:30. At any rate, I'd have several hours to work. Even still, I knew it wouldn't be enough. Put me in front of a TV and some editing equipment, and time just evaporates.

I had combed my wet hair so it would dry into something presentable, and I'd put on a T-shirt and khaki pants when I heard a knock on my door. I answered it, only to find a pale-faced Collin on the other side.

"What's up?" I said. "You need something? Because I'm sort of in a hurry to get going."

"You haven't heard yet," he responded in a whisper.

"Haven't heard what?"

He walked past me, inside now he took my hand and gently pulled me over to my hideous couch. I made a mental note to myself for the millionth time to replace it. I sat down as he turned on the television. "What? Did somebody shoot George Bush or something? That would be a shame," I said, with sort of a laugh.

Then I looked at the electronic images dancing in front of me. It was the most horrific dance I had ever seen, full of fire, loss, and terrible, terrible, waste.

I sat, watching, trying to make sense of how the world can change so drastically in an instant. I had no idea how much time had gone by, when I noticed that Collin was still sitting next to me, holding my hand. When I looked at his face there were tears streaming down it.

How could I be so selfish as to think only of my immediate, generic loss, the one I was sharing with the rest of the country and the world, when Collin was suffering next to me? "Oh my God. Dave would be down there, wouldn't he? I suppose there's no way you'll be able to hear anything for a while."

He nodded. Dave was his favorite first cousin, and Collin thought of him as a brother. He lived in NYC, working as a firefighter.

"Oh, Collin. I'm so sorry."

He reached for me, hugging me so tight I could feel his heartbeat. Even after everything, it was the closest we'd ever been.

Spring 2006

I leave my dad's hospital room with the excuse of finding something to eat. For the past few hours we have been catching up with my mom, chatting about her travels and telling inside, family type jokes that are over a decade old.

My dad is still smiling as I walk out. The important thing is that he's happy. She makes him happy, and that's all that matters. And I would be lying if I didn't admit to being happy to having her back as well. I'll save the tough questions for later.

I make my way to the cafeteria, and buy an apple, a grilled cheese sandwich, and a large diet coke. I pay ($10, can you believe it?) and look around the dining area for a place to sit. Then I see him, sitting by himself, drinking a cup of coffee. I walk over, place my tray down, and sit across from him.

"How did you find my mother?" I ask.

"I hired a private detective," Collin replies.

"For real?"

"I figured it was the fastest way of letting her know, and I thought time was of the essence."

I take a bite of my sandwich. It's a slice of semi-melted American cheese in between two pieces of white bread, which are soggy with butter because they weren't on the grill long enough. It's delicious. After I swallow, I speak. "Okay. But why?"

"What do you mean," he says. "Why, what?"

"I know you love my dad, but why are you doing this? Why are you spending entire days at the hospital, being so nice, and working so hard to bring my family together?"

Collin doesn't answer, so I continue. "I mean, I realize this isn't about me. You're doing this because you love my dad, I get that. But you're going awfully far. How much did that private detective cost? And how did my mother get here so fast? Plane fare from South America isn't cheap. Did you help her?"

Collin leans back in his chair, spreads his arms out, and rests his right ankle on his left knee. It's his ultra-relaxed pose that he takes on whenever he's feeling nervous. "Yeah, I picked up her ticket," he says breezily. "But you know money isn't an issue for me. Besides, she wasn't in South America, she was in Mexico City, so it wasn't even that expensive."

I press further. "Okay. But you still haven't told me; why?"

His face looks so stolid, save for a slight twitching of his left eye. "I don't have to tell you. You already answered for me."

"Collin, come on."

He scoots back closer to the table, takes a final sip of coffee, then absently starts to peel the Styrofoam cup apart into a curlicue, like how some people peel oranges, but I've never been able to master that technique. "Okay. Before Davey died I was supposed to fly out for his son's first birthday celebration. I thought it was silly. Evan was going to be one, it's not like he'd remember or even notice whether or not I was there. So I didn't go." Collin chokes up a little as he adds, "And I'll always regret not taking that last opportunity to hang out with Davey. I can't tell you what I'd give, what I would sacrifice, for one more chance to see him, to tell him I love him, and to say goodbye."

A handful of tears have made their way down Collin's face and he brushes them away. I hand him an only slightly used napkin, but he shakes his head. "I'm fine," he says with a sniff.

"So you did this for my mom, who you don't even know, so she can say goodbye in case my dad dies on the operating table?"

Collin reaches across the table, takes my hand, and squeezes it. "I don't think your dad is going to die, Sam. I really don't. But you know what they say—life is precious, and it can be defined by single, vital moments. Not to sound cliché, but that's so true."

"But why do you care so much about my mother?"

He sighs and shakes his head. "Sam. Get real. What do you think?"

I look at him, and I know he's trying to communicate something to me, something deep that ought to be crystal clear, but I refuse to pick up on it. Maybe I'm dense, or maybe I need to affirm my suspicions of what I think he's feeling by hearing him say it. I'm not sure—stress and fatigue have made me dumb. "Sorry," I say. "You're gonna have to spell it out for me."

He sighs again. Still holding my hand he says, "I don't want your world to change irrevocably before you've had one more chance to have your family together. On the off chance that your father doesn't make it, at least the three of you will have been together again. One last time."

I push my words out, past the lump in my throat. "So you did this for me?"

"Of course I did."

"But," I ask, "Why?"

He smiles at me in this really sad way. "Isn't it obvious?" he says. "I still love you, Sam."

26. Melody

It's 10:30 on Saturday night, and I am not at a party or social event of any sort. Instead I am home, in my craphole of an apartment, and Brady Williams is breathing down my neck as I finish his paper on the fall of communism for World History. We've been working on it for an hour.

It was therefore, a combination of internal and external forces, which brought about the Romanian revolution, and thus proved to be the final brick in the wall of freedom.

"You're shitting me, right? 'The wall of freedom?' There's no way Mrs. Johnson is ever gonna buy that. That whole last line has got to go."

"Fine," I say, through gritted teeth. I press the delete button on Brady's laptop and erase the last sentence.

The revolution in Romania was caused by different stuff, and it was the last step towards getting rid of communism.

"That's still too good. Put in some mistakes, and get rid of the words 'revolution' and 'communism.' They sound too smart."

"You're not serious? How can I get rid of those words when they're the subject of your paper?"

"Just do it. Make it sound right, or our deal is off."

I try one more time. *So there system wher you don't pay for stuff and your supposedly equal is garbage. All the people fought the government and that was the last time before things changed for forever.*

I mean that as a joke, but Brady's face turns happy as he reads it. "That's more like it. Remember, make it just good enough for me to pass. Any better than that, and Mrs. Johnson will know it's not Brady's."

"Got it," I say. I know some girls think Brady is cute, but I can't figure out why. At nineteen (he's a super senior - i.e. someone who failed and had to repeat his senior year) he's still battling the occasional bout of acne. I guess it does sort of blend into his face, so it's not that noticeable. But he wears those big baggy shorts that hang halfway down his butt, and he tries to act all ghetto when he is, in fact, about as white as a person can get. The worst part though, is he actually refers to himself in the third person. I mean, who besides Elmo does that?

I continue typing. *The president of Russia was Gorbachev, and I think he'd died already. And our president was Ronald Reagan. There friendship changing things changing the world.*

Brady is breathing down my neck as I work. I want to swat him away, or better yet, smash him flat the way I would if he were a fly. I can smell his cologne, which, combined with the scent of his hair gel, is really powerful in a really bad way.

And in other nations, like Bulgaria and Checksovalkia, they had revolutions too. All these revolutions combined made the fall of communism.

"I told you not to use that word."

I stand up, pushing Brady away from me on one side, and his computer away on the other side. I need air and space and more air.

"I can't not use the word 'communism' if you want me to write you a passing paper. What I'm typing right now is worse than fourth grade work."

"Nah. Your standards are just too high. Trust Brady on this one."

He smiles and tilts his head, then winks at me. Ick.

"Brady, no offense, but I think I'll do better if you let me work alone. It's hard for me to concentrate when you're here."

"No problem. Brady gets it." And he must, because he gets up to leave. "It's about time to head over to Abby's party anyway." He chuckles, and rubs his hands together, reminding me of an overdone villain in a bad movie. "I've been practicing saying that shit you wrote out for me. This is going to be tight!"

"Do you want to practice it one more time?" I ask.

"Sure. Hold on, let me get into character." Brady walks the short lap around my living room, his head hanging down. If I didn't know better, I'd say he was concentrating. He picks up an empty water bottle and puts in my hand. "You be Abby for a minute, and pretend this is beer."

I silently agree, and Brady does one more lap around my living room. Then his head jerks up, his eyes lock into mine, and his every muscle is tense. He walks toward me, and he doesn't stop until there is less than an inch between us. He grabs the plastic bottle from my hand and hurls it across the room.

"I know you're ashamed of us, Abby. You're ashamed of our love. But I love you anyway. And Brady's not gonna let you drink your guilt away. I'll never let you go, babe. Brady will never let go." Then he seizes both my shoulders, leans in, and lunges for a kiss. Panic and visions of Axel and forced encounters go rushing behind my eyes. I push him away, perhaps a little too hard, and cry out.

"Get off me!" I yell.

Brady loses his balance and lands on the floor.

"What's your problem? I was only rehearsing."

"You can spare me the stage kiss," I say, faking a laugh. Reality comes back, and I remember where I am and who I'm with.

"Sorry." He mutters.

I extend my hand to help him up. "You should get to Abby's party while it's still in full swing. You want to make as big a scene as possible."

"Right." Brady walks over to the mirror that is hanging in my entry way and starts primping. He runs his fingers through his hair and adjusts his shirt. "So, when Abby freaks out and calls me a liar, what do you want me to say?"

"We went over this. Just say things like, 'Stop pretending nothing happened between us.' Then, if you could start crying and act all hurt, that will make you seem really believable."

"Got it. And you'll have my paper for me on Monday."

"I'll have it tomorrow. You can get it after you tell me how tonight went down."

"Make sure nothing happens to Brady's lap top."

Without saying goodbye, Brady strolls out of my apartment, and on to crash Abby's party. This performance has not been Kelsey-approved, but that's because I decided it was best not to bother her with the details. Besides, she's been squeamish lately. All of a sudden she's worried about hurting Abby's feelings. I don't get it, but I know Kelsey will thank me later when Bobby is hers. And what am I getting out of this? I suppose it's simply the satisfaction of a job well done.

I go and sit back down in front of Brady's computer. I figure I may as well get his paper done now, while the apartment is peaceful. Surely Brady can't mean what he said—if I make his paper as bad as he was saying I ought to, he'll fail for sure. I delete what I wrote and start again.

In the late 1980s a lot happened in the world, but the most important thing that happened was the fall of communism. It started in the USSR but then all the smaller countries in the eastern block followed there example till the Berlin Wall came down. It was very tight.

There, that's a good start. Historically accurate, yet realistically written by someone like Brady. I smile at my brilliance, and am about to continue on when there's a knock at my door. I figure it's Brady, having forgotten his cell phone or something, but when I answer the door I find Kelsey. This is her first visit to my apartment.

"What are you doing here?" I ask. "Shouldn't you be at Abby's party? Why are you turning down an opportunity to move in on Bobby?" I stand in my doorway, blocking her entrance. It's not just that I'm ashamed of where I live (which I am), or that I have lied in the past about the quality of my apartment (which I have); I don't want Kelsey to come in because she really should be at that party. I had talked her into going because it's important for her to be there and lend Bobby a shoulder to cry on after Brady makes a scene. Step four of my foolproof plan.

"Can I come in?" she asks. "I need to talk to you."

"No. The party is happening *now*. You need to be there."

"That's what I need to talk to you about." She forces her way in, and walks the short distance to my living room. She barely looks around before choosing the most uncomfortable chair—one from an old dining room set with no arms, found at a garage sale. I collapse into my mom's recliner, and lean my weight back to force out the footrest. From the purposeful look on Kelsey's face I get feeling this conversation isn't going to be short, so I may as well be comfortable.

"Okay. What's the problem? Is it that I'm not going with you to the party? We already established that I'd only mess it up. I'm still too controversial."

"It's not that," she says. "It's your plan. I'm sorry, Melody. I know you've put a lot of work into it, and I appreciate it, I really do. But I think we should stop."

I lean forward, and the easy chair automatically folds into its upright position with a thud. "What? Why should we stop when we're so close? You're crazy. We're not stopping."

Kelsey twists her fingers into little knots. "I can't be a part of this anymore. It's just not right."

What the heck? When did Kelsey find her moral compass, and why now, when it's so inconvenient for her to have one? "How can you say that? It's not like we're stealing or something. We're only using information that's true, and setting up the situation so you'll look good. Bobby isn't going to be forced into anything."

Kelsey's face is red, and she looks like she's constipated or something. "But. Still. It's not right."

That's the best she can do? This won't be so hard. "Okay, you've said that already. I don't get it. What isn't right about it? Have we killed anyone?"

"Of course not."

"Right. But Abby could have. She's lucky she's not in jail for manslaughter. Do you know how many people die each year in alcohol related incidents? Tons. And you're worried about her? Give me a break."

"It's not Abby that I'm worried about. It's Bobby. It's like we're manipulating him."

Please! Bobby is no saint, this I know without a doubt. "Oh, I get it. It's okay for him to manipulate you every day, playing with your emotions and flirting with you, then making fun of you to his friends. That's okay, but convincing him to treat you well, to treat you like a *girlfriend* instead of an idiot, that's manipulation?'

Kelsey jumps up, tears in her eyes. "Bobby doesn't make fun of me!"

"Wake up Kelsey! *Everyone* makes fun of you!" She looks like I've just slapped her. Am I too harsh? I don't think so, but I soften my voice to soften the blow. "This is high school, and people are cruel. And I'll tell you something; the world is cruel. If you don't learn to take care of yourself now you never will, and you'll be one of those idiots who gets stabbed in the back because you were too nice to say no when somebody asked you to turn around. Why can't you claim what is yours and stop waiting for your fairytale ending?"

I'm half expecting her to run out of my apartment wailing at this point. But sometimes Kelsey surprises me. She lifts her chin and responds, "Just because I'm not you, that doesn't mean I'm weak, or that I'm an idiot, or any of that other stuff you just said. It's my life and my decision, and I'm not doing the plan."

Then Kelsey turns around, and her ass looks no smaller than usual, despite the air of dignity her words just gave her. Despite my anger, I have to admit, I didn't know she had it in her. Still, I'm not one to let things go easily, so I shout after her, "That's what you think. My plan is in motion, Kelsey. Stopping it now would be like messing with gravity. You don't mess with fundamental things like gravity—not without repercussions!"

Kelsey has continued out of my apartment and down the stairs to outside. I'm sure I sound like a freak, yelling at the air. No matter. I always win in the end.

27. Samantha

Night has invaded the hospital. During the day it's possible to believe a hospital is a semi-cheery place if you concentrate enough on the coffee shops and gift stores, or the smiley nurses in their patterned scrubs making pleasant conversation with the patients and their families. But at night a quiet darkness settles in, and the loudest noises are the beep of the machines the sick are hooked up to. During the day recovery seems more than possible; it's the obvious happy ending to the movie that is your life. But at night, death is just around the corner, waiting in hushed tones to leap out and smother you.

Am I being too melodramatic? I can't help it; I'm sitting at my father's bedside the night before his surgery. While I'm trying to think positive thoughts, I can't push away the thought that this could be the last time I ever see him alone. My mom and Collin both left to get some sleep, and when they left my dad was asleep as well. But I worried that he would wake up and feel scared, so I opted to stay. My instincts were right on target; he woke up desperate to chat. "I'm glad you're here," he said immediately after he opened his eyes. "Because I wanted to tell you that I'm sorry."

"Sorry for what?"

"For being such a crab, among other things. And I need to tell you this, so pay attention. There's a fire-safe box in the basement, honey. It may be hard to find, but it's there—mixed in with the camping gear, old boxes of your stuff, and all the dishes we never use. In it is your

169

birth certificate, the deed to the house, my will—all the important papers that you might need if I pass on."

I take his hand in mine. "Dad, don't talk like that. You're going to be fine."

"We don't know that for sure, sweetheart."

"Dad…"

My father squeezes my hand. "Samantha. Life doesn't always turn out the way you think it ought to. You know that by now, don't you sweetheart?"

"Of course. But…"

His soft voice cuts me off, as he squeezes my hand. "I fully intend to survive this surgery. This isn't goodbye."

I wipe the tears that are already coursing down my face. "Okay. I love you, Dad."

"And I love you, more than anything. You need to know how proud I am of you. I know I don't always show it, but I am."

"Thanks, Dad."

"However, there's still a lot of room for improvement."

The pleasant yet moving soundtrack to our conversation, the one that was playing in my mind, screeches to a halt. "Huh?"

"Don't take this the wrong way, Sam-Honey, but it's time you grew up a little. You have a great heart and a good mind, and it would be a waste for you not to live up to your potential. That's all."

"That's all? What does that even mean, Dad? How am I not living up to my potential?"

He sighs, as if to indicate that I'm being simple. "You're clinging to a man who isn't giving you what you need because you refuse to let him. And you're looking for redemption where there isn't any."

Okay, what sort of drugs is my father on? Would the doctors have given him something before his surgery? Maybe Collin brought him more than the hard candy he had promised. "Dad, I have no idea why you just said that."

"Yes, you do."

I look at him, his face bathed in a pool of dim light. I see a half smile spread across his lips. He looks almost serene. Or, maybe he's stoned. Same difference. I sigh. "Whatever. Your wife abandoned you twenty years ago yet you took her back. Are you really qualified to give me marriage advice?"

If my words angered him, he doesn't show it. He actually sort of laughs as he answers. "I don't have to be qualified to give you advice, I'm your father. And I wasn't talking about your marriage." He gives my hand one more final squeeze, then closes his eyes and rolls over, falling back asleep.

"Dad, I'm sorry. I'm confused. Tell me what you mean."

His steady breathing is my only answer.

I am sitting in the hospital waiting room while my dad is in surgery, and I am leafing through a copy of *Better Homes and Gardens* from several months ago. There is a feature on Valentine's Day: recipes to create the perfect meal for you and your sweetheart. Back in February I would have tried them. The main course is this chicken dish with pine nuts and sun-dried tomatoes—very 1980s, but sounds tasty nonetheless. The side dish uses heart of palms (get it—hearts for Valentines Day) and the dessert is raspberry mouse with dark chocolate drizzle.

Does anyone actually use these recipes, and if so, do they present the food in the casually impeccable way in which it was photographed? It's hard to imagine, but somebody must, or else they wouldn't keep printing stuff like this. If I was a better person I would, on a regular basis, cook food like this for Nate, and by the time it was all ready, the dirty dishes would be rinsed off and tucked away from sight in the dishwasher. Nate Nate Nate. Every time I think of him, a guilt bubble inside of me expands, pops, and creates hundreds of baby guilt bubbles.

It's not a good cycle.

I throw the magazine off to the side, and stare up at the clock hanging on the wall. It says 11:45. Dad has been in surgery for four hours.

My mom is in the chair to my left. She is knitting. When I saw her pull out her knitting needles for the first time, a couple of hours before, I asked her, "Since when do you knit?"

"Oh, I started years ago. It calms me, and it's practical too. It's hard to find decent sweaters in Mexico."

Do people need decent sweaters in Mexico?

Collin is across from me. I can't look at him. I don't know how to respond to that "I still love you" bomb that he dropped the day before yesterday. But until I can find the words to express the emotions I'm unable to identify, our eyes cannot meet. Period.

Meanwhile, Nathan is incommunicado. I'm not sure if that's because he isn't calling me, or if it's because I'm not calling him, but we haven't spoken. My cell phone is working again, so I can't blame his not calling on that. The battery had just fallen out of place. I almost wish it was really broken; then there would be a reason why he hadn't called.

A wave of nausea rumbles through me. I reach into my bag and pull out my saltines and lemon drops. They're both supposed to help—I shove three saltines into my mouth first, chew, and swallow. Then I suck on two lemon drops at once. The sweet acidy taste does distract my senses a little.

"How far along are you?" My mother asks.

"Huh?"

"You're pregnant, right?"

I fake a laugh because I am so not in the mood to have this conversation. "Yeah, whatever, Mom."

"You're eating saltines, your breasts are enormous, and last night at dinner you didn't order anything to drink. It all adds up, honey."

If Collin is paying attention to our conversation, he isn't giving any indication of it. He is stubbornly looking through an issue of Newsweek with Al Gore on the cover. God knows how old it is, but Collin appears entranced.

"You're not about to become a grandmother, so don't worry." I say this in a stage whisper, hoping it's quiet enough that Collin won't hear but loud enough to make my mom back off. Anyway, I'm not lying.

My mom looks me up and down, and I wilt under her stare.

"Why are you lying?" Her question may as well be an alarm clock in a library; I swear she raised the volume of her voice up at least three or four decimals. Collins puts down his magazine, and looks directly at me. Damn it, our eyes meet for an instant, but it's enough - enough to create that crazy warmth in my heart and nether regions that he's always been capable of generating just by looking my way.

"What does Newsweek have to say about Al Gore?" I ask.

"Don't change the subject, honey. Tell me what's going on." My mother rubs my shoulder with the palm of her hand, and her touch stings like shampoo in my eyes. I swat her away.

"Don't you think it's a little late to be playing the concerned parent?"

She picks at the lavender yarn, which is now resting, in her lap. "Sam, don't be like that. I just want to know."

"Well, lay off. Now is not the time."

Mom picks up her knitting, squeezing it all together, and the needles and yarn glop together. "Honey, I'm sorry I was gone so long. But I want us to be close again."

"We should be focused on Dad right now, okay. We can save all the other conversations for later."

"But…"

"He says he isn't going to run for president again." Collin's voice thrusts itself into our conversation. We both turn our heads towards him.

"Really?" I ask, with way more enthusiasm than I would usually have about Al Gore, "that's so interesting. What about all the people who think he could save the Democratic Party?"

Collin folds his magazine in half. "He doesn't address that. The interviewer didn't ask."

"Sam…" my mother begins again, leaning in towards me and trying to block my focus from Collin, "I really think…"

Collin interrupts her. "But if you ask me, there are no easy answers anyway. How could one person alone have the ability to save the Democratic Party? I mean, everybody is replaceable, right? Don't you agree, Sam?"

I stammer. "Umm… I don't know. But I do think Al Gore is better off, not being president. He's probably more influential and happier out of the White House." As I say this I am aware that maybe Collin and I aren't really talking about Al Gore at all, but the day is too confusing to worry about double entendres. Whatever. My mom looks from me to him.

"I'm sure being a multi-millionaire helps," says my mother. "But have you seen him lately? He's gained a lot of weight."

The doctor enters the waiting room. "Mrs. Stromwell?" he looks toward my mother. Doesn't he know that of the three of us, she's the last one who should be addressed first?

"Yes!" she cries and jumps up simultaneously. "How is he?"

"Phillip is doing well," he says, and Collin, my mother, and I all breathe a collective sigh of relief. "The surgery went fine. We cleaned out the arteries, and now he's resting. You'll be able to see him in a few hours."

"Thank you," my mother hugs the doctor through her tears of gratitude. He looks like he's endured lots of hugs like this, and no matter how uncomfortable they may make him, I would bet the alternative—telling loved ones of a patient's demise—would be far, far worse.

The doctor manages to make a smooth exit, and my mother's arms are empty and looking for a new occupant. I won't fill the vacancy. Suddenly, sure as anything, the saltines I ingested moments ago are making their way back up. I dash for the bathroom, finding a toilet to puke in just in the nick of time. After weeks of nausea, I am finally throwing up. It seems like all the food ingested during that time is coming out, for I don't just puke once, but over and over, and with it, comes tears of anger, regret, and relief. After what feels like forever I am finally done, and I barely have the strength to flush the toilet and stand up.

But I do it anyway.

I leave the stall, grateful to be alone in the bathroom. I am splashing water on my face when my mother enters.

"There you are," she says. "Are you okay?"

"No."

"Why not?" she asks. "What's wrong, honey?"

Fresh tears spill from my eyes. I want to tell her and I don't want to tell her. It's so unfair.

"Momma," I say, still leaning over the sink. "I think I'm really lost."

She places a warm hand on my cold and sweaty back. "That's okay," she says. "I know right where to find you."

Hours later I am standing in my father's kitchen, fresh from a hot shower. I am wearing boxer shorts and a T-shirt and nothing else because I plan to go to bed very soon. But first I need to eat something greasy and salty, like potato chips. I'm not finding any. I'm contemplating making toast with lots of butter when Collin walks in. He has on the same outfit as I do. We could be a print ad for Hanes.

"Hey," he drawls, in a voice as smooth as sherbet. "How's it going?"

During my relationship with Collin there had been many a late night when, after a long day, I would be standing in the kitchen and he would come in, wrap his arms around my waist, and nuzzle my neck with his nose, cheek, and lips. On those nights I would sigh in relief, and mumble my fears into the safety of his chest. Then he would kiss away all the ugliness in the world, and I would be left only with the beauty of him.

How much would I give to have a moment like that right now? I shouldn't want to, and if I were to answer *his* question honestly, I would say, "Well, my husband hasn't returned any of the three messages I left him today after my dad's surgery. I have no idea what is going through his mind, but it's obviously not thoughts of me. He should be here, not you. You're my ex, and you're here, and you're so close right now that it almost makes up for all the distance that has ever been between us. But you are not my husband. Not. My. Husband. You need to go now. Now. Now." But I do not say that. Instead I settle for, "Fine. When are you leaving?"

He does a double take. "Wow. You're welcome."

"I'm sorry. Am I supposed to be thanking you for something?"

He shakes his head and laughs. "See if I ever do you another favor. By the way, how's Cheshire?"

"He was fine when I left."

"Great, but how's he doing now?"

I decide on toast after all. I take two slices from the bread bag and pop them in the toaster. "As far as I know, fine."

"As far as you know? Haven't you talked to your husband lately?"

I replace the twist tie onto the bag, and keep busy by putting the bread back in the refrigerator and fishing for the butter. Collin just leans against the kitchen table, watching me. "Collin, you may find it hard to believe, but your fish's well-being is not on the top of my list of concerns. If you're so worried about him, you should go home and see how he is for yourself."

"Really?" he asks with the casual arch of an eyebrow.

"Yes, really. Look, I appreciate all that you've done. Obviously I can never thank you enough for driving down to take care of my dad, and for bringing my mother home—all of it. But my dad is okay now, and I don't think it's appropriate for you to be here any longer."

He mocks me by repeating me. "You don't think it's appropriate?"

"I'm married Collin. And what you said, the other night…"

"About how I still love you?"

I close the refrigerator door, place the butter on the counter next to the toaster, and reach into the cabinets to find a plate. "Yes, that. That's not appropriate. We can't have conversations like that." I've found both a plate and a knife, and now there is nothing to do but stand here and wait for my toast to pop up.

"But we did." He moves closer to me. I can smell his skin. "I'm sorry. I realize that my loving you is a huge inconvenience - for both of us. Believe me, I've tried to stop. But I can't make it go away. Every time I'm with someone else I'm so hopeful that it will work out. But eventually the same thing always happens." His gray eyes challenge me to ask the question.

I relent. "What always happens?"

"I resent her for not being you."

"Collin…"

He steps forward, close enough to run his finger along the rim of my T-shirt. "I know what you're going to say. We don't know how to be together."

"Well, we don't. God knows we've tried too many times."

He looks back up into my eyes without letting go of my T-shirt. I know I should break away. I've just forgotten how. "I don't know how to be with you," he says. "But I can't be with anyone else. Where does that leave me, Sam?"

He doesn't give me a chance to answer his question. Instead he's pulling on my T-shirt, pulling me towards him. My mind has emptied of all thought; being held by him is pure sensation. I am in his arms and my heart is pounding. My arms are wrapping around his neck and shoulders and my blood is pulsing. His head is leaning down, down, towards mine and my limbs are liquefying. Our lips are just about to meet when it happens.

My cell phone goes off.

The sound I have waited for all day has finally materialized, and it shocks me back to reality. I push him away, and run to the living room, where I left my purse. I fish for my phone, and see Nathan's name appear on the tiny screen. Relief courses through me as I flip open my phone.

Yet as I'm talking to Nathan I am aware of Collin standing in the door-less doorway between the two rooms, unabashedly listening to my conversation. And I know I feel guilty, but I can't quite pinpoint why.

28. Melody

Monday morning. The number of Monday mornings left in my high school career is quickly dwindling down. If my mom and Kenny don't break up in the next six days, then she is moving us to Green Bay. That means I now have six days to secure Mr. L, and to convince Kelsey to let me live with her for the rest of school year. Difficult: yes. Impossible: Not at all.

The first thing I do is stop up in Mr. L's room to say hello. Since our conversation at Subway we have been communicating on a whole new level. It's like he's given into the familiarity between us. He hasn't called me Miss Madsen once since that night; he calls me Melody or nothing at all. And he's touched me on the shoulder three times; once his hand rested there for more than a second. But most importantly, we've started eating lunch together. I've been packing a sandwich and bringing it to his room, where we sit, talk, and eat together like it's the most natural thing in the world.

But the weekend lasted forever, what with all the Kelsey drama, the writing of Brady's paper, and the aftermath of Abby's party. I'll deal with all of it in good time, but right now I am walking into Mr. L's room, where he is sitting at his desk. When he sees me he smiles and waves, but says nothing. He is on his cell phone, apparently listening to a message. Then he flips it shut.

"Important call?" I ask.

"No, just an update on my father-in-law," he says.

"And that's not important?"

His jaw sets into this clenched position. "There's nothing I can do about it from here."

"And your wife didn't want you there?"

He's nearly gritting and grinding his teeth. "No. Her ex-husband is there with her, so she doesn't need me."

"Oh."

"I'm sorry." He gets up and moves towards his whiteboard, then takes out a marker and begins to write the day's activities for each of his classes. "I shouldn't be talking about personal stuff with you. It's not appropriate."

I laugh. "Don't worry about it. We're friends."

"That's where you're wrong," he says. He is carefully scrawling in neat horizontal lines:

English 10—

A.   *Journal Prompt*

B.   *Essays handed back/discussed*

C.   *Read from House on Mango Street.*

I don't know how to respond, so I say nothing. He can feel my eyes watching him; I know he can. But he keeps writing as he speaks. "We can't be friends, not as long as I'm your teacher. That would be crossing a line."

"Isn't it a little late to be worried about that now?"

He sighs. Then, as if in defeat, he leans his body into the board. His feet have not moved but his forehead is pressed against a clean white spot, so that he is standing at an angle. Looking down at his toes, he says, "Probably."

I move closer to him. It's a risk, I know, but I put my hand on his back. My palm is flat against his blue oxford shirt, and the delicious feel of what is underneath is burning through the cloth. "Maybe this is one line that ought to be crossed."

He's still looking down. "Oh Melody…" he says. He sounds resigned. Or maybe just tired. I'm not quite sure.

But whatever—this is good. It's got to be. It's like his resolve is a physical creature that is shrinking into nothing before my eyes. I am so tempted to wrap both of my arms around him to give him a hug from behind. I am actually contemplating doing just that when I am shocked by a very shrill voice.

"Mr. Linden! I have a question about my paper." Becki Birkland is standing in the doorway, with Lana Gretch behind her. Mr. L jumps, literally jumps away from my touch and twirls around to face her, dropping his marker in the process. "Oh. I'm sorry, am I interrupting something?" Becki asks.

"Not at all." His laugh is a nervous, jerky burst of sound as he reaches down to grab his marker. Becki and I meet eyes. I widen mine and raise my eyebrows at the same time, as if to dare her to say anything to anyone about what she just saw. She squints. She may as well have said "Game On!"

Mr. L stands up straight. "What was your question, Miss Birkland?"

Becki looks away from me, and focuses on him. "I spent a really long time on this. Why did I get a B-?"

"Um, well, let's look it over." He leads her over to his desk, and I make my silent exit.

I need to find Kelsey.

She is at her locker, checking her lipstick in the magnetic mirror hanging on the door. I walk up behind her. "Hey!" I say. She jerks a little, startled, then she turns around. "You never called me back. Did you go to Abby's party?" Kelsey frowns, and her mouth turns into this perfect little horizontal line, like she can't decide what to say or how to say it. I was expecting that, and my plan of attack is to pretend that it's all good between us.

"Of course I didn't go to the party," she says hotly. She opens her mouth to say more, but I start in before she can get any words out.

"That's cool. I talked with Brady the next day, and I guess he was so convincing that Bobby hit him. Can you believe it? But it's actually good that you weren't there, because we need to execute step four of my plan. It's not enough to make Bobby mad at Abby; we need to destroy her faith in him enough that she'll break things off with him. After that, you just move directly on to step five, where you find him alone, vulnerable, and broken down. And girlfriend, you'll know what to do then! Hang in there, Kells, we're in the homestretch. Bobby is going to be yours! You can thank me later, when it's all done."

I squeeze her shoulder, as she stands there, stunned.

"Well, gotta get to first hour! I'll talk to you soon." I leave before she can respond. Besides, I really do need to get to class. I've already made notes on how to destroy Abby's faith in Bobby, but I need to go over them and make sure there are no flaws in my plan. I only get to practice this once, after all.

The day goes by in a jumbled haze, the way busy days often do. It became necessary to skip gym class for two reasons. One—I know if I see Kelsey, she will try to talk me out of executing the final stage of the plan. Two—it's my best shot to sabotage Bobby. Now, I thought long and hard about how I should do this, and in the end, I decided to take a page from the book my mother wrote. Not that she ever did anything *exactly* like what I'm about to do, but let's just say my plan is inspired by how she originally stole Kenny away from his crazy ex-wife. (She claims that she really did think she was pregnant at the time, but I doubt that's true.)

First I go to the counseling office, where there is a wall of glossy brochures on everything from STDS to how to quit smoking. I pick up whatever there is about pregnancy and teen parenting. Then I go and ask Edith for a pass to the media center. She loves me, so she gives me one without even asking why I'm not in class. Once I get there I find a computer in the corner of the room, and I quickly set up a hotmail account, which takes, like 5 minutes. Then I write an e-mail to Abby (I got her address from the background check.) This is what it says:

Subject: Thought you should know
Dear Abby —
*We go to the same school, but I'm not ready yet to tell you who I am.
I've always thought you were straight up, so I'm doing the decent thing by
giving you the 411. When you were out of town on the band trip Bobby
and I hooked up. We were both wasted. But now I'm pregnant, and he's
my baby's daddy. If you don't believe me, just look in his backpack. You'll
get what I mean once you look inside.*
I just thought you should know.

I press send, close out the screen, and then I race down the senior
hallway to Bobby's locker. I'm glad I thought to look up his combination the week I was helping Edith in the attendance office. Actually,
I would be praising myself for my brilliant foresight if I hadn't made
a habit of looking up the combos of everyone I thought I might use
some day. Anyway, I open up Bobby's locker while there is nobody
to see me do it, and I shove the brochures into his backpack, deep
into a pocket where he won't find them right away. At least, not until
Abby searches through it.

The crowning glory of my plan? I happen to have heard whispers
in the hallways that Lindsey Davenhook is pregnant. I have seen
Bobby and Lindsey flirt with each other, but he flirts with just about
everyone, so that's no biggee. Yet, it gives the whole thing an air of
credibility, which is why the e-mail account I set up is *LuluDA@
hotmail.com.* I figured that was ambiguous enough not to be overly
obvious, but all the same, Abby is no mental giant. I had to make it
easy enough for her.

Fourth hour arrives, and I beeline for Mr. L's room, making sure
to get there before the bell rings so people can see me walk in. This
time he's playing with his cell phone, flipping it open and shutting it
closed in one fluid, continuous motion.

"You're not eating anything today?" I ask.

He doesn't smile this time when he sees me. "What are you doing here?" he asks, like it's totally weird for me to be around at this

time of day.

I ignore his rudeness. "I felt bad about this morning. I wanted to make sure everything's okay between us."

"You shouldn't be here," he blurts. Desperation is leaking out of him. "And I need to call my wife."

"Sure," I say. I feel like I'm backing away from a growling dog. "I get it. I'll see you next hour." I turn to go.

"Melody!" He cries. I turn back around.

"Yeah?"

His voice softens. "Maybe you should help Edith next hour. I don't really have anything for you to do."

"I sort of need to talk to you," I say. "Please, can't I come to your room?"

He's still playing with his phone. Then, he snaps it shut a final time and shoves it into his drawer. "I'm sort of busy."

"Yeah, you look really busy."

He physically responds to my sarcasm by contracting into himself, taking up less space than he was a moment ago. "Ms. Madsen," he begins. "I hope you remember that above everything else, I'm your teacher. You should be treating me as such."

I cough, not because I'm mucus-y or anything, but I need to stall for a second while I decide on what to say back. "Mr. L, I mean no disrespect," I say. "And I hope you know I'd never do anything to hurt you. If you don't want to see me, that's okay. I just wish you'd be honest about why."

"I am being honest."

"You're not."

He stares down at his desk and sighs "Okay. I can't argue with you anymore and I can't change how you think. But I also know that if people continue to see you and me talking together alone, rumors will spread, and that's something I can't afford."

Softly I say, "I understand." I feel a lump rise in my throat, and I try to swallow it away. "It's just, I really do need to talk to you. Maybe later? When people aren't around. I'm going to be here late for newspaper layout. Maybe I could swing by afterwards? If you say yes, I promise I'll never bother you again."

He squeezes his eyes shut as if he has a headache. "Fine. Come talk to me when you're done. I'll still be around." Now his eyes are open, and he's staring at the drawer that contains his phone. It doesn't matter; soon he'll be looking only at me.

"Great. I'll see you then."

29. Samantha

It's hard for me to explain just how or why I was so easily tempted by Collin. If I could understand it myself, it might be easier to justify and forgive myself for my near transgression. If Nate hadn't called, I very well could have let myself be kissed by my ex. And he's my ex for a very good reason.

After 9/11 Collin and I slipped into an easy friendship. I traveled with him to New York for his cousin's funeral, and his entire family assumed we were a couple. We did nothing to dispel that belief; it just seemed easier to let them believe we were together. So we slept side by side in the same bed for three nights, and it wasn't unlike the many nights we were together when we were too tired, bored, or estranged to feel passionate. The only difference: our bodies were in constant contact. If we weren't holding hands then one of us was spooning the other, or our toes were touching, or an arm was draped carelessly across the other's chest. We barely spoke, but he shed many silent tears while in my arms.

Once we got back to Shannon, Collin slept in his own bed and I slept in mine. Yet our dynamic had done a 180. There was no more small talk in hallways, no more stopping down to retrieve lost books or sweatshirts. But on the first Friday in October there was knock on my door. When I opened it I found him, a box of pizza in one hand, and a copy of *Taxi Driver* in another. "It's criminal," he said, "for a film buff like you to never have seen *Taxi Driver*."

He invited himself in, and we sat and watched and ate. The following week it was Chinese takeout and *The Deer Hunter*. A week later, burritos and *Godfather II*.

"Enough!" I cried. "I can't take any more of these boy movies."

He laughed at my belligerence. "Sam, these are classics. They're all in the American Film Institute's top 100."

"I don't care," I said, crossing my arms across my chest. "Most of the critics who rated them so high are men. Of course they're going to pick violent, male-centric films as their favorites."

"That just shows how much you know."

His next few picks were *Singing in the Rain, Gone With the Wind,* and *Casablanca*. "They're all in the top ten," he said, "and they're chick flicks."

In early December we watched *Citizen Kane*, and for the life of him he couldn't understand why it was rated as the best movie ever. "There's no sex, no violence, swearing, or intrigue. What do people like about this film?"

"I think it's the cinematography and the circular structured story-telling," I replied.

"Whatever. It's boring."

I couldn't argue with him. Well, I sort of could. But for once I didn't want to. I had come to look forward to our movie nights. They were so uncomplicated. Never did Collin look deep into my eyes and offer to give me a backrub. Never did he make a sideways comment intended to push my buttons. And most significantly, he didn't show up stoned and the strongest thing we drank together was root beer. After our evenings were over I'm sure he probably went upstairs and drank or smoked alone, but that wasn't my concern. For years my relationship with Collin had subsisted on angst and friction. No more. Now we were in harmony.

Until Collin got a girlfriend. Tammy. She was twenty-three years old, blonde, and really, really nice, except when she was angry. I never experienced her anger, but Collin told me stories. I think he liked the roller coaster of being with her, at least in the beginning.

Anyway, Collin had this idea that we'd continue movie night, but that we'd include her. So they both came over, and the first week we watched *China Town* (Collin's choice), and the second week we watched *Moonstruck* (Tammy's choice). Both times they held hands and cuddled on the couch, and I felt like a chaperone on their date. The third week I lied and said I had plans.

To be honest, I cried a few times about the demise of movie night and the materialization of Tammy. But I never let Collin know my true feelings, and I tried hard to move on. I joined an online dating service, and a book club, and on Friday nights I took walks with the Sierra Club where most of the participants were either upwards of fifty, married, or completely undesirable. I figured it was exercise and it got me out of the house. Besides, I wasn't unhappy.

And when I saw Collin we would smile at each other; sometimes we would even hug. And, whenever he and Tammy had one of their many, many fights, he came to me for advice. I should have told him to leave her, because after a certain point her anger started to sound abusive. However, I was afraid he'd take it the wrong way, like I wanted him for myself, or something. And that would have only been partly true.

Then came Christmas of 2004.

I usually drove to Chicago to see my father, where, on Christmas Eve, he and I would go shopping together in the expensive stores along the Magnificent Mile and buy each other extravagant items like $40 soap or tins of caviar. On Christmas morning I would cook an elaborate brunch, and in the afternoon we'd go see a movie. It had been our tradition since my mother left for Mexico, when my father and I had found it necessary to celebrate in a way that didn't bring to mind memories of her.

But that year my father's oldest friend, who was recently widowed, convinced him to go on a cruise. "You can come with us, honey. It will be your Christmas present."

"And impose myself on the adventures of two swinging bachelors?" I said. "Not a chance."

"You know it's not like that, Sam. Walt's going to need some time before he can date again. And, in case you forgot, I'm still married."

I shook my head and rolled my eyes, confident he couldn't spot such gestures over the phone. "I know, Dad. But don't worry about me. Just go and have a good time."

Truth was, I was really rooting for my dad to meet someone on the cruise. It seemed past time for him to let go of his supposed marriage to my mother. But I knew there was no chance of that happening if I came along, so I opted to stay home. My plan? Christmas day would be one of extreme indulgence. I stocked up on a vast array of chocolate, and went grocery shopping for all the foods I love but rarely allow myself to eat (like pork sausage, cheesy garlic bread, and cream-based tomato soup.) I also bought myself *The Davinci Code* in hardback, which seemed like a huge deal, since I usually only buy paperbacks or wait for them to come to the library. Finally, I stopped by the video store, where I was careful to only pick out the trendy movies that weren't on the AFI's top 100 list. (I wound up with *You've Got Mail*, *Erin Brokovich*, *Pirates of the Caribbean*, and *Bad Santa*.) I picked up a job application while I was there as well. It turns out they were hiring.

On Christmas morning I got up, made myself chocolate-chip pancakes, and read the first three chapters of *Davinci Code*. At 10:30 I took a shower, did some yoga stretches (nothing that would make me sweat) and was debating which movie to watch first when my phone rang. I was expecting it to be my Dad.

"Hey! How's the cruise? Have you gotten a tan yet?"

"Sam, it's me. Thank God you're home. I need you to come get me."

I looked out the window. It was gray outside, but inside, on my ugly brown couch, I was wrapped in my favorite fleece blanket, content to squander away the day in the warmth and safety of my apartment.

"Collin, I'm sort of busy."

His voice raised at least an octave above its normal pitch. "Please! Christmas has gone horribly wrong. I'm begging you."

"Don't be so dramatic. Did you and Tammy have a fight? Just tell her you're sorry."

"It's more complicated than that. Please. I'll explain everything on the ride home."

"Did her father catch you smoking pot?"

"No. It has nothing to do with drugs or alcohol, I swear. Sam, if you do this for me I will be forever in your debt."

"And if I don't do this for you?"

"Then we should say our goodbyes now, because I'll be a dead man by morning."

Curiosity alone compelled me to grant his request. I got the directions to Tammy's parent's house, and made the twenty-minute drive to pick him up. When I arrived Collin was sitting outside on the curb, his duffel bag at his feet. He was shivering in his flannel-lined shirt. Collin has never liked wearing coats; it used to be a point of contention between us. He would go out in winter without one, then complain later when he was freezing. Seeing him suffer like that now only made me feel annoyed rather than sympathetic.

I pulled the car up and he climbed in.

"Okay," I said. "This had better be good."

"Her father was going to kill me," Collin said in a puff of air. "Seriously." Collin's elbows were resting on his knees, and his head fell into his hands. "I'm such a screw-up, Sam. I don't think I can fix what I've done."

With one hand on the steering wheel, I reached my other hand over to pat him on the head. I wasn't in the mood to deal with his tears, not on my day of supposed luxury. "There, there. I'm sure it's not so bad. Tell me what you did and I'll tell you how you can fix it."

Collin's raised his head. "It's a long story."

"Yeah, well, I'm too curious now. You have to tell me."

With resignation he began, keeping his gaze down. "You remember when I told you about that fight we had, when Tammy said I look at other women too much?"

"Right…"

"Well, I guess she never totally believed me when I said I was sorry and that I'd stop." He stuck his lip out, reminding me of a little kid pouting. "I tried, really, and today wasn't even about that."

"You were looking at another woman on Christmas?"

"We went to a church service this morning. I thought I saw Elaine Altmer, from college. But I wasn't sure if it was her or not, so I kept looking over during the sermon, which was pretty boring. Anyway, I don't know if it was Elaine, or just some woman who was into me, but she started making eyes at me. Tammy noticed and freaked out."

"What do you mean? How did she freak out?"

"We were sitting towards the back, and she pulled me out into the lobby while they were taking collection. She said, 'I can't believe you're flirting with someone on Christmas, at my parent's church, no less! Have you no shame?'"

I suppressed a giggle, and took my eyes off the road for a moment to glace over at Collin. "Come on. She didn't really say *have you no shame*? Nobody says that when they're seriously angry."

Collin slapped his knee in agreement. "Exactly! I thought she was joking. So I laughed. That made her even angrier, and she started hitting me. I tried to stop her by grabbing her fists, telling her to calm down. So she slams all her weight into me, and I fall back into the manger scene that the church had set up. We make this huge crash. Baby Jesus, Mary, and the animals are everywhere, and I'm struggling to get up while I swing my arm out to try and catch Tammy from falling too. But she doesn't see that coming, and she just continues to fall at the just the right rate for my hand to make contact with her face. That's of course the moment that her father chooses to come find us, to see what was going on. Tammy is in tears, sporting a bright red cheek, saying I hit her on purpose, that I'm a philandering jackass, and I've ruined Christmas."

"You're not serious."

"Would I have had you come pick me up if I wasn't?"

I made an effort not to laugh, but it escaped out of me anyway. Collin didn't join in—too soon, I guess. But the harder I tried to quell my laughter, the more powerful it became, like a force unto itself. Soon my snickers were so loud they took up the entire car, and I was wiping tears from my eyes.

"I'm glad you find my misery so funny," he said.

"Oh, lighten up. The shelf life for your relationship with Tammy had expired a long time ago anyway."

"I really tried with her, Sam." He had raised the volume of his voice until it bordered on a yell. "I thought I had finally grown up enough that I could make it work."

"Collin, did it ever occur to you that *Tammy* wasn't mature enough to 'make it work'?"

I had stopped laughing, and Collin regarded me with the look of an interrogator, sort of like how Chazz Palminteri looked in *The Usual Suspects* when Kevin Spacey was duping him. "No," he replied. "It never did. After being with you I guess I'm just used to everything being my fault."

"Ouch," I said. "I don't think that was necessary."

He squinted at me. "Wasn't it? Tell me one thing that went wrong between us that was actually your fault."

I wanted to answer, but I had no idea what to say. Collin watched me as I wrinkled my forehead, trying to come up with something. "I knew it. You can't name one thing that you did wrong, can you? You still blame me for everything."

My resentment was really beginning to fizz. "So what if I do? Maybe everything was your fault."

"Right," he said in his condescending voice that he reserves for arguments. "And you did an excellent job of convincing me of that, demolishing my self-esteem until it was nonexistent. No wonder I haven't succeeded in any other relationships."

"So your break up with Tammy is my fault?"

Collin didn't answer. In my book, to neither confirm nor deny is to passive aggressively confirm. I hate that. I pulled the car over to the side of the road. "Get out." I said.

"Oh, come on. I was kidding. I don't think it's your fault."

"Too late. *Get out.*"

Collin's face turned red. He unbuckled his seat belt, and preemptively wrapped his flannel jacket tightly around his body. "Fine. I'd rather walk anyway." He got out and slammed the door.

I sped off, trying to make my tires squeal. Asshole.

When I got home I changed back into my pajamas, and turned on *Bad Santa*. Any movie with a romantic theme would have been ill advised, and I was determined to forget my anger by laughing at something stupid. But it wasn't working. I couldn't concentrate, and after twenty minutes I turned off the movie and went into my bedroom, where I buried my face into my pillows and screamed. Once I was out of breath I lifted my head up and started hitting my pillows, imagining that my fists were making contact with Collin's face. But soon I was too winded and exhausted to keep going, so I collapsed on my back and stared up at the ceiling.

Then I heard the lock in my front door turn. I jumped up in a panic and ran into the living room. Of course, I found Collin standing there, his face humble and wind-burned. In one hand he was holding a convenience store rose pin that you can buy at the check-out counter, in the other he was holding barbeque Pringles, which he knows are my favorite.

"Merry Christmas, Sam. I'm sorry about before."

"Ever hear of knocking?"

"I thought about it, but I knew you wouldn't let me in."

"I might have, if I thought you were somebody else."

He smiled, and gently walked towards me. "Who else is going to be knocking on your door on Christmas?"

I would have taken offense to his question, if I could have given him a reasonable answer. As it was, I just shrugged my shoulders and stood there.

"Anyway," he said, close enough to me now that I could smell the cold on his skin. "I am sorry. I had no right to say what I said, especially since everything that went wrong between us, was in fact, my fault."

Okay, should I dive into the deep end of this conversation Collin seemed poised to pursue, or should I stay in the safety of the shallow end? I couldn't decide because my head was already swimming.

Not knowing what choice to make, I made a bad one. "Do you want some wine?" I asked.

I know that was a stupid thing to do, and I don't know why I did it. Maybe I was just tired of thinking so much, and for once, I wanted to act on impulse. But if, up to that point, everything bad about our relationship was Collin's fault, well, that was now no longer the case. You see, there are very few single moments, single decisions that we can look back on and say, with some authority, "If I hadn't done that, everything would be different."

I have a few. Offering Collin wine tops the list.

"Sure," he replied. "I'd love some wine."

"I have a bottle in the kitchen. Have a seat and I'll go open it."

Rather than following orders and walking towards the living room, he walked towards me instead. Handing me his convenience store gifts, he said, "Thanks for picking me up. I know I was a jerk before. But Sam, there's nobody I'd rather be spending Christmas with than you." Then he grabbed me in a hug, which I probably would have eagerly returned if my hands hadn't been full. But as they were, I broke away after a couple of seconds.

"Let me go get that wine."

We went through that first bottle and another one after it; for every one glass I put away, Collin had two or three. By the end of the evening it was so much easier to fall into the comfort of old habits and the familiarity of each other's touch than to spend yet another night alone. "There will never really be anyone for me but you," he slurred, and I was tipsy enough to want it to be true. "I know I'm flawed, Sam. But nobody is ever going to love you the way that I do."

Who doesn't want to hear that? I couldn't answer him with words, so I kissed him instead.

That night, I got pregnant.

"So why did Collin drive back to Shannon?" My mother's question jars my nerves. I'm driving us to the hospital, which was a mistake. I don't know why we didn't take the EL. Navigating traffic and unfamiliar routes has never been my strong point.

"He had to get back," I reply. "There are some maintenance problems at the apartment building that he needs to get to."

"Oh." I can tell she isn't buying it, but I don't care. Truth is, Collin left early this morning without saying goodbye. Last night, after Nathan called, Collin started packing. I was aware of what he was doing, but was too exhausted and upset from talking with Nathan to care. "So what is going on between you two? Are you completely over?"

"Mom, how can you even ask that? I'm married, remember?"

"Right. Of course. I guess I forgot. Why hasn't what's-his-name, your husband, been around?"

"You know, you can't take off for years on end, come back, and then expect me to fill you in on every intricate detail of my life."

My mom wraps her arms across her chest in exasperation. "I'm not asking for the intricate details. I just want to know why Collin is acting like your pretend husband when you've got a real one back in Shannon."

I grit my teeth, and grip the steering wheel. "That's not how it is, Mom."

"Oh no? Then why didn't you want Collin to know you're pregnant?"

I'd forgotten she has this innate ability to read situations. My head snaps towards her in surprise. She looks so innocuous: pink sweatshirt, faded blue jeans, brown hair in a ponytail. The only hint of her age is the few strands of grey, and the laugh lines that have weathered her face. She's the way I hope to be when I'm approaching sixty, except for one small detail. She's the devil.

Problem is; it's as easy to love the devil as it is to hate him (or her).

"Okay, Mom. I guess you have it all figured out."

"No, only partially. I need you to fill in the blanks." She gives me her most cunning grin, the one that says, "I'm not giving up."

"Fine, you win. Collin was acting like my pretend husband because he says he still cares about me, but more than that, he still loves dad. Nathan, my husband, isn't here because things are complicated in both our lives and I told him not to come. And yes, I'm pregnant, but not with my child. I'm acting as a surrogate for my best friend."

"Wow." She whooshes out a breath, implying that my explanation has exhausted her. "And Nathan's okay with this?"

"Yes. He thinks it's great."

She nods her head, processing. "But you don't think Collin will feel the same way?"

"Collin doesn't know yet. I wanted to tell him, but, like I said, it's complicated."

Her head nod turns to a headshake, like she's physically rejecting my answer. "Why? If you two aren't together anymore…"

I raise my own voice to drown out hers. "Because, I was pregnant with Collin's baby. It didn't work out."

For once, my mother knows better than to ask for more details. "I'm sorry, honey." She sits silently, watching the cars and the buildings go by. I turn into the parking garage and pull into a space. "Ready to go see Dad?" I ask.

"In a minute." She places her hand on my arm. "Sam, I'm sure you know what you're doing. But even if you don't, I realize I gave up the right to give you advice a long time ago."

"Good. Thanks. Let's go see…"

"However," she interjects. "Have you thought about how hard it's going to be, giving up the baby that's growing inside of you?"

I answer with my gaze and my voice low. "Of course I have, Mom. I'm prepared for it."

"I hope so. Because I can't imagine anything is harder than giving up a child."

I exhale in a little huff. "Really? You didn't seem to have much trouble with it at the time."

She sighs. I can tell that she's restraining herself from getting angry, because her face looks like the one that Shirley McClaine wears in *Terms of Endearment* every time she's about to tell off Debra Winger for being flakey or irresponsible. "Honey, I know you think I deserted you, but to borrow a word that you just used, things were complicated."

I feel my mouth harden into a cynical smile. "And you wouldn't let it go at that. So I'm not going to either. Come on, Mom. Tell me why your life was so complicated that you had to leave for years on end."

She sighs, heaving her shoulder and chest up and down. "I can't."

Her face is turned away from me, and that angers me more than her refusal now to talk. "Yes you can. I think I deserve an explanation, after all this time."

She sits silently, and seconds pass. But they're not normal sized seconds, they are weighted and inflated at once, and they crowd us as we sit in the tiny car. After what seems like forever, she turns to me, and I see tears in her eyes. "Honey, your father and I had been together for twenty years before I left. Things happen—that's all I can say. But it wasn't easy to leave him, and it wasn't easy to come back."

"What about me?" I whimper. "Was it easy to leave me?"

"Of course not." She reaches out to squeeze my shoulder, but I lean away. My physical rejection registers on her face, but she continues. "You were always closer to your father than you were to me. I knew as long as you had him, you'd be fine. Besides, I didn't take off before you had become a fully formed human being. You already were complete when I left."

"That's not true," I say. "I've never been complete. Who is?"

"I don't know, honey." She smiles, like what she's about to say is meant to be funny. "Maybe Al Gore's complete?"

"Right, Mom." I unfasten my seat belt and reach behind me for my purse. "Let's go.

"Seriously, honey. I think people like him, who have accepted that life is unfair, but have maintained their dignity and are still going after what they believe in, they're the ones who are most likely to feel complete. That's all I was trying to do when I left, you know."

"I know."

We sit together for a moment in silence. My mom takes my hand, and I let her. "Sam. I just hope you don't think that having this baby for your friend will somehow make up for the one that you didn't have."

"Mom, even if I do, isn't a little late to be worried about it?"

"Perhaps." She looks at me, and I'm reminded of countless talks during my childhood and adolescence, when her eyes would glimmer as she only said what she thought I needed to hear. "It's just—no matter how painful not having that baby was, giving away one that you gave birth to is going to be a thousand times harder."

30. Melody

I'm awake before my alarm rings. It's because I didn't sleep at all last night. By the time I got home and went to bed it was early morning anyway. Then I tried to get some shut-eye, but I couldn't. I'm like that when I'm angry. My fury turns into this enormous ball that is way too hot to touch. It keeps me from sleeping, feeling, or thinking about anything other than why I am so mad.

I get up and get dressed, not caring for the first time in months how I look. I skip breakfast; my stomach is sizzling and unable to digest anything anyway. I grab my book-bag and head out early so I can stop at the printers on my way to school. It's my job to drop off the proofs for this month's edition of the school paper. Last night it had actually been easy to attend layout. Mom was over at Kenny's, packing. She called me on my cell phone, to let me know she'd be out all night. "Just thought I'd let you know," she said, in an unusual show of consideration. "I'm also reminding you that time is running out. You have till the rest of the week to prove that you've snagged that teacher. Otherwise, say hello to Green Bay."

That last, snotty part, is more like the mom I know and (sometimes) love. If she hadn't made that comment, maybe I wouldn't have felt so pressured to do what I did last night. But she had and I did, and now I'm walking to the printers, about to do something that could ruin lives.

Yeah, right, you're probably thinking. *You're just in high school, how could you possibly even have the power to ruin somebody's life?* Well, that depends on whose life it is that I'm ruining. What if the answer was, my own?

A couple of years ago I was walking home on a beautiful fall day. I stopped at an intersection and looked both ways. To my left was this blue truck, making its way down the street at what I'd guess was thirty-five miles per hour. I remember consciously thinking, *That truck is too close. Wait for it to pass.* But I didn't. I stepped out into the street. The driver saw me just in time, slammed on the breaks, skidded off to the side, and just barely avoided hitting me. Then he yelled out the window to watch where I was going, and drove off. To this day, I can't explain why I did it. Were my feet simply acting independently of my brain? Was I curious about what would happen? Or, did I have some bizarre death wish? I doubt that. I'm not the suicide type—it's like admitting to the world that you're defeated. No thanks.

But now, as I'm walking to the printers, I admit to myself that I'm about to step in front of another blue truck, and, again, I can't say why. I know my anger is urging me forward, but even that isn't enough to justify my future actions. So I replay last night's events inside my mind, and they play out like a bizarre after-school special.

I didn't even go home after school, instead I went straight to Ms. Corey's room, where Elle, Trudi, and Meg were already hard at work on getting the layout done. It's good there were three of them on the job, since collectively, their intelligence is about equal to mine (I was tested—142. Not lying). Since they seemed to have layout covered, I did some last minute editing on the cover story, which as I said, was on SAT testing. Elle broke away from her little trio and noticed what I was doing.

"Why are you changing Trudi's story?" she asked, in this super loud voice that was meant to be heard by Trudi.

I didn't stop typing, or even look away from the computer screen. "I'm not changing it," I said. "I'm just tweaking it a little so it fits. There are some unnecessary words and information that's been repeated."

Trudi wandered over. "Um, I already went over that?"

"So? Are you saying it can't be improved?"

"It's how I want it," she replied in a watery voice.

"Oh, I apologize then." I looked her directly in the eye and smiled. For a second she smiled back, believing I was genuine. "I didn't realize that everything's about what you want."

Trudi's smile vanished and she stammered for something to say. Her skin is made of tissue paper. She's so easy to have fun with; it's one of my favorite things about her. "Ms. Corey!" she cried, tears catching in her voice, "Melody is messing with my story."

Ms. Corey sighed and got up from her office chair, acting as if to do so was as difficult as, say, relinquishing the last brownie to your fat bratty cousin who gets brownies everyday, and you were saving that brownie for yourself, but you know he'll start screaming if you don't give it to him and it's not worth the trouble.

"Melody, what's the deal?" Ms. Corey asked.

"I just wanted to make it fit better," I said. "It's a good article, but there are some little improvements that should be made. I don't understand—aren't we supposed to proof each other's work?"

"Not without informing the author that we're doing so first," Ms. Corey said.

"Sorry." I said to Ms. Corey.

"Trudi, you can look over her changes before anything is made final, okay?"

Trudi sniffed and nodded her head. Then she went back over to Elle and Meg, where the three of them began to whisper and send me dirty looks. I pretended not to notice.

I exhaled and got back to work. The hours went by quickly. Trudi, Elle, and Meg bickered over how to place the articles and photos, Ms. Corey sat at her computer pretending like she was doing work instead of writing e-mails, and I proofed everything. It's a thankless job, but at least it's something I can do independently.

At 7:30 I took a break. I found a quiet place in the hallway and gave Kelsey a call.

"Hey!" I said as soon as she picked up. "Are you busy?"

"Um… I'm sort of doing homework."

"Oh good, then you're not busy. I need you to do me a favor."

"Umm, now's really not a good time."

"It won't take long. In about an hour I need you to come to school with your camera."

She doesn't say anything for a second, then answers with a wound up, "Huh?"

I try to soothe her with my reply. "I'll explain the rest when you get here. So I'll see you in about an hour?"

"Melody, I can't," she snarls.

"Yes, you can," I insist, "…and you will. I set Abby and Bobby's breakup in motion today. You owe me."

"I told you I didn't you want you to do that."

"Well, it's too late. And unless you want me to tell the whole school about *our* plan and *your* involvement with it, I suggest you get yourself and your camera here in an hour. Find me in Ms. Corey's room."

I pressed end on my cell phone and put it away. There is a definite advantage to being universally disliked—I have nothing left to lose. I am like one of those suicide bombers (although I realize it's kinda distasteful to compare yourself to a terrorist). I don't care about the consequences of setting off some dynamite, because my world already sucks. If other people, like Kelsey, care - then that is to my advantage. But I only stood to benefit from an explosion.

At 7:45 I had been back at work for a couple of minutes when Trudi, Elle, and Meg claimed to be done. "We just need the prom description, but everything else is finished," Meg said to Ms. Corey.

"Oh, sorry," I said. "I need to completely rewrite it. There's a ton of mistakes." The prom story was done by a sophomore in Ms. Corey's journalism class, so I wasn't stepping on any toes present in the room. Still, Elle groaned in frustration.

"Ms. Corey, I have three tests tomorrow. I need to get going. We all do."

Ms. Corey looked at the clock. "That's okay girls, you can take off. I'll stay here while Melody finishes up."

"But, what about Baker's Square?" Trudi griped. "You can't not come. This is the last time."

"You gals go ahead. I'll meet you there. And maybe Melody will join us this time." Unlike the three of them, Ms. Corey still pretended that she wanted me to come.

"Okay…" they muttered as they shuffled out. Ms. Corey returned to her computer and I returned to mine. We had nothing to say to each other. At 8:10 I told her I was done. We made the final additions to the layout, and headed out. She handed me the proofs.

"I believe it's your turn to drop these off at the printers?" The staff rotated that responsibility. I had volunteered for it first back in September, so it had cycled back to me now. I wordlessly took the proofs from Ms. Corey while nodding my head. She added in, "Now are you sure you don't want to join us for some pie?"

"I really need to get going. I have an economics test tomorrow…" My voice trailed off as I made a face.

She noticed my scowl. "What's wrong?"

I shake my head and fake exasperation. "I forgot my book. I need to go back."

"Oh." She sighed, turning her head towards the door, but not her body. "Do you need me to unlock the room?"

"No, no. I'll just find a janitor."

She looked relieved. "Okay. See you tomorrow."

She headed out and I headed back in. I got Randy, the night janitor, to unlock the journalism room for me and I told him I needed to use the phone as well, so he didn't stick around. Then I sat and waited for Kelsey. She showed up at 8:30 on the dot.

"Alright, I'm here." She plopped down in Ms. Corey's seat. "I brought my dad's camera because it's like, ten times better than mine. What do you want me to take pictures of?"

Kelsey was dressed in khaki pants that actually fit her and a black tissue T-shirt. She almost looks kind of pretty when she isn't dressed in hoochie-mama clothes. "What?" she said in response to my stare.

"Nothing," I said, shaking off my observation. Kelsey was here for a reason, and I needed both of us to stay focused. I was not naïve enough to think she'd go along with my plan without an explanation first, so I was prepared to come clean with her. It was the only way. I launched in. "Okay, first of all, my mother is insane."

Kelsey pinched her face. "What?" she asked, as if I was the insane one.

I just continued on. "So remember that while I'm asking you for this favor. I need to prove something to her, and this is the only legitimate way I could think of to do it."

I explained the mission to her.

"No, no way. We could both get in real trouble." She said.

"Kelsey, I swear, the only person who will see the picture is my mom. Then I'll erase it."

She refused at first, but my power of persuasion proved to be too much for her, and she relented. Then she quietly followed me down to Mr. L's room.

I silently cursed the rushed timing of this whole venture. If only I had more time. I could have gotten his wife to leave him, and then he'd really have been mine. Not that I was giving up on that idea, but it wouldn't happen in time for my mother to feel she's gotten proof of our relationship.

His door was open. I took a deep breath. It's so rare that I feel nervous; I actually had to stop and identify the emotion, because the sensation associated with it is so foreign. Oh well—nothing ventured, nothing gained. I walked in, leaving the door ajar—enough that Kelsey could listen without being seen. Ironic, that my fate was in Kelsey's hands. She had better not screw this up.

The only light in the room was coming from the lamp on his desk. Mr. L must have gone home and come back. He was wearing worn blue jeans and a gray sweatshirt that's frayed at the collar. He was in the back of the room, sorting through student projects—big posters with an *Animal Farm* theme. His back was to me, but he must have sensed my presence, because he turned around.

"Hey, Melody." His voice was flat, like a worn tire that has given up. I personally like flat tires, because it's fun to put air into them. It's hard to find anything else in this world that's so easily brought back to life. And I have to say, it would be wonderful to inflate him.

"Are you okay, Mr. L?"

He scratched his forehead and brushed away a tendril of hair. "Yeah, I'm fine." God, he's a bad liar. "Come in. You wanted to talk to me about something?"

"I wanted to apologize."

"For what?"

I took a good look at him before I plummeted into my answer. I wanted to trace his entire body with my fingers, starting with his beautiful face. I didn't know if my feelings were going to make this easier or more difficult, but what the heck.

"Everything. I never meant to make you feel about bad your marriage, or put you in any sort of uncomfortable situation. And I certainly didn't mean to create any fuel for gossip. I know our relationship is pure, but other people, sick minded people, they might not. And when I think about how all of this could have hurt you, how I could have hurt you, when all I want is to see you happy, it makes me crazy. You've only ever been good to me. Nobody, not even my own mother, has ever been as nice to me as you have."

He half-laughed as he shook his head. "Melody..."

No! Condescension would not be permitted. I stepped forward, closer to him, as I raised my voice, both in volume and in urgency. "I know you think it's no big deal. But it is to me."

His shoulders sagged. He whispered, "I'm not nearly the man you think I am."

I moved closer to him still, and dared to cradle his cheek in my hand. "Yes you are. You just don't realize it. You're smart, and brave, and kind. I wish—I wish you weren't my teacher. I wish we were the same age and we had met at a bar or through a mutual friend or something. And that you weren't married. Then I'd have had half a chance. Not that I could ever deserve a man like you..."

He grabbed me by both my arms. "You have to stop."

"I don't know how." Tears were streaming down my face. Wow. I didn't remember deciding to cry.

He let go of me, retreating. I wouldn't allow that. I flung myself in his direction, impounding him in a hug. At first his body was stiff, but then I felt him relax and wrap his arms around me. "It's going to be okay," he whispered as I cried into his shoulder. He ran his fingers through my hair. So divine. I almost forgot about Kelsey, right outside.

I lifted up my head, and he didn't recoil. Then his thumb traced a path down my cheek, wiping away a tear in its journey.

"Melody," he said, "You're a great girl. Really. I admire your strength, and you're so wise…"

"Stop," I whispered. "Please don't say anything else."

"But…" he continued, "this absolutely cannot happen."

His body language contradicted his verbal language, as he had not pulled away. So I stood up on my tippy-toes, and compelled his mouth to meet mine. For a single, miraculous moment he kissed me back, and the world was sublime. Then the flash from Kelsey's father's camera lit up the room.

Mr. L pushed me back. "What the hell was that?" He looked disoriented, moving his head from side to side.

"Huh?" I said, playing dumb.

"What was that flash of light?"

"I don't know what you're talking about. I didn't see anything."

Mr. L hurried toward the door, probably to investigate the hallway. I ran after him, making it to the door before he did, and I stepped in front of him. "Please don't leave me," I said.

"Melody, get out of the way."

I stroked his shoulder. "But we aren't done talking."

He put his hands on me again, this time to move me out of his path. That was okay; by now Kelsey should have had enough time to make a quick exit to the downstairs women's bathroom, where she was to wait for me in one of the stalls. Feet up, door locked. I prayed that she could follow instructions.

Mr. L was out in the hall, searching in vain for the flashing-light culprit. He was looking through the glass windows to various locked classrooms, and walked into both of the bathrooms nearby. I knew I was smart to tell Kelsey to run downstairs. I was hoping she actually did, so I breathed a sigh of relief when Mr. L came out after a few seconds, alone.

"Um, what's the deal?" I asked in a meek voice.

"I think somebody took a picture of us." He said. "There was a flash, like on a camera."

"Are you sure? Who would do that?"

"Who knows? Anyone!" He cried. "But whoever it was, they're probably gone by now." He started pacing around in circles, breathing as if it took all his concentration to do so. "I'm fucked, do you realize that? I am completely and totally fucked."

Gosh. I'd never heard a teacher swear like that before. "Mr. L, it's going to be okay."

He stopped moving. Now his hands were on his knees, and he looked like he was about to hurl. "Did you (breath in, breath out) tell Becki Birkland (breath in, breath out) that you were coming here tonight?"

"No, of course not. I never talk to Becki."

"Then who did you tell?"

"Nobody."

He stood up straight, and approached me, taking up all my personal space. This time it wasn't so pleasant. "Don't lie to me, Melody. You must have told someone. There has to be a *reason* why someone was camped outside my door with a camera."

"No, I swear to God." I started to cry. His fury made it easy enough to squeeze my tears out.

"Stop lying to me!" He shouted. "And stop crying! If that picture gets out, my life is ruined. My career will be over, and so will my marriage."

I looked up at him, and I lost control. "So what? You don't love your wife anyway. She's lied to you. She doesn't love you like I do! Leave her! We'll go away together. You can get a different job, and we can be together."

I expected him to melt at this point, to capture me in a passionate embrace, and we'd walk off into the make-believe sunset. But that was not what he did. "Grow up!" he shouted. "For such a smart girl, you're being really, really stupid."

I was speechless. So I stared at him, my mouth hanging open. "Did you really think I'd leave my wife for you?" He laughed, an evil, bad-guy sort of chuckle. "You believe there is anywhere we could run away to? We'd have to run away from ourselves. I can tell you from experience, that's impossible."

"But…" I stammered.

His face loomed above mine, like a scary red balloon I wished I could pop. "Listen to me," he said with soft urgency. "You and me—there is nothing between us. I don't love you. I barely even like you. I feel sorry for you, that's it."

Suddenly I was reminded of another night when I was in this ominously darkened hallway, feeling threatened by a beautiful male I thought I could trust. So I immediately erected a wall inside of me. Because after Axel tried to rape me, I promised myself that I'd never feel intimidated again. I don't ever break my promises.

Mr. L continued. "Now, I'm not stupid enough to believe it's a coincidence that a camera went off at the exact moment you kissed me. I know you have something to do with it, which means you have the power to stop that photo from getting out. And if you don't, you'll be sorry."

I stuck my chin out. "Really? Is that for the record, Mr. L?"

He didn't say anything, but his eyes glared hatred into mine. Then he turned on his heel and walked away. I watched as he went back into his classroom for a moment, then he came back out, clutching his car keys. There were several feet between us, but his calm voice reached my ears without much effort. "I don't know what you stand to gain from this, Melody. If you tell people, if you show them that picture, you'll only hurt me. How does that benefit you?"

I said nothing.

He responded to my silence. "If you have any amount of dignity or human kindness, you'll destroy the photo." Then he walked away, down the darkened hallway, out of my life.

I went to find Kelsey.

She was, sure enough, waiting for me in the downstairs bathroom.

I ignored all her questions, grabbed her camera, and ran back upstairs where Ms. Corey's room was still unlocked. I uploaded the photo. It came out well. Then I sat down at my computer and began to write.

Kelsey was hovering over me. "Melody, what are you doing?"

I didn't stop to answer. Maybe if I had some dignity and human kindness I'd have taken the time…

My memories of last night are not likely to fade any time soon. Now, on my way to the printers, I am carrying two versions of the front page. One carries a story about the SATs. The other is my story. I honestly don't know which one I'm going to drop off.

31. Samantha

"Cheshire is dead." I'm talking to Jane on my cell phone. It's late afternoon, and I'm in my dad's backyard. Spring is in full swing—birds are chirping, the sun is shining, and the smell of honeysuckle in the air. Why couldn't it be rainy and dark outside? There is only silence from the other end. Jane is driving somewhere while holding her phone to her ear.

"Did you hear me," I insist. "Nathan killed Collin's fish. I just don't know what to do."

"Crap!" I hear her yell. Then her voice returns to normal. "Sorry. I was making a tricky turn. That's too bad about Collin's fish."

"It's more than too bad. Cheshire was Collin's test case. If he could keep Cheshire alive, that would have meant he was ready for a more serious relationship. But Nathan forgot to feed him, and now he's dead. Can't you see the symbolism in that?"

"I get it, Sam," she says, punctuating each syllable. "What I don't understand is why you're so upset about Collin and his relationship status."

I rub my neck and roll my head. Can't get rid of this tension. "I feel like I've ruined his life."

"Don't be silly. This is a fish we're talking about. You can buy him another one for a few bucks."

"That's callous. It wasn't about the money. He was attached to Cheshire."

"Sam, why are you focused on this?" This time her yelling is directed at me. "You should be relieved that your dad's okay and your family is back together. You're so terrified of being happy that you are willing to find any little thing to obsess over."

I look down at my feet. They're dirty because I took my shoes off and started squishing them into the muddy ground several minutes ago. I should really get off the phone and go wash them.

"Sam?"

"Everything feels off."

"Okay. You're going to have to be more specific. So this is about more than Collin's fish?"

"Nathan called me last night. He sounded very weird."

"What did he say?"

"He told me that he had made a huge mistake. He was crying. I'm like, 'Just tell me what happened. We can work it out.' Then he didn't say anything for a long time. So I said the same thing over and over, 'Just tell me. It can't be so awful.' Finally, he tells me that he forgot to feed Cheshire, and that he's dead."

"Isn't he being sort of hard on himself?"

"No. I don't think that's what he was really crying about. I think he knew…" My voice trails off. Sometimes it's hard to be completely honest with Jane. She's such a good person. I just don't measure up.

"You think he knew what?"

I breathe deep, physically yielding to my guilt. "When he called, I was about to kiss Collin. I think Nathan sensed it somehow."

"Oh, Sam."

"I know! Whatever you're about to say, I know. I'm a rotten, weak, horrible person. But I didn't kiss Collin. I got off the phone with Nate, told Collin about Cheshire, and that was it. We both went to bed separately, and in the morning Collin drove back to Shannon."

"So when are you coming home?"

"Today. My mom says she wants to take care of my dad, so I'm leaving in a few hours."

"And how did you leave things with Nathan?"

"Vague. Very, very vague." I curl my toes into the mud once more. "How do I fix this, Jane?"

"I can't tell you that."

"But…"

"Sam. You haven't been honest with Nathan about so many things. I know you have your reasons, but come on. You sound more worried about Cheshire than you do about your husband. So before I can give you advice on how to fix your relationship, you need to decide which relationship you want to fix."

I run my fingers through my hair, trying not to be mad. I know she's telling the truth, but still, that doesn't mean I want to hear it. "Aren't you being a little harsh?"

She starts to reply, but her phone goes dead. She must have dropped it or something. Oh well, I'll talk to her soon, anyway. I wipe my feet against the concrete; it's an unpleasant sensation, scraping my skin. The bottoms of my feet would be more callused if I hadn't treated myself to a pedicure last week. Stupid, stupid me. Calluses are hard-earned and necessary. Why did I pay to get rid of them?

Now, just to be clear. I didn't intentionally lie to Nathan or with-hold the truth about my marriage to Collin. It's sort of like in *Pretty Woman*, how even though Richard Gere knew that Julia Roberts was a prostitute, he didn't hear all the dirty details of her workday. There's a reason for that; she liked the way she looked in his eyes. I know that their ultimate acceptance of each other is sort of the whole point of the movie, but I'm not naïve enough to believe life ever really has a Hollywood ending. I'm also not a prostitute, but after the final, brutal ending of my romance with Collin, I felt sullied enough to be one.

Later, after my phone conversation with Jane, I am driving back to Shannon, willing my car to go slower. But the minimum speed limit is forty, and if I go at that pace the other cars will run me off the road. I've played with Jane's words over and over, and have come to an inescapable conclusion: Once I'm home, it will be time to tell Nathan the truth. About everything.

As the highway stretches out ahead of me, I review the final chapter of my story with Collin—the one that Nathan will soon be forced to hear.

"Marry me," Collin said when I held up the stick with two little pink lines.

"You're insane."

"Possibly. But you love me anyway. And I love you. Why shouldn't we have a baby and live happily ever after?"

"Do you want my list of reasons?" I asked. "Hold on, it's in the bedroom. I'll go get it."

"You didn't seriously make a list," Collins called out after me. "You're joking, right?" I didn't have to answer, because walking back into the living room with my notebook was response enough. "You made a list about why you shouldn't marry me, before I'd even proposed?"

"My period is never late," I replied. "Last night I was lying in bed, thinking 'What if?' I know you, and I knew what you would say. Turns out I was right."

Collin sighed and shook his head. "Fine," he said. "Let me see this list. I'm betting I can argue away every reason on here."

"Great," I handed it to him. "If you can do that, then I will marry you. But if you can't, then you'll accept my answer of 'no' without protest."

"No problem. This will be the easiest thing I've ever done." His eyes scanned my list:

My list of reasons for why I shouldn't marry Collin:

1. *He's an addictive personality and I can't change that.*

2. *We've broken up too many times before and it's always painful.*

3. *I know his flaws too well and he knows mine.*

4.   *I want to leave Shannon and make films and he's too lazy and complacent to ever want to do that.*

5.   *Other than our history, we don't have much in common.*

6.   *I hate how he's obsessive about trimming his toenails but he'll let his fingernails grow so long that they get dirt underneath them, then he'll peal them off at inappropriate times, like when we're at a restaurant, then he'll leave them there for the waitress to clean up.*

7.   *We're incapable of staying together.*

"Only seven reasons?" He said with a grin. "I was expecting twenty-five, at least."

"Like I said, I made it last night when I was in bed. I got tired; otherwise I would have written more."

He studied the list a little longer, wrinkling his brow in concentration. I gazed outside the window as I waited. A drizzly Sunday evening and dusk had settled in. Why are Sunday dusks so much more weighted down than any other day of the week? "Okay," he tapped his finger against the notebook. "This is even easier than I thought."

I sat up in attention and focused. Collin spouted off. "Number one—I'm an addictive personality. You're right, but I haven't done drugs for a couple of years now. Yes, I still drink, but most of the time I can handle it. And I promise to be good." He gave me an angelic grin before he continued. "Number two—Okay, I know our breakups have been messy, but if you marry me, it will be for the rest of our lives, so we'll never break up again, which makes that reason completely moot."

I just continue to stare at him, but he isn't fazed. He moves on, as if we're competing to see who can hold their breath longer, and he's winning. "Number three—Knowing each other's flaws is a good thing. It's the couples with a too idealistic image of each other who don't make it. You know that. Number four—You still want to leave

Shannon?" He pauses to give me a chance to answer. When I don't, he isn't bothered. "Okay, I don't get that one. We've been broken up long enough for you to have had plenty of opportunity to leave. So honestly, Sam, I don't really buy it. But hey, if you want to leave, let's go. We can move next week as far as I'm concerned." He looked back down at the list, his brow furrowed. "Where was I? Okay, number five—Maybe we don't have a lot of similar interests, but our minds work in the same way."

I broke my silence. "No they don't. My mind is completely different from yours."

Collin raised his eyebrows. "Then how come I totally understand how you think?"

"You don't totally understand how I…"

"Yes I do."

"Fine. Prove it. What am I thinking right now?"

His eyebrows furrowed; that always happens when he's exerting himself, mentally or otherwise. "Right now you are thinking, 'Damn it, why did I show him this list?' But it wouldn't have mattered if you had hidden it, because eventually I would have found it and argued against it anyway."

"Not ah." I said, only because it was the best response I could muster.

"Yeah huh." He replied back. "You always make stupid lists, and you always keep them in the notebook by your nightstand. By the way, I love that you labeled it as 'My list of reasons.' Because you label all of your lists like that." To prove his point he started flipping through my notebook, reading off other pages. "My list of groceries for the week,' 'My list of things I'd like to accomplish for the new year,' 'My list of things to avoid saying to people I've just met.'"

He laughed and leaned forward. "I label my lists like that too. I think I picked up the habit from you. So I'm not even surprised or distressed that you wrote a list. I think it's endearing." He flipped back to his original page, and read it again, running his fingers through his hair. Then his ears grew slightly flushed, a clear sign that he's annoyed. "Alright," he huffed, "I have never pealed my finger nails in a restaurant and left them for the waitress to clean up."

I grabbed a pillow and squeezed it into my lap. "Yeah, you did! We were at that fancy seafood place with the expensive cocktails. I was so grossed out."

"You're thinking about somebody else."

"No I'm not!"

"Sam, I would remember doing something like that."

"No you wouldn't! Because you do it all the time. You don't even realize you're doing it! And yet you're a maniac about clipping your toenails."

"I'm trying to be considerate! I don't want to accidentally scratch your legs when we're in bed."

"Well that's all very sweet and nice, but would it kill you to trim your fingernails every once in a while?"

"Well, you should have said something about it sooner, rather than listing it as a reason not to marry me!"

I sighed in frustration and threw the pillow from my lap. After a moment of tense silence he said, "Maybe we should come back to that one, and move on to number seven for now."

"Okay," I said, though my voice had an edge that contradicted my answer.

Collin's shoulders sagged, but he pressed on. "Number seven—We're incapable of staying together..." His head dropped down, and his silence made me think he had given up the fight. Was that disappointment I was feeling? Couldn't be. Surely I was mistaking disappointment for relief. I do it all the time. Then he spoke up. "…Sam, I'm sure you're right on that one. I know from experience that you're right. But I also know, with absolute certainty, that we're equally incapable of staying apart."

He let gravity pull his last answer down, sinking it into the floor, bringing my heart with it. I refused to let the instant tears his words had triggered escape, even if on the inside I was a blubbering idiot. But externally, I was still one tough cookie. "That's the best you can do?" I asked, with the voice of a petulant teenager.

His face crumpled. "Yeah, I guess it is."

"Well, I would not qualify your last two answers as 'arguing away' my reasons."

He looked off to the side, at my bathroom door, away from me. "So your answer is no."

"Collin, look at me." He turned his gaze back towards me, and our eyes locked. An electric current shocked me at least every other time that happened—how I wished his effect on me could be minimized. Or gotten rid of all together. If I didn't love him. "You give up way too easily," I continued. "Now, let's go back to reason six and see if we can't find some common ground."

Two weeks later we flew to Las Vegas for a whirlwind wedding/honeymoon four-day weekend. We got tickets to go see the Blue Man group, which I loved and Collin found creepy. I of course couldn't drink, and out of consideration, neither did Collin. But we both soaked up the sun sitting poolside, and one evening we blew $100 gambling. Neither of us finished the night with anything in our pockets, but it didn't matter. We were in love again and we had each other. When we got home Collin carried me over the threshold to our apartment—an apartment we had already laughed, cried, and fought in countless times. Yet somehow it felt like a new beginning. It's not that I really believed things would be perfect, or even all that different. But I was optimistic that we had grown and changed and matured. I trusted we at least had a chance.

For a month I read books on pregnancy like *What to Expect When You're Expecting*, made lists of my favorite baby names, and scoured catalogues for ideas on how to decorate a nursery. Collin stocked our refrigerator with healthy, organic food like fruit, yogurt, and hormone-free chicken breasts, and every morning he insisted on making me these power-smoothies, which he refused to tell me the ingredients for. I actually sort of liked them, and Collin said, "That's great, Hon, but you might not if you knew what was in them."

Then I started to worry that these mysterious shakes were like something out of *Rosemary's Baby*, and Collin was feeding me some weird concoction that was preparing our child for the devil. So I silently snuck into the kitchen one morning while he was making one. I watched as he poured rice milk, prunes, and bananas into the blender. "That's it?" I wondered. "What could be the big deal?" Then he reached high into the cabinet and pulled out a baggie full of dried dandelions. He poured a tablespoon's worth into the mix.

I tiptoed back into the bedroom, and was sitting up in bed, reading, when he brought me my shake. I took one sip, then said, "You know what this tastes like? An early summer morning of my childhood. Either that, or weeds."

Collin smiled. "Okay, Smart-Ass. I know you were spying on me. You're a really loud walker, by the way. It must be all that weight you've gained."

In one, swift action I threw my drink at him, and covered his face in yellowish goo. "Never. *Ever* make jokes about my weight, understand?"

"I understand." He said, his face dripping onto his shirt. "But you still have to finish this shake. It's good for you. It will keep you healthy and regular."

"Why the dandelions?" I asked.

"They're supposed to prevent birth defects. I want our baby to be perfect."

"Got it," I replied. Then I pulled Collin to me, and commenced to licking what remained of my shake off his face.

"I think I'll give you your shake like this every morning," he said. And I laughed.

Then one day our sewage backed up. Our entire building had to vacate, because the floors were covered in icky brown water. Professional plumbers were called in, and Collin had to be around to supervise the mess. It turned out that the root of the problem had come from the apartment directly above ours. The guy who lived there, Rudy, had tried to flush a huge bag of cocaine down his toilet. Of course, the police were called and Rudy was arrested. Collin swore to me that he had nothing to do with it, and I believed him.

At first.

On the third day of staying at the Holiday Inn, I was watching TV when there was a knock on my door. I opened it to find two policemen. It was just like in the movies; there was a pleasant looking one, who was tall and sandy haired and reminded me of my cousin Ned. The other one was shorter but also broader, and had jet-black hair and bright blue eyes. He looked sort of like a compact Pierce Bronson, only with a sour look on his face. He stayed quiet most of the time.

"Hello, Mrs. Chayton, we were wondering if we could ask you a few questions." The sandy-haired one smiled and flashed his badge at me.

"Is there some sort of problem?" I asked.

"We just need a couple minutes of your time," sandy-haired one responded.

I stepped aside, and let them into my hotel room, which was littered with dirty clothes and take-out containers. Sandy-haired one sat on the edge of the bed, and the other guy remained standing.

"You heard about the cocaine that was flushed down your tenant's toilet?" Sandy-haired one asked.

"Um, yeah. Of course. But he wasn't really my tenant. My husband manages the building, but it's my uncle-in-law who owns it."

"Sure." He scribbled something in his pad. "Mrs. Chayton, is it true that your husband was convicted for possession of marijuana back in April of 1994?"

"Uh…well, I'm betting you already know the answer to that since you obviously have access to his police records."

"Has your husband ever done cocaine, Mrs. Chayton?" Sandy-haired one asked me this question with a smile; he could have been asking me if I'd ever been to Disney Land. I had to work to be more offended.

"I don't know what that has to do with anything," I said.

"I think you do."

"Collin wasn't doing cocaine with Rudy. Collin doesn't do drugs."

Sandy-haired-one laughed. His face looked like Ron Howard's. "Mrs. Chayton, I have all sorts of information that tells us the opposite."

"Like what?" I demanded.

Pierce Bronson-one spoke up. "Like from Mr. Ellison himself."

"He's lying," I said.

"Rudy Ellison was dealing. Nobody in possession of that much cocaine isn't. We've been following him for a while, trying to bust him. He was onto us, which is why he flushed his stash. What we're trying to figure out now is, was your husband in on it? We have reason to believe he was."

I don't remember which one said that. All I remember is the instant sensation of my world crumbling to bits.

My interview with the cops didn't last long. Shortly after they left, I left too. I got into my car and drove around in circles, trying to put my thoughts together. For a while I stopped at the library, and sat, staring off into space for I don't know how long. Then I went to the self-help section and found books about marriage. I leafed through several, but they all said the same thing. It's only possible to make your relationship work if you're fully committed.

It was after midnight when I returned to our hotel room. Collin was sitting up in bed, watching a rerun of *Everybody Loves Raymond*. I think it was the one where Ray and Debra get into a fight about something his mother said.

"Where have you been?" Collin asked in a quiet voice.

I silently walked over to the television and turned it off. I remained standing in front of it, directly opposite of Collin, so he was staring now at me.

"Are you okay?" He asked.

"No. No I'm not okay. I had a conversation with a couple of cops today."

His face had grown pale. "Yeah, they questioned me today, too." His voice lacked the indignation of the innocent. He wasn't even going to try.

My stomach turned and I made a beeline for the bathroom, reaching the toilet just in time to throw-up. Collin came in, grabbed a washcloth, wet it in the sink, and kneeled down beside me, pressing it against the back of my neck.

I swatted him away. "Don't touch me. Get away from me."

He sat back. I flushed the toilet, closed the lid, and rested my cheek against the cool porcelain.

"Sam, it was only one time. And it was before we had gotten back together."

"You told me you hadn't done drugs in years."

"It was only one time."

I stood up. I stood up over him, wishing I could step on him and squash him like a bug. "You lied to me! And you knew he was dealing from our building. Were you in on it?"

"No!"

"That's not what the police think!"

He struggled up, grasping at the rim of the tub to stand in the enclosed, claustrophobic space. "I wasn't in on it! Rudy just named me to try and lighten his own sentence."

"I don't believe you!" I turned around and walked away.

"Sam. I swear to God."

"Save it, Collin. It's too late." I grabbed my suitcase and flung it on the bed. Then, frantically, I started gathering all my belongings and threw them in. "Even if you're telling me the truth, you're still an accessory to a crime. I bet you never turned him in because you wanted to keep the option of buying drugs open. Which means you're reprehensible, and you're still addicted. Jesus, how could I be so stupid to think you had changed?"

"I have changed. You can trust me."

"No. No, I'll never trust you. Ever. Again."

I stopped my packing for a moment, and our eyes met. No electric current this time. Just anger. And hurt. "I want a divorce." I said.

His eyes welled up with tears. "No. Please don't say that."

"It's too late, Collin. We're over."

"How can you say that? We're having a baby."

"No. No, we're not. I don't want to bring a baby into this world whose father is a drugged out liar. I'm getting an abortion tomorrow."

His body recoiled. "You wouldn't do that." He gasped.

"Yes I would. But only because I'll be sparing all three of us a lot of pain." I zipped my suitcase shut and headed toward the door. Collin grabbed my arm, forcing me to stop.

"Sam, don't. Please. Don't. I'm begging you. Give me one more chance. I'll do anything."

I yanked my arm out of his grasp. His face was streaked with tears. His desperation had physically transformed his face and his body so that he was barely recognizable. If anything, that made it easier.

"Goodbye, Collin."

The door shut behind me, and the clicking of the lock was the most final sound I had ever heard.

The next day I made an appointment for the abortion. I still can't completely pinpoint what drove me to do it. I was hurt, angry, and yes, vindictive. I was also terrified of forever tying myself to a man who seemingly could only bring me pain. But in my darkest hours, I fear that it was weakness alone that propelled to take this unthinkable step.

But it ended up not to matter. The morning of the appointment I woke up in Jane's guest bedroom and found that I was bleeding. I wouldn't have thought that a few weeks of pregnancy could result in so much blood and cramping, but it did. I was sure it was my body's way of punishing my soul-lessness, and I almost welcomed the pain. I convinced myself that I had willed myself to lose the baby, and that I was no less guilty than I would have been had the procedure been done.

Jane nursed me through the entire thing, putting aside her own pain around the issues of motherhood to tend to me without a hint of judgment. For that, I owe her everything. Having a baby for her now seems like the least I can do.

I'll never be able to say for sure if I would have gone through with the abortion or not, but I never told Collin about my miscarriage. It was just so much easier to let him hate me rather than feel sorry for me. I wouldn't have been able to handle his pity.

A week later I returned to our apartment, mostly because I didn't know where else to go. When I got back I found our apartment cleared of all his stuff, and I assumed (correctly) that he had moved back upstairs into a vacant unit. We didn't speak, I slipped into a depression, and even the smallest tasks, like preparing something for breakfast or driving in my car, seemed huge. At one point I made a half-hearted attempt to look for another place to live, but I soon found that nothing was going to be as cheap as the rent Collin was offering me, and with my meager salaried job I wouldn't be able to afford living anywhere else. Besides, after our breakup I never saw him. I guess we were both so determined to avoid each other that even chance encounters didn't happen. Soon I became complacent in my assumption that Collin was out of my life, even though he obviously was not.

One day he knocked on my door to tell me that the police hadn't found enough evidence to convict him, so he would get away scot-free. But, he added in a teary voice, he would have gladly done prison time if I had stayed with him and kept our baby. When I told him that I was no longer pregnant, he just shook his head and cried. Two days later, I started divorce proceedings.

On the day we went to sign the papers, he approached me after. "You know," he said, "I'll always only blame myself for this. And I still plan to make it up to you." I didn't, couldn't respond. There was no way he could ever make it up to me. He had turned me into someone I didn't even recognize—vindictive, mean, and petty.

Then I met Nate and married him. We lived in my apartment because once he found out how inexpensive my rent was, Nate suggested we stay with my apartment for a year or two, as we saved to buy a house. I agreed, because to do otherwise would have required me to explain to him about my relationship with Collin, and I didn't know how to do that without scaring Nate away. So I said nothing. But now, way too late, I see how stupid it was to start a relationship anywhere close to my previous romantic failure.

A few miles outside of Shannon, and I'm crying at the memories playing and replaying in my mind. I swat away a tear that has run its course down my face. I sniff, loudly, glad that I'm alone in my car. Glad that right now, the only person I have to answer to, is myself.

When I get home I'll tell Nathan the whole story, and I'll give him the epilogue as well.

Every morning now I wake up, wishing there was some way I could reverse things and bring that baby back.

I guess that's what I've been trying to do all along. But now I'm the cliché of the person who is digging a hole in the sand, and the further I get, the more buried I become.

32. Melody

(As Published in the Shannon High Tribune)

Teacher Caught in the Act!
My Story—By Melody Madsen.

Everything I wrote here is the truth. Nobody, not even Ms. Corey, knew about it. I publish it only to prevent other students the pain of what I have gone through.

It is a fact of life; students look up to their teachers. We rely on them, not just to teach us history, math, and science, but also to serve as an example of maturity. I personally have never known my father, so I admit to being more in need of a male role-model than most young women my age. That is why, when Mr. Linden took a special interest in me, I was flattered and receptive to his attention.

He asked me to be his student aide, and I enthusiastically agreed. I spent hours in his room, alone with him. I came in on Saturdays to help grade papers at his request. "Isn't it against the rules for me to grade other students' work?" I would ask.

"There's no such thing as privacy," he would respond, always with a smile.

How right he was.

I first began to question whether his attachment to me was appropriate and in line with the normal relationship between teacher and student when he came to my work place, Subway restaurant.

He arrived one night right when we were closing, and wouldn't leave, demanding to talk about problems he was having with his wife. The next morning I stopped in his classroom before first hour began and he was distraught. He told me all this personal stuff about his marriage, including his wife's romantic history prior to his relationship with her.

Samantha Linden, 35, is ten years older than Mr. Linden. She was previously married to Collin Chayton, the caretaker of the apartment building where the Lindens presently reside. Mrs. Linden's marriage to Mr. Chayton was short-lived, ending soon after she terminated a pregnancy in 2005. She is now pregnant again, although Mr. Linden is not the father of this baby.

This of course, has left Mr. Linden emotionally distraught, to the point where he has crossed a line in seeking solace from me, a student. On one occasion he even asked me if I thought he should leave his wife.

On another occasion he said, "She never told me she had been married before. And she had an abortion. I don't know if I can forgive that."

Then he put his face against his whiteboard and started to cry. I felt bad, so I put my hand on his back to comfort him, and that's when two students came in. They saw us touching, and I was sure they had the wrong idea.

Except, I was the one with the wrong idea.

That afternoon, Mr. Linden demanded that I come to his classroom later that night, after everyone else had left the building. I was hesitant, but he told me the whole school already believed we were involved. If I wanted his help in dispelling that rumor, I had better meet up with him later. That is what he said.

Still, I was uncertain, so I brought a good friend, who shall remain anonymous, along with me for backup. Once I was in his room, Mr. Linden started freaking out, saying we ought to run away together, and leave his wife and the school behind. When I said no, he grabbed me and said, "You'll do what I tell you to do."

I tried to get away, but he grabbed me and kissed me, hard on the mouth. That is when my anonymous friend had the foresight to snap a picture, which you can see, printed above.

Mr. Linden noticed the flash of the camera, but did not react in time to catch my friend. However, he did say, "I'm not stupid enough to believe it's a coincidence that a camera went off at the exact moment we kissed. I know you have something to do with it, which means you have the power to stop that photo from getting out. And if you don't, you'll be sorry."

Perhaps I will be sorry. But I'm guessing he's the one who will truly regret his words and actions.

33. Samantha

I pull my car up to the curb, turn off the ignition, and get out. I unlock the trunk, and lug out my suitcase. Slightly off balance, I walk towards my building.

I try to focus on my breathing while simultaneously ignoring all the physical symptoms of nervousness: butterflies in my stomach, perspiration, and the shakes. "Damn it," I say to myself. "He's your husband. You should be able to tell him anything."

But as I'm trudging up the stairs with my suitcase close behind, I have to acknowledge my lameness. After all, confessions are only valued when made in a timely manner. Even then, they're not always welcomed by the recipient. "Oh well," I grudgingly admit, "too late to worry about that now. It's time to come clean."

I open the door. Nathan is sitting on the couch, staring at nothing. His face is chalk-white.

"Hi." I say. "I'm really glad to see you."

He looks up at me, like he doesn't even remember who I am. I walk into our apartment, but it feels like I'm entering uncharted territory. "We have a lot to talk about," I tell him. "But the first thing I need you to know is that I love you. Very, very much."

I place my suitcase down, and sit beside him. I kiss him on the cheek, then on the mouth, but his lips don't respond to mine. I pull away.

"Nathan, what is it? What's wrong?"

He still won't look at me.

Okay, this is going to be even harder than I thought. "Honey, there's something I need to tell you. It has to do with Collin. There are some things about my relationship with him that I never told you..."

"You were married to him, pregnant, and had an abortion."

I swallow my shock, and assume that Collin must have told him the whole story when he came to pick up Cheshire's bowl. I never would have thought him to be that spiteful

"No. I was pregnant. Things didn't work out and I was going to have an abortion but then I miscarried, and I went in anyway so they could, you know..." I don't finish the statement and neither does he. I roll my head around. Suddenly my neck is really tense. "Did Collin tell you?"

"I read about it." Nate pulls out a copy of his school's newspaper and puts it in my hands.

I can't quite register what Nathan is saying because I'm looking at a picture of what looks like Nathan kissing some girl who isn't me. Why is he showing me this? I try to make sense of it, but there's a roar in my ears, like the sound of the ocean, only louder, scarier, and not soothing in the least. Like how the ocean would be if it was in hell. It's drowning out everything else, so much so, that I barely hear the phone ring.

"Don't answer it," says Nate. "We need to talk about this. I can explain about the picture."

His words don't completely register, and somehow I can't ignore the phone. I pick it up, still staring at the ghastly picture of Nathan. "Hello," I say faintly, trying to hear myself over the noise inside my head.

"Sam, it's Jake. I have some bad news." He has bad news? Worse than what's going on in my life? I want to hang up, but it's Jake. Jane's husband. And he sounds horrible. It must be something truly awful.

The roar in my head has turned into a ring, and it's as harsh a noise as finger nails on the chalkboard. My heart leaps up and catches in my throat. I can't speak and time is moving way too slowly.

I struggle for air. "Has something happened to Jane?" I gasp.

Nathan must know, he must see the look in my eyes because he takes my hand. It's wet. Or is it my hand that's wet? "There was an accident." Jake says.

I hear someone ask him, "How bad?" Then I realize I'm the one who said that.

"Bad," Jake says. "Jane's condition is serious."

I exhale. Jane. Hurt in an accident. I know I need to be with her. Nothing going on in my life can compare to this. I try to speak calmly. "Where are you, Jake?"

He tells me where to find him, and I hang up the phone. I free my hand from Nate's, place it on my belly, and I get up. Without looking at him, I say, "I have to go. Jane's been hurt."

"It's always someone else, isn't it?" he asks, not bitterly. But still.

"She was in a car accident, and it sounds bad. I have to go. Do you want to come?" Now I do look at him, and honesty floats above us like a poisonous gas.

He shakes his head. "No." Then he looks down. "Sorry."

I don't tell him it's okay. I just turn around and go.

Part 3—Six months later
34. Melody

It's Halloween and I have no plans.

Normally, this wouldn't bother me. It's a stupid holiday anyway. People dress up so they can be someone other than themselves for a little while, even if that means being a murderer or a whore. Most Halloween costumes fall into one of those two categories, and the ones that don't are usually even more lame than the ones that do. And could somebody please explain to me why I am required to hand out free candy to a bunch of kids who come around, rudely ringing my doorbell? The kids in my neighborhood often don't even bother with a costume, and most of them are nearly as tall as I am. Because of the day, they are somehow entitled to free candy.

I can't remember when I've ever been entitled to anything.

My mother seems to think I am now. She believes the school owes me (i.e. her) some sort of settlement because I was emotionally traumatized by the relationship between Mr. L and me. So she postponed our move to Green Bay to sue the school district.

"I'm doing this for you, honey." She said, with more pride in her voice than I've ever heard before, at least where I was concerned.

Of course, that was six months ago. In the meantime, I was sort of expelled. The administration saw my act of renegade newspaper publication as unforgivable. In addition, Brady got busted for plagiarism after I wrote too good a term paper for him. Not only was he willing to name names, he also implicated me in the whole Abby/Bobby debacle. It seems Abby attempted suicide (by taking half a bottle of Aspirin, which at the most, made her ears ring a little) after she received that e-mail I anonymously sent. Anyway, I looked kind of bad, and as the principal said, my absence would be as much for my own sake as it was for theirs.

Then he suspended me for three weeks when there were only three weeks of school left. I did my remaining assignments at home, but my GPA suffered for it. In addition, they assigned me 100 hours of community service, and I won't have technically graduated until I complete it.

Whatever. Now I don't have my diploma, and all the colleges I applied to (late, I may add, because I had so much trouble scraping together the application fees) won't even touch me now. So I'm stuck in Shannon with nothing to do but work in Subway and wait for this stupid lawsuit to go away. I don't even have Kelsey to hang out with anymore.

She's actually still in town, still living with her parents. She's going to school here in Shannon, but any spare time she has is either spent with her new college friends, or with Bobby, who is now her boyfriend.

That's right. My plan worked. Not on myself, but on Kelsey. If ever you needed proof that life is unfair, there it is.

I exhale loudly to shake off these thoughts. What good is reflection, anyway? I look up at the trees towering over me; their leaves are gold, orange, and red. I'm walking to my next community service assignment, which is at a house in one of the wealthier neighborhoods in town. Some of the houses I pass by have done a lot to decorate for Halloween, with ghost and ghouls littering their front lawns. A big colonial-style home has hung orange pumpkin lights through all their trees, erected a mini-graveyard to the right of their driveway, and put up what looks like a witch crashing her broom into their big oak tree. Huh. I wonder how much time and money they spent on all that.

A few more houses down and I find the address I'm looking for. I look at my watch. 2:00 p.m. That means I'll be leaving at 6:00. I still don't get why I need to do four-hour shifts, when I'd much prefer shorter ones. I'd come more often, of course. But I get no say in how this is set up. I never do get any say in anything, though.

I ring the doorbell. A plump blonde woman wearing jeans, an American flag T-shirt, and bare feet answers the door. She gives me a sort-of smile.

"Are you the hospice volunteer?" she asks.

"That's me," I say.

"You look awfully young."

"That's because I am young," I say. "Are you going to let me in anyway?"

She gives a soft little grunt and moves to the side so I can enter the home. Immediately I'm in the living room, which has beige carpet and matching sofas. There are family photos hanging on the wall, many with a dark haired boy who looks vaguely familiar. On both the sofas are bright, multi-colored throw-blankets, which look homemade. There are also several pillows, all in suede or fake suede earth tones. It's the sort of room that makes me want to curl up and take a nap.

The next thing I notice about the home is the smell. The other homes I've gone to have had this stale, hospital type of smell—I suppose it's what looming death is supposed to smell like. But this house smells like lavender, and I don't know, freshness. There are a lot of plants, either hanging in the windows or on top of cabinets and tables. Maybe that's why.

"I'm Mindy," says the woman who let me in. "I'll probably always be here when you are, because I'm the full-time nurse. If I'm not here, then her son will be."

"Okay," I say. "As long as someone is else is around, that's fine. You were told that I'm just supposed to provide companionship, right?"

She smirks at me. "Don't worry. You won't be expected to empty any bed pans."

I shrug my shoulders. "Where is she? Can I meet her?"

"Yeah, come on back."

She leads me down a hall to the left of the kitchen. After passing a bathroom, study, and small bedroom, we reach the master bedroom, which is where we're headed. Mindy leads me in.

"Daphne, you have a visitor," she says. "Are you up for a little company?"

Daphne nods her head. She's lying in bed, nearly swallowed by her pink satin comforter and oversized pillows. Then again, she's so emaciated that it's hard to imagine her not being swallowed up. She's wearing a flannel nightgown with flowers on it, the sort you'd expect a grandmother to wear. Her hair is stringy, her face is gray, and her skin looks like it's sagging off of her.

"She can't talk very well anymore, lung cancer will do that," says Mindy. "But she likes to play Scrabble, and she likes to be read to. You'll find her games and her books underneath her nightstand."

"Thanks," I say. I approach the bed. "Hi, Daphne, I'm Melody." Her breathing is of course, heavy and strained. "Would you like me to prop you up with some pillows, so we can play scrabble? I love that game too."

She gives me another nod. I gingerly put two of her pillows beneath her back, then I get out the Scrabble board and set everything up. "Okay, Daphne. I'll let you go first. But just to warn you, I'm really, really good at Scrabble. I play to win, and I'm not going to cut you any breaks just because you're dying."

She makes this weird, guttural type of sound, and at first I'm scared that I've upset her. Then I realize she's laughing.

My visit with Daphne marks hours eighty-four through eighty-eight of my community service stint. When choosing my community service assignment, there weren't a lot of options. I don't do kids, animals, or highway cleanup. So I chose to go into the homes of dying people and keep them company. My job description is specifically "not hands-on," instead I'm simply supposed to provide entertainment for the patients while their family members take a break.

The first guy I visited, Saul, was a ninety-year-old stroke victim. He didn't do or say much, and I mostly just watched television with him or read aloud from the newspaper. He died after my fifth visit. Then I was sent to Matilda's house. She had Alzheimer's disease, and was convinced I was her daughter Jackie, who died in a car crash forty-five years ago. I held her hand a lot and played along when she told me stories about Jackie's childhood. Her surviving daughter, Carol, filled me in on some of the details so I could feed Matilda's delusions. Carol's philosophy was, if it made her mom happy, why not?

Matilda hung in for sixteen of my visits. When I went to her funeral, Carol came up to me and said, "You have no idea how happy you made my mom."

"I only made her happy because she thought I was Jackie."

"But you gave her a chance to say goodbye. That's a huge comfort. Thank you." Carol wrapped me into a tight hug. It didn't bug me the way Kelsey's hugs used to, and I was actually able to not pull away for a whole three or four seconds.

Now I've been assigned to Daphne, who has cancer. They didn't tell me how long she has left; hopefully she'll last through another three of my visits. It would kind of suck to go to another new person; besides, I like Daphne's house. It's very inviting.

After a round of Scrabble, and half an hour of reading aloud from *The Time Traveler's Wife*, I notice Daphne has fallen asleep. I close the book and put it back underneath the nightstand, having marked the place where we left off. Then I sit and watch her sleep, just in case she wakes up and wants to be read to again. After an hour or so I decide she's out for a while, so I tiptoe out of her room, and find Mindy in the living room, drinking a diet coke and watching *Access Hollywood*. There's a story about Paris Hilton on.

"How is that girl famous?" she says. Then she looks at me, waiting for my answer. I had thought it was a rhetorical question.

"I don't know," I reply. "Some people just thrive on negative attention."

"Huh, I wonder what that's like."

I'm sure I could enlighten her, but even I have better things to do. "Um, Daphne's asleep, and it's nearly six, so would you mind signing this for me?" I hand her my community service time card, and she takes it from me.

"Huh," she says, after studying it back and front. "Why do you need proof of your hours if you're a volunteer?"

"I was assigned community service," I answer, with as much

dignity as possible. No need to care what Mindy thinks.

"Why? What bad thing did you do?"

"That's really none of your business," I tell her. "I just need you to sign my card."

She gives me a stony look, then searches for a pen. I reach into my bag and hand her one. But before she finishes, the front door opens and in walks the dark-haired boy from the pictures that are hanging on the living room walls. In the flesh he's a lot easier to recognize. It's Carter Wilkin, my old spelling-bee nemesis.

"Melody?" he says. It's been years since we've spoken; once we reached high school our paths rarely crossed. However, recent events have made me infamous among the high-school graduate crowd, so I'm not surprised he knows me. "What are you doing here?" he asks.

"I'm the hospice volunteer," I say. "How are you, Carter? Is Daphne, um…"

"She's my mom." His words drip out of his mouth like sleet.

I know by now how hard family members can take a loved-one's death, so I try to be sympathetic. "I'm sorry. I didn't realize."

I notice how red is face has grown. "Yeah," He says. "I'm sorry too." He seems more than sad, more than uncomfortable. There's this heated attitude coming from him that's causing my skin to crawl. Surely he's not still mad about the spelling bee?

I'm determined to stay nice. "Well, Carter. It was good seeing you. Maybe you'll be around on Thursday? Perhaps then we can catch up."

"Yeah, I don't think so," he mutters.

I square my shoulders. "Oh. Okay. Well, another time, then."

"That's not going to happen, Melody."

I reach down for my bag, pretending to be consumed with arranging myself so I don't have to look at him. "Umm, okay."

He remains rigid. "I don't want you to come back. My mother deserves better than a volunteer like you. You're here because you have to be, right?"

Mindy pipes in. "She was assigned community service. See, she has a time card that I need to sign."

"I figured," says Carter, grabbing the card. "Tell you what,

Melody. It's your lucky day." He takes the pen from Mindy's hand, and initials every remaining box. "Just fill in the rest of these with made-up hours. You're off the hook."

"But," I stammer. "Then you won't be able to get anyone else in here. They'll only assign you one volunteer at a time."

"I guess that's for me to worry about, isn't it?" Carter ushers me out the front door, rather forcefully I might add.

"Take care, Melody," I hear him say as the door slams behind me.

I look down at my time card. I really am off the hook.

I begin my trek home. Dusk has fallen and I pass several trick-or-treaters on the way. One little girl, who is probably around five, is dressed as a princess, complete with a shiny pink dress, tiara, and wand. Only the young and innocent, who are secure in their own beauty, can look as happy as she does. She's holding onto her mother's hand, and the mom is trying to prevent her from tripping over the sidewalk or over the hem of her fancy dress. However, when she steps down from the curb, she does start to take a tumble, but the mom pulls on her arm and steadies the girl just in time. They walk on.

I'm off the hook. With this time card, I can finally get my diploma and find a way to leave Shannon. "Yay, me," I whisper to myself. Then the tears begin to fall.

35. Samantha

It's a Monday morning in the first week of November. I'm standing on Jane's doorstep, knocking, hoping she'll answer. Jake called me because the school called him. She didn't show up to teach her class this morning and nobody could get hold of her.

"Can you go check on her?" he asked. "I'd do it, but I've left work one too many times lately."

"No problem," I said. So here I am knocking, trying not to panic. Her car is in the driveway. Why isn't she answering?

My knocking turns to pounding, until finally, after yelling her name a couple of times, she opens the door.

"Hey," she says, looking bleary-eyed. "What's up?"

"Didn't you hear me knocking?" I say. "I've been out here for several minutes. And before that I tried calling you. So did Jake."

"I was asleep, and I had my phone off," she still looks dazed. "Why did you guys need to talk to me? Did something bad happen?"

I shiver. It's cold and wet outside, and Jane hasn't invited me in. Months ago I wouldn't have waited for an invitation, but now, something has shifted. Ever since her accident she's been different. The doctor says she probably bruised the frontal lobe of her brain, which isn't uncommon in accidents like hers and can cause short-term memory loss, depression, and erratic behavior. So I've been trying to be as patient and accommodating as possible, knowing she'd do the same for me were our situations reversed. But our old familiarity is gone. I wrap my arms around my chest, trying to hug away this chill.

"Jane," I say, trying really really hard not to sound accusatory, "you're supposed to be teaching and you didn't call in. We were worried about you."

She wrinkles her brow in confusion for a second, but shakes away her doubts almost immediately. "It's Monday. I don't teach today. You guys have it wrong."

"No, Jane. It was last spring when you didn't teach on Mondays, remember? This term you have an 8:00 a.m. class."

She looks down and away, like there's nothing she'd less rather see than my face. "Whatever. How am I supposed to remember my schedule all the time when it keeps changing? It's an easy mistake."

"Okay."

"Look, I should wash up and get going. So you can stop worrying. I'm fine." She starts to close the door on me.

"Wait," I say. "Do you want me to stick around? I could give you a lift. I'm going in that direction."

Jane heaves her chest in an exasperated sigh. "I'm not a child, Sam. I can drive myself."

"Okay."

"So you can stop treating me like a child, okay?"

"Okay."

"Good. See you later."

She closes the door before I can say goodbye. The first time she treated me like this I was devastated. The second, third, and fourth times also sucked. Now I'm used to it. I walk to my car, and squeeze myself and my huge belly inside. More than anything else, I just feel tired.

"Life doesn't always turn out the way it's supposed to. I was lucky, but not everyone is. I can't imagine the pain of wanting a baby so badly, but not being able to have one. I don't know what I would do if that happened to me. This probably sounds really cheesy, but perhaps my purpose is to do this for someone. God blessed me with the ability to get pregnant easily and bring a baby to term. Plus, I love being pregnant. Why shouldn't I help women who aren't as blessed as I am?"

The woman talking is on the television screen in front of me, and she's wearing a smock-like Laura Ashley maternity gown because she's very, very pregnant. Her pale complexion has a rosy glow, and her blonde hair is pulled back with a wide headband. I bet she's a great mother.

I press the stop button, creating another clip and I drag the footage I've just watched into the timeline of my film project. I'm close to being finished with editing all the footage I've shot so far. And, so far, so good. I joined a Yahoo! group for surrogate mothers, and I was able to find quite a few who agreed to be interviewed. They were all very amiable about it, which I suppose goes with the territory. If you're agreeing to carry someone else's baby, chances are you're accommodating by nature.

It's kind of frustrating actually. I need to represent another side of surrogacy—the difficult, painful side. All the mothers I've spoken to are happy. They had already had kids of their own when they agreed to carry another couple's baby, and pregnancy and labor came very easy to them. And I couldn't find anyone who was carrying a baby for her best friend, only to have that best friend get into a life-altering car accident a third of the way through the pregnancy.

I blame myself for Jane's wreck. She was talking to me on her cell phone when it happened. There was traffic ahead of her and she didn't slow down in time, so she rear-ended another car. Luckily both cars had airbags, and everyone escaped with their lives. But Jane had severe whiplash, a concussion, and a couple of broken ribs. Those injuries have healed, so she's "lucky." Apparently, countless people have died or became severely damaged after accidents like hers. Jane's problems are miniscule in context. But since the accident Jane has been forgetful, rude, and unconcerned with her impending motherhood.

I look at the clock. 2:42. I have to be at work in eighteen minutes. I grab my half-eaten bag of Fritos, water bottle, and my pink notebook (where I keep all the notes and list of contacts for my project) and stuff them into my bag. Then I turn off all the equipment, and head out. On my way I pass Neal, the manager of Shannon Community

Access Channel. He's wiry, with a goatee and clothes that always look too big. He looks up from his *Entertainment Weekly* as I pass by.

"Hey, Sam," he cries. Damn. I was hoping to make it out without having to talk to him. I stop. "When are you going to have something for me to broadcast?" he asks.

I plaster on my sweetest smile. "Soon, I promise."

He flips the page of his magazine. "You know the rules. You use the equipment, you let us air what you've done. You've been mooching off us for months with nothing to show for it."

"Neal, we've been over this before. It's a piece about pregnancy. It won't be done until I'm no longer pregnant, which as you can probably tell," I point down to my huge belly, "won't be much longer. Then, I swear, you'll have an amazing two-hour feature that you can broadcast to your heart's content."

"And right after you have that baby, you'll be in here, working?" He's so condescending; I want to squeeze little his throat until he goes away. But he keeps talking. "Won't you be too tired with midnight feedings and stuff? And who's going to watch the baby while you're in here, finishing up?"

"That's not your problem, is it Neal?"

He gives a grunt in response then returns to his magazine. As I walk out I make a mental note to bribe him with another pan of brownies the next time I come in, which most likely will be tomorrow. I hate to be nice to someone so rude, but it's necessary. Lately, my time spent at Shannon Community Access Channel is the only thing keeping me sane.

"I can't believe you're going to continue with the film!" That was Nathan's response, the first time I spoke of it after Jane's accident. "Don't you think that's in poor taste, after everything she's been through?"

"Jane wants me to finish it," I said, fighting back tears.

Actually, I'm still not sure that's true, because she hasn't said either way. But I know beyond a doubt that if Jane were herself she'd want me to finish it, so I'm sticking with it. One day she'll emerge from this fog she's in, and we'll watch the movie together, and her baby will be in her lap. That's just how it has to happen. Until then, we all need to hang on to what we have as tightly as we can, so none of it will disappear while we aren't looking. That's what I've been trying to do, and it's exhausting.

I sigh, and waddle into my car. I don't want to be late for work. Once Nate lost his job, I saw no other option than going back to Bravo and begging Hal for my old job back. Something in my eloquent plea must have moved him, because not only did I get rehired, I got the promotion I was being considered for before I walked out. "We've had a terrible time filling the position," Hal told me. "Neither of the people we placed in it lasted."

That's probably because the pay is abysmal, but the hours and responsibility attached are significant. I work most days from 3:00 to 10:00, and I'm responsible for taking inventory and keeping the books. I also get to place the orders, which is sort of fun. Besides the new releases, we have a small budget for classic or art films, and I enjoy picking out new additions to our library. My goal is to make Bravo known as the hangout for true film buffs.

I get to work, and do what I do everyday upon walking in. I put my purse back in the office, bring my water bottle up to the counter, steal a box of thin mints from the candy aisle and rip it open, and shove several in my mouth at once. Then I grab the copy of *Sophie's Choice*, and replace it with whatever was playing (today it was *Hitch*. Blah. *Sophie's Choice* is a huge improvement.)

"No. Not again," says Naomi, who is working her afternoon shift, in the job I used to have. "I can't watch *Sophie's Choice* again for the hundredth time. It's too depressing."

"Life is depressing, Naomi. Deal with it."

She huffs and puffs, slamming things around while putting re-turned DVDs away. Whatever. I refuse to watch some stupid, mindless Will Smith dribble that paints the world as rosy and perfect. Falling in love with a man who turns out to be insane, battling illness and hunger, choosing which child to have killed while you're standing in line to be killed yourself—that happens to people. That's real life. If Naomi can't accept that, well, then she needs to grow up.

I start organizing the area behind the counter. Naomi can be such a slob; there are stray DVD cases and receipts everywhere. It's so irresponsible. I need to talk to Hal about it. Or should I just take care of it myself? Perhaps that would be better—put the girl in her place. I can give her what for, that's for sure. She won't know what hit her.

"Sam."

Nathan's voice startles me out of my thoughts. I hadn't heard him come in.

"Hey," I say, not bothering to hide my surprise, and okay, discomfort. "What are you doing here?"

"You used to come visit me at work. I thought I'd do the same."

"Oh, okay." I look at him, really taking in his appearance. He must have shaved and showered today, and he has on a clean shirt and tie. "You look nice. Are you on your way somewhere?"

Annoyance skips over his face. "I told you, I have that job interview at Sylvan today. I'm on my way right now."

"Sorry. Of course. I just forgot." How could I forget? Ever since Nate lost his job, he's had a terrible time getting any sort of work at all. After the local paper ran their own version of Melody's story, complete with details about the lawsuit her mother is pursuing and the original picture of him kissing Melody printed in the school paper, Nathan became known as "that guy who had an affair with his student." We considered moving, but knew that was an impossibility until after I had the baby and the lawsuit was settled. So when Nathan applied to the Sylvan Institute he thought he probably had no chance. It's a place for rich people to take their under-achieving kids for extra help in reading and math, and it was as close to a teaching job that he could even hope to get in this town. The other day, when he told me he had been called for an interview, was the happiest I had seen him in a long time.

Nathan looks up at the televisions. "*Sophie's Choice*? Haven't you been watching that at home, too?"

"Only a couple of times."

"Isn't that the one where she has to choose which of her kids will die?"

I fiddle with a DVD case, and answer him, looking down. "Yeah, that's the one."

"Yeah. I heard that's, like, the most depressing movie ever made. You should be watching something happy, honey. Something that won't get you down."

Naomi overhears and pipes in. "I agree. Let's watch something else. *Anything* else!"

"How about *Roman Holiday?*" Says Nate. "You like Audrey Hepburn, right?"

I glare at him, and grind out my words. "I'll change the film, but I refuse to watch *Roman Holiday.*"

He lurches back in response to my harshness. "It was just a suggestion. You watch what you want." He leans over the counter and gives me a kiss on the cheek. "Wish me luck!"

"Luck!" I cry, and wave to him as he walks out the door. I watch through the window as his car pulls away, and I give a silent prayer. "Please, please let him get this job."

"So, then, I'm putting *Hitch* back on." Naomi says, loudly.

"Um, no. You're not."

"You said you'd change it!"

"That's right. *I'll* change it." I head straight to the drama section, and pick out the only other movie I can stand right now to watch. I put *Mommy Dearest* in the DVD player. I don't mind; Meryl Streep and all her weepiness was beginning to get on my nerves anyway.

36. Melody

His office looks exactly like you'd expect it to. Terrance Taylor must watch a lot of lawyer television shows, or at least his decorator does. The carpet is deep blue, and matching blinds hang from the two windows. Above his desk I see his diploma from the University of Minnesota law school, which I guess is supposed to be good, but I doubt it's top tier. Everything else in this room has an air of sterility, including his huge, shiny-top desk, which is bare, save my file, a silver clock, picture frame, calculator, and one of the metal ball thingies where the balls are suspended by strings and if you pull and release one then it sets them all in motion. All of it reminds me of that overpriced store, The Sharper Image, that I like to visit at the mall so I can sit in one of those back- massage chairs. Terrance almost seems like he could come from there himself. He's trim, with slicked-back hair, a pointy nose, and a perfectly fitted suit.

Mom and I are sitting in black leather chairs with metal armrests facing his desk. Mom keeps crossing and uncrossing her legs, then primps her hair, and afterwards she'll rub her hands together. Then she repeats the cycle. All of this is done, of course, while she's talking.

"He took advantage of her," she says. "Melody felt this hero-type worship for him after he saved her from that kid, Axel, and Mr. Linden totally played on that and she fell for it. The school shoulda never allowed any of it to happen."

Terrance takes notes as my mother jabbers on, yet he's able to respond and ask questions simultaneously. I've never seen anyone who can write and talk at the same time. I can't, unless I'm writing and saying the same thing at once. I'm sure that he isn't. Without looking up he says, "And the school never contacted you after Melody's attack?"

"I guess they left a message or two, but Melody felt so ashamed she erased them. You know how victims of rape often blame themselves. And the school never bothered to keep trying, to speak to me directly. That's criminal. If I had known what happened, maybe I could have offered my girl the support she needed, and she wouldn't have fallen prey to that teacher." My mother crosses and uncrosses her legs again as she finishes, a triumphant smile on her face.

"Uh huh," mumbles Terrance. "And Melody… you're willing to verify everything you published in that article as the truth?"

Before I can say yay or nay, my mom answers for me. "Of course she can. What could she possibly have had to gain by exposing him for the poor excuse of a man that he is? Melody is like, what's that woman's name, you know …" my mother snaps her fingers, trying to recall.

"Monica Lewinsky?" asks Terrance.

"No, no, not her. She actually did blow the president. That black woman. She spoke out against that judge."

"Anita Hill," I say.

"Right, Anita Hill. She never got anything but abuse, poor thing. Nobody wanted to believe her, and that asshole judge got the job anyway, didn't he? And what could she have possibly gained by stepping forward, other than seeing justice served? My Melody only wants to prevent other girls from being hurt like she was, don't you babe?" My mother reaches over and squeezes my knee.

"I suppose," says Terrance, "that the considerable sum of money you hope to win through this lawsuit hasn't even entered your daughter's mind?"

"Of course it has!" my mother cries. "The settlement will be her college fund. But that wasn't her motive at the time she published the story. She didn't even want the lawsuit. I had to talk her into it, didn't I sweetie?"

My mother's face is turned towards me, and I've never wanted to ram my fist into it more. I don't answer, but nod my head in reply.

Terrence stops writing, places his silver fountain pen down on desk, and speaks directly to me. "If that's the case, Melody, we may have a problem. Even with that photo, there are no guarantees. It's your word against his, and because you seem unable to find a character witness or anyone who will vouch for you, we might have a hard time convincing the school to settle. Then our only choice will be to go to court, where the burden of proof will be on you. I need to know you're committed to this."

"You're committed to this, aren't you hon?"

My mom and Terrance are silent while they wait for my conformation. The only sound in the room is the ticking of the clock. I know what the right answer is, this should be easy. Yet, when I form the word "Yes", it catches in my throat momentarily, and comes out sounding sort of like, "Yerk."

They look at me like I should be on the short bus. Okay, Madsen, try again. You can do this. "Yes." I say.

My mother smiles and Terrence nods his head.

"Yes," I say again, this time in a whisper.

We leave his office, and my mother drives to work. I start to walk home, but without even making a conscious decision I veer from my path toward the nicer area of town. Funny, after leaving our appointment with Terrance Taylor, all I wanted to do was go home and take a shower. Now, not so much. Now the idea of sitting in my crap-hole apartment with nothing but bad TV to keep me company makes me want to put a gun to my head.

It doesn't take me long to get to Daphne and Carter's house.

I ring the doorbell. There's no answer, so I ring it again. After around twenty seconds, he answers.

"What are you doing here?" There is no more friendliness in his face or tone of voice than there was the last time we spoke, when he threw me out for no reason. Oh well. At least I'm used to being unpopular.

"It's Thursday," I say. "I'm here for my shift."

"I already told you…" he begins, but I cut him off.

"I know what you told me, Carter. I'm not good enough to sit with your dying mother. But did it occur to you that maybe she feels differently? We played Scrabble. I made her laugh. I read to her from that book, which was so good, I went to the library and got my own copy." To prove it, I reach into my bag and pull out *Time Traveler's Wife*, which I packed earlier that day in case I needed to kill time in Terrance's waiting room. Carter is silent in his shock. "You're probably right, you know. I've never loved anyone the way you obviously love her. And I'm sure she'd rather spend all her remaining time with you. But if you'll let me, I'd like to get to know her before she's gone."

Carter's head falls forward, as if his neck can no longer bare its weight. He speaks into his chest. "Every hour you spend with her, that's one hour that I've lost."

My heart feels like it's being squeezed. "I'm sorry," I murmur. "I can't imagine…"

But I can't finish my thought. Damn it. I'm crying again. This has got to stop. "I should go," I say, turning around.

"Wait," he says. I stop. "Come in."

So I do.

37. Samantha

The apartment is quiet when I get home, and the door to our bedroom is shut. Nate must have already gone to bed. I find he has left me a note on the kitchen table. *Sam, Jake called again. Wants to know when your next OB appointment is. Can you call him back already? –N*

I crumple up the post-it and throw it in the garbage. Jake should know when it is; I called over there already and told Jane, asking her to write it down. She said she'd let Jake know, but obviously she didn't. But why does Nate automatically assume this is my fault? I ruminate over this as I head to the bathroom, where I relieve my bladder for the millionth time today. I also brush my teeth and wash my face, avoiding my reflection in the process. Lately the sight of my own face really bugs me. No matter what I do I have this weird expression, sort of like a caged horse barring its teeth. Not attractive.

I'm not sleepy, and I'm tired of looking at the television, so I grab my book of classic fairy tales and start reading. I'd always heard that the original versions of these stories were much more violent and disturbing than the Disney-fied ones we were spoon-fed as children. So far, I'm not disappointed. In *Cinderella* one of the evil stepsisters cuts off her big toe in order to fit her foot into the golden slipper. It works at first, and she tricks the prince into taking her away to be married. But he looks down and notices the blood seeping out of her shoe, and takes her back home. Then the other stepsister chops off a portion of her heel, and again, the prince, who can't be too bright, is fooled until he notices how her shoe is also over-flowing with blood. Then the prince finally ends up with the real-deal, poor motherless Cinderella, who happens to clean up well and has exceedingly small feet. He takes her to get married, and the stepsisters come along, to be bridesmaids or something, but birds peck their eyes out before the wedding, so they're left toeless/heelless and blind. Justice is served.

So there you have it. You've got to be pretty and sympathetic in order to get a decent man. Forget having enough drive to saw off portions of your feet; men aren't impressed with such antics.

I'm just about to begin reading *The Little Mermaid* when the bedroom door opens and Nate emerges from the dark.

"Hey," he says. "How long have you been home?"

I keep my head buried in my book. "Not long. I thought you were asleep."

"I was. Then I woke up."

"Oh."

He sits on the armchair across from me. "In case you were wondering, I didn't get the job."

I lower my book. His face is solid resentment. "They told you so soon?" I ask.

He grunts out a tough little laugh. "I was half way through the interview, and it was going fine. Then somebody, a manager I guess, interrupted, and asked to speak privately to the lady who was interviewing me. They go into the other room. The lady comes back after, like, just a couple of seconds, and she tells me the position has been filled."

I don't know what to say, so I reach for the most benign words I can think of. "Oh. Well, that's bad luck."

"Bad luck?" Nate challenges back. "Luck had nothing to do with it. The lady who called me in for that interview just didn't realize who I was at first, but once she was enlightened, that was it."

"Okay…"

He leans forward, his body contracting into an arc of tension. "Don't pretend like it was otherwise. My name is mud."

I laugh before I realize I am doing so. Nate shoots me a hateful look, and instantly my laughter evaporates, like hot water does when thrown into sub-zero degree air. (I tried that once on a particularly cold winter day. The water turned to mist before it could reach the ground. It was pretty cool.) "Something funny?" he asks.

"Sorry," I say, and I mean it. "It's just, 'My name is mud' sounds like something my grandfather would have said."

Nate seems to appreciate the joke about as much as my dead grandfather would. "Well, in this case it's true, and it's not a joke.

"I don't know what to tell you, Nate."

"Tell me we can move away."

"You know we can't."

"We can't stay here!" He cries and jumps up from the couch simultaneously. "There is nothing for us here."

I remain calm, sitting, looking up at him. "You mean there's nothing for you here."

He paces around the room, doing circles around me. "Oh, that's right. I forgot. You have so much keeping you in Shannon. Your ex-husband, your fantastic job, the baby you're going to be a mother for now."

"That's unfair!" I yell. I have to yell. At eight and a half months pregnant, I can barely move, so I need to overcompensate in other areas. Nate stops and looks at me. Our eyes meet. I narrow mine and say, "Collin and I are through, my job is the only thing paying the bills, and I am *not* going to be this baby's mother. Jane is."

Nate shakes his head. "You live in denial."

If I were a snake, my cheeks would be puffed out and I would be coiled and erect, poised to attack. But there's nothing reptilian about me, so with venom I spit out, "Don't put this on me. Nobody forced you to kiss Melody."

His shoulders sag. "She set me up."

"And it worked, didn't it! How could you have been so stupid, Nate?" Then I do my best Nate imitation. "Oh sure, Melody, come by my room late at night when nobody else is around and we'll talk. I realize you have a huge crush on me and that by inviting you I'm feeding your unhealthy fascination with me, but hey, what the heck? I love the attention!"

He glares at me. Then wordlessly, he turns and enters back into our bedroom, slamming the door behind him.

This is how our fights go.

It's sort of like that Bill Murray classic, *Ground Hog Day*, where he is doomed to repeat the same day over and over until he finally gets it right. For six months Nate and I have been having variations of the same fight, but we never resolve anything, and somehow we're incapable of moving on.

The night when everything changed now seems so long ago. Nate and I were in the middle of what was going to be the most important and revealing conversation of our marriage, when unfortunately we were interrupted by news of Jane's accident. I think Nate is still mad that I walked out on him to go to her, but what could I do? I promised him and myself that we would finish the conversation later, but no matter how much we try, it's like we're incapable of doing so. I'm sure I'm equally at fault, and my guilt over almost kissing Collin has been silently eating away at me. That's nothing though, compared to the guilt I feel for being on the phone with Jane and distracting her so that she got into that accident.

Two days after Jane's accident, I came home from the hospital and Nate insisted on making me spaghetti because I hadn't eaten all day. I sat at the kitchen table, making ribbons out of the blood-red tomato sauce by tracing the edge of my plate with my fork. We sat in silence: me not eating, and Nate watching me not eat.

Finally, he said, "So, you were married to Collin."

"I was going to tell you." I whispered.

"And the abortion." His words were a statement, not an accusation. I said nothing. "Is that why you volunteered to help Jane? To make up for it?" I still didn't respond, and he let his frustration slip out. "Sam, stop playing with your food and look at me."

I put down my fork, deciding to humor him. "What?" I said. "What do you want from me?"

"I want to know if you married me to get over someone else. I want to know if all our choices, the ones that affect both of us, are based on secrets you've kept from me. I want you to tell me that I have it all wrong."

"And I want to trust you," I said. "But I've forgotten how." I got up and put my plate full of spaghetti in the sink. "I'm going to bed," I said. "And I'd appreciate it if you slept on the couch tonight."

Then, closing the door behind me, I buried my head in the pillows, and cried loud and long.

Now six months have passed, and I'm on the other side of that bedroom door, but the distance between us is still the same.

Two days later I'm at Jane's house, showing her tapes of my recently edited footage. Jane is sitting on her couch, picking at the peanut butter and jelly sandwich that I made when I got to her house. I made one for her and one for myself—I was starving. But while I have been expanding and feel ready to explode, Jane has diminished. She's lost interest in so many things, including eating. At the moment I'm more concerned that she focuses on my footage than on food, so I pause the tape that we're watching.

"Do you think I should leave in the part where she starts to cry? Or is it just too annoying?

She doesn't look up. "Sure."

"Sure, what? Sure, it's annoying, or sure, I should keep it?"

Jane shrugs her shoulders. "I don't know. Whatever. Do what you want."

"But I don't know what I want. That's why I'm asking you."

"Well, I don't know either. It's your project."

I know I shouldn't pursue this, but something in me is unwilling to let her off the hook this time. "But you have a stake in it," I say, with just the slightest of a quiver.

Jane's voice certainly isn't quivering. "Not really."

I can't find the words to respond. There's a lot I wish I could say, but I have to be careful. Finally I simply say, "Jane, come on."

She borders on a yell. "Sam, you're asking too much of me. I don't know."

So now I yell back. This has become a real fight. Our first real fight. "How am I asking too much of you? It's not that hard to have an opinion. I just want to know what you think."

"What I think is that I'm tired of talking about babies and thinking about babies. It's all anyone wants to focus on and I'm sick of it. I can't handle it anymore."

"Jane, you have to handle it. You're going to be a mother soon."

Her words are furious and full of tears. "I don't feel like I am. You're the one who's pregnant. You're the one who's experiencing my husband's child growing inside of you."

"Yes, but Jane…"

"No. You have no idea what that feels like. Maybe the two of you should just go off together, make it easier on all of us."

Shock prevents me from forming a quick, deft response. I try to laugh off what she said, but my laughter sounds weak and unnatural, even to me. "Come on, you're being silly," I mutter.

"Don't condescend to me!"

"Jane." I'm crying now too, albeit silently. The unfairness of having lost my best friend—especially when I'm carrying this baby for her—comes crashing down. I need her right now, and she's somewhere else. I pull myself together enough to say, "Let's talk later when you're a little more calm."

I grab my stuff and walk (waddle) out, hoping fruitlessly that she'll yell out an apology and tell me not to go. But she doesn't, so I climb into my car, turn the key in the ignition, wipe away another tear, and drive off. But as I'm driving through the streets of Jane's neighborhood the baby kicks inside me.

And my heart breaks a little.

How is it possible that in a couple of weeks I'm going to be handing this creature over to someone who has lost interest in being a mother? I always imagined that giving her up would be hard, but I never thought it would feel as impossible as it does at this moment.

I slow to stop because there is a red light in front of me. Perhaps I should make a turn at this intersection rather than going straight. I could head out of town, go some place where nobody knows me, and raise this baby as my own. Wouldn't everybody involved be just a little relieved?

The baby kicks again, and the light changes. My palms are sweating, and I pause before accelerating; indecision and anxiety are paralyzing me. The car behind me honks, so I drive forward, straight forward, sticking to my familiar route. Because deep down I know, I'm not brave enough to do otherwise.

So I rub the spot where she kicked me, absurdly wishing she never had to come out at all.

38. Melody

The smell of enchiladas cooking is making me hungry. Carter pops his head into Daphne's bedroom, and whispers, "I think dinner is ready. Is she still asleep?"

"Yeah," I say, getting up. Daphne has been dreaming (of something nice, I hope) for the last few chapters of *The Time Traveler's Wife,* so I just sat there at her side and read to myself. Carter says she gets disoriented easily, so he likes to have someone with her as much as possible, even when she's sleeping. He requested a volunteer from the hospice agency so Daphne could have constant companionship while he and Mindy might have the occasional break.

Still, even with my eight hours a week they were feeling overwhelmed. So I said I would come in more often. "You don't have to do that," said Carter.

"I know," I replied. "But I have nothing better to do. You already know I have no friends, no life. Other than working at Subway, I have nowhere to be but home. Believe me, I'd much rather spend time with your mother than with mine."

Carter smiled in response, which I took as a Yes. I started just dropping by.

Today I've been here a couple of hours. I arrived after working a full shift at Subway, and I reeked of baked bread when Carter opened the door to find me in my Subway uniform.

"Do you want to wash up?" he asked, as diplomatically as possible.

So I took a shower and borrowed something of Daphne's to wear, just a pair of old jeans and a green sweatshirt.

"I hope you like Mexican food," Carter says as I walk into the kitchen.

"It smells great," I say. Mindy has already set the table, and is sitting down, so I join her by sitting down as well. Carter pulls the pan out of the oven and dishes out the mixture of melted cheese, sauce, and seasoned beef onto our plates.

"Do you want beans?" he calls out to both of us.

"Sure!" Mindy says.

"No thanks," I reply.

Soon he has placed our plates in front of us, and he is sitting down. Then the three of us dig in. After Mindy and I proclaim how good everything tastes, we sit and eat in silence. It feels so nice, to be sitting at a kitchen table sharing a meal with people who aren't crazy, I don't even notice Carter isn't eating. But Mindy does.

"Carter, aren't you hungry?" She inquires

He rubs his eyes and shakes his head. "Sorry," he says. "One minute I'm fine, and then all of a sudden it hits me, and I think, how can I enjoy eating or sitting or doing anything, when mom is dying?"

"That's natural," Mindy replies. "It's human to feel that way."

His voice is completely flat. "Yeah, well, I'm tired of being human."

We're silent again. Mindy resumes eating. Carter attempts a bite, but it looks like it's painful for him to chew and swallow. "So Carter," I say. "What are your plans?"

He looks at me like I've spoken in some crazy foreign language.

"What do you mean?" he asks.

"You know, your plans. What are you thinking you'll do after your mom has died?"

"Melody!" Mindy barks, horrified.

"What?" I say. She glares at me, punishing me with her eyes.

Carter doesn't seem nearly as bothered as Mindy is by my question. "You're the first person who has asked me that," he states, neutral and quiet.

"Surely not," I say.

He pushes his hair back from his forehead and sits up a little straighter. "She got sick about a year ago. It started out as breast cancer, you know. At first we thought she was going to be fine. She went through chemo and radiation, and the doctors said she was cured. Then, like a month later, she went back in because she felt lousy, and they discovered it had spread to her lungs and brain. They gave her, like, a few weeks. The day after we found out, I graduated from high school. Nobody's asked—everyone was too polite. Everyone knew, with my dad remarried and totally focused on his new family, I'm all she has. My plans have always been to take care of my mom."

"But before, were you going to go to college?"

"Art school," he says.

"Oh. That's cool. To do advertising?"

He laughs. "No. To be an artist."

"But is there money in that?"

"I don't know. I don't care."

"Huh." I say, trying to comprehend. How can he not care about money?

"So what about you?" He asks.

"What about me?"

"After you're done suing Mr. Linden for sexual harassment, what are your plans?"

"To leave town. Start over. Beyond that, I'm not really sure."

"You're suing someone for sexual harassment?" Mindy inquires.

"My mother is. On my behalf. I don't know. I'm not even sure why I agreed to it."

Mindy speaks with her mouth full of beans. "Well, is he guilty?"

I look towards her, blocking Carter from my view. "I don't know."

"How can you not know?" asks Carter.

I turn to meet his eyes. "I guess when nobody bothers to ask you the important questions, it's easy not to have the answers."

Silence again.

Carter drinks from his water glass, then sets it down with a thump. "So, Melody, were you hoping to find them here? The answers—I mean."

I'm still looking at him when I start laughing. "Yeah, right. You're so full of wisdom. And Daphne, who can't talk, she's really set me straight on a lot of my issues." As soon as I say it I realize I've been too harsh. All I was trying to do was make him laugh.

Carter silently gets up and leaves the table. Behind me, he walks down the hallway to Daphne's bedroom. I hear him enter. Mindy gives me another one of her looks—I swear she was a schoolmarm in a past life. Or an executioner. I heave a sigh and get up too. Damn, dinner was really good and I am hungry.

I find Carter sitting by Daphne's side, holding her hand. If he hears me enter, he doesn't turn around. "Poignant," he says. "P-O-I-G-N-A-N-T."

"Huh?" I ask, sitting down next to him. I notice his cheeks are stained with tears.

"That's the word I lost on in the spelling bee, remember?"

"Okay. I came in here so you could yell at me. Why are you thinking about that awful spelling bee?"

He sighs. "I don't know. I guess I've always felt bad about how it turned out. The petition, and …everything." Carter is much more tactful than I am. His sweetness prevents him from mentioning the true ugliness of the event, and that's fine by me.

"It's okay, Carter. My God, it was so long ago. Who even cares any more?"

"I've been living in the past," he says. "It's the only place where I can find my mom. I keep reliving the good times. And she was so proud of me that day. But not my dad. He yelled at me for losing on an easy word like poignant." Laughing quietly, he says, "Ironic, really, since the man has never appreciated a poignant moment in his entire life." He looks at me. "You know, you remind me of him."

I feel like I've been slapped. "Ouch. You don't have to be mean."

"Sorry," Carter says. "It's just, you're nicer than I thought. And I'd hate to see you end up like him." I say nothing, so he goes on. "He's not a good person. Refusing to admit to mistakes can ruin a person, Melody."

"What makes you so sure I've made a mistake?"

He's inches towards me like he's inside an airplane—it happens so fast, I have the illusion he isn't really moving at all. "You're human. Everyone makes mistakes, right?"

"Maybe I'm tired of being human."

He smiles a sad little smile and looks back towards his mother. All at once I envision both of them as younger, happier, healthier. I can see the resemblance between them; they have the same jaw, the same hair color, the same dimple in their chin. She's beautiful and in her company, so is he. My throat closes up and I can't speak. But somehow, I know I don't have to.

And I'm not stupid enough to say I told you so. Because I realize, if I pointed out to Carter just how poignant this moment is, well, that would be defeating the purpose, now wouldn't it? So I lay my head on his shoulder instead, and close my eyes. I'm safer than I've been in a really long time. Maybe ever.

39. Samantha

Friday afternoon and my feet are in stirrups and there is gel on my belly. Jake is standing to my side, and the midwife, Meg, is crouched between my legs. Marta, a former student of Jane's, is standing in the corner of the room, filming. She's willing to help for free, just to gain experience. The little room is crowded, what with three people and all the camera equipment. Still, without Jane here it feels empty.

"Everything looks good," Meg says. "I would guess she's around seven pounds, and the head is in the correct position." She stands up and snaps off her rubber gloves. "Now let's listen for the heartbeat." I take my feet out of the stirrups and move the sheet further down to cover my body up. I suppose modesty at this point is irrelevant, but I can't help it.

After a moment the fetal monitor picks up the swishing sound of her heart beating inside me, and Jake's face looks torn between joy and sorrow. I know what he's thinking, how he's feeling. Happiness is both fundamental and unfeasible. However, on the way to this appointment I vowed to myself that'd I stay strong. I'll pretend that everything is fine, and if I pretend hard enough, maybe it will be. So I share the moment with Marta, who gives me a thumbs up when I glance in her direction.

"Okay, Sam, you can sit up," says Meg, and she hands me a paper-towel to wipe my belly off. I do so, and Jake helps me into sitting position. Meg sits on the little stool by her desk, and addresses us both.

"You are already dilated two centimeters and are 40 percent effaced."

"What does that mean?" Jake asks, his complexion turning white.

"It means," Meg says, "that Sam is opening up and the baby's head is dropping down in preparation for the delivery."

Jake gasps. "So, it could happen at any time."

"She's thirty-six weeks. If she delivered today we'd consider her full-term. But just because she's partially dilated and effaced, that doesn't mean she'll deliver tomorrow. I've seen women looking like she does wait weeks for the baby to make an appearance." Meg, who is completely filled-in on our unusual situation, looks back and forth between us. "Do either of you have any questions?" Jake and I both shake our heads no. "Do you have a birth plan all set?"

"No, we're behind on that." I say. "We need to talk to Jane."

Meg addresses Jake. "But you and Jane are both planning on being there, right?"

"Of course they are!" I say. "Right, Jake?"

Jake hesitates, and he tries not to look at me. He talks directly to Meg. "Actually, Jane is having a hard time lately. She's been unable to deal with stressful situations, and, uh, anyway… She's thinking that being there would be a bad idea."

Meg nods her head. "I see."

"What?!" I yell, startling everyone. "When did she decide that?"

"Um, yesterday. We, um, had a talk, and uh…"

I cut off Jake's stammering. "No. This is unacceptable. She's going to be there. I don't care if I have to handcuff her to me, she is going to be there when this baby is born."

Jake sighs. "Sam, you need to cut her some slack. You know she's suffering."

I heave myself off the table, and stand directly in front of Jake, hands on my hips. "I don't care. It's time for her to rise up. One day this baby will grow up, and she'll want to know why her mother wasn't there when she was born; what are you going to say?"

Jake looks over towards Marta. "Can you turn the camera off, please?"

Marta stops filming, and quickly exits out the room. Meg says,

"I'll let you finish discussing this privately," and leaves the room as well. Now it's just the three of us: Jake, me, and our mutual frustration.

Quietly Jake says, "She's terrified, you know."

I put my hands on my belly as if it were a visual aide for our conversation. "Jake, don't you think I'm terrified too? We all are, but you and I are dealing with our terror. She needs to, too. For the baby's sake."

Jake looks like he's reaching for his words, hoping for something meaningful from the sterile environment we're standing in. "It's different for her. Jane doesn't recognize herself anymore. She knows how bad her memory is, she knows she can't control her temper, and she's convinced that she shouldn't be alone with a baby." He rubs his forehead. He looks so sad. "I don't know what to tell her. I can't fix this, I wish I could, but I can't. So all I can do is try to give her what she wants."

"What about the baby?" I say, and my voice is barely louder than my breathing. "Shouldn't you give the baby what she wants?"

Jake squeezes his eyes shut for a second, then opens them back up. They're red with circles underneath them. "Of course I'm going to give the baby what she wants."

In almost a whisper, I say, "The baby is going to want a mother."

He turns away, like he's about to leave, but stops at the door. "Well, you have the power to give her one, not me."

It takes me a second to catch his drift, and once I do, I need to catch my breath. I can barely admit to myself that being this baby's mother is what I secretly want. If I admit it to him, all is lost. Because no matter how much I want her to be, she's not my baby. "I can't," I say.

"It wouldn't be forever," Jake says. "Just for a little while…"

My palms are sweating and my heart is racing, and I don't know if it's because I was scared he'd say something like this, or because I was scared he wouldn't. "Jake, you all of people should understand. It's because it wouldn't be forever that I simply can't do it."

Jake hangs his head then looks up. He sounds so defeated when he says," I do understand. But right now I can't put the baby's needs first, anymore than you can. So just try to understand, I'm doing my best."

Jake quietly leaves the room and I get dressed to go. *I'm doing my best*, he said. I wonder; can I, truthfully, say the same?

Later, Marta has gone to load today's footage onto the computer at Shannon Community Access and to do some preliminary editing, and I'm at work, trying to block out thoughts of anything that causes me anxiety, which is basically everything, so I'm attempting to name all the state capitols off in my mind. When I was in fourth grade I knew all of them, but now I can't even remember all of the states. So I turn my attention to the movie that is playing. Due to complaints made to upper management, I'm no longer allowed to show *Sophie's Choice* or *Mommy Dearest*. So I have on *My Life Without Me*. It stars Sarah Polley as this married trailer park mom who discovers she only has a few weeks to live. So she makes this list of things she wants to do before she dies, which includes having an affair and finding a new mother for her kids. Miraculously, she meets Mark Ruffalo at the Laundromat, and they get it on, and a nice, pretty woman moves into the trailer park, and she hits it off with Sarah Polley's kids and husband. And the story is supposed to be profound and life affirming but it's just silly. I mean, how often do we make lists only to have the items just magically fall into our laps? If there's one thing I've learned, it's that there are no easy answers and sometimes life is just messy. Yet I still make lists. Huh. Ignoring my work, I decide to make a new one right now. It's called, *my list of things to do after the baby is born.*

Item number one is to have my own private banquet, consisting of sushi, chocolate-chip cookie dough, Caesar salad dressing, tuna, espresso, and lots and lots of alcohol—all things I had to give up during this pregnancy. Item number two is to lose fifteen pounds. I've just started writing down item number three when a solid look-ing girl, with a pretty face and fancy highlighted hair, walks in and comes directly up to the counter.

"Hello. Can I help you?" I say.

You would think we were in a drug store and she'd come up to pay for condoms or vaginal itch cream, that's how embarrassed she looks. "Um. Hi," she says. "I heard you're married to Mr. Linden?"

I gulp. This has better be good. Anyone who still refers to Nate as "Mr. Linden" is no friend of mine. "Yeah, he's my husband. But if you've come here for more gossip, you've come to the wrong place."

"O-Okay," she stutters. "Um, my name is Kelsey. And, I wanted to talk to you about Mr. Linden. To help, actually."

I squint at her. "I really doubt there's anything you can do to help. Thanks though." I turn around, and grab some of the mail I'm behind on going through. But she doesn't get the hint and stays standing there.

She speaks a little louder this time, to my back. "I'm the one who took the picture of him and Melody kissing," she says.

I turn back around. "Why did you do that?" I command.

Her face twitches. "You—you don't know Melody. She's, like, this really manipulative person. I thought she was my friend, but ..." Kelsey looks down and for a second I think she's about to cry. She looks back up at me, her eyes dry and determined. "...But, then she helped me get what I thought I wanted. And in the process I wrecked this perfectly fine relationship, and I can't be happy because I feel so guilty, every time I look at Bobby I think about Abby swallowing that Aspirin, and it's too late to fix it, but I started thinking about you, how bad you must feel, and it occurred to me, I should tell you what I know, because I know stuff about Melody. I thought maybe, if your marriage still has a chance..."

The mention of my marriage makes me flinch, and I cut her off. "Okay. You've lost me. I don't know what you're talking about, and I think it would be better if you'd simply mind your own business."

She stands up straighter. "I just wanted to let you know what really happened. But if you're not interested, well..." Her voice trails off but her confidence stays put.

I sigh. "Maybe I'm interested," I concede.

"Would you like to meet with me sometime? We could talk, and I could tell you some stuff that might make a difference."

My back is aching, and the baby has been kicking me in the same spot all day, and for the last few days and I have had the worst case of gas ever, and I'm really not in the mood for this. "Why?" I breathe out, as much an accusation as a question.

After a pause she answers back loud and strong. "Because it's past time to do the right thing."

Instantly I am shamed. When it comes to my marriage, I have no idea what "the right thing" is anymore. But I do know that despite everything, Nate is fundamentally a good person. If this girl, who has no real stake in Nate's future, is willing to go out on a limb for him, than I ought to, too. "My break is in an hour," I say. "Let's meet at the restaurant across the street and we'll talk."

40. Melody

It's late Friday afternoon, and I'm getting home from my early shift at Subway when I see the message light flashing on my answering machine. I press it, thinking it will be Kenny, berating my mother once again for not moving out to Green Bay with him. Or maybe, hopefully, it will be Carter, asking if I'm going to stop by later. Ever since the other day when I put my head on his shoulder, the air between us has been slightly charged and I no longer feel completely comfortable just dropping by unannounced. Then again, his mother is dying, so I doubt me and my stupid charged air are the number one things on his mind.

"Hello, this message is for Melody Madsen. Melody, this is Eileen Mitchell, from the *Pittsburgh-Post Gazette*. I'm calling in reference to the newsroom internship you applied for. Please call me at your earliest convenience…" After leaving her contact info, there's a click and the message is over.

Last September, when it looked like I was never going to graduate high school and getting out of Shannon was an impossibility, I scoured the internet for opportunities to pick up and leave town. After typing, "newspaper internship" into Google (one of the many types of internships I typed in), I found a list of internships to apply for by city in Pennsylvania. I sent off my writing samples and cover letter to every single paper that didn't require me to be in college, have prior experience (other than high school) and or be a minority. I chose Pennsylvania for the sole reason that it was the only state organized enough to list the internship opportunities in that way.

I pick up the phone and type in the numbers left for me by Eileen Mitchell. And I get voice mail. Damn. She probably won't be at her desk until Monday, which means I'll have to wait at least a couple of days to talk to her. Still, this has to be good, right? She wouldn't call me if wasn't interested, surely. After replaying the message a couple of times to analyze Eileen's voice (it does sound sort of encouraging) and making triple sure I have her contact info written down correctly, I erase the message. Thank God I heard it before Mom did. Then I begin to wonder how many other messages may have been left for me that I never received. Man, why didn't I just list my cell number, and leave the home number spot blank?

Speak of the devil, the door to our apartment opens and in walks my mom, carrying a bag of groceries. She's home so much more, now that Kenny's no longer around. "Hey, Sweetie," she says when she sees me. "I just finished talking to Terrance. The date for the hearing is set. One week from today."

She strolls into the kitchen and begins to put away the contents of her bag—diet coke and eggs into the refrigerator, cereal (Lucky Charms), canned soup, and goldfish crackers into the cabinets, and frozen pizza, ice cream, and TGI Fridays artichoke dip into the freezer. Ever since Kenny's left the picture, and the prospect of a huge settlement has loomed over us, Mom has morphed into something resembling a real mother. Grocery shopping for semi-real food is only one of her new and improved mom bits; she's also taken to cleaning the apartment every once in a while and last week she took me out for dinner at Applebee's, where she attempted to ask me questions about myself—like who my friends are, what I'm interested in, and what sort of job I'd like to have. College didn't come up.

But maybe we all just need the hope of something better in order to make our day-to-day lives bearable. My mom has lived for so long without that—perhaps she's just tired, and the idea of more money and the opportunity to do something nice for me is what she needed to become a nice person. Maybe.

I walk into the kitchen and watch as she puts things away and straightens up. "I can't wait," she continues. "All you got to do is say the stuff we've gone over, and…"

"And we'll be in the clear?" I finish. "I know."

"Thirty thousand dollars, honey!" she cries. "Just think what we could do with that money. We could buy a house!"

"What about Kenny and Green Bay?"

"Forget Kenny and Green Bay! I never realized how much I wouldn't miss him until he left. I'm talking about you and me, sweetie. We could get a lovely little two bedroom and fix it up, all girly-like. We'd be like that TV show, *Gilroy Girls*, you know, with the young pretty mother and her smarter than average daughter? And everyone thinks they're sisters because the mother looks so young and they hang out together all the time because they're best friends… that could be us! Wouldn't that be fantastic?"

Her face is beaming. I don't ever remember her getting so excited at the thought of spending time with me. Sure, her idea of us being like *Gilmore Girls* is overly idealistic, but I find myself unable to burst her bubble. This could be a turning point. So I do something I haven't done since I was a little girl; I wrap my arms around her in a hug. "That would be fantastic, Mom."

Several hours later I'm lying in bed, reading, when my cell phone rings. It's Carter.

"Hey," I say. "I can't believe you're still awake. I thought about calling you earlier, but I know you like to be asleep by midnight, so I didn't. How are you? How's Daphne?"

He doesn't say anything back, but I can hear him crying.

"Carter, what's wrong? Is Daphne okay?"

"No." He says. And I know without needing to hear anything more. I just know.

"Do you want me to come over?" I ask.

"Yes."

"Okay. I'll be there as soon as I can." I hang up and get out of bed, throwing on jeans, a sweatshirt, and my work shoes. Then I escape through my bedroom window. I haven't had to sneak out in a long time, so I feel awkward making my way down the wall of the building to the little ridge where it's sort of safe to jump the rest of the way down. I walk to Carter's house, finding my path in the quiet darkness. Cars drive past and some of the homes I go by have lit windows. But mostly the homes are dark, and I'm guessing the people who live there are warm and safe in their beds, dreaming of the tedium of their days. I read once that most of our dreams are about stupid things, things we get bored of when we're awake. I wonder why that is. Shouldn't we have enough control over our minds to at least lead interesting lives in our dreams?

Then I start wondering, how many people behind these closed doors are experiencing heartache tonight? Has anyone else just lost their most important person, or is Carter the only one? I suppose it doesn't matter. As far as I'm concerned, Carter may as well be the only one.

My journey feels shorter than usual, and before I know it, I'm standing at his door. I don't knock. I don't need to, for it isn't locked, and I make my way inside. Somehow I know exactly where to find him, and my intuition guides me to Daphne's room, where he's sitting in the dark beside a now empty bed, his head in his hands. It's so quiet, and I swear I can feel her surrounding us; maybe she's looking down at her little boy, longing to ease his pain. So I do what she would if she could, I hold him, wishing my arms were enough to make everything okay.

41. Samantha

Saturday morning. 8:00 a.m. My phone is ringing. I open my eyes and see that Nate isn't on his side of the bed. I pick up the phone.

"Hi, Dad." I say.

"How'd you know it was me?"

"Because you're the only one who calls this early."

"8:00 a.m. is not early, honey. But I'm sorry if I woke you."

"That's okay, I wasn't really asleep. Just sort of dozing. What's on your mind?"

"I was wondering if you're going to want your mother and me to come down once you're in labor. We should have some sort of a plan if you do."

I stare up at the ceiling and try to keep my cool. This is the third time he's called me with this question. I know he's hoping I'll finally give him what he wants and say, "Yes Dad, please come down," but this time I can't change my answer just to soothe him.

"Dad, that won't be necessary. Besides, I don't want you getting all excited about a baby you're not ever going to see."

"But I want to be there for you, honey."

"That's sweet, but I'll be fine."

"Will you?"

"Of course. Now can we drop this issue? I'm not going to change my mind."

He chuckles. "Like you ever change your mind. Once you're set on something, that's it, isn't it?"

"I don't think that's true."

"What about Collin?"

Blood rushes to my face, and I'm glad I'm alone so Dad can't see me blush. "What about Collin, Dad? I know you love him, and I hope you realize that I gave him chance after chance. But now I'm married, so I had to tell him no. Sometimes relationships just need to end."

"Sam," he says, with a twinge of disdain, "I know you're married. That's sort of my whole point. I don't want to see you make the same mistake twice. What if I had given up on your mom as easily as you like to give up on people?"

"In what universe did I give up on Collin easily?"

My dad ignores my question, like he hadn't heard it all. "She wouldn't be back," he says, sounding rehearsed. "But I was patient and I waited and she finally forgave me, and now here we are, happy again. Sometimes things can work out, Sam."

I struggle to sit up. "What do you mean, she forgave you? She took off on you, and you're the one who needed to forgive her, which, if you ask me, you did remarkably well. Perhaps I'm just not as good a person as you are."

The phone line is staticy for a moment, and I can't tell if he's talking and I just can't hear him, or if he isn't saying anything at all. But then his words reach my ears. "Honey, I thought you knew."

"Knew what?"

"About the affair."

I'm sitting up now, but inside me I feel a collapse. "Huh?"

He takes a breath, and I can picture him physically bracing himself. "I cheated on her. It was stupid and I regretted it right away. But what's done is done, and your mother threatened to divorce me. I begged her not to. She said she wouldn't, but she needed a little time. That's why she went away."

"But she was gone so long."

"Because every time she came back it was too difficult to stay." He's silent for a moment, and I suspect he's fighting tears. He resumes, with a choked up voice. "She and I, well, when you've been married a long time, it's not always easy."

I can't process what he's saying. It's all jumbled, like the adult-speak in Charlie Brown cartoons. I swallow some air. "Why are you telling me this now?"

"I thought you knew."

"No you didn't. This isn't the sort of thing you just casually mention then forget about later. Why didn't you ever tell me?"

"Weakness?" He says it like it's a joke, but it isn't. "I wanted you to like me."

"Oh, Dad." Pause. Neither of us speaks, but I'm sure we can feel each other as if we weren't hundreds of miles away. "So why tell me now? What are you advocating for?"

"I'm not advocating for anything. It's just, well, you're at a crossroad, aren't you honey? I thought a change in perspective might help."

Leave it to my dad. Somehow the confession of his worst mistake causes all of mine to come crashing in around me. Or maybe it's just hormones, stress, and fatigue. I start to cry. Not just the trickle of a tear, but full-out, dam-bursting-type crying. It goes on for a while, several minutes anyway. Dad waits till I've quieted down a little before he speaks again.

"So I was wondering," he says, "do you want your mother and me to come down when you're in labor?"

A moment ago crying was my physical release, but now, accepting help is an even greater one. "That would be great, Dad."

I can hear him smile. "Okay, then we should have some sort of a plan."

It takes me a while after hanging up the phone to get out of bed. I let my thoughts wander.

"I bought you a new one," I said to Collin, holding up the clear plastic bag with a bright orange fish swimming inside. It was a week after Jane's accident, and I hadn't run into Collin once. So after visiting the pet store, I went and knocked on his door.

"That wasn't necessary," he replied, his face stony.

"Take it anyway." I shoved it into his hands. But he dropped it, accidentally I believe, and the bag burst, leaving the poor little fish flapping around on the floor of the entrance to his apartment.

'God Damn it!" I cried, reaching for the fish, gingerly picking him up by the fin. "Quick, get a bowl of water!" I shouted to Collin, while I desperately tried to keep hold of the fish without hurting it. Collin ran into the kitchen and came back with a full glass. I dropped the fish in, and immediately it started swimming around the new confined space.

"Hey," I said, "I think it's going to be okay."

"Doubtful," said Collin. "I'm betting he'll be dead in a couple of hours. The water temperature will do him in. You're supposed to put the bag of water they come in, into the bowl, and let them adjust slowly."

I stared at the fish. He really seemed fine. I couldn't picture him belly-up two short hours from now. Or maybe I just didn't want to. "Well, only time will tell."

Then Collin and I stood, looking at each other, him holding the fish, and neither of us moving. "Was there something else you wanted?" he asked.

"No. I just, you know, I'm sorry about Cheshire, and I wanted to thank you one more time for all your help with my dad, and well, I guess that was it." I gave a half smile, and turned around to leave, confident he wasn't in the mood to talk, when he spoke from behind me.

"Your husband showed me the newspaper."

I stopped, frozen in my tracks. My throat suddenly felt really dry. Nate hadn't mentioned showing Collin the article that had exposed our personal lives for all of Shannon West High to see.

"Why would he show you that?" I wondered aloud.

"Because it concerns me too!"

I was startled by Collin's response, but I didn't reply with what was going through my mind. Nate showed him that article to hurt me.

"Your timing was perfect, you know." His tone burns through me. "Right before you married Nate I entered rehab. I've been clean for a while, working to make myself good enough for you. You thought I was doing drugs and selling drugs when we were married…"

I turned around. "Because you were!"

"No. Not then. I'm telling you the truth, Sam." His eyes were wild but the rest of him was calm. "I bought some coke from that guy in our building once, before you got pregnant. And then after, after you had the abortion, yeah, then I really started back. But I never sold drugs, ever, and when I started using again, it occurred to me that I was digging my own grave. So I decided to change, thinking it was the thing to do whether it got me you back or not. Then you married Nate, which almost broke me. But instead I've been attending meetings and I have a sponsor… but now… now you're pregnant again, right?"

Collin looked like every cliché of every betrayed husband or lover in every bad movie I've ever wasted two hours of my life watching. Unexpectedly I regretted it all.

"It's not what you think."

"It doesn't matter what I think," he said. "We will still be over, won't we?"

"We've been over for a long time," I said, gently, putting on a bandage instead of ripping one off.

"Yeah, but I finally get it now." And he slammed the door in my face.

The memory recedes. How have I let my most important relationships escape me? My mom. Collin. Now Nate, and now Jane. I pick up the phone and call her, and I tell her she's meeting me for breakfast. "You owe me this much," I say. Something in my voice must be persuasive, because she agrees to be at the coffee shop in 30 minutes.

We arrive at the same time and greet each other in the parking lot. Silently we walk in together and we're seated instantly. As we sit down she asks me how I'm feeling.

"I'm fine," I say. "But I didn't call you to talk about me. I called you for one reason. You need to be at the birth…"

I don't finish my sentence because she cuts me off.

With an angry frown she lays into me. "You have no right to tell me where I need to be, and you have no idea what I'm going through."

I reach across the table and grab her hand. She tries to pull it away, but my grip is too strong. "Maybe you're right, Jane." With a squeeze, I say, "So tell me."

"I can't."

"Try," I command.

"It's not that easy."

"I don't care," I respond, but I try to do so in a gentle, kind way. "Jane… I need you to be strong right now, and so does the baby. I'm sure it's not easy, but what choice do you have?"

She sniffs, and her shoulders sag in resignation. With her hand still in my own, she finally begins, after months of silence, to tell me what's on her mind.

"I hate myself now, Sam. I mean really, I have this deep self-loathing that just won't go away." She looks at me to gauge my reaction, and I try not to look away or to blink. "I can't focus on anything for more than a couple of minutes, I forget things all the time, I get angry at stuff that never would have bothered me before, and it's like I can't control myself. I don't even realize how mad I am until after I've said or done something terrible. How am I going to be with a baby? What if I…" she breathes deeply, her chest heaving up and down. "What if I hurt her? I just can't imagine anything happening that would be worse than that."

I contemplate her, so broken and deflated. And I decide all at once that if she can come clean, so can I. "You know, I sort of do know how you feel," I say.

"You don't," she demands.

"Well, obviously not the brain injury stuff. But the fear. This baby—your baby—has been growing inside of me for nine months, and in a couple of weeks I'm going to have to let her go. Part of me can't wait, but then, at the same time, I don't know how I can possibly say goodbye." I blink several times, trying to keep the tears at bay. "This may sound crazy, but it almost feels the way it felt before, you know?"

Jane cocks her head in confusion. "You mean, the miscarriage?"

I nod. "How can I give up another baby?" I ask. "What sort of person am I, that would do that sort of thing twice?"

Jane smiles, which strikes me as odd, given what I just said. I'm about to chalk it up to brain damage, but then, miraculously, the old Jane is back for a moment when she responds.

"You're the best kind of a person there is," she says. "And you have nothing to feel bad about. What happened before, that wasn't your fault."

I shake my head, and she leans in and squeezes my hand the same way that I had previously squeezed hers. "It wasn't your fault, Sam. Anyway, I have absolute confidence that you wouldn't have gone through with the abortion."

I'm tempted to laugh, but I hold back, because I'm pretty sure that sad, bitter, laughter caused by cynicism would go over her head. So instead I ask, "But what if I had? What sort of person would I be then?"

"A very confused and depressed person?" she offers.

My nose is running and my eyes sort of are too, so I let go her of hand, grab a napkin, and wipe them. "Maybe you're right," I say. "Maybe I would never have done it. But what if the baby knew somehow what I was planning? And what if that's what caused it?"

"Oh, Sam…" Jane is teary now, too. "Do you think that's how it works?"

"I don't know," I say. "But every morning I wake up with this fear, that it does work that way." I sigh and look up at the ceiling. "So the deep self-loathing that won't go away… that I can understand."

At first she says nothing in response, and when I look at her, I see that the old Jane has disappeared again. Her eyes aren't as engaged as they were just moments ago, instead, she has the slightly vacant stare she's been sporting lately.

"You don't have to feel that way," Jane says. "You can be the baby's mom." Finally the words that have been hanging in the air since Jane's accident have been spoken, and by the only person entitled to speak them.

"No." I shake my head. "No I can't, Jane. You are her mother. I don't care how damaged you are. Because I'm damaged too. We all are. Except her—she's not damaged, not yet. And it's you who needs to love her and take care of her."

Jane continues to cry, silently, wiping her face with her sleeve. I can see her thinking, processing, and I know I've won. Not so much because I'm incredibly persuasive, but because, I expect, on this particular issue, she wanted to lose. All she really needed was someone to engage her in battle. Finally she looks up and meets my eyes. "Okay," she says. "But I need you to help me." I nod my head, knowing that I am promising Jane the world as I am sinking into the ground. The idea of being a pseudo-mother to this baby feels about as feasible as the idea of a painless birth.

But then, again, as I said to Jane just moments ago, what choice do I have? Losing a baby once was hard enough. Losing a baby a second time is inevitable, but I see now that the rate at which I lose her is not up to me. At least this way, I won't hate myself in the process.

The waitress approaches us. If she notices our tear-stained faces, she gives no indication of it. "Sorry about the wait!" she chirps, "what can I bring you ladies?"

I order the big house stack of five pancakes, sausage, and orange juice. Jane orders coffee. After the waitress walks away, Jane offers me a weak smile. I smile back, and we sit in comfortable silence. Five minutes go by, then I say, "The baby is kicking, do you want to feel?"

Fear passes over Jane's face, but she nods her head, and moves over to my side of the booth. She places her hand on my belly, and the baby kicks beneath it.

"Oh, Sam," she whispers, and she sounds like a delighted child. Although I have to believe that one day Jane will be Jane again, right now, I feel like a mother to her and to the baby as well.

The moment passes, Jane straightens up, and moves back to her seat. My food and her coffee comes, and we attempt to talk about normal things, as if our lives haven't recently been turned upside down.

"How's Nate?" she asks. Jane hasn't been keeping up with his scandal, so I lie and tell her that he's fine. And my mind begins to wander.

It's time for me to do what I've just demanded of Jane. I need to step out of my comfort zone and help the person I promised to love above all others. Which means, it's also time to call Melody Madsen.

42. Melody

My feet are tired. Once again, I'm walking. This time I'm walking home from work, and there's a cold drizzle and bite to the air. November has definitely moved in and I really need a car. If insurance weren't so expensive, I'd buy one. I have a lot saved up; all those hours at Subway, working for college tuition money that will probably never be used for its original purpose. None of the colleges I wanted will touch me now, not after that near-expulsion thing.

Then again, if we get that settlement, Mom and I could get a house and I'd still have enough to take classes at UW-Shannon and buy a car. I suppose that prospect is why I haven't yet called Eileen Mitchell from the *Pittsburgh Gazette* back. Sure, I've been busy; Carter has needed a shoulder to cry on, and there's still work and preparing for the hearing and now that mom wants to spend time with me, I have that to deal with too. Still, I know I should call Eileen Mitchell back.

I get out my cell phone, and see there have been three missed calls. All from the same number. She's not leaving messages anymore, just calling and calling. I wonder if this would qualify as harassment; maybe I should ask the police. I round the corner to my apartment building, and the first thing I see is her - this really pregnant woman standing on the street, like she's waiting for someone. Like she's waiting for me. It was months ago when I saw her for the first time, but she's especially recognizable now. I stride up to her, my cell phone in hand.

"Hi, Melody," she says.

"You're stalking me, and I'm calling the police," I say. "So you had better leave."

She laughs. "Give me a break. The police aren't going to do anything. I'm just standing here on the street. That's perfectly legal."

If she thinks she has the patent on cool and collected, she's wrong. I draw myself up, and even though I'm a couple of inches shorter than she is, I am holding myself so well we may as well be the same height. My voice stays even. "You've been threatening me."

She cocks one eyebrow. Damn! I wish I could do that. It's hereditary. I know, because no matter how hard I try, I can't master that skill, sort of like rolling my tongue. Can't do that either. Anyway, she's staring down at me, like we're in a duel or something. "I've been threatening you," she says. "That's rich. I've been calling you. You haven't returned any of my calls, so here I am. All I want to do is talk. And since I'm nine months pregnant, there's no way I can be a physical threat. So I suggest you hear me out, because I'm not leaving until you do."

I cross my arms and shift my weight to the side. Then I silently give her my, *Okay talk*, expression, with a side of, *But I don't have to like it and I certainly don't like you.*

"You're going to drop the case." She says.

I toss her a smile full of poison. "Really?"

"Yes. My husband never did anything to hurt you. He only tried to help you, and you used him. Your friend Kelsey told me everything, about your five-step plan, about the background checks you ran with her credit card number, about the bet you had with your mother, and what she heard outside my husband's door on the night you kissed. And she's willing to repeat it all at the hearing. So I suggest you drop the whole thing, and we'll all move on with our lives."

Absently I scratch at my collarbone while I try to ignore the earthquake erupting inside me. Kelsey came forward? I guess I underestimated her, and I hate it when people exceed my expectations. It takes all my self-control, but I don't let my voice betray me by leaking out any shock or horror. "Kelsey's lying," I say. "And even if she wasn't, it doesn't matter. He still shouldn't have kissed me. He led me on, he crossed a line, and he should pay."

She moves in, invading my space. She sticks out her index finger and pokes me in the chest. "For what, exactly? Not loving you back?"

If she wasn't pregnant, I'd clock her. I want to, really, really bad. But I spew out these words instead. "You're one to talk! Look at what you did to him, the misery you put him through, and for what? Why did you even marry him? I bet you never loved him the way I did, and I'll also bet you've destroyed his life way more!"

Score one for me. Her face goes white and I can tell I've hit her where it hurts. She steps back, and I continue on. "Besides, it's the school district we're suing, not him. So lay off, and go worry about yourself and all the ways you've damaged your husband."

But it's not over yet. I can tell by her face and her body language that she is figuratively getting back up for another round before the make-believe referee counts backwards from ten. I have to give her credit; she's a worthier opponent than I thought. "You don't get it," she says. "You've ruined his career! They asked him to leave because of that article. If he left without protest then the school promised not to give him a negative reference. But that won't matter if you and your mother pursue this. He'll never work as a teacher here, not ever again. But if you drop the case maybe he could work somewhere else."

"And would you go with him?" I demand.

"That's none of your business."

"Pardon me. But I don't feel like giving up more money than I've ever had just so you can feel good for fixing something that shouldn't have been so easily broken."

She wrinkles her forehead and bites her lip. "What's that supposed to mean?"

"It means," I say, as if I'm talking to a stupid child, "that my five-step plan was awfully effective. Too effective. If he really loved you, tell me why it was so easy to lure him in. You can lie to him, and you can lie to me, but sooner or later you're going to have to be honest with yourself. What was wrong with your marriage that it couldn't hold up to something like me and my silly five-step plan?"

She clenches her fists, and for a moment I think this is going to turn into a hair-pulling, nail-scratching, catfight. But she comes at me verbally instead. "Listen, you little brat. Maybe nobody has ever told you, but you're not as special as you think you are. We barely know each other, but I know this; you've hurt me, you've hurt my husband, and neither of us has ever done a thing to hurt you. I don't care that you're poor, I don't care that you've led a shitty little life, and I don't care that you're unloved and unappreciated. The time has come for all of us to move past our issues and do what's right. And I'm telling you, your time is now. This is your chance, and if you blow it, yes, Nathan and I will suffer. But you will never recover."

"Wow. Thanks for your concern. My life finally makes sense now!" I gush.

She just stands there, trying to decide if she wants to say anything more. It doesn't matter; I'll still manage to have the last word. But she just nods her head, turns around, and goes. I watch her and all her baby weight shuffle away. Then I go inside, up the stairs to my apartment, and collapse on the couch.

It used to be that winning a fight would leave me exhilarated, ready to take on the world. But now I just feel tired…and defeated. Sort of like I lost.

Three days later I'm in Terrance Taylor's conference room. For a private hearing there's a lot of people: school officials, lawyers, secretaries, Kelsey, Mr. Linden, Samantha Linden, and of course, my mom.

Ever since my run-in with Samantha Linden my thinking has been all jumbled, sort of like I'm on cold-medication. It's like there's this wall between me and the rest of the world, and I can't seem to break through. I don't like to waste a lot of time on guilt, after all, what's done is done. But now I'm sitting here, and the thoughts racing through my head are even making it difficult to breathe in a normal way.

People start talking, but I don't hear any of it. Instead, like a deaf person whose sense of sight has been heightened, the faces in the room loom before me, every pore, every feature, every muscle twitch exaggerated and inflated. My eyes fall on Mr. Linden. He looks trapped.

Hurt. Nothing like the man I thought I fell in love with.

Then I notice, all the sound in the room has evaporated—everyone is looking at me. And I know it's a cliché, I know it's stupid, but Samantha's words echo in my ears. "This is your chance, and if you blow it, you'll never recover." I close my eyes and see the light in the hallway; I'm running from Axel, and I find Carter sitting in the dark. And without thinking it through, I open my eyes and my mouth, and shock everyone, but most of all myself, by saying, "Mr. Linden never came on to me. I came on to him. It was all my fault, and I'm dropping the case."

The room erupts again with noise, chatter, everyone is talking at once and it's impossible to decipher single words or entire meanings. I don't stay to hear any of it. I run away. This time, I have somewhere to go.

43. Samantha

After the hearing we go out for lunch. Nathan is smiling for the first time in months. It's like he's been trapped underneath a rock, and it's finally been lifted and the sun has come out and he can move again.

"I can't believe she dropped the case," he says. "I wonder what caused her to do that."

I try not to wear my secret meeting with Melody on my face. And I've resolved not to say anything—some things are just better left unsaid. I run my finger along the edge of my water glass, causing the condensation to dribble down the side. "Maybe she finally developed a conscience."

He laughs. "Well, whatever the reason, thank God! I can find a job somewhere else. Soon the baby will be born, and we can get out of here and start over. I hear they need teachers in places like Utah and Alaska. What do you think? I don't care, as long we're not here and as long as we're together."

I don't know what the right thing to say is, and I struggle to find words. They come out in a bubble, floating above us and vulnerable. "That's really sweet, Nate."

He starts to take a bite of his hamburger, but stops when he sees my face. He lowers his burger to his plate and his smile is erased. "What's wrong?"

Maybe I'm a coward, but I've convinced myself that it's better to do this in a public place. There's no need to let things get ugly. But now? Perhaps I should have let him be happy for a few more minutes, but the air has already been contaminated by my negativity, so I might as well proceed. And it's so hard, because I know there will be no going back. "I never should have married you." I say.

He flinches. "We've been through a tough patch, Sam, but we can get through this. I can forgive you and I'm hoping you can forgive me."

"It's not about forgiveness," I say. Then I launch into the speech I've rehearsed in my mind multiple times during the last few days. Funny—every time I went over it I would cry, but now my eyes are staying remarkably dry. "Nate, almost a year ago I fell in love with you, hard, and I thought you were the answer to everything that was wrong with my life, with everything that was wrong with me. But that was so unfair to you; no one person should be expected to be what I had set you up in my mind to be. I was looking for a way to feel better about myself and the world. You were so pure and good, and I thought being with you would erase some of my badness." I pause. His face is blank, and he blinks at me—a non-answer to what I've just said. So I continue. "That's why I didn't tell you about my marriage to Collin and the abortion. Because, when I looked at myself through your eyes I actually liked what I saw. But I brought you down with me."

"Don't be silly," he pushes his plate aside and leans forward, taking my hand. "We both played a part in what happened. So we learn from our mistakes and move on."

I slide my hand out of his. "Nathan, listen to me. I'm only going to say this once, because it's so awful to have to say. I love you, but…"

"But you love Collin more." He states this like it's the answer to a really obvious equation that only a truly dense person couldn't figure out. "Isn't that what you've been getting at?"

"No. That's not what I was going to say. Nathan, listen to me…"

"Be honest, Sam!" His intensity shames me into silence. "You married me because I was a less screwed-up version of Collin. I didn't realize it at the time, but I get it now. You wanted a do-over. You wanted to be with someone like him. And you wanted to start fresh, free from all your mistakes."

I hang my head. This is so not the way I wanted this conversation to go.

"Right?!" he demands. I can't answer.

He scrunches up his face, and I can tell he's weighing his words. "Sam, if you're going to leave me, okay. I'm not going to beg you to stay. Because as much as I love you, the truth is, you're a real pain in the ass. I could go somewhere else, start over on my own, find someone new, and still have the life I pictured for myself. But you at least owe me the truth."

Wow. Harsh. I don't know if he said that out of anger, or self-preservation, but I guess it doesn't really matter. I grab a napkin and wipe my eyes. Suddenly I'm Kate Winslet, nearly frozen to death and close to drowning after the *Titanic* sank, holding on to the hand of poor, frozen, Jack. Only in my case, letting go will save both our lives, not just mine. So even though my heart is breaking, I tell him what he needs to hear.

"It's more complicated than that. But yeah, I still love Collin." Nate shakes his head, crooks his jaw and studies his fingers. I wish I could say something that will make him look at me the way he used to, just one more time. "I met Collin forever ago, and he's shaped my life in a way nobody else has. But that isn't why I married you. Even though it's not working anymore, what you and I had was real."

Nate gives a quiet little chuckle and shakes his head again. "Oh, Sam. You only think that because you live in a fantasy world." Nate takes his napkin from his lap and gently folds it and places it on the table. He gets up, hands me the car keys, and kisses me on the cheek. "I'm walking home. Then I'm going to start packing."

And he disappears into the frozen abyss of TGI Fridays, and past the sinking ship that's our marriage.

It's in bad taste, I suppose, to go find Collin right away. If I were smart, I'd wait until Nathan left town, and the baby was born, and I'd had a chance to collect my thoughts and evaluate what I really want and blah, blah, blah. I tiptoe past my apartment and walk upstairs and down the hall to Collin's. I knock on the door. *Please, please let him be home.*

He is. When he opens the door all the loneliness and confusion I've been feeling hits me in the face and for a moment it physically hurts. Then I can see my own pain mirrored in his beautiful gray eyes.

"Hey, I just wanted to tell you something," I say.

"Um, this isn't the best time…"

"I'll be quick." My words come out in a furious jumble, as if I'll lose the courage to say them if I don't say them all at once. "It's Jane and Jake's baby, not mine. I told Jane I'd be her surrogate because I thought she'd be a good mother and I guess I felt I owed the world a healthy baby. I should have told you right away, but I never meant to hurt you and I'm sorry. I'm probably too late. But I just wanted to tell you that I love you too."

I stop to catch my breath. Then I notice that Collin hasn't said anything back.

"I'm sorry," I say. "You said it was a bad time. I'll come back later." I start to leave, but then he speaks.

"That's okay. It's no big deal," he says, "It's just, well, I was about to feed Rocky." He holds up his box of fish food for me to see.

"Rocky?"

"The fish you gave me after Cheshire died." A crooked smile forms on his face. "I named him that because he's a survivor. Also, I figured since we watched Rocky together and you gave him to me, well…"

I move in, wrap my arms around him, and kiss him so hard that by all rights he should pull away. But he doesn't. He holds me, big belly and all, pressing me to him as if we were meant to be an extension of each other. And our mouths and tongues and hearts move together in unison, and finally I can exhale, even though the only air I have is coming from him. Briefly, I pull away. "So I'm not too late?" I ask.

He smiles and looks down at his non-existent watch. "Sam, you're right on time."

Then the screen fades to black and the credits roll.

Okay, the only part of that that's real is the very last part, as I am at work and the movie I put in, *The Boy in the Plastic Bubble*, has just ended. If you've never seen it, it's a real classic. John Travolta and the dad from *The Brady Bunch* star, and it's about this boy, who has to live in a germ-free environment, but then he falls in love with the girl next door, and he discovers that living in a bubble can really suck.

It's been a few days since Nate and I separated, and he's moved out, temporarily living with parents until he figures out his next step. Meanwhile, a combination of guilt and fear has prevented me from knocking on Collin's door. Instead, I've been imagining different versions of our tearful reunion. But they never feel quite right. I did call him, twice actually, and both times I left a message saying that I would love to talk to him, and to please give me a call back.

But he hasn't.

No matter, I have no idea what I'd say anyway. I'm sure it's a terrible idea to get back together one more time. And how could I assume that he'd want to, anyway? Sometimes it really is too late. Besides, I have enough on my mind with my impending labor. I don't know when it will happen, but at least now Jane, Jake, and I have our birth plan ready. The most important part is that we're all going to be there. Well, okay, the most important part is that I'll get an epidural when I want it. But Jane being there is really important too.

Naomi walks through the door, ready to start her shift. "Hey," I say. "I'm glad you're here. I have a lot of office work to catch up on, so I'll be in the back."

She grunts her okay, and I head towards the safety and confinement of the office. I lower myself into the chair and rub my belly. All day I have been feeling off—like I have indigestion and would have diarrhea if I was eating much of anything. Suddenly, a pain shoots through my abdomen. "Huh, that was kind of weird," I think, but I dismiss it as gas and start going through my office work. Ten minutes later it happens again. "Ouch," I say. Then I get back to work. Then, ten minutes after that, I get yet another pain, and I think, "Huh. I wonder if this is what labor is like."

In movies pregnant women will be walking along, completely fine, then they'll grab their bellies and with a look of surprise, shout, "Oh my God, it's time!" Everyone will rush to the hospital, and then in the next frame, the woman is in the hospital bed, happy, holding her baby.

But maybe this is one of those times when there's a big disparity in truth between movies and real life. I suppose it's worth checking out, anyway. I find the number for the midwife on call, and pick up the phone.

"Yeah, it sounds like you could be in pre-labor," she says, after I've described my symptoms. "I wouldn't eat any rich foods, and you'll want to be ready to come into the hospital when necessary."

"How do I know when it's necessary?" I ask.

"Your contractions will be a lot closer together, like three minutes apart or so. Start timing them now. But I'd say you have a little while."

I thank her, and hang up and call Jake. I tell him there's no rush, but to be ready because the time is approaching. He does his best to stay calm. Then I call Marta. "Maybe plan on tomorrow morning?" I suggest. "The midwife didn't seem to think there was any cause for alarm."

"I'll call in sick tomorrow," she says, "and I'll get to you as soon as I can."

I thank her and hang up. Then I consider calling my dad, but think better of it. No need to let him know until it's really time. I've heard labor can take hours and hours. So if I call him as soon as it's really set in, that should give my mom and dad enough time to get here for the exciting part.

I finish out my shift. By the time I'm ready to go home, my contractions are eight and a half minutes apart, and fairly intense. Later, after I've taken a shower and eaten some soup, they're back to ten minutes apart, and they don't really hurt so much. Then they go to twelve. Then they go away.

At midnight I give up, thinking the baby has changed its mind. I call Jake, who I was right to believe would still be awake, and tell him it won't be tonight. Then I try to go to sleep.

At one a.m. I am still wide-awake. I have been lying in bed, unable to turn off my brain, going over the many, many failures of my life. I'm thirty-five years old, soon be divorced for the second time, and my greatest achievement is managing a video store. But what's worse is, I have no shoulder to cry on. Feeling more alone than I've ever felt before, and longing for a type of comfort that I haven't had in years, I reach for the phone. I don't even realize who it is I'm calling until she picks up. "Hello?" she croaks.

"Mom, it's me."

"Sam. What's wrong? Are you having the baby?"

My voice is full apology. "No. Not yet. I just needed to talk."

"Okay. Let me put your father on. He's asleep but I'm sure he won't mind…"

"I actually wanted to talk to you."

There's silence. Then, "What's wrong, honey?"

Words are in my throat like they've been standing in line for the last six months, and now that I'm talking to my mom, it's finally their turn. "I'm scared, mom. About this baby, and about my life. What do I do?"

Her breathing is even. "You take it one day at a time. That's all anyone can do."

Heavily, I breathe out my anguish. "What if that isn't enough? I screw things up, Mom. All the time. But now there's this baby and everyone seems to think I'm responsible for it, even though that was never the plan. And I've already destroyed one baby's life. What if I do it again?"

"Sam," she says, "Listen to me. You are a good person with a wonderful heart. And you're stronger than you realize, much stronger than I've ever been. Whatever is being asked of you, you can do it. I know you can."

How I long to believe her, to let her voice become a compass, setting me back on track. Oh God. Am I still so immature that all I really needed, all this time, was to hear my mother tell me that I'm good enough? I hiccup.

"Mom, I'm so sorry. Dad told me about, you know…"

"Don't." Her voice is severe. "Don't apologize. You did nothing wrong, and for all you knew, I took off for no reason. Don't ever apologize to me. Just know that, flawed as I am. I'll always, always love you."

I sigh. "I love you too, Mom." Saying that to her is like lifting an anvil off my chest. Suddenly, incredibly, I feel light.

"Good. Now get some rest."

"Okay. Bye."

"Good night, Sweetie."

We hang up, and finally, I am able to close my eyes and sleep.

Until 4:00 a.m., when I wake up and my sheets are soaking wet. But that's the second thing I notice. The first thing I'm aware of is that I'm in more pain than I've been in before. It's like I've hit a wall and I can't go back and I can't go through, so I'm just forced up against this impossible unbeatable thing.

Abruptly, but with absolute certainty, I am clear on what I need. I need to see Collin. Calling him won't do, I need to look him in the eye and say everything I've never said but ought to have. I get out of bed and begin the tortuous journey to find him. I'm not sure how I do it; it's like those stories of super-human strength when mothers rescue their children by single-handedly lifting up a car that their child is trapped underneath. Okay, maybe my walking up the stairs to bang on Collin's door isn't quite that amazing, but it feels like it is.

Please let him be home, I say to myself.

He is. When he appears all the pain is still coursing through me, vibrant, overbearing. But now, like always, his gaze reflects back exactly what I need to see.

"Sam?" is all he says.

"Please," I grunt out. I quickly make an executive decision that our heart-to-heart discussion can wait. "I'll explain everything later. I just need you right now." Then I'm doubled over in pain, yelping like an animal. He gently grabs my arm and helps me to stand upright.

"I'm here," he says between my cries.

It's dark. My epidural has set in, but they turned it down so I could feel my contractions enough to push. Jake is on one side of me, Collin is on the other. Meg is at the foot of my bed, and standing next to her is the delivery nurse. They all talk in hushed tones. Jane is somewhere, in the corner of the room, I think. I don't care, because I know she's here.

Every time I feel the beginning of a contraction I squeeze Collin's hand. He gives Jake a silent signal, and together they help me to sit up. Then I channel all my strength and determination and I bear down, down, as far as I can and as far as I know. When I can't push any more I collapse back, and Meg or the nurse looks at the monitor and says something like, "You're doing great, Samantha," or, "She's really moving, you're almost there."

It's like running after I'm so winded, and I want to stop but need to get to where I'm going. And I know that crossing the finishing line will be a defeat, because I'll be losing her.

I squeeze Collin's hand. Another push. "You're so strong, Sam," he says. I know he's lying. As I lay back down I want to say, *this isn't strength, this is cowardice.* This is me living in a fantasy world, never stopping to think what I'd do when she came. I turn to Jake. He just looks at me, and I see him look in Jane's direction with affection overflowing from his eyes.

Meg looks at the monitor again. "I think you can be done with this next push. Give it everything you've got, okay?"

Have I ever given anything, everything I've got? "Everything" is one of those concepts that is beyond the human imagination, like the endlessness of outer space or the finality of death. I don't even begin to know what everything is. But now is the moment to find out. Now is the time to push ahead because going back is impossible or at the very least, ill advised. So I push and in an explosion she's here, crying and suddenly, her cry is the best sound I have ever heard. It means she's real, she's complete; she's alive. And now I know what everything is. I lie back, and see that Meg has caught her, and there's a flurry of activity as they cut the cord and wash her and wrap her in a blanket.

Then Jake is holding her, crying. "Jane!" He cries. "We have a baby. Come see our baby girl!"

Collin is by my side, stroking my hair, and I lie here, certain I'll never be the same again.

"Hold her," he says. "It will be okay. I promise."

I look at him. I've never wanted to believe one of his promises more. Maybe that's the reason why this time, I trust him.

"Okay," I whisper. "In a little bit."

Collin sits with me while Jane and Jake hold their baby. He holds my hand while she is washed and weighed. But finally, after what seems like forever, he gets up and returns with the baby in his arms. He places her into mine. I look at her, convinced that I'm seeing perfection.

"Hi," I say.

She doesn't say anything back. That's okay. We have plenty of time to get to know each other.

44. Melody

It's been a week since the hearing and my mother still isn't talking to me. She's moving to Green Bay to be with Kenny. She probably assumes I'm going with her, but we haven't discussed it. Obviously, it's sort of hard to discuss anything when you're not speaking. But we've both been packing.

She just doesn't know where I'm going.

After the hearing I called Eileen Mitchell, and miraculously, the internship was still open. We did a phone interview, and I got the job. I start at the beginning of the month. They only pay $250 a week, which won't be enough to live on, but I figure I'll get a waitress job or something. Worst case—there's got to be a Subway in Pittsburgh that's hiring. Plus, I have enough money saved to put down a deposit on an apartment and pay for moving expenses.

So I've dropped by Kelsey's house to say goodbye. When she answers to the door she has that scared look in her eyes that I sort of miss; for a moment she is the Kelsey of olden days, the one that was so easy to push around. But quickly her eyes change, and she becomes her newer, stronger self.

"If you've come here to yell at me, don't waste your breath. I should have stepped forward much sooner than I did."

"That's not why I'm here," I say. "I just wanted to say goodbye, I'm moving soon. And, I wanted give you this."

I hand her an envelope. She looks in it, and finds two one-hundred dollar bills.

"What's this for?" she asks.

"The background checks—you know, when I used your credit card number."

"Oh, well, thanks." She looks over her shoulder, squirming a little. "Look, I'd invite you in, but…"

"That's okay, Kelsey. I should get going."

I smile and start to leave. God, surprising people is fun. Never in a million years would Kelsey have expected me to do the right thing.

"Melody!" She's steps out of her door and stands across from me on her front walkway. "Just out of curiosity, why did you do it?"

I carefully regard her. "You mean the whole thing with Mr. Linden?"

She puts her hands on her hips, shifting all her weight to her left side. "Yeah, was it because of the bet with your mom? Or did you actually love him?"

Kudos to Kelsey for such a bold question. I look her up and down. She's maybe lost weight, although, come on, her ass will always be large. Still, there's an air of dignity about her now, and I'd like to think I'm partially responsible. Maybe the silver lining in all of this is that Kelsey grew a pair. Well, whatever the cause, she at least deserves the truth.

"I don't know," I say. "Maybe a little bit of both?"

Kelsey nods her head, and a line forms in her brow as she considers my answer. For a second I think she's going to ask me something else, but she simply responds with, "Take care," she says. "Stay strong."

I raise my eyebrows at her. "Hey—if there's one thing I'm good at, it's staying strong."

Kelsey gives me a smile. I know she'll never forget me.

When I get home I find my mother's car parked on the curb, packed up with all her clothes and prized possessions, like her music library (an eclectic mix of bands such as WhiteSnake and Dixie Chicks), her George Foreman grill, and her shot glass collection. She's also included the television, the blanket her mom knit for her (it was the last thing she knitted before she died), and several framed photos and albums that document years past. I also notice my favorite pair of brown leather boots—ones I splurged on a year ago, and have barely seen because they quickly found a home in mom's closet. Ha. Mom left the car door unlocked, so I reach in and grab them. But as I'm doing so, she emerges from the front door, carrying her purse and a cooler. She looks me over silently, then walks around me.

"Are you going somewhere?" I ask.

She ignores my question and opens the backseat door, then shoves the cooler inside. Okay, at first the silent treatment was peaceful, and considering the alternative, highly desirable. But now it's getting old.

"Mom, what's up?" I demand. "You're not leaving right now, are you?" She gives me a dirty look and climbs into the driver's seat.

"Wait a minute," I shout. "You can't just leave without saying anything!" She starts the car and pulls away from the curb.

I don't know if it's from boldness or stupidity, but my body temperature grows hotter and my head begins to swim. I jump in front of the car, blocking her path. "Come on, Mom," I say. "Talk to me."

She stops the car, and stares daggers at me through the windshield. I step to the side and over to her window. I put my boots down and she begrudgingly rolls the window down.

She sounds like one of those computerized voices, perfect but devoid of any emotion. "Kenny called. He wants me with him, and since he's the only person who's ever been loyal to me, I'm going."

I feel the ground swing, like I'm on one of those crazy rope bridges at a playground, and I clutch the side of the car for balance. I know what's coming. "What about me?" I ask, sounding more pathetic than I'd like. Maybe I don't want to come with, but that doesn't mean I don't want to be wanted.

"We're through," she bites back.

I shake my head. "You can't mean that, Mom."

"You're not my daughter, Melody. My daughter wouldn't give up the way you did, not when we were so close."

I won't cry, I tell myself. I'm crouched down, trying to be short enough to make eye contact with her while she's seated in the car.

It's a ridiculous fighting stance, and the fact that she's not looking in my direction doesn't help. She stares forward, as if she's already on the highway. I search for the right thing to say, the words that will make me her child again. But my breathing is coming out in short little bursts, and all I can think to say is, "It wasn't right, Mom. He didn't do anything bad. You know that."

"What I know," she hisses, "is that you're a disappointment. And I'm done." She turns the car back on and I grab at the window before she can roll it up.

"Wait!" I shout, regaining my senses. There's more to think about here than my silly emotions. "What about the apartment? You can't just leave it with all our furniture and stuff."

She gives me her menacing "I win" grin. "I'm not. I transferred the lease into your name. It's your mess to deal with now."

She drives off, and I'm left, numb, standing in the street. There's a muddy November sky, and the trees lining the sidewalk have lost their leaves. Sort of how I feel inside.

Is there some fundamental flaw in my personality, in who I am, that explains why even my own mother doesn't love me? Because let's face it, she never has. Still standing in the middle of the street, I consider just staying there, waiting for another car to come along and run me over. After all, nobody would miss me. But the wind blows through me, and my desire for comfort outweighs my desire for gloom and doom, so I head inside, picking up my boots as I go.

When I enter my apartment I am struck with the mess she left me. Possessions thrown here and there in pursuit of the ones worth keeping. Drawers pulled and emptied out onto the floor. All the nice stuff is gone, and all the crap remains. But hey—she didn't get to keep the boots. At least I have the boots. It's almost enough to make me smile.

And she didn't take the furniture. I guess Kenny already has everything they need in Green Bay. But cleaning all this up and dealing with the landlords is going to take more time than I have. There's no way I can be in Pittsburgh in time. I heave a sigh and collapse on the couch. What now?

45. Samantha

After the baby was born there was a lot to do: getting me cleaned and sewn up, doctors examining the baby, moving me to another room, and trying to teach both the baby and me how to breast feed.

I still have doubts about the breast-feeding. I have doubts about all of it. But Jane insists that she wants me to, that above anything else she wants what is best for the baby, and she's convinced we can both love her and she can love us both. Whatever. My mind has turned to glue, which is probably good, because I am unable to analyze anything. So I am sitting with little Chloe, trying to get her to latch onto my nipple, when my parents come in.

"Hey," I say, covering myself. "Did Collin call you?"

"Yeah," says my dad, as he comes over to kiss me on the forehead. He looks at the baby. "She's beautiful."

"I know," I say. "I mean, people say that about every baby, but in her case it really is true."

My mom gently laughs, and sits on the edge of the bed, next to me. "We're so proud of you, honey."

"I didn't really do that much, Mom. I was just the vessel."

My father's voice sounds choked. "Sam. What you did was amazing. I'm sure Jane and Jake would agree."

My mom strokes my hair. "And you've been so strong."

I tear up. "Yeah, well, I have a feeling that the tough part is yet to come. But you both warned me."

Mom extends her arm around me, pressing her side to mine in a hug. "It's going to be okay. You'll see. I'm not saying it will be easy, but it will be okay."

I let my head drop to her shoulder, and for a moment, all of my fears are at bay.

Jake and Jane enter the room with both sets of their parents. After a brief round of introductions and a few tearful thank-yous Jake approaches the bed. "May I?" he says, as he gently takes her from my arms. Then the four grandparents gather around a beaming Jake, while my parents look on, their physical presence a welcome comfort to me.

Jane approaches my bed and my parents retreat. She leans down and kisses my cheek. "Thank you," she whispers.

"You're welcome," I say. There will be more for us to say, later. But for now, this is enough.

And before I drift off to sleep, it occurs to me how lucky this baby is. She's less than a day old, and already she has nine people who love her.

Later on the room is dark because night has fallen and people have gone home. Even Jane and Jake left to get some shuteye, which I don't begrudge them one bit. They have a lot of sleepless nights ahead of them. I'm flipping through channels on the TV when Collin comes in, carrying a brown paper bag.

"Hey," he whispers, noticing that little Chloe is asleep in her bassinet. "I brought you a burrito. I know how bad hospital food is and I thought you might be hungry."

"Awesome!" I say, ripping open the bag and tearing into the burrito. With everything that happened today, I actually sort of forgot to eat, and I never forget to eat. But the smell of Mexican food reminds me how hungry I am.

Collin sits on the chair next to my bed, a quiet, shadowy figure in the dim light that surrounds him. "How are you?" he asks, his voice soft and a little sad.

"Okay," I say, through a full mouth. I finish chewing, suddenly feeling shy. "Hey, thanks for everything. You were great."

"Don't mention it," he mumbles.

I place my hand on his arm. "No, really. I can tell you have that EMT thing going on. You stayed so calm, and you really helped me focus and get through it."

"I'm glad." He gets up and strolls over to look at the baby. "She's really something," he says, and his voice catches on what must be tears trapped in the middle of his throat.

My heart sinks. Of course he's thinking about the baby we didn't have. I push my burrito aside and all at once I'm flooded with shame and regret.

"I'm sorry, Collin," I struggle to say.

He remains focused on little Chloe. "For what?"

Pause. "Everything." Another pause. "But especially about our baby."

"Yeah, me too."

I open my mouth to speak, and without meaning to, I make my greatest confession. "I miscarried before I had the abortion, you know."

He turns from the baby, and now his eyes are on me. Under his gaze my breathing is heavier. "I had made the appointment, but on the morning I was supposed to go in, I woke up bleeding." I pause, noticing how close the air around us now feels. What am I hoping to gain by telling him this—forgiveness? Pity? I know I don't deserve either, so quietly I say, "I realize that none of that matters now."

His response feels like a lifeline. "Of course it matters."

I bite my lip and inhale deeply through my nose. "But I lost our baby, and either way, it was my fault."

He shakes his head. "It was never your fault."

"You give me more credit than I deserve."

"You can't blame yourself for a miscarriage, Sam."

"Yes, I can. I have been for all this time. Besides, I made the appointment..."

Neither of us says anything, but I'm crying now and so is he. After a couple of minutes I work up the nerve to ask, "Do you think you can ever forgive me?"

He points to Chloe. "Isn't that what she was about?"

"She's about a lot more than that. But I guess I thought by having her, I'd be able to forgive myself."

He walks back to the bed and sits next to me. "Did it work?"

"I…I don't know. But forgiving myself isn't the same as being forgiven by you."

Collin bows his head, takes my hand, and gently plays with my fingers. "Really? I thought it was."

I twine his fingers together with my own and our hands form a double-sized fist. "Collin, I don't even remember a time when I didn't love you. And I've tried so hard to stop."

"What about Nate?" he chokes out.

I shake my head. "We've both moved on."

Collin nods but says nothing. I continue. "It makes no sense for you and me to get back together, you know. We both have our problems, and now I have a baby that isn't really mine, but she's part of me anyway. You probably don't want that sort of baggage. And God knows, we've tried so many times to make it work and it never has."

He lets go of my hand and looks up. Our eyes lock together and without a doubt I know. In his eyes I am somehow accepted and redeemed and it's in fundamental ways that only he can offer. Now all I want is to offer him the same.

I raise my hand to brush away a lock of hair that has fallen onto his forehead. He collapses first his head then his entire body so that he's now pressed against me, his head fitting into the nook of my neck. "So," I whisper while stroking his back, "Do you want to get back together?"

The sound of his breathing, in synch with my own, is his only answer. And in this moment my entire world is contained within the walls of this room, in the sound of his heartbeat, in the feel of little Chloe sleeping nearby. And that's when I discover, when you truly love someone, you create your own silent language.

46. Melody

Another shift at Subway. For a little while there I didn't mind them so much because I was sure they weren't a permanent fixture in my life. There was an end in sight—one that resulted in me moving to Pittsburgh and starting my career in journalism. But now everything is ruined. I'm stuck with my mother's apartment and in turn, her debt, and there's no escape. I'll probably be working at Subway for the rest of my life.

I'm making sandwiches, hating every customer who walks in with their desire for tuna or roast beef or spicy Italian on whole wheat with lettuce and mustard but no tomatoes, and it makes me want to go postal, upturning trays of vegetables and firing off the bottles of chipotle sauce and horseradish like they're semi-automatic rifles. I want to rip my visor from my head along with all my hair, and when this moron asks for a six-foot sub I almost scream at the top of my lungs, "It's six-inch! Six-inch you stupid retard!" But I smile sweetly and pretend there is nothing I would rather do than serve him and the other lowlife, unwashed, and uninspired patrons who visit here.

Then he comes in. He's dressed in jeans and a grubby sweatshirt, and through the windows I see a U-Haul parked outside on the street. I'm like a deer caught in the headlights as he approaches, stuck, desperately wishing to run or hide or to dissolve into a pool of oil and vinegar. There's a sudden lull in customers, so I don't even have the excuse of business to move him along.

So I'll just have to stick my chin out and be strong. "Hi, Mr. Linden." My voice is loud and pleasant, like the hostess of a society party.

He seems neither angry nor particularly happy to see me. He opens his mouth and the words roll out. "How are you, Melody?"

I'm having a bit more trouble forming sentences. But I manage, "Okay. You?"

He attempts to clutch the glass over the bread, meats, and vegetables. Could it be he's nervous too? "Good," he says, like it's necessary to convince me against what I'm probably thinking. And okay, I'll mention the elephant in the room.

"Really?" I ask. "I—I was worried I may have ruined your life, or something. After you lost your job…"

He shrugs his shoulders. "It looks like I've got another one. There's this teacher in rural Wisconsin who is going on maternity leave, and since I'm willing to relocate for a short-term gig…"

I cut him off. "Oh. I'm glad. Look, I'm really sorry, for everything."

He bites his lip. "Me too," he says. It's not the response I was expecting, and it's not the one I deserve.

"What are you sorry about?"

He looks like he wants to physically shake off all his thoughts and this whole encounter in one big, loud spasm. So I have to admire him for keeping his cool and continuing on. "That night, in my room, it never should have happened. I was the adult, and I ought to have stopped it from happening long before."

Out of pure curiosity I ask, "Why didn't you?"

He stretches his neck and rolls his head a little, still obviously wishing he could be somewhere other than here. But I guess something inside him is saying, "No, you have to be here." It's like I'm a dentist appointment, or something. Unpleasant, necessary, and so good to be walking away from. "Melody," he says, "I wish I could give you a good answer. It would mean I could explain it to my wife, and to myself. But all I can tell you is, you don't magically become perfect once you're an adult. You still have an ego, and weaknesses, and errors of judgment. Which, I admit, sounds lame. So the best I can do is take responsibility, and hope that we all can move on."

I nod my head. He continues talking. "But I appreciate what you did, dropping the case. It made a huge difference."

"Did it?"

He meets my eyes, and winks. "So, can I get a six-inch chicken on Italian Herb with tomatoes, green pepper, mayonnaise, and salt and pepper?"

With a little laugh I say, "Sure." I make his sandwich, wrap it up, and put it in its plastic bag and hand it to him. He gets out his wallet to pay.

"Please," I say. "I think after everything, you deserve a free lunch."

He accepts the sandwich. "Hey," he says, "there is one thing I'm curious about. What made you decide to say what you said at the hearing?"

So his wife never told him about our showdown? I think back to our last encounter at Subway, when Mr. Linden begged me not to tell him what I knew about her. But I did anyway, and look how well that turned out. And even though I'm not dying to grant Samantha Linden any more favors, I have to wonder if there are some secrets worth keeping.

"I don't know," I say. "I guess I just knew it was my moment to do the right thing."

He gives me a smile, the type he used to give me back when I was his favorite student. "And now?"

"What do you mean?"

"What's your next step?"

I look down at the trays of food. "I wish I knew."

He smiles in a way that looks genuine. "You'll figure it out. Don't settle for being ordinary, Miss Madsen. Because you're not."

He waves goodbye, and I watch him walk out the door. Through the windows I see him climb into the U-Haul, driving out of Shannon and towards the skyline of some small hick town. And I know I'll never see him again. My perfect man, my knight in shining armor, my destiny: the one who was going to fix everything that's wrong in my life—is gone. I almost wonder if he was ever here at all.

Later that day Carter stops by my apartment. It's not the first time he's done so; I think being in own his house reminds him too much of Daphne. I'm sorting through some of the junk my mother left behind: a sewing kit without any needles, the attachment to a hairdryer, a pair of shoes that are too tight, and some exercise videos and hand-weights. I shove them all into a garbage bag. Life lesson #1—there's always crap to wade through.

"I suppose you're in a similar situation," I say to Carter, who is sitting in the armchair, watching me throw stuff out. "Hopefully your mom wasn't as big a pack-rat as mine."

"We always had a garage sale once a year," he says. "And every Christmas she would insist that I donate to charity at least two of my toys that I no longer played with."

"Really? Wow. She sounds great."

"Yeah, she was." Carter tears up—again. It doesn't faze me anymore; it's just what he does. I get up and squeeze his knee as I walk past him, heading into the kitchen. I open up the refrigerator and grab a couple of cokes, and return to the living room.

"Here." I say, handing him one of the cokes. "Are you thirsty? I am."

He wordlessly takes the coke, opens it, and takes a swig. I do the same. He looks around the apartment, as if he's really noticing for the first time what a crap-hole I live in.

"What are you going to do about this place?" he asks.

I sigh. "I have no clue. It's just another one of my mom's messes that she's forcing me to clean up."

Carter perks up a little, and he's slightly more awake and present. "What do you mean?"

I fight exasperation. I've already told him all about this, more than once. I know mourning can distract a person, but come on. "She took off. Left the lease in my name. Now there's no way I can take that newspaper internship in Pittsburgh."

A wrinkle of confusion forms between Carter's eyes. "Did your landlord have you sign anything?"

I think for a moment. "No."

He leans forward in his chair. "Then how could the lease possibly be in your name? I mean, legally, wouldn't you have to sign something?"

"I don't know. I guess since we have the same last name…"

He raises his voice and his face actually looks animated. "But if you didn't sign anything, I don't think it's possible for the apartment to be in your name."

I sit there, playing with the metal tab on top of my coke can, letting the significance of what he just said sink in. Perhaps my mom lied to me. It wouldn't be the first time.

When Carter speaks again, he actually sounds happy. "Melody, you haven't said anything to the newspaper people yet, have you?"

Despite my having sipped a coke, my throat feels really dry. I shake my head and struggle to respond. "No. I've been putting it off."

He comes and sits next to me on the couch. "So maybe you should just go. I mean worst case, you'll owe a couple months rent and your mom will lose her deposit. Big deal."

My shoulders tense. I knew this was too good to be true. "It is a big deal if you don't have any money."

His voice softens, like he's delivering bad news. "I can loan you the money if it comes to that. I think you should go."

I say nothing. But Carter must be able to read the fear on my face, because he says. "What? What are you afraid of?"

My eyes travel the area of the room. "If I abandon this apartment, my mom will kill me."

Carter reaches for my hand. "No she won't. She might get angry, but so what? You can't live your life trying to please her. Besides, it doesn't sound like she's the type who will ever be happy, no matter what you do."

"I suppose."

He cocks his head. "But?"

"But, maybe I don't want to go to Pittsburgh anyway."

"Why wouldn't you?"

I don't know how to express this feeling I have, the one that I ignored ever since it took residence in the pit of my stomach. "I won't know anyone."

"You'll meet people."

"What if I fail?"

"Then you'll try something else. It isn't the end of the world to fail."

I look at him. Suddenly a memory flashes through my mind. Kindergarten. The class was playing with a big parachute. We all stood in a circle, and raised the parachute up as high as we could, then quickly moved towards each other and sat down. For one perfect moment the parachute gave us this magical shelter, before it gently collapsed around us. And sitting across from me, a huge smile lighting up his face, was Carter. Is it possible I've always felt this way about him without realizing it? "Would—would you want to come with me? I'm sure they have art schools in Pittsburgh." I playfully punch him in the shoulder. "We could be roommates."

That wrinkle between his eyebrows forms again, like he's thinking really hard. He leans back against the sofa and stares up at the ceiling. "Maybe. I don't know. I have to finish up here first. Sell the house. But maybe after that."

Then we sit together on the couch. We aren't looking at each other, we aren't touching, but the air feels as magical and perfect as if that parachute was still surrounding us. "Carter, I think you're the first real friend I've ever had."

His head turns towards mine. Then, in one slow fluid motion, he runs his hand through my hair. "I'm flattered. But I'm sure I won't be the last."

47. Samantha

The months go by quickly. I suppose that's what happens when you're happy.

I'm actually amazed at how well everything has worked out. Because of my management position at Bravo I can determine my own schedule, and I've kept my mornings free to spend with Jane and Chloe. I also spend the odd evening with them, and all-day Sundays too. Jane's still nervous about being alone with Chloe, and after she decided to undergo treatment and rehab for her brain injury, there isn't a lot of money to spare for things like nannies. So my helping out is good for everyone, including me. My dad was right; I've fallen in love with that baby. But I'm confident that even as Jane gets better, (and I think that slowly, she is), there will still be a place for me in Chloe's life.

Of course, my new busy schedule has made it hard to finish my film, but with Marta's help I've finally managed. We're looking around for contests to enter, and it's been playing on Shannon public access, to much acclaim. Now Marta has an idea for a new project, and I'm trying to figure out times to work with her on it.

I suppose the hardest part of my new schedule is that I don't have much time to spend with Collin. Ever since he enrolled in nursing school it's been tough. However, we've found enough time to take care of the important stuff, like buying a house together and getting me knocked up. Yeah, that's right. I'm pregnant again. I guess women can still be fertile when they're nursing. Then again, I have a feeling that I'm just highly fertile anyway.

So it looks like I'm stuck in Shannon for good. It's funny how sometimes, the life you're trying to escape is actually the one you should've been living and embracing all along. I ruminate on this at work, as I stack DVD cases back on the shelves. Then I overhear a snatch of conversation, and I can't believe I didn't instantly recognize the young woman who came in with the dark-haired boy when they walked in.

"If I had known you were going to be so bossy about which movie to watch, I never would have come to visit you in the first place." She says this playfully, flirtatiously even, and I realize why I didn't recognize her. She looks softer, almost kind.

The guy she's with laughs. "Get used to it. Once we're roommates I'm going to commandeer the remote."

"Um, doubtful. Do you know who you're dealing with?"

"Yup. And you don't scare me one bit."

They both laugh, then, as if they're suddenly aware they're being watched, they look my way. Her face falls once she sees me.

"Oh, hi," she says. "I didn't know you worked here."

"That didn't show up in background check you did on me?" I ask, clipping out my syllables in little bursts. Her face turns red, and she looks over at the guy. She's embarrassed in front of him, and il-logically, I feel kind of bad.

After a moment of tense silence, I ask. "Did the two of you need help in finding a movie?"

He speaks first. "Sure. Do you have any suggestions, something we would both like?"

I pause before answering, and Melody's eyes meet mine in a silent plea. So this guy is important to her, huh? I suppose that means I now have the power to make her miserable, even if only for a moment.

What should I say, how can I embarrass her the most? I stall for time, trying to figure it out, and pretend to look at movies in order to recommend one. My eye passes over *The Graduate*, and without warning a question pops into my mind. *When did I stop being Elaine, and become Mrs. Robinson? How am I no longer the ingénue in my own story?* My hand grazes over my belly, and I look back over at Melody. Try as I might, I can no longer convince myself that she's the cunning, marriage-destroying villainess I've believed her to be. She's simply been starring in her own life-movie, and it was in conflict with mine. Something like forgiveness washes through me, as I notice that she and her guy-friend are around the same age as Collin and I were when we met. Only I'm guessing they haven't clicked in quite the same way. Not yet. It looks like they're still in the friendship stage, but perhaps wanting more.

"Have you seen *When Harry Met Sally*?" I ask. "It's really funny, and usually appeals to both men and women."

He turns to her. "What do you think?" he asks.

She shrugs her shoulders. "Sure."

"You can find it in comedy." I say. He takes off to find it, leaving Melody and me alone, faced off once again.

"It worked for me," I say.

Her face is perplexed. "Huh?"

"The movie. It worked for me. I watched it for the first time with the love of my life."

She regards me, and simply asks, "Not Mr. Linden?"

"No. He's a great guy, but…"

"…but he wasn't the answer after all, was he?" she says.

I let her question sink in. I would be offended, if she wasn't so spot-on. I answer without apology, "No. He wasn't."

"Yeah, me neither." She gives me a half smile. "Good luck, you know, with the love of your life."

I gesture towards her guy, lost somewhere in aisles of films. "Yeah, you too."

Then her cockiness returns. "Oh, I've never been one to rely on luck." She saunters off, and I'm left standing where I was, where I've always been, and where I expect to be for a long time.

And that's okay with me.

A Reader's Guide to Starring in the Movie of My Life

Questions for Reflection and Discussion:

1. When do people need redemption? Which characters in *Starring in the Movie of My Life* need redemption, and how do they find it?

2. The main connection between Melody and Samantha is that they are both looking to be "saved" by Nathan Linden. What were the differences in how they wanted to be saved, and what were the similarities? Does Nathan actually save either of them, or do they save themselves?

3. Think of the male leads in this story: Nathan, Collin, and Carter. Which ones were you rooting for? Were any of them worthy romantic partners for Samantha and/ or Melody? Did any of them deserve their own happy ending?

4. Was Samantha's sacrifice in carrying a baby for Jane a good idea? If you were in a similar situation, what would you do?

5. Both Samantha and Melody feel estranged from their own mothers. How does that affect their other relationships, and how does it affect their daily actions? Does this story have any "good mothers"?

6. Consider the flashback scenes that depicted the evolution of Collin and Samantha's relationship. Can true love be so conflicted? How do you define true love?

7. Which characters did you find likeable? Are any of them ones you would want for a friend?

8. Where do you see all of the main characters of *Starring in the Movie of My Life* ten years after the novel finishes?

9. Samantha likes to compare her life to movies, and Melody likes to orchestrate her life as if she is at once the director, screenwriter, and the star. Is either outlook healthy or productive? Is either one something you yourself have done?

10. If this novel actually was a movie, who would you cast in the main roles?

Acknowledgements:

Thank you to all my students, past and present, who taught me about personal strength and fortitude. Melody's good qualities were inspired by you.

Thank you as well to the people who provided feedback during the writing of this book. You know who you are.

To learn more about Laurel Osterkamp
and her writing, visit her website:

LaurelOsterkamp.com

PMI Books
Boulder, CO
www.pmibooks.com